The
Rabbit
Girls

The Rabbit Girls

Anna Ellory

LAKE UNION

PUBLISHING

Published by Lake Union Publishing, Seattle

www.apub.com

Amazon, the Amazon logo, and Lake Union Publishing are trademarks of Amazon.com, Inc., or its affiliates.

ISBN-13: 9781542007238 (hardcover)
ISBN-10: 1542007232 (hardcover)
ISBN-13: 9781542094191 (paperback)
ISBN-10: 1542094194 (paperback)

Cover design by Emma Rogers

Printed in the United States of America

Dedicated to the women that time forgot.

Turning and turning in the widening gyre
The falcon cannot hear the falconer;
Things fall apart; the centre cannot hold;
Mere anarchy is loosed upon the world,
The blood-dimmed tide is loosed, and everywhere
The ceremony of innocence is drowned;
The best lack all conviction, while the worst
Are full of passionate intensity.

W. B. Yeats, 'The Second Coming'

January 1945

It couldn't be rushed.

Crouched on the end of the bed, focused only on the uniform in her lap, she unpicked an inch from the hem with fingers fat and numb. Very, very carefully she pushed the slip of paper into the pocket.

It needed to lie flat. Completely hidden within the folds.

She fed another all the way along the seam as far as it would reach, checked the front, the back and the fold. Then another and, finally, the last one.

The final one.

Time was slipping away, rushing by. It was the end.

Her fingers raced to thread the needle but the eye was small and the thread thin. The calls and screams thundered closer, louder, each one more urgent than the last. Her hands shook, a tremble mirrored in her chin, her lips and her heart.

They were hidden.

Safe.

She rolled the thread nimbly around her fingers and placed it into the seam. She wove the needle through the hem, locking it in.

There was nothing left to do, except . . .

1

MIRIAM

December 1989

The Wall between East and West is open. The door between her and the rest of the world is closed. Locked and checked, twice. She runs her finger along the gap between door and frame to find the tiny, soft feather in place. Her fingers trace the grain of the worn wood down to the handle. To check for a third time. Locked.

She lifts the intercom phone and listens.

Silence.

Thick carpet lines the hallway to his room. Without glancing at him she smooths the velvet curtains before opening them to a lavender sky. The rain has washed the air clean and she welcomes the breeze.

'It's a beautiful day,' she whispers, wanting it to be true. The building opposite looms in all its classical primacy, facades stark, windows shut. Light seeps out through cracks, barred from reaching across the street by old twisted railings. *Berlin is Berlin again.* And Miriam is home.

The cobbled pavements of Klausenerplatz glisten from night rain. When the rasp of the pressure mattress fades to white noise she withers away from the window to the man in the bed. Arranged flat on his back, white sheets tucked around his body.

She pauses.

The circuits connect and with relief her body follows the familiar pattern.

'Did you sleep well?' She does not let her mouth run quiet for fear that in the silence, her thoughts will ignite.

From the bedside table she unfolds *B.Z.*, the newspaper is dated 10th November, she hasn't purchased another. The smell of words creates a sharp nostalgia.

She reads the bold headline '*We all thank God*' and turns the page. Faces smiling, laughing, crying, people hugging each other, bottles of beer raised, and in the background: the Wall.

'What do you think, Dad? Do you think this,' the paper crinkles in her hands, 'is an act of God?' She smiles, for she knows what he would have said. Or she thinks she does.

'They are calling them wallpeckers, the people battling through with a hammer and chisel. It'll take them a decade to reach the other side this way, but look . . .' She turns the paper so that if he were to open his eyes he could see the picture, black and white, of a small boy and an even smaller hammer. She imagines the *tink-tink* as the wallpeckers young and old chip into the wall. 'You should see this,' she murmurs.

There is no response, not even a flicker of recognition.

He had always been busy; never still. Until now. He had a quick mind, but regularly knocked into things, his body betraying his age, while his mind was vibrant.

Miriam folds and replaces the newspaper, suspended in time. The world continues to turn around her; the magnitude of the news is so big, it's incomprehensible. The euphoria, the joy . . . The Berlin Wall is down, but the news is of little consequence, the emotion out of reach for her, because she is cleaning, caring and changing.

A cycle which will end, and soon.

'I'm lifting you.' She leans on the bed and holds him under both arms, avoids looking at his face. She can lift and nudge with her body weight into his chest to hoist him a few inches up the bed. She fluffs his pillows and shuffles him up. Guided by her small hands, he rests, semi-reclined.

'There we go,' she continues and pours the water from a plastic jug into the cup. 'Small sips,' she says. She positions a clean hand towel under his chin.

According to the medical staff, the slanted rim and two handles of the cup make it easier for him to drink, but the water bypasses closed lips and trickles down his beard. The doctors also say words like 'Fluid Balance', 'Hydration', 'Comfort'. Their faces show boredom. Disinterest. Repetition. They look, they do not see. They talk, but cannot hear. He should remain comfortable, hydrated, and all input and output should be measured. Yet he was not meant to live longer than a few days. Weeks later he still breathes, but the prognosis is death. Attempting to make this a *'comfortable'* experience feels as futile as sticking on a plaster.

'A few sips now. A bit more.'

The nurses encouraged her to shave him when he was in hospital, but it felt too intimate an act, so his beard continues to grow as water drips from it into the towel.

Miriam empties the catheter bag into a kidney-shaped bowl and carries it out, conscious of the step between bedroom and bathroom. The fluid swooshes as a smell that is acid to both the nose and the stomach rises around her; she tries not to heave. Once flushed away and the tray disposed of, she sits on the side of the bath, waiting for the water to warm. It falls over her fingers and she resists the urge to wash her hands while she waits.

Collecting the water in a bowl, she moves back into the bedroom. In the bed, she sets about undressing and bathing him. She does not speak through this process.

Not once.

She washes, dries using a soft, white towel, and places the cream for pressure sores on the affected areas. The mattress shifts as airflow changes to support his body as it moves.

Taking his left arm, Miriam pushes it through the sleeve of the clean pyjama shirt. As she turns his wrist she notices his watch has stopped. Tapping on the face does not yield movement. His old watch, gold hands and gold face with black numbers, dissolved into tiny outlines over time.

Turning his wrist over she places it on the bed, trying to find the clasp. Its wide gold strap has no links to unfasten. Bending closer she runs her fingers along its rim.

Engaged as she is in the watch, her fingertips caressing for a hook, she doesn't notice his breathing change. She doesn't notice the shift of movement. She doesn't notice his other arm move.

She doesn't notice any of these things until an icy hand grabs at her wrist.

She looks to his face, his head still slack. His eyes still closed.

Until they are not.

His grip tightens and transports Miriam to a younger, brighter version of herself. Late teens at the zoo with friends. A big group of blurred faces, forgotten names. A colourful image of tie-dye, eye shadow and feathers.

The 'petting area' was a small enclosure with a shin-high wooden fence. The air was hot and thick with the sawdust that covered the floor. She was pushed forward to face an enormous bird of prey. She looked to her friends who had 'volunteered' her and felt claustrophobic. The gloves provided did nothing to disguise the solid bird on her arm with its leather-like feet and sharp claws. The bird's eyes moved this way and that. Everyone was watching her. People started to move across her vision, creating a kaleidoscope. But the bird held on, even tightening its grip as everything went dark.

Miriam tries to use her free hand to loosen his, but knocks the bowl to the ground and the suds splash up in a wave. Having grown comfortable looking at his eyelids, his open eyes are too white and too deep. She wants to look away. Anywhere else. But his gaze holds her, he is staring through her.

'What is it?' she asks gently, although his grip is tight. He pulls on her wrist. Again, her body moves closer as he pulls himself up the bed higher until they are level.

'What's the matter?'

His breath has a rancid, sweet smell, like decaying fruit. She tries to pull herself away, yet it spirals on her cheek. She feels her pulse quicken in the trapped hand then thrum as the circulation slows. Her eyes are still locked into his when his look changes and he focuses on her. His features soften.

'It's okay. I'm here.' Her voice splinters as it rushes out.

'Frieda,' he says like the whisper of a fallen leaf. 'Frieda.'

His voice reminds her that this is *Dad*, the man who sang her to sleep, read stories and smoothed her hair. *Dad*, the man to whom she has not spoken for ten years.

She clears her throat. 'Dad, it's Miriam,' she says gently.

A millisecond of recognition and she places her free hand on top of his, which still grips on hard. He coughs and the sound vibrates around the room.

'Dad?'

'*Frieda!*' he calls like a long, low foghorn over a crowd. '*Frieda!*'

His body won't cooperate as he tries to move out of the bed. He struggles, scrabbles, plucks at the fabric, unable to get free. An act so futile, she cannot look away. He calls out 'Frieda' once more before slowing. Deflated. Eyes closed. His right hand now lies over his left wrist, holding the watch.

She waits for his inhale.

Exhale.

Pause.

Inhale.

And she exhales shakily. Not moving for some time, just watching his chest rise and fall, a rhythm to suffer by. His face relaxes and saliva dribbles from the side of his mouth. She wipes it away with a cloth.

HENRYK

'Dad,' she calls. I can hear a woman's voice as soft as lilac.

But I am lost . . .

Lost in the past.

Lost with *Frieda* . . .

It was 1942 and she had been in my class almost six months. She rarely spoke, never smiled, but listened with an intensity that would make any professor feel exuberant, any professor, that is, not teaching within a Nazi regime.

Instead, her acute awareness of the subjects I taught, the texts we studied, made me more and more nervous.

She was attractive in the same way everyone in the class was. Male and female. Fair and strong. But she *commanded* my attention, and I was desperate to know what she was thinking. What did she think about the texts? So far, I had yet to hear a single word from her mouth.

The snow fell in heavy sheets outside the window and the class was fractious, bored; like a bundle of puppies they wanted to be outside.

I was pacing around behind my desk, chalk in hand. I had written *Schmerz* – Pain – on the blackboard and my fingertips were dusty.

I had delivered the theory behind death, dying and 'the greater good'. All acceptable. Then I happened to glance at her and took a huge risk.

I went off track. For her.

To see if she had a reaction.

'When thinking of pain . . .' I formed the words, rolling them in my mouth before committing to them. 'Contemporary writers cannot depict pain like those in earlier centuries.'

She looked up, directly at me, and I stopped, frozen to the spot right in front of her desk, but continued: 'Pain is an old entity and . . . well, perhaps we could learn something from the Russians after all.'

'How to starve,' said one of the men to a slight chuckle. I looked at him until he sank back in his seat.

'Russian writers *feel* their pain to allow their readers to suffer,' I said.

The class laughed, although I wasn't sure I was being funny.

'They'll all feel the pain of the Führer soon,' another student offered.

'No,' *she* interrupted. 'Surely you mean that we *feel* their pain as if it were our own.'

It was the first time she had spoken out and the rest of the class looked at her, as I did, with intrigue, astounded she had spoken at all. One of the students wolf-whistled and the class dissolved into laughter and chatter.

Yet she had spoken, to me, and she continued, lowering her voice conspiratorially, and I leant closer. 'The power of the writing is not in the words or the actions, but a creation of every nuance of feeling that another has felt, do you agree, professor?' she asked *in French*.

I checked the class, but they were busy mocking her. I perched on my desk.

'I agree,' I said, carefully framing my words in French, thinking this may be a trick. The French words felt refined but rusty in the back of my head.

'If we look at Russia, France and Ireland, we can explore a pain that we cannot imagine.' She was speaking in a loud, husky voice that belied her age, still in French. As I listened the language became fresh, exciting, freeing. The class was fidgeting again and watching our exchange.

I lowered my voice. 'Our history is also full of pain.'

'It is,' she said. Then changing from French to English she added, 'But our history is also subject to whomever is in charge; it becomes less fact and more fiction, open to the whims and fancies of a flatulent *Schwachkopf.*' She used the word in German and the shock on my face reverberated around the class. None of them could understand the rest of our exchange, but that word *Schwachkopf* seemed to ricochet. She looked at me. Challenging me.

'Look at page seventy-six,' I said to the class in English. She laughed and I switched to German, giving the instruction again, adding, 'Discuss with your partner the techniques employed by the author to describe pain.'

The class rustled and mumbled about it, before lively chatter ensued. I moved closer to her desk and bent low.

'What are you doing?' I asked.

'It is only when we understand language that we can truly immerse ourselves in the collective pain of that culture and read the text as it is intended. Not like these assholes.' She went back to speaking French. 'These *connards.* Factory-made buffoons who cannot think for themselves: yes sir, no sir,' she mimicked, and as I looked around many students were looking out of the window and others flicking through the text in front of them.

'This is very risky, Fräulein,' I said in English, again following her shift. English landed better on the tongue, but it was slower to form in my head. I cherished the complexity of the languages that I hadn't had an opportunity to practise in years. Switching back and forth was incredibly difficult, yet my brain sparkled with the challenge.

'Risky?' She smiled as though the thought of taking a risk amused her. 'I would have thought, as a professor, that you would want an actual conversation. A . . .' But then she changed into another language and I was lost; I watched her lips as she spoke, but I didn't understand.

She laughed. 'Not Dutch then, maybe . . .' She reeled off words so fast they sounded like bullets.

'How many languages do you know?' I asked.

'A few,' she replied, in French this time.

'You need to be careful speaking the language of the enemy at this time,' I said, lowering my voice, speaking English again.

'Are they the enemy?' she asked slowly. 'Or the people who are going to free us?'

I looked around, but the class was busy chittering away and when I looked back at her she had returned to looking at her book as if she hadn't spoken at all.

'Thank you, Fräulein . . .?' I said, wanting to keep her talking.

'It's Frieda,' she said, not looking up.

'Frieda.'

MIRIAM

Frieda? she thinks. *Who is Frieda?*

Her father's hand still rests on the watch. She goes to unclasp it, but changes her mind, not wanting to disturb him again. Her hands work as fast as her heart to button his nightshirt.

His eyes, although closed, swell from their sockets, held by paper-thin eyelids like hot air balloons tethered by pegs. His mouth is wide open and she moves away from the direction of his breath, yet guilt forces her to remain. And woven into that guilt to remain by her father's side is her mother.

Her mother would have cared for Dad better, known what to do, what to say. Mum never blundered or froze; she was always there with exactly the right thing, but when Mum had needed her, Miriam hadn't been there.

She wasn't there when Mum died and won't believe that she also suffered like this. Instead she imagines a single window shimmering dust like glitter across a starched, white sheet. Perfectly covered by blankets in her 'good' nightdress. The back of her father's head bowed as he knelt holding Mum's hand in both of his.

Miriam holds Dad's hand in both of her own and looks at the watch; it reads ten past four. Hands still, but the watch itself has moved.

Miriam sees an ashen line of skin at the top. She turns the arm over, alert to any reaction from him.

And sees it.

She has seen this before in textbooks and on the television.

But now. Here. Black on white, hidden under gold.

On her father.

Numbers.

Grey-black numbers, each one no more than a centimetre in length, perfectly square, tattooed into his skin.

He was *there*.

She returns the watch to its usual position and squeezes his hand tight as tears form. Bending to kiss him on the head, she changes her mind and gives his hand a final squeeze before turning away.

In the kitchen, she turns the tap and allows the water to flow before resting her head on the cool work surface. Rat feet of fear scuttle up her spine. The numbers. She recalls the videos and pictures she saw as a child, of stripes, hollow faces, piles of bodies. She cannot imagine her father's face as one of the many.

She thinks of Mum. The only one who could help her right now. Wishing for her, for just a moment.

A moment where she wasn't so alone.

Closing her eyes, she sees her. So clear and so deeply felt, the memory turns back time. An apron covering one of her most beautiful sunflower-yellow dresses, her high heels clicking on the floor of the kitchen, where food had nourished the soul before it was tasted on the lips.

Turning off the tap she wipes her face in the rough mashed-potato smell of an old tea towel. Holding the tea towel to her side, a comfort to hold something, she is drawn into her mother's room. Thin, yellow cotton curtains allow what light there is outside in. The walls and furniture floral and the room made up, blankets and sheets on the bed and the wardrobe full.

Full of Mum.

She sits down in the large wardrobe, pushing the shoeboxes away. The curtain of dresses closes in, a rainbow of colour and texture, shrouding her in the scent of orange blossom and sweet pastry. The dresses hang still, as though waiting for her return.

She sees Mum's hand, the way she held a lipstick brush, her baby finger raised as if she were drinking a fine tea. The hand pale, like a glove, then as she grew older becoming flecked and marked. The twist and turn of inspection of a new dress in the full-length mirror hidden in the old wardrobe. Mum resting her leg across the opposite knee, pressing first her toes then heels into a pair of shoes, as carefully as if they were glass slippers.

Each image, too great to be contained, flashes for only a second, like a lighthouse, before illuminating the next one. Spinning around each flare, shining a bright, white light on her loss. Now held, paused, as though seen through one frame.

The tomb of absence that used to be Mum.

Her heart, fisted, batters at its cage. Unable to quieten her mind, she crashes out of the wardrobe, pulls dresses down from the rail and knocks shoeboxes into the room.

Avoiding the large mirror that hangs over the sink in the bathroom, she forces herself to slow down as she loosens the hot tap. She places her hands under the water, as if in an inverted prayer. The water is cold. It trickles over her fingers and into her palm. As soon as she can feel some heat, she turns the water on full.

Then the soap.

Held in her closed palms she waits for it to warm.

She scrubs and rubs until she has achieved a great lather; placing the foaming bar back in its rack she scours her hands, scraping her fingernails and knuckles into her palm, rubbing and scrubbing and vigorously pressing her hands into each other. Enough that the soap, no longer silky, becomes coarse to her skin.

Noticing the familiar pain build, she continues, allowing its voice to take over the others. Something concrete. Filling her where absence cinders like a forgotten flame, just waiting for a spark to ignite it.

Her hands, held small in Mum's. No more.

The soap, like Velcro, pulls against the supple skin, removing memories of a touch that had been everything.

She places her hands back under the water, and the heat from it makes her gasp, bringing her thoughts back to the present. She holds her hands steady. Allows every bubble to wash away.

When her hands are bright pink, with no soap left on their surface, she stares at them for a long time. And imagines the pulse that runs violently under the skin. She takes the nail brush under the flowing water, and scrubs.

Each nail brushed, left, right and top, but the bristle sticks into her thumb at the wrong angle. A small drop of blood flows a little pink and swirls down the drain.

She rinses the brush under the steaming water before placing her hands, one then the other, under the tap. Under the scalding pain. She counts.

Three.

Two.

One.

Then slowly turns off the tap, tight, and tries to calm her racing heart. Placing her shiny hands into the towel to pat them dry. Drying each finger and inspecting the damage to her thumb.

'It'll be okay,' she says to herself. And she feels calmer, relaxed and soothed by the water and the tingle of her hands. She allows her thoughts to surface, the panic subdued.

For now.

2

MIRIAM

She sits in the old chair, relocated from the office when he had first come home. It was a chair she'd sat in when her feet couldn't reach the ground. One on which she twirled the loose fabric at the seams between newly painted fingernails. She had retreated into it on many occasions with a cushion held tight to her chest.

The rain patters on the window, Miriam turns the dial and tunes in the radio as the pips chime out.

'This is the eleven o'clock news.' The newsreader's voice is loud and she turns the volume down. 'East Berliners are exercising their new-found freedom to travel into the West and long queues can be found along all the major checkpoints. This freedom . . .'

She zones out the reporter and thinks of freedom. How has she exercised her new-found freedom?

There is a little café across the road and the coffees and selection of cakes, she recalls, used to be wonderful. It has been a long time. Would it still be the same? Could she go?

Standing at the window she watches the far corner of the street where people are milling around and she thinks perhaps she could collect something and return home, she wouldn't be more than a few minutes and Hilda says he can be left for a few hours. She says it a lot, but Miriam hasn't left the house.

Until now.

'I'm going out,' she says, and is surprised by the surety in her voice. 'I won't be long.' Bringing the smell of fresh coffee into the house will do him good, she thinks. As she pulls on her boots and takes her coat off the hook, the phone rings. Its shrill noise pierces through the flat and stops Miriam dead; she is taken back to a month ago, another phone call and another door . . .

That night she picked up the phone, the news was still showing images of people dancing on the Wall, drinking and singing.

Unbelievable to think that was a month ago, and yet . . .

They had been watching the scene for hours from the sofa, two hours away from Berlin, two hours away from her father.

'Frau Voight?' a woman on the other end asked.

'Yes,' Miriam whispered.

'You are named as the next of kin for Herr Winter. I'm sorry to say your father is gravely ill.'

As the woman kept talking Miriam sat on the stair, her eyes on the back of *his* neck. He was watching the television. He didn't turn around.

She listened as the woman spoke. *Stroke. Inoperable. Prognosis.*

His hairline nestled in the collar of his shirt.

The front door was ahead of her. Directly in front of her. Five footsteps and she would be at the door. Six, she would have left.

Five steps. She imagined each one, how they would feel; would they be any different because they were walking her to freedom? In the end, however, they had been five steps too many.

Miriam heard the dial tone in her ear yet still held the phone tight. At the front door, her shoes and coat were next to *his*, a matching pair hung side by side, never quite touching. And then *he* was in front of her.

He took the phone from her ear and listened.

'Wrong number,' she said, and stood, not looking up, before returning to the sofa. He replaced the phone, his footsteps soft as he walked up behind her. She took a deep breath and could smell his hand, both paper and oil, as it gripped her shoulder.

The faint smell of oil still clings to her, arresting her, and she steps back. Taking off her boots she checks the door is locked.

Then returns to the chair and to avoid giving her fingers rein to crawl and scratch at her skin, pulls a cushion to her chest. The day passes in a blur of Bach, Brahms and symphonies she hasn't heard before, punctuated with the pips from the radio and the same news, over and over again.

As the haunting strings of the *Kinderszenen* play out, a lump forms in her throat. 'I didn't know,' she says. 'I didn't know you were . . . there. Why didn't you tell me, Dad?'

She reaches out to touch his hand. 'I don't understand why, how . . . and Mum?' She shakes her head and starts turning him over so he is facing the chair.

'You were right, about everything, I'm sorry.' A voice long lost, emerging. 'And it's too late now.' She pulls the blanket and curls his white hair behind his ear.

'This is the final journey, Dad. So please let me help you.' She sits and squeezes his hand in hers, feeling the bones.

'Please, Dad, if you can hear me. Who is Frieda?'

He makes no response. She watches his eyelids flicker and tries again.

'Is this Frieda someone you knew when you were . . . imprisoned?' she varies the sentences, over and over.

Nothing.

'Where were you? Auschwitz? Bergen-Belsen?' There were many, she thinks, all over Europe, but she cannot remember the names. 'It was so long ago,' she says. Trying hard to recall her school years. She can only remember the lesson about the rise of the Third Reich and her entire class silent under the heavy weight of knowing that their parents and grandparents had lived in a time of fascism, and may well have been supporters of Hitler. Even her father, a teacher himself, hadn't spoken to her of the war at all.

HENRYK

Emilie and I considered it lucky that by the spring of 1942 I still had a job. The expulsion of professors at the university had started almost as soon as I arrived. Some forced to leave, others through 'choice'.

I stayed, I kept my head down, I taught what they said I could teach. *'German* – Nazi approved.' *German* language. *German* history. *German* literature. I swallowed it whole. Emilie wanted a baby, I needed to provide for a family. But it was a bitter pill.

I looked at my class, each student a replica of the next.

Surrounding the students, desks facing me, were propaganda images. All eyes following me around the room. I was under scrutiny, a light reflecting all the sharp angles of the sun, and me in the spotlight.

Alone.

Until Frieda.

The secret whisperings of her voice drew me to the university day after day. I played the games the faculty required so that I could stay on. I taught the approved *literature* and didn't quibble when my book list for each term came back from the head of department with half the books crossed off it. I did all these things for the conversations in English or French with her. She had me up long into the early hours recalling what she had said and rehearsing what I could say next.

I read with a ferocity that I couldn't understand; I consumed all the books I owned that were written in English and French; I read aloud to myself and Emilie who, although she loved me for my idiosyncrasies, thought I may have gone a little far with my new obsession with language.

I wanted to teach, really teach, so I handed Frieda my copy of *Ulysses* in English, hidden within the end-of-term papers. She said nothing, as though the heavy weight of the volume passed to her was undetectable.

The following week we talked in hushed whispers, in English, while the other students worked, and I realised that I had not found a willing pupil to teach as I had hoped. Instead Frieda, who was ten years younger than me, challenged me and continued to surprise me far beyond any of my peers. More often than not, we talked long after class had finished, the rest of my students leaving without me noticing.

We talked in books, in words, in secrets. Never venturing off the texts, but exploring and pushing the other in our examination of them. *Les Misérables*, French edition, but only volume two; neither one of us could find the first volume. Hemingway neither of us liked. Then the most battered, smouldered and falling-apart André Gide, and I knew possessing this literature would have us both imprisoned. The risks were growing with every week that passed and every book that we exchanged.

Then, at the start of spring term, she handed me *Karl and Anna*. I had never read Leonhard Frank. I made a pretext to call her into my office so we could look at the book together.

'It's too dangerous,' I said. 'No more. This could cost me my job, and you your place here.' I handed her back the book, desperate to read it, to hold it, to turn its pages and get lost in prose that was banned; a prose that was free. 'It's over. I'm sorry.'

'It's never over,' she said, and left.

Leaving the book behind, a heavy weight on my desk.

MIRIAM

As the evening draws in, she turns him on his back, offers him water and empties the catheter bag. The silence of the apartment grows into a roar. She pulls out a bottle of wine with a coating of dust on its neck to pour into a large glass and returns to his side with both the glass and bottle.

'Do you remember when I came home early from the zoo? When I fainted that time?'

She drinks and the liquid both soothes and burns.

She thinks back to first meeting *him*. A white, open-topped shirt, sunglasses tucked into the tip of the 'V'. His chest hair tickled her cheek as he lifted her away from the heat, the sawdust and the punctuated way the bird kept looking at her. He'd taken her outside where the air was blue and fresh with grass.

Her friends followed and stood around watching. But *he* spoke to her. He was older and tall and his eyes had been on her alone. He had treated her like a woman. For the first time, she had felt seen and the object of admiration. 'Beautiful,' he had called her.

But not for long.

She takes another sip, which turns into a gulp.

'It was such a long time ago.' She paces the room, taking large swigs from the glass then topping it up from the bottle. 'I introduced him to you and Mum that Christmas . . .'

An internal tick of diminishing time. Wanting to hold each moment, but knowing every day brings *him* closer. She has no fear of death; the thought of dying is a nothingness.

She shivers and drinks half a glass to try and drown the echo of memory. To try and stay present.

'Was Frieda your mother's name? A sister maybe?' She sits heavily back in the chair and lifts the glass to her lips as her breath ripples, red, along the surface of the wine. 'I didn't know anything, did I?'

Caressing her thumb across the veined and spotted skin of her father's hand, it wrinkles, almost reptilian; she smiles tightly.

'I am still here,' she says, more to herself than to him, watching the change of his skin moved by her thumb.

'You must.' His voice wraps around her in the dark and the drink spills on to her hand as she sits sharp.

'You must . . . leave.' His voice soft, each word a wisp, leaving dry lips. He rests his head back on the pillow. Skeletal bones, loosely covered by skin, are all that remain. Head drawn back, jaw slack, his eyes still closed, lips parted. She moves to touch his face, but brings her hand back, unsure where to put it.

'I did leave, Dad. I have left him. It's over now,' she says, and she means it.

'It's. Never. Over,' he says, the words peppered by static breaths.

She jumps up excited. 'But Dad, it is . . . the Wall . . . You said it would never happen, but it did. It's down. It is over.' But as she looks at his face she realises he is lost; he didn't hear what she said. She sways and places her glass on the table.

He pulls at the watch on his wrist, his fingers gain no grip and it looks like he is plucking the metal links as though they were feathers. She tries to calm his hands, but he continues.

'The ceremony . . .' He wheezes, the words strain with effort. 'Of innocence . . .' His chest rattles. 'Is drowned.' Tears pool in his eyes then flow, gathering speed and momentum, across his cheek.

She tries to stop his hand but he bashes blindly at her. She feels the sob that comes from his chest mirrored in her own.

'My. Love. My. Light,' he wails, the torture in his voice so horrific she holds a hand over her mouth, shaking her head. Watching the tormented.

He becomes still, silent.

Her feet grip into the carpet and her hands ball themselves up in her sleeves.

Taking a step closer she says, 'Dad?'

Tears wet the pillow and his hair is stuck to his forehead. His cheeks are flushed and a low murmur of a howl vibrates in him.

'Miriam?' he asks, still here, with her.

He begins to sob with abandon. His breathing, thick and fast, tumbles over itself.

He touches her arm to bring her closer.

'Frieda,' he starts.

Before she can say anything, his head arches back, his body stiffens. He jolts, buckles and crashes back on to the bed.

She steps back, alarmed.

Then again.

Every sinew of his body taut. Vibrating. The bed ricochets with the force. His hands claw. Teeth grind. His head knocks against the pillow, faster and faster.

'No,' she cries. Then she thinks.

She moves to the bedside table. Shin knocking on the bed.

Midazolam. The pressure plus alcohol has turned nimble fingers into thumbs as she opens the lid and draws up a millilitre of fluid.

The air in the bed whistles and groans. The base rattles. The noise echoes. Hollow.

Saliva leaks out from the corner of his mouth.

Placing the syringe between his lips, she angles it, squeezing the fluid into the inner cheek, and massages it around his bristly jaw into his gums. His teeth are clamped shut in a grimace.

She is supposed to reassure him with her voice, but finds she doesn't have one.

She waits.

Hoping.

Praying.

His body still twitching but, she notices, with less force. He breathes in long, loud rattles.

Tears fall, hope leaking from her eyes.

She is overwhelmed by the need to hug him, to have his strong arms around her and feel safe; just once more.

She moves him into the recovery position and goes to the phone in the lounge. With fumbling fingers, she calls an ambulance, hangs up, then calls for Hilda.

3

HENRYK

From the moment she left my office, Frieda didn't speak to me again in the class, yet I had been drawn into her sphere. She licked her finger to turn a page, I was aware. She moved her thumb across her bottom lip, I was aware. Her pencil moved, I was aware. Wanting to *know* what she was thinking, what had caused the urgency to press the pencil deeper into the paper. She pressed her lips together when she concentrated and when she wore her hair long, curled slightly at the ends, she would bat it away from her eyes. And all too often I became caught in the vortex of those eyes; forest deep.

She was not without admirers, but she went around with a boy named Felix: tall, thin and as skittish as a beetle. I could not see what she saw in him. I tried not to think about it, but thoughts of her seemed to consume me.

As I walked into my class each day I looked to her desk first. As I read the dry papers I was supposed to teach, I saw them through her eyes and made a point to mention Yeats or Joyce, to offer her *something*. Her eyes bored into mine, telling me something I could not know.

I wanted to take back what I had said in the office, to run the risk of being caught with banned books so that I could hear her voice, listen to what she had to say, absorb the languages that rolled off her tongue. It was dangerous and I knew it, yet I continued to be riveted by her every move.

There seemed no other way.

MIRIAM

By the time the ambulance has been and gone, Dad sleeps, pale as bone, and Hilda, creased and colourful as ever, drinks from a delicate cup and saucer. Mum's best china: white with a sapphire trim.

'You did well,' Hilda says. 'I think it's coming to the end now; it's always tough, but you did well.' Her tone commands Miriam to look at her, so she lifts her head before returning to watch his breaths fog up the oxygen mask, askew on his face. 'He's comfortable.'

'There is so much I didn't know,' Miriam says.

'It can feel that way, but it's really normal,' Hilda says, raising her cup. 'To want more time.'

'He was talking earlier, something about drowning, innocence . . . a ceremony,' Miriam says, her voice shaking. 'And he has numbers.'

'Numbers? A tattoo?'

Miriam nods and puts both hands, hidden by sleeves, up to her face. 'I thought they were together,' she says, muffled by the clean fabric of her jumper.

The smell of ironing evokes a time, aged ten or twelve, when she was sprawled in the middle of the bed watching the steam rise from clothes as Mum pressed every crease into oblivion.

'What did you do in the war?' little Miriam had asked brightly.

'The what?'

Mum replaced the iron and turned her back to find a hanger from the pile.

'War, Mum, you remember.'

'Why do you ask?'

'We talked about it in school today.' When Mum didn't respond in a heartbeat, Miriam's estimation of the appropriate time to do so, she continued, 'Anita's parents fled France for England before coming back and Dieter said that his grandparents were in a camp, like a death camp. Were you a nurse back then too?'

'Hmm.'

'We are reading about . . .' But Mum's head was low, her fingers playing with the intricacies of a collar button.

'Please don't cry, Mum.' Miriam moved to the side of the bed.

'I'm fine, love,' she said, dashing tears away with her thumb. 'Did you talk with your father?'

'No – he's . . .' He was in his office. She had poked her head in and realised it was the start of an *episode* as cigarette smoke enveloped him in a cloak of fog. She had kissed his forehead and opened the window before joining Mum in the bedroom. It was best to let Mum find out about the episode for herself. 'What happened? If you want to say, that is.'

'I worked at the hospital, helping wounded soldiers back to the front line,' she offered, busying herself with another shirt. After a long pause, she continued, 'We lived in a small place not far from the hospital, in an apartment with no windows, it was so small you couldn't fling a cat in there.'

'Swing a cat,' Miriam corrects.

'Why would you swing a cat?'

'Why would you fling one?' They laughed together.

'Can you go and stir the soup for me?' She came around the ironing board to the edge of the bed and planted a kiss on her forehead.

'I thought they were together,' Miriam says again.

Hilda takes large strides around the bed. 'I have cared for a lot of survivors.' She places an arm around Miriam's shoulders. 'It is very hard on the families, especially if they didn't know.'

'He isn't Jewish, so why would he have been . . . there?'

'There are some records, it's surprising how much you can find out now.' She gives Miriam a considered look. 'You can leave your father for an hour or two, you know? It'll do you some good to get out too.'

The idea of leaving the safety of the apartment makes her mouth dry and she licks her lips with a dry tongue and tries to swallow.

'I'm sorry, Hilda, but I . . .' Her words form then change and form again. She thinks, double-checking, rethinking how to say what she wants to say. Double-thinking. Triple-checking. Wringing her hands in her jumper. Her mind jumping from feathers, the grip on her wrist, Frieda, her mother, and finally landing on *him*.

'I can't,' she says. 'But thank you, Hilda.'

Hilda looks at her then changes the subject. 'I think he's over the worst of it. He needs to sleep it off, but you may find it happens more.' Hilda looks at him and, as though linked to what she said, both his legs tremor slightly. 'This may be the way he goes.'

Miriam places her hand over her stomach to stop the fracturing within.

His legs stop shaking, as he mumbles, '*Frieda.*'

HENRYK

A Wednesday in March, it came to be that I was no longer employed by the university. It was a day her seat was empty.

They didn't tell me at the end of the term, the end of the week or even the end of the day. The head of department, Herr Wager, a formidable ex-officer of the Third Reich, with the scrawny dean of the university, Erik Scholl, by his side, entered the classroom.

'Apologies, Herr Winter, but your class has finished. You are no longer a member of this faculty. Please collect your jacket.' He placed an enormous hand on my shoulder and turned me forty-five degrees towards the door.

'Why?' I asked, but I supposed it didn't matter why.

'Sorry, Henryk,' Erik said. 'Only Nazi officials have the required education to teach at this facility now.' He stood taller as he rubbed the blackboard clean of my writing and started filling it with his own.

I gathered my jacket from the back of the chair. Some students watched with interest, others with pity and many focused on their books as I shut my briefcase.

'Can I get my things from my office?'

Erik turned his back and started addressing the class. *My* class.

I was pushed through the doors and into the corridor. Our shoes the only noise as I was escorted to the main double doors. Herr Wager opened them for me, but remained inside.

'Don't leave Berlin, there will be questions for you,' were his final words. And in that moment, I thought it must have been Frieda, she must have reported me.

Two large hands squeezed my arms, leaving their imprint behind. 'Goodbye,' Herr Wager said.

A sting lodged in my eyes and throat. And a spike of ice formed across my chest. They would find *the* books, they would arrest me. I walked away from the university, fear giving my feet wings, and turned the corner away from the entrance, which had just become my exit.

I saw her out of the corner of my eye coming towards me.

'Professor,' she called, and on impulse I turned towards her, even though I knew I should turn away.

Her hair blazed out behind her, white in the sunshine. She was running towards me, and I stood motionless, unsure of where to place my feet. I wasn't sure if I should run away, duck and cover, or run towards her. What I did know was that I forgot to breathe, so that when she caught up to me, I was as breathless as she.

'Professor,' she gasped, and her voice dropped an octave. 'I have something for you.'

I kept my arms crossed at my chest, to try and get some command over my body in the presence of her so close to me. We were the same height and the intimacy of being unable to look away from her face, to hold her entirely in my vision, was unnerving.

'Haven't you done enough?' I said. She looked wounded and I dropped my hands to prevent them from reaching out to touch her. Despite fearing she had caused all of this, I couldn't master myself enough to walk away, to run away, as I should have done.

She was the image of my demise.

MIRIAM

The image of her father fitting until he dies, and there being nothing that anyone can do about it, sits heavily with Miriam. The silence
expands until Hilda swallows the dregs in her cup, places it down with
a tinkle and picks her bag from the floor, knocking the newspaper from
the table as she does so.

Hilda taps on the headline. 'God, indeed.' And she laughs.
'Speaking of which, I had a discussion with your father's doctor, Dr
Baum, today. I was going to talk to you in the morning, but now I'm
here . . .'

Miriam looks up, meeting Hilda's eye.

The turn of conversation makes her senses sharpen.

Full alert.

At the mention of his name, even though ten years have passed,
comes the familiar sting. Dr Baum sat behind his desk, the bustle of the
waiting room behind the closed door. The doctor illuminated as the sun
streamed through the window so she could never really see his features.

She digs her nail deep into the nail bed and pulls at the loose skin
she uncovers. Her mind runs so fast through all the '*meetings*', as if
they were one. The stale coffee, the thick pile of her medical notes,

the antiseptic and the prescriptions, and her husband's clammy hand clasped over hers.

An overwhelming need to wash her hands grips Miriam like vertigo. To peel the layers of skin away, to turn back time, to when *his* hands had never touched hers.

Trying to force air into her lungs so she won't faint now, with Hilda in front of her, Miriam can smell Dr Baum's office. She knows she is not there. She is in her father's room, she is home, Hilda is in front of her, a creased worried expression on her face, yet the air is permeated with the smell of the thick, wool-covered foam seats of the doctor's office.

She can feel her husband's hand like a glove over her own, smell his hot breath and hear Dr Baum clear his throat as he theatrically placed his glasses on the notes, offering his sympathy and his prognosis. Discussing options *for her*, agreeing a way forward *for her*, shaking hands and leaving with pills.

For her.

She clasps the fabric covering her stomach, a soft nylon, almost sheer, it hides her fingertips as they touch her warm flesh, to help her find her centre.

'There is a care plan meeting happening next week,' Hilda says.

The words fall like heavy drops.

'I'm not sick.' She looks to Hilda, to see if she *knows* her past. And her present. But Hilda is taking her father's pulse.

'It's for your father. Routine. To check we are doing everything to support you.'

Miriam moves her fingers on her stomach. Thumb. Forefinger. Middle. Ring. Baby. Pressing each one into her skin, then back. Baby. Ring. Middle. Fore and thumb.

'You did really well, it's not nice seeing them like this. I do understand.' Hilda consults her watch. 'It is very late, or actually it's very early. I shall leave you to rest.'

Hilda picks up her bags.

'Remember, keep an eye on his respirations, call the paramedics again if you need to. Plenty of fluids once the midazolam wears off. And Miriam . . . sleep for you, okay?'

She manages a faint smile. Hilda is a wave of fabric and colour, her glasses perch in her curly hair like a bird in its nest. She hugs Miriam, who stands solid, Hilda's perfume creating a floral smog. 'Stay where you are, I'll see myself out.'

As soon as she hears the door close, Miriam rushes to lock it and turns the catch. She sees her feather, which lives between the door and its frame, on the floor with a snatching of dust and places it in her pocket.

4

MIRIAM

The next day, her father is settled and flush-faced. Unable to find the energy to sustain her usual verbose rubbish, she cares for him in silence. Her eyes are red and heavy, having not slept, just rested in the chair, watching him. The world seems harsh in the morning light.

The kitchen cupboards are almost empty: crackers, coffee, but not much else.

'I'll have to go out today,' she says to herself as she pulls out a pack of crackers. Wandering into the living room she switches the television on. East meets West is still, after a month, the only news.

'I was terrified.' A young man with a mop of black hair and wearing a denim jacket is speaking to the camera, a microphone close to his mouth. It's old footage, she has watched it already, but as she watches it again, she eats.

'Once I'd taken the first step, well, I thought they would kill me. Shoot me right there and then,' he continues. 'But I just kept walking.' He looks away from the camera back to the Wall behind him. 'And I won't be going back.' The camera pans back to the reporter as the man is carried off on the wave of the crowd.

'And the festivities continue. Christmas really has come early here at Checkpoint Charlie.' The reporter signs off and they cut back to the studio.

As pictures of Helmut Kohl, Gorbachev and President Bush flash on the screen, Miriam hears the post arrive through the letter box.

She turns the television off and leaves half a cracker on the kitchen side before collecting a letter addressed to her father in close-knit writing, familiar.

Herr Winter, it says, but it's for her.

It seems to weigh heavily as she stumbles back to his room.

Dad sleeps.

She is alone.

She kisses his papery cheek. 'Please don't leave me,' she says, smoothing hair off his face, and places an extra blanket from her mother's bed over him. She picks at the scab that has formed over her thumbnail and stares at the floor, the effort of breathing is enough. She cannot do anything else but wait.

Time pressed down on her before, like a silent companion, but after last night it has started to tick. And it's loud.

'I'm sorry I haven't been here for you,' she says to her father. 'I want to help you.' She slices the envelope open. It doesn't matter what is inside. She knows it's from *him*.

She pulls out the back of a polaroid. Reading her name in tight print. *Frau Voight* on the back, the only content.

Frau Voight. The back of the picture reads. But Dad's name is written on the envelope.

'He sent this to *you*,' she says, alarmed at the image of herself. A heat starts in her chest and races to the top of her head.

She stands abruptly and walks to Dad's office, the place most of her memories of Dad reside.

Opening the door, his office smells old, stagnant as a library in summer. Full of words and thoughts, committed to paper, then forgotten.

She heads straight for his heavy, walnut desk and looks for his matches. The desk occupies the entire end of the room. The writing pad still holds indents of words written by his hand.

A photo of his parents, sepia. The creases along the centre and through the middle divide, yet the picture is one of togetherness. Held in a frame, the only ornament. Mum's touch never entered this room.

The desk obstructs the sash window, which overlooks the street lined with skeletal oaks and horse chestnuts. The cafés have their red, green and blue awnings rolled in and their tables and chairs stacked away, but the bakery, she can see, has its billboard out announcing fresh loaves.

The bricks of rye, wholemeal and country bread are walled up behind the glass counter and she remembers that sweet treats line the inner counter. She had pushed the door to a sing of the bell and, with both hands on the glass, deliberated over which iced doughnut was for her, and which would be for Dad, while Mum chatted with the baker about holding with traditional rising agents and such.

Her stomach grumbles as she turns from the window.

Bookshelves full of heavy titles in many languages line either side of the room to the back wall, which is bare. Four imprints in the carpet are shadows of where the chair had stood.

She finds the matches in the top drawer of his desk and lights one with shaking hands, kissing the flame to the corner of the polaroid. Then, as it catches, she places it in his ceramic ashtray at the back of the desk and watches as the picture curls and folds, blackening first the image and then, finally, her name.

The smoke hangs in the air and strangles her.

She opens the window as the ashes curl grey and she thinks of the chimneys. The images of smoke and ash. The camps. And her father, there.

Standing in his study, where everything is him, she starts to rummage in the drawers, pulls out ledgers, thick books, paper and more paper. Looking for answers.

She scans each document for his handwriting. The papers seem to be accounts with dates starting from the sixties, some notepads in shorthand, mostly scribbles in pencil.

Miriam discards all she looks at into a pile in the middle of the floor. Before long she is lost in a warren of his work, puzzling her way through notebook after notebook. When all the contents of the desk are on the floor, she moves to the bookshelves.

She scans along the titles, many shelves full of texts in German, English and French. Educational as well as fiction. Poetry, essays and plays.

Translated collections of Yeats stand resolute, side by side with English originals. She picks one up, *Michael Robartes and the Dancer*, and rubs her fingers over her lips. The shelf just under it has more Yeats. The same book. The entire shelf full of the same volume, in many editions and translations. She pulls out one at a time and looks at them, opening the cover. *Property of Berlin State Library*. And another. All the same. She counts twenty copies. Most from the library. What had her father been doing? Why did he need so many?

She carries one back into his room and drops into the chair.

The rhythm of his breathing becomes hypnotic. She opens the cover and wafts the pages around his face. Old, worn and good. 'The last sense to go is smell,' said one of the ever-changing faces in the hospital.

She flicks through a few pages and comes to the first poem, named the same as the collection.

She reads and the words dance around the alcoves of the room like a child's hanging mobile. Knights with spears, dragons and the lady she imagines with a tall hat and veil.

After the first stanza, she looks up.

'I remember this one, do you?' She reads on, gently touches the golden sheets of paper as the book bends in her hands. A muscle memory for her fingers of when she had held the pages before.

'Get yourself to school, Miriam,' Mum had said, leaving the apartment. 'I'm on a twilight, I'll see you in the morning.'

'What about Dad?' Miriam picked up toast from the table.

'He'll sort himself out.'

She went to his room. Curtains closed and air clotted with sleep. He was in bed.

'Morning,' she said, and bounced on the bed next to him, kissing his head. He smelled over-warm, his soft skin unwashed.

It was an *episode*.

She kicked off her shoes and shimmied up the bed to sit on the pillows and put her feet under the duvet.

'What shall it be today?' she asked, but saw the Yeats on the table. 'Oh, this is my favourite.' Picking up the book she said, 'If you are sitting comfortably? Then I shall begin . . .'

And she had, she read to him, always during his episodes, she would skip school and spend the day by his side, making him better. She had never thought why he had episodes of inertia, he just did. She thinks back to the childhood version of herself. She hadn't questioned it. It was just as it was. She read poetry to him. And it worked.

Her mother never knew.

'*They say such different things at school*,' she finishes the poem.

Tears wet her face and the words on the page swim around. If this helps, then this is what she will do: read to him to help him come back.

She has never thought to ask him about his life before her. Hitler killed Jews and her parents weren't Jewish. She has never thought about it any more than that. History, as horrific as it was, has never been this close to home.

HENRYK

Frieda and I stood not far enough away from the university building on what was my last day. Her hair was floating towards me, over her neck and shoulders, on the air of early spring. It wasn't cold yet she was in a heavy cotton dress, beads of perspiration threaded through her hairline.

'Haven't you done enough?' I said.

'Actually, I haven't done nearly enough.' She squeezed my arm. The same place Herr Wager had gripped, she warmed. 'Here.' From the satchel heavy on her shoulder she drew out book after book, launching them into my arms. All the covers and first few pages had been ripped off long before they had come into my possession. But I knew them as well as my own hands.

'How did you get these?'

'I stole them back for you; you'd have been arrested if they'd found them.'

'What are you doing?'

'Returning them. I wasn't sure which ones, so I got as many as I could and all the papers from the locked drawer in your desk.' She paused. And like a parent who finds their lost child, I felt both infuriated and yet relieved beyond measure.

'Here, you may as well have the bag.' She took the bag off her shoulder and passed it to me, but with my briefcase and the books stacked in my hands I couldn't take it. She laughed, a deep rumble, which I mirrored in an instant smile. As she smiled back at me, her face changed. Her eyes, unframed against pale lashes, were large and emerald.

'Let me help,' she said, and placed the books back into the satchel before handing it to me. I was surprised by its weight. 'I couldn't get everything,' she continued. 'I only found out this morning and it took me ages to get into your office.'

'I thought the burning of books was over. I should never have kept them in my office,' I said, placing the satchel over my shoulder.

'If they burn books, it's not long before they burn people too,' she said with an emptiness in her voice. She looked to the ground and I followed her gaze the full length of her dress to her brown shoes. And before I knew what I was doing I placed my fingertips to her chin, palm up, and raised her head to draw her eyes back to mine.

I jolted in shock at the charge of the connection beneath my fingertips. And like forked lightning, flames of electric heat stunned me and I took a step back, dropped my hand but not my gaze.

'I don't understand,' I said. 'Why are you helping me?'

She beamed. 'I also have a leaving gift.' She blushed scarlet, which only made me want to touch her skin again, to radiate in its heat. She pulled out a desperately weathered book from her backpack. *Michael Robartes and the Dancer*. 'Do you have it already?' I looked around, aware of my surroundings now. Uncertainty made me pause, but she placed the book into my hands.

'Yeats? No, I haven't,' I said, admiring the slim volume. 'Thank you.'

'See you again, professor,' she said, looking relieved, and walked away.

But she was walking my way. I held back, aware of the contraband I was carrying. Now they were in my possession again I wanted to get them home, not past the university, nor further into the belly of the beast. When she obviously wasn't going back into the building I had no choice but to follow her path.

'Excuse me, Fräulein Hasek,' I called over-formally. 'We are heading the same way and it looks like I am following you. Perhaps you could slow a bit and I can escort you instead?'

'My name is Frieda,' she said.

'I know.'

'Then don't call me by my family's name when you know mine.'

'I . . .'

'We all have a family,' she continued, 'but that doesn't mean I want to be associated with mine, does it?' And although her words were hostile her eyes shimmered.

'Apparently not,' I started. 'So, Frieda?'

'Yes.'

'May I escort you for as long as our paths remain the same? I'm Henryk,' I said.

'Nice to meet you, Henryk.' Her voice became lower, deeper and more sensual than anything I had ever heard as she said my name.

We walked in silence. I didn't know what to say to her, nor what I would say when I returned home, but what was really playing on my mind was how I could get her to say my name again.

'You went to a lot of risk getting these.' I tapped on the bag.

'Not really. I do some filing for Herr Wager and I overheard his conversation before class this morning, so I slipped into your office and took everything I could.'

'Still, you could have been caught,' I said.

'One small act of defiance.'

'Stealing my books was political then?'

'No, it was judicious,' she said.

I couldn't reply as I followed the well-trodden path home. I turned on to my street as she continued walking.

'Thank you, Frieda,' I said.

'See you again, Henryk.' And she smiled before walking away.

I wanted to shout back, *But when?*

I walked up the path to the front door, knowing I had just experienced a life-changing moment. The thought fleeting, yet the apparent cliché didn't make it any less true. I watched the main road, hoping to see her silhouette, hoping she would return and hoping to delay the inevitable truth. That I was now under suspicion, that Emilie and I were in danger and I would now have to make it real, by speaking it out loud.

Feeling my feet centred on the concrete step, the key felt heavier in the lock as it turned and the door hushed open. The smell of wood polish and orange blossom, Emilie, drifted through the door.

The road was empty as I looked back for the second time, and I knew that to taste heaven would lead me to hell. *Heaven and hell?* I shook my head, trying to shift the fog that had gripped me.

A fog by the name of Frieda.

5

MIRIAM

She comes to a line of poetry that he uttered last night.

'*The ceremony of innocence is drowned.*' It is in this collection, and all the other copies he has from the library. There is something more to this poem, but she doesn't know what. Maybe this is the way to Frieda, to find out what happened to her father, maybe this will help him to move on.

'Move on,' they say. But what they mean is die. But maybe, just maybe, there is a way to get him back?

She shakes the notion away.

'Hope doesn't belong at a deathbed,' Mum had said in her matter-of-fact way after difficult shifts, and she was right, of course. 'All we can do is offer a peaceful, unburdened passing.'

He will die. But perhaps he's holding on for something? She looks at what he has become and as she turns and offers him water, she thinks of what Hilda said. There were records. Maybe her father was searching for something within the library itself, and if not, maybe she can understand a bit more about his past. After all, it is one that is shared by millions, although few as lucky as her father to have survived.

She looks at her father's sleeping form before collecting her coat and boots. She stares at the front door. 'I won't be long,' she reassures herself. 'Just a few bits, and the library. I can do this.'

He knew where she was, but she had left him. That was the hard part and now . . . now, she was going out.

She replaces the white feather between the frame and door, its plume thick and missing in parts, the quill bent at the end. She draws her finger enticingly over the surface, feeling the internal snap, made without creating a sharp edge.

The key turns in the lock. It crunches and clunks. She moves away, feeling the comfort and pull of home even as she walks through the empty hall, down the stairs. Lionel is at his desk.

'Afternoon,' he says, looking up. 'Christmas shopping, Fräulein?'

Miriam nods.

'How's your father?' he asks.

'Stable,' she says, pushing the main doors.

The rain of yesterday has eased. A carpet of autumn cushions the road as she walks through the landscape of her childhood.

Nothing has changed, structurally, yet the feelings it evokes have altered. No longer safe, every corner is a risk, an unknown. When she gets to the main square, the shops and cafés are loud: voices, music and lights. Kids playing on the street, carrying portable machines that boom at her, and cyclists splash water up near the curb.

They all blur into one thing. Not *him*.

Once on Neufertstraße she is treading in unfamiliar territory, her eyes searching not for landmarks, but for recognition. She allows her feet to walk while she scans all who pass her from shoes to face. She is looking at everyone. Behind every hood, under every hat, she searches for his eyes, his face.

Him.

The shop on the corner is full of people, trolleys, food, radio blaring from speakers. Her thoughts swirl, her eyes wander, darting from one thing to the next. Holding an empty basket, she stares at the shelves and finally collects brands that are vaguely familiar. At the counter she picks up a newspaper: '*Freiheit*', the headline shouts at her. *Freedom*.

Miriam fumbles for the money and walks away without her change. Taking some deep breaths back outside on the street she takes a step. 'The first step was hardest' – she remembers the East Berliner's words – 'but they got easier.' She must keep going.

To see if she can find any answers.

HENRYK

I didn't have to wait long to see Frieda again. After a turbulent week when Emilie wept in my arms each night, we tried to work out what to do next. Neither of us slept. She had found us a new place, a tiny apartment with an open loft hatch. We weren't in hiding and yet we had found an apartment which could hide us. Emilie paid six months' rent in advance and gave her maiden name to the landlord.

To leave Berlin under suspicion meant greater risk. To be caught trying to leave meant certain arrest and, since neither of our hearts were in leaving the only city we had ever called home, we stayed. Telling ourselves that the only way was to wait it out.

We said goodbye to our home, reluctantly leaving the key with Frau Voss, who clicked her teeth in what I hoped was sympathy, but may have been eagerness to 'care' for our neglected belongings.

I wasn't sure we would ever see the house again and I felt empty. With a lot of bags, we moved into the half-apartment where we were safer. Emilie still sobbed, but the tears brought her sleep. I listened as her breathing relaxed, and held her as she slept. I couldn't rest, knowing they were on every corner and up every street; it only took one wrong turn and they would be after *me*.

I didn't know what was next and had no idea, under every eventuality I could imagine, how I would protect her.

Emilie was nervous to continue her work, but she went every day, and she held her head high. Nursing was what she did, it was who she was, and nothing would keep her from her job.

When she left for the hospital I would walk, trying to find a bit of peace, knowing that if I didn't force myself to leave the apartment, I wouldn't.

MIRIAM

The bus from Sophie-Charlotte-Platz is full, everyone heading to the centre, bursting with lively talk and cheer. She rolls her ticket between her fingers, shopping in her lap, and allows the conversations to roll over her too.

Her feet echo heavily on the marble floor of the library entrance, the pillars blocking the view of those snuggled into sleeping bags, escaping the rain. She notices the bullet marks on the inner wall, a reminder of the past; untouched. She has never been here before, there seemed no need, what with her father having a library at home.

A wet heat envelops her as she wanders around the library shelves, like walking into an open book. Many people are milling around and she feels a little out of orbit.

A woman in a warm-pink cardigan is at the desk, a long queue forms behind her. 'And what I am saying . . .' the woman says hotly, leaning her arms on the counter.

Miriam walks past the desk to study the dark shelves. The building is vast and illuminated over multiple levels; stairs reach around and jut out of nowhere, taking Miriam up and around a different floor, before finding another staircase again. She follows a sign for 'History', then 'Europe'.

There are a lot of books and she feels intimidated by the sheer volume of them. Her eyes jump to 'Holocaust' written in large, bold letters. She takes the heavy book and sits at a table close by. Her hands shake and she chews on her inner cheek until she can taste blood before turning the page.

Faces.

People.

She turns each page, scared at what she will find. Scared of what she is looking for. She looks at every one, at every face. Looking for Dad and for Mum. But after a few pages, she feels sick. Each person was a mother or a father, a brother, sister, son or daughter. She has never looked at them this way before and each page she turns makes her feel worse. Her head is spinning, yet she doesn't look away. Just trying to absorb something that cannot be comprehended.

'Excuse me.' A woman appears at her shoulder. The same woman who was at the desk. 'You're sitting on my coat.'

Miriam springs up out of the chair, apologising profusely.

'That's okay,' the woman says. 'Hard stuff.' She nods to the book on the table.

'I'm just . . .' Miriam starts, but cannot finish the sentence.

'You just come over the Wall?' the woman asks.

'Oh no, I . . . I . . .' Miriam blunders. The woman has cropped hair, white but with some blonde of youth. Her skin is bronzed and she has a hard look.

'I was one of the first over,' she says. 'I lived in Leipzig, I thought I'd see what all the fuss was about.' She straightens her white top under the deep-pink cardigan and Miriam sees a beautiful red beaded necklace that gets tucked into the top as she adjusts.

'Fuss?' Miriam asks.

'Yes, the West is Best attitude . . .' The woman wears no make-up but looks strong and healthy. Miriam pales in contrast and pulls at her sleeves, scratching at the skin along her inner wrist as she crosses her arms. 'Not sure I believe it. This library is built on lies, built on the back of the Nazis' pillage. These books are stolen from the people.' The intensity of her gaze makes Miriam look away to the book on the table. She picks it up and puts it back on the shelf.

The woman continues: 'It's hidden away, forgotten. All of it. As Stalin said, one death is a tragedy, one hundred thousand a statistic and six million . . .'

'Six million,' Miriam says to fill the silence.

'Indeed. Anyway, I'm sorry, I will leave you to it.' And before Miriam can say anything else the woman walks away.

Miriam looks at the shelves and shelves and shelves, wondering how many books were in this library. She drags her fingers across the spines; how many homes must these books have had before landing here?

She walks down aisle after aisle, past students studying at tables that run along the width of the room in rows. As she passes, many look up. Their glasses bigger than their faces, they resemble baby owls blinking in the daylight. Others remain bent double, their focus on their notebooks. Their studious faces remind her of her father at his desk.

She thinks back to the images in the book and a curl of anger balls in her stomach. He must have been rounded up, put in a cattle wagon and then . . . As she looks around she thinks if every book was a person . . . But the sheer volume is incomprehensible.

The library is too big, and now, all she wants is to go home.

6

MIRIAM

The stale smell of wet coats and damp people rises in a condensing fog. She wipes the window with her sleeve and contemplates removing her coat, but her entire body is fatigued. She allows herself to be rocked as the bus moves along. Her thoughts lost on the faces and the stripes and something intangibly hollow about the way they looked into the camera, almost begging, but angry, looking for . . . something: recognition, or maybe just a record.

Dad has a number. He was there too. But he survived. And in her mind, she sees him twisted up and on the floor. Calling out for her. Shouting *her* name. Needing her. Sweat trickles down her back, and she shifts impatiently in her seat as the bus struggles its way through traffic.

She starts chewing the skin along her fingernail and picking at it. The shopping bag twisted and twisted in her hands. As the bus chatters, Miriam counts the stops for home. She has five stops to go, when the same woman from the library gets on. Miriam shifts to make space for her and smiles. 'Hello again.'

'Hi,' the woman says and Miriam returns to looking out the window as the traffic stalls around the main junction to Brandenburg Gate. There are so many people milling around she can hardly see the Wall. She watches people with their cameras taking pictures. Once a concrete wall, now a tourist attraction, and the thought makes her sad. History made into show.

Miriam puts all her concentration on keeping her hands still in her lap. On breathing in and out. And not thinking about her father.

Four stops until home.

'Did you find what you were looking for?' the woman asks.

Miriam shakes her head. 'I don't really know where to begin.'

'Something in particular?'

'Sort of, but not really. I just . . .' Miriam shifts her weight closer to the window under the scrutiny of the woman next to her.

'I'm Eva.'

'Miriam,' she says, shaking Eva's warm hand.

The bus jerks to a halt and the driver swears loudly. A giggle runs through the bus and both Miriam and Eva smile.

'To be honest, I'm not sure what I am looking for. I feel really stupid that I don't know what they went through.'

'The victims of the Holocaust?'

A feeling drifts over Miriam like a haze that won't lift. *Victims?* How could her father have been a victim? Tears fall unbidden and, as Eva sits and gives her the space to cry, a calm comes over Miriam, her hands relax and she says, 'I found a number on my father. I think he was in a concentration camp. I suppose I wanted to find out more, but . . .'

There's a very long pause in which the bus stops and people exit and enter in a jumble of bodies.

Three stops.

When the bus rattles on again, Eva says gently, 'Only Auschwitz tattooed.'

'Pardon?'

'Your father would have been in Auschwitz at some point if he has a tattoo,' she says.

'Oh God.'

'No, no God.'

The bus is full, yet more people mill on to it, despite the lack of seats. They stand and sway as the bus heaves along.

Two stops.

'Auschwitz,' Miriam repeats.

'The books in the library will have some details about Auschwitz for you, if that's really what you want to know.'

Miriam looks up.

'I don't know. It's just so horrific,' Miriam says, and feels Eva's hand on her shoulder. Tears fall from worn-out eyes. They keep falling and Miriam cannot find a way to make them stop. Eva rustles in her coat pocket and hands Miriam her handkerchief. It is grey with lace along the outside, folded neatly into a square with a blue flower on its front.

Auschwitz.

'Eva?' she asks as the bus slows. 'How could my father have been in Auschwitz? I mean . . . he isn't Jewish, nor was our family.'

'Not all prisoners were Jewish.' She perches on the end of the chair, her feet in the aisle. 'In fact, the camps were homes for asocials, criminals, political activists, gypsies. You name it. If they didn't agree to Hitler's regime, they went in a camp.'

'Would they have stayed together? My parents?' she probes. 'They were married before the war.'

'No. In all circumstances men and women were separated.'

'My mother never spoke of any of this. She didn't have a tattoo though,' Miriam says with certainty.

'There were other camps. Ones that didn't tattoo their prisoners. Camps specifically designed for women.'

'I . . . I don't know anything about this.'

'That's okay. Where is the tattoo?' she asks.

Miriam looks confused.

'On his body,' Eva clarifies.

'His wrist.'

'That means it would have been after 1942, they stamped the tattoo on the chest before that.' Eva sounds so matter-of-fact it makes her head spin.

'They did?'

Eva nods and pushes the arms of the chair to raise herself to her feet. 'This is my stop.'

She has learnt more about her father's past in a short bus journey than she had in her entire life to date. She wants to thank Eva, but cannot find any words, so just looks up at the woman. Her eyes are bright and unframed and Eva, aware she is being studied, smiles and offers her hand.

Miriam in confusion passes her the handkerchief back. Eva pockets it and walks off the bus. She lifts her hand as if to wave from the pavement as the bus blunders on.

One stop.

The palace, and the River Spree is on her left as the bus swooshes by, the evergreen trees painting a striking contrast to the grey canvas around them.

HENRYK

Exactly a week after I left the university I headed to the Palace Gardens. Completely absorbed in my own troubles and weary beyond thought, I didn't see Frieda until I had almost walked past her. She was sitting on a park bench overlooking the Spree, in the shade of tall evergreen trees, just off the main path. She held a cup in her hand and another was by her feet. She wore a sky-blue dress and her brown leather shoes. Her hair was tied up, plaited, and weaved around itself into a knot. She relaxed into the back of the bench and the pine, the grass and the hint of flowers in the air made me feel dizzy.

'How did you know I would be here?' I asked.

'I didn't.' She looked at me until it was my turn to blush.

'Sorry, I was being presumptuous. That one is not for me, is it?' I said, indicating the second cup on the floor. She shook her head. 'My head is a little full and . . .' I continued, 'I'm not making sense. I'll leave you to your . . .' My words drifted off.

'That's okay. Here.' She offered me the second cup. 'You can join me, if you like. Felix seems to have forgotten our arrangement.'

I took the cup, the one that hadn't touched her lips, and she poured coffee from a flask into it. I tried to shake my thoughts into something cohesive. Admiring a beautiful woman was fine, slavering over a beautiful woman like an ape was not. She drank from her cup, her lips full and wide, and when she took the cup away, she smiled as I sat next to her.

'It's coffee,' she said as if I had looked uncertain.

'Thanks.' I took a gulp. It was warm and strong.

'What happened to Felix?' I asked.

'He's off doing his own thing.'

'You two are a couple though?'

She took a considered sip of her drink and I watched her lips close over the rim again. She took the cup away.

'You're staring,' she said.

I cleared my throat and caught her eye. I watched her lips part as she brought the cup to them again. She smiled, lowered the cup and licked her bottom lip deliberately. She laughed, a boom of pleasure, and caught up in its contagion I laughed along with her.

'Couldn't resist,' she said.

'Neither could I.' Then, desperately trying to gather back some clarity, I said, 'You were talking about Felix.' I turned away from her to face the Spree and, across the bank, leaves were emerging from skeletal branches. Leaning back into the bench, we were side by side. Close, but not touching.

'I was? Felix and I look like we are together. We are good friends. But for all appearances, looking like a couple is mutually beneficial.'

'Why? If you don't mind my asking?'

'Parents. Both of ours. So being together keeps our parents' "plans" at bay.' I must have looked puzzled. 'Marriage,' she clarified.

'I understand.'

'Did your parents push you into marriage too?'

'No, my parents died when I was a boy. They were political activists after the war and were at rallies or marches more than they were at home. Although she never said so, my grandmother was ashamed of my mum, but she loved me. I was born somewhere in their war between

59

love and duty,' I said, nerves turning my thoughts into speech without pause. 'I don't remember them. It was my grandmother who wanted me married, but she wasn't so keen on Emilie.'

'Because . . .?' she prompted.

'My grandmother was . . . conservative, Emilie isn't.'

'Ah, but you married her anyway?'

'I did. It's been eight years now and . . . she is . . .'

'You love her?'

'Very much.' The truth made it more bearable, to be saying this to the most intriguing person I had ever met. Sitting next to Frieda didn't diminish how much I loved Emilie, nor did she cease to exist.

'I'm sorry your parents are being difficult, it must be hard for you,' I said, trying to turn the focus away from myself.

'I think they are worried I'll end up like my Aunt Maya. A dyke.'

I laughed, but she looked unhappy. 'Is that the reason for Felix?'

'To hide my sexuality? No. His? Maybe.' I must have looked shocked. 'Don't tell me you are as conservative as your grandmother?'

I laughed. 'No. What happened to Maya?'

'We were so close. She was a linguist and she taught me everything.'

'So that's where the languages come from?' I asked.

'Yes. Aunt Maya travelled and returned with language; I was a willing student. But they killed her, I'm sure of it.'

'Your parents?' I said, alarmed. My mind faltering, trying to make sense of what she was saying. She was close to me. Next to me. When she lifted her cup, she brushed my arm with hers.

'No.' She turned on the bench so we were face to face again. 'The "cleansing". She would have been arrested long ago; she stood up for what she believed in. I wish my family would do the same. Cowards, the lot of them.'

'Everyone deals with times like these in different ways,' I said, trying to be supportive.

'Sure, but I'd have more respect for them if they had some backbone.'

'I'm sorry about your aunt and your parents.'

'I'm sorry about yours.'

'Surely your parents can see you're too young to marry.'

'Am I? You are married.'

I nodded. 'I suppose I must have been your age when I married Emilie.'

'What's your wife like?'

'Small, dark, sharp tongue and even sharper mind,' I said with a smile.

'How did she take your news? Being fired?'

'Not well.' The understatement seemed hilarious and I laughed.

'I'm sorry,' she said, laughing too.

'Don't be, it's me who will be sorry.'

Her laugh gravitated towards me like a hug and I instantly felt better. As if the depth of her laugh had taken some of the weight off my shoulders.

A light shone in her eyes, like an incredible force pulling me closer. Towards those eyes and those lips. Our laughter stopped.

I placed my cup on the ground and raised her chin with my fingertips as I had before, though this time the jolt didn't make me jump back in alarm. I saw myself in her eyes. And there was something else there. Something I couldn't understand. Her skin under my fingertips grew warm, an electrostatic wave of heat that charged me somehow, as I tried to understand if what was happening in me was happening to her.

'What are you doing?' she whispered.

'I don't know.' But as I said it I did know, I knew as sure as my heart was beating. This was something new. Something unfounded in me reflected in her. Something I could not walk away from.

She was framed in my eyes. The scenery obliterated by the contours of her face. I moved my fingertips across her jaw, her pulse jumped as I brushed past her neck and cupped her face in my hand.

She had a tiny mole almost hidden behind the curve of her upper lip.

I watched her reaction as I tilted my head towards her, she didn't move. She questioned me with her eyes, but her lips parted the tiniest amount and her bottom lip was moist. I moved towards her mouth, capturing her top lip in both of mine.

I shifted back to where I could see her eyes again. As my hand skimmed the back of her head, into the nape of her neck, I pulled her forward and she melted into me.

She brushed both her lips along mine, a touch feather-light on the surface, but it resonated deep in me.

It was a power that eradicated any other thought.

Her lips on my lips.

She pulled away first and a heat crawled through my limbs, to keep her close to me. I moved in to kiss her again, but she caught my eye and somehow shut me out, so I shifted my hand around her shoulders and drew her into my arm. We faced the park together.

'You are married,' she said.

My heart buzzed in my throat. But when she said nothing more I swallowed.

'The country is at war,' I countered.

'What does that have to do with anything?' She slipped out of my embrace.

'They are facts, are they not?'

'Yes.'

'A fact is an absolute,' I said.

'What am I then?'

I paused for a nanosecond, because I knew, instantly. 'Frieda, you are light itself.'

Our eyes connected and although she didn't say it, I could see her thinking, and she flushed. I wanted to kiss her again. I wanted to touch her.

'I have to go back to the university,' she said, getting up. 'Or I'll be late.'

I stood up with her and tried to arrange my thoughts cohesively. She smoothed her dress and put the cups back in her bag. 'Thanks for the coffee,' I said.

'I enjoyed *talking* to you, Henryk.'

Goosebumps travelled up my arms and tingled over my neck as she said my name.

'Maybe again?' I offered. 'Same place?'

'Same time?'

'Tomorrow?'

She smiled her assent and left.

7

MIRIAM

'Auschwitz,' she says. Leaving the shopping in the kitchen, she offers her father water and moves him as he rests.

She spends a long time washing her hands, thinking of the word, 'Auschwitz'. Three fingernails bleed by the time she has finished and she feels sick from the pain of the water.

Exhausted beyond words she pulls a blanket over her knees in the chair and falls into a dead sleep.

She wakes in the middle of the night. Guilt crawls at her skin as she quickly attends to her father's needs, offers him water, which he gulps down, and some food, which he doesn't eat. Once he has resettled she looks out of the window. Saturday night. She hears sirens and voices, but her street is quiet. Under cover of night she gently moves his watch.

She looks at the number for some time. As if to seek the answers from the grey lines that mark his skin.

The newspaper article from earlier today shouted *Freedom*. The Wall may be coming down, but had her father ever been free? She covers him again and goes into the kitchen to unpack the forgotten shopping and washes the dishes that have accumulated on the side. She cannot find the tea towel, nor a clean one in the drawer. She dries her hands in the bathroom and takes a deep breath before switching the light on in Mum's room.

The mess she made the day before remains and she finds the tea towel amidst the dresses that heap and overflow from the wardrobe. When she was little she hid in this wardrobe trying on Mum's shoes and playing with the tassels and fabric of the dresses that fell around her like rain as she waited out the impending storm brewing in the rest of the apartment.

She places the shoes back in their boxes and hangs Mum's dresses back up on the rail, they are creased and she feels guilty as she smooths them, trying hard not to touch them with her damaged fingers.

She stacks her mother's shoes: dancing shoes, best shoes, summer and winter shoes. Even the shoes Mum wore to Miriam's wedding. All immaculate and cared for. But something has been dislodged and they won't stack straight. Miriam takes them all out and starts again, but finds the handle of an old carpet bag that has fallen over at the very back, which topples the boxes.

It is heavy and nothing she remembers seeing before. Putting it to one side she restores order to her mother's wardrobe. Turning to find the carpet bag waiting like a patient lapdog, she twists the clasp with a flick, popping the mouth of the bag open.

She pulls out a yellow sheet, dull, like a faded daffodil, and sits on the end of the bed. The more she unfolds the sheet the stronger the scent of urine, sweat and soil rise out of the cloth. The sheet is large and the contents drop into her lap. A navy-and-grey striped shirt. Miriam pulls the fabric out and the shirt turns into a dress. It is long and thick, coarse cotton.

It has a triangular collar, and three buttons down the centre. She opens the yellow sheet fully to a single-bed size, gets up and lays the sheet out on the floor, before placing the dress on top.

Like a shadow in the sun, she cannot look away.

The dress has holes in it, frayed in places and creased as though it has been kept folded for a long time. It is a striped dress. A uniform.

She carries it into his room.

'What happened to Mum?' she says. 'Dad . . . I found . . .' she starts, then folds herself into the chair, dissolving into tears of exhaustion, loss and something else.

Fear.

HENRYK

I stayed at that bench by the Spree for what felt like all day and watched as ducks flew by and herons waited for a catch. I watched the world move. Finally, when I knew Emilie would be home, I got up. Thinking the entire walk back about how I could tell her, how I could frame the feeling so that she could understand. I had always told Emilie everything. Like breathing, we talked. Not telling her this seemed unthinkable, but despite my meandering walk home, I hadn't come up with a single thing I could say.

'Henryk, is that you?' she called, anxious, from the tiny space that was now the kitchen. Our flat had become a boudoir, stuffed with all the little luxuries that had been spread out in our old house, but here flowers, paintings and books were hoarded everywhere. And there was my wife, in her apron, strings loose at her back.

'Hi.' I walked to her and kissed her cheek.

'Where have you been?' she asked.

'Walking.' I pulled the loose knot and retied it, smoothing out the hospital uniform underneath. I placed my hand on her wrist and spun her into my arms. I guided her small body out of the kitchen and into the overcrowded lounge. I hummed tunelessly as I led her into a rather fast waltz.

'Henryk, what are you doing?' she laughed.

'I'm happy,' I said, and was about to explain, to allow the words to dance out, to share this feeling with her and make her part of it with me, when she stopped abruptly.

'What is there to be happy about?' she asked, standing on her tip-toes, her eyes so deeply etched in pain, it sliced me to the quick. She placed her hand on my cheek and kissed me, before walking back to the kitchen. And the truth of it hit me so hard I felt winded: the reason for my happiness would be the very thing that would devastate Emilie.

MIRIAM

The dress, the uniform, is on her lap. Dad is sleeping and night hangs in every corner of the room. She touches the buttons, smooth and round. The front pocket is frayed and something is poking out of the corner. She places her hands inside the dress and the fabric rustles, but there is nothing on the inside that would explain the sound. Nor an opening to the pocket.

'There's something in here,' she says, her voice rebounding in the darkness.

Miriam retrieves her mother's sewing scissors from the drawer in the living room. She feels the cold silver seep into her warm hands, the soft way the steel curves at the handles, the tiny screw that allows the blades to be held together, yet move apart. Her fingers caress the blades until she reaches the tip, barely touching it, she hovers her fingertip over the point.

The pressure of the metal pinches into her flesh and as soon as blood oozes, her body relaxes as if lowered into a warm bath. She watches the drip as it forms on the tip of her finger. She breathes deeply. An unnamed mass of something unravels.

Its familiarity welcome. An old friend.

She clears her throat and places her finger in her mouth. The iron taste a pinpoint on her tongue, its warmth lining the roof of her mouth.

Taking the scissors to the seam, she cuts a few inches, reaching her fingers inside she finds a slip of paper, folded. No bigger than a match box.

Unfolded it is exercise-book size, but as thin as tissue paper. The writing is in the tiniest script Miriam has ever seen. It is almost illegible. She places the letter on her lap and turns the lamp so that it showers light down on her, and the dark of her skirt allows the grey pencil to stand out. The paper has no margins, no paragraphing, just corner-to-corner writing. Both sides.

She looks closer. Pinpricks shiver up her arms. Miriam lifts the paper into the light, an intricate spiderweb of words, and reads.

Dear Henryk,
Eugenia Kawinska believes she no longer exists, she died the moment we became nothing more than a number.

Actual dying and turning to ash is irrelevant now.

I listen to her, but I cannot let her words penetrate. I am trying to maintain hope. But hope, here, is like wishing on stars; a whimsical, childish fantasy. It is naivety. It is no more than a memory.

A memory of the red-brick bridge of Gleis 17, of a time before.

Now we are swallowed by the fumes of our bodies. The wool blankets seem to rise, cloaking us in an unwanted fabric of stagnation. The only movement is my breath hanging, limp and dull, in the summer twilight. I hold my pencil, to guard it with my life. While many pray, I cannot find any other way to keep being, to keep being me without this, so I press my pencil firm and strong to mark the paper and save a life.

Eugenia started to speak, almost to herself, and held within the confines of our own air, we listened.

She told of her capture.

Hiding in a box, painted white and concealed behind curtains, in the back of a shop in her home town of Lublin, she waited. Listening to the earth quiver in rage as soldiers gutted, raped and burned the entire town. Every person was killed or shipped out.

Eugenia said it felt like a bad dream, one where you need to run, but you cannot, legs numb and unmoving.

It is how I feel here, every minute of every day, without you.

Eugenia is a Catholic girl. You'd like her; there is something warm and comforting about her face. Before this I imagine she looked like the angels we saw in the picture of the Virgin of the Rocks: peace and calm beauty. Her face has endured the hardships, her brow furrows and her eyes move too fast, but when she speaks, she holds a room. She is so composed. Graceful. She even has the curls of an angel in the hair and the lips.

Eugenia said that she switched off to the roar of the death march. No longer asleep nor awake. Hearing voices, whispers and fast feet, a separate compartment lid of the box she was hiding in opened and illuminated her. Unable to lift her head she looked ahead along the stretch of the wooden box. She saw shoes, blue shoes with green thread laced in the sides. Baby shoes. One lace loosely knotted, the other not tied at all. Little grey socks peeking over the rim, and pink, chunky legs.

It was a mama and a baby.

Eugenia tells of how the mama tried to hush the baby, but he squawked when she placed him in. The little

71

shoes and their baby legs tried to leave the box, to clamber out, but he was too little. The mama spoke quietly. She told the baby to lie down, but he stood. He held a rag tight and reached up for his mama as soon as his bottom touched the ground.

The mother wore no shoes as she climbed in and, though only wearing a light dress herself, she took off her jacket, swaddling the baby twice over, like she was tucking him into bed. She lay down and curled around him – there was no space for her to lie flat. She positioned her body as if protecting him from every angle: his cushions, blanket and bed, all in her. They lay together and she pulled the lid shut. They were all in the dark again.

Henryk, I write her words here to capture them, for she speaks this in such a way . . . this is her story not mine.

'I didn't want to see her face. It was quiet for a while, the mama whispered to the baby, her words were sooth-ing. Hearing the smallest tones of the simplest of plea-sures, I felt this hollow dip grow in me. I was falling into it, turning my stomach upon itself. The baby must have asked for nursing, I heard the healthy suck and swallow, loud at first, then softer. He must have drifted off as the hurricane entered.'

Miriam leans back in the chair, silent.

8

HENRYK

The platforms at Berlin-Grunewald station were safe before the war started. A place that people flocked to for a chance to leave everything behind; for a chance of freedom. But 1944 was not a safe year and leaving was no longer a holiday.

Forced to travel. To a destination unknown.

Sweating and with a thirst that smothered the rising bile of hate in the pit of my stomach, Frieda and I found a small place to sit, but we could not rest. Moved and jostled and moved once more.

It wasn't until late on the night we were arrested, after being marched through streets for hours, that we leant our backs against the red brick of the station bridge. Looking out at the wooden cattle wagons lined up on the tracks, I felt able to look at Frieda. Her eyes were wet with tears, but none fell.

'I'm sorry,' I said.

We were in the eye of the storm. Waiting. Gleis 17 held hundreds of people, all like us. Keeping out the night chill the best we could. The hushed tones of uncertainty were punctured with leather boots on cobbles, shouts and shots. Hundreds of people together, some with luggage, most, like us, with nothing but each other. She was shrouded in my coat, its navy collar turned up around her ears and her hair falling loose over it. I felt her heart beat as though connected by an invisible thread, each pulse charging my own. A conversation of hearts.

With Frieda, my words never allowed me to articulate freely in the manner I was accustomed to. I hid behind the words of great poets, the best artists time had offered us. I could not rely upon my own words, for they cracked my lips and coarsened my tongue. I should have spoken words that were my own to her, but often, I did not need to. I would mumble and falter to tell her how raw and new my feelings were. She would challenge me with her eyes, drawing my gaze away from my own fingers, busy knotting themselves up, and see me. Right into the depths of me.

For a professor of literature, a man proficient in three languages, I found myself devoid of any skill. As frustrating as using water for ink, I jabbered senselessly. She, however, led me to understand the language of silence and the poetry of eye contact.

I closed my eyes to the world around me and just listened to the beat of her heart, like rain pounding on the open road.

She smelled of a warmth that was home.

I couldn't sleep waiting at the platform, so I laid my fingers on the rough collar of my old coat. I held Frieda close to me as I cocooned myself in memories, because to live in the past meant I could survive the night.

MIRIAM

The phone rings.

She stares at the paper lying on top of the dress, the uniform, at the end of his bed until the haze of morning casts it in shadow.

'Both of you?' A tear falls, but she doesn't wipe it away. She allows it to drop and become swallowed up in the fabric of her skirt.

The phone rings again, but this time it doesn't stop. Miriam leaves the dress, the letter and her father to answer it.

'Hello?'

There is only static on the other end.

'Hello?'

Nothing. Her heart hammers in her ears. 'Who is this?'

Goose pimples rise at the nape of her neck. As the silence grows louder, it seems to shake the walls around her and she drags the phone from her ear and rests it on the hook. Her hand clutches the plastic.

She runs a bath in the early morning light and shivers as the steam rises. She is entombed. Frozen. Deep in the bath water her goose pimples are scalded away. Like single drops of water, her thoughts accumulate until they flood.

Dressed in a lined cotton skirt and a pullover, she returns to the room. The phone rings again. She picks it up slowly and places it to her ear.

'Hello?'

'Miriam,' a voice answers. A familiar voice. *His* voice.

Axel.

Miriam quickly replaces the receiver. She stares at it, at the perspiration made by her palm. She unplugs the cord and stands over the table: the lamp with its oversized shade, the box of tissues, a pad of paper and now the phone.

Silenced.

She sits in the old chair, reupholstered more than once, now covered with a corduroy fabric. Her small, thin fingers run across it and then back, changing the texture of the surface from a deep maroon to a wine red.

Back and forward.

Over the years, she has laughed and cried in this chair, talking to her father's back, or to his face.

Back and forward her fingers move, faster and faster, over the ridges of fabric, digging her nails to create a satisfying crump. Her thoughts circle to the letter and the person who wrote it as her hands transform into paws to claw at the chair.

Her wedding ring is the only blemish, its thick, gold band sucks her finger into it and then spits it back out again, making her knuckle look deformed. She stops pulling at the chair and starts pulling at the ring instead. Having never taken it off, not once, just the idea makes her look around the room.

Dad looks peaceful, fast asleep, on his side.

She nudges the ring up and over the knuckle. It pings off and lands heavily in her lap. Her finger now pale and open to the elements seems to shine a brilliant white. She smooths the new skin across her lips.

Unsure what to do with the ring in her lap, she picks it up between thumb and forefinger and draws up her feet, her arms around her knees, the ring perched on top. She stares at the empty circle, its unending band.

The intercom buzzes and as she jumps up, the ring skitters along the floor. She collects it from the corner of the room, where it glints at her, and places it in the silk lining of her navy skirt pocket for now.

'Frieda,' her father mutters; his feet twitch like a dog in sleep.

The intercom is followed by a knock at the door and a voice calls through the letter box. She cannot hear it over the noise of the bed and she doesn't care.

Actual dying and turning to ash is irrelevant now.

She is Frau Voight, nothing more than a name as Eugenia was nothing more than a number. But the uniform, the letter, it means Mum was there too.

Mum is gone. And Miriam never knew, and Dad . . . and who was Frieda?

She is all alone with her questions.

'It's too late,' she says. 'I'm too late.' There is nothing she can do to scrabble the past back, to ask the questions, to understand, to really *know* them. Because this . . . this dress, changes everything; every memory and everything she thought she knew has fallen away.

There comes a bang at the door and a voice she knows.

'Miriam,' the voice calls, and on stiff, cold legs she wobbles out into the hallway.

'Hilda?'

Miriam opens the door and Hilda gently touches Miriam on the arm as she walks past and through to the bedroom. 'Are you okay?'

'I . . . was asleep,' she says, following Hilda into the bedroom.

'Of course. Your father looks rested.' Hilda turns to her father. 'And how are *you* this morning, Herr Winter. Henryk, you are looking good today.'

Miriam rubs her eyes as Hilda blunders to the bedside.

'I'll make you a tea? Coffee?'

'Coffee, please.' She opens her bag.

Miriam puts the kettle on and stands in the kitchen. When it screams and the water splashes on to the hob, she jolts to remove it, unsure how it came to boil so fast. A fragment of time, lost.

Flick. Gone.

She takes the boiled kettle off. 'Sleep, I just need some sleep,' she says and dabs the tea bag as it bobs around the cup.

'Need any help?' Hilda removes her gloves at the doorway as Miriam scoops the teabag on to the side sending an avalanche of tea over the edge too.

'No coffee?' Hilda asks.

'I wasn't thinking, sorry.' She goes to pour the drink down the sink.

'No problem.' Hilda intercepts the cup and holds it with both hands. 'All done here.'

They walk back into his room.

'How has he been?'

'Quiet, but okay.' Miriam looks at his shrinking body and the bag. The dress no longer at his feet. 'Where's the dress?' she says. 'The dress that was at his feet, where is it?'

Hilda points. 'Just there.'

Miriam rushes to the chair and lifts the dress with both hands. Holding it against her chest.

'What is it?'

'It's a uniform, I think.' A shiver runs up her spine. 'She was there too,' Miriam says. 'They both were. I found this . . . and a letter inside it.'

'Is everything okay?' Hilda asks. When Miriam doesn't answer, she continues, 'Why don't you get yourself up and out today? I only have your father on my list this morning and you could . . .' They walk into the living room, which smells of wood polish and dusty sunshine. 'It's a beautiful morning out there.' Hilda opens the curtains and then the windows to prove it. The light shines into the long-forgotten room and dust floats unbidden around her.

'I can't leave him,' she says. 'I . . . I've missed so much. I won't leave him again.'

Hilda sits and places a hand on Miriam's arm. 'They didn't want you to know. If they had, you would have known. Here, go for a walk. It'll clear your head.' She warms to her idea and nods. 'I'll be here.'

And although every part of Miriam doesn't want to move, she is pushed into a coat and boots and out of the door. 'It'll do you good. Now go,' Hilda says. 'We'll be fine.'

A biting cold hits Miriam as she walks down the street. Breathing clean air, the world is waking up, and the lack of traffic means it must be a Sunday. The world keeps moving. As do her feet.

She hasn't walked without a destination for so long, and the further she goes the more her muscles unclench. At the junction, she turns right on to Dancklemannstraβe, the classic Berliner residential build-ings shine white from the morning light. All the shops and restaurants are closed and the bike racks empty. The glass-fronted buildings link to each other like a bumbling carriage. She walks past a clothing shop, an Italian restaurant, a second-hand book and vinyl shop. The residents in the apartments above remain sleepy quiet.

She walks to the beat of a train on tracks, to the beat of her heart, but her head is lost in a letter from the past.

It mentioned Gleis 17. The picture of cattle wagons in the book she saw at the library. And the footnote, Grunewald station. Where they shipped people, her parents too, no doubt, off to camps.

When she nears Lietzensee, she turns right on to Sophie-Charlotten-Straβe. She is going back to where it started. For they both survived, even if they were separated, they made it out alive in the end.

She walks to Grunewald, her breathing erratic, her heart pumping in her ears. The station is quiet as she enters the brick building, the flo-rist closed, and for a place designed for footfall, the lack of noise rattles her. A white sign with large black letters directs her to the track. She takes a deep breath and follows it.

9

MIRIAM

The track is rusty, covered in leaves and stones. As she stands on the platform the wind roars like a living thing, grinding, whistling and softly growling through the trees. The tips of her nose and ears tingle and pulse. She waits, as though for a train from the past.

Three wooden sleepers lie across each other, haphazard, with a bronze plaque screwed in to the top commemorating the deportations that happened here. Years ago. A lifetime ago, she thinks. Her hands grow cold, her feet numb and she stands. Waiting.

Stems of roses are played with by the wind. Once laid in memory, their petals join the leaves and big grey stones underfoot. A rose petal floats across her feet, once red, now crumpled black. She bends and picks up a stone and runs her finger over its jagged edges, its heaviness comforting.

Millions were deported, killed. The bringers of the roses come to remember, but her parents chose to forget. Why?

She places a stone on the sleepers.

'For Mum,' she says, then chooses another stone to lay beside the first, so they touch. 'For Dad.'

They survived. When most died. They chose to have a life free of the past, but she cannot understand why Mum would keep the uniform. The clouds gather overhead and the wind swirls.

'But if you chose to forget,' she whispers, squatting low so that she is level with the stones sitting together on the sleeper, 'why did you keep the dress?'

She presses her lips together hard. 'And the letter.' She didn't know a Eugenia. Why would she keep a letter that didn't really 'belong' to her?

Her memories shift like smoke, changed by the current, and suddenly dissolve at the crunch of footsteps on stones behind her. She struggles to stand on cold legs. A couple, both in long, dark coats and fur hats, have come with flowers and Miriam nods to them, before noticing the stones. So many stones, so many people. Why would her mother keep a dress with just one single letter?

There must be something more.

Something else, maybe.

And just as she stamps life into her feet, she feels momentum. To leave a place stuck in the amber of memory and return home, to the present, to Dad and to the dress. To find out what happened to them. Her breath steams ahead as rain falls.

Through the station and out, the sky rains grey and she is soaked before she has walked to the end of the car park, her hood drips water on to her face. She finds a solitary taxi about to pull away and hails it.

The jingle of tinsel cheer that rings both from the radio and the driver stun Miriam into silence. It is an assault on the senses after the clear, crisp quiet of the platform. The peaceful respect of the past scratched away by cheap music.

'Where to, love?' the driver asks, turning the rear-view mirror so he can see her. She tells him and sees the smear of fingerprint left on the mirror. It fragments the light into a unique pattern that keeps catching her eye as they wash through empty streets. The screech of windscreen wipers creates shooting stars from raindrops across the screen. Closer to home, she wonders where Axel is and feels nauseous without any warning, just thinking of him.

'Don't mind if I turn up the radio, do you?'

The false cheer pulses out at her from the warbling driver.

She pays the driver. He wishes her a Merry Christmas and pulls away, leaving her on the step of the large five-storey apartment block, shadowed by oak trees on either side, their leaves littered on the cobbled ground. The front door a white light guiding the ship lost at sea home.

Unlocking the main door, she continues up the stairs, the fur of the hood tickles her damp skin. She moves as fast as she can, but her feet hold her back, each step weighted, like walking through water.

She finds the key in her bag, turns it in the lock and pushes her way into the apartment.

Time moves through frames like snap shots. Blink. Snap. Move. Her thoughts circle around and around. She hears the mattress and the radio in the background.

His door glides open and he looks dead.

She takes a step in, unsure yet eager, but stops as the smell of over-ripe fruit, more pronounced by leaving, hits her like a wall.

His chest rises then falls.

She smiles at Hilda in the chair. The radio is playing a quiet violin solo and Miriam can hear the haunting, sharp notes as they cascade, reminding her of journeys and of goodbyes.

'The weather turned, eh?'

She nods.

'I had a thought,' Hilda says, getting up. 'Now that you are here to stay, perhaps you would like to see a doctor?'

Miriam takes off her coat and kisses her father's papery skin.

'There's nothing wrong with me.' Miriam's voice rises, then falls fast, as she somehow loses her centre. Unravelled somewhere between the purpose she felt at the platform looking at the stones and now, back in the apartment.

Hilda packs her glasses into her bag. 'I think you are doing an amazing job. But it would be wrong of me not to offer you some support, medical or otherwise.' She closes her bag and puts it on her shoulder. 'Think on it, okay?'

Miriam looks at her father, a sheen across his forehead and his cheeks pink. She touches the back of his hand with her fingertips.

'If this *is* what you want to do?' Hilda continues.

A fireball of frustration rises so fast she feels she may launch herself at Hilda and tear into her.

'There are other places, hospice perhaps, if you are finding this too tough. And it wouldn't be a reflection on you, just . . .'

The internal fire is extinguished with a hiss.

'No. I have to. I want to,' she implores Hilda.

'Then we need to look after you too, so you can look after your father. I can make you an appointment.' Hilda gives Miriam a kiss on both cheeks as though to seal the conversation, then sees herself out.

The soloist is still playing and Miriam turns the radio off, cutting the harmony dead.

HENRYK

The memory of Frieda in my coat, the colour of midnight. I know if I can remember, if I can hold on . . . I search for a memory that kept me alive.

It will keep me alive again now.

And among the shadows I find it, as easily as knowing my own name.

Yeats.

The images bounce like the raindrops did as I shook off my coat and hung it over Frieda's bathroom door.

'They burnt your books today.' Frieda passed me a cup of black tea as I sat on the end of her bed, brushing a hand through my wet hair. The bed, which also doubled as a sofa, was the only furniture, aside from the coffee table. The room had been painted a worn rose colour, deep, rusty pink. It felt warm despite being cold.

Her apartment faced east and was part of the central block of flats in the building. With only one window, situated in the bathroom, no natural light also meant no natural heat.

'And you have ten thousand marks on your head.' She sat opposite me on the low table, and blew the steam, which climbed like smoke from her cup. Our knees were close, but not quite touching.

'Ten thousand marks?'

'Yes. Think you're worth a bit more?' She laughed.

'No. More and you'd hand me in yourself.'

'Don't speak like that.'

I touched my knee to hers but she pulled away. 'My books. All of them?' It stung, although I knew it shouldn't.

'Don't worry too much, you were in great company. I imagine the clouds will be full of text in the morning. Look up and the world can read your words.'

I sipped my drink and looked into the cup.

'What's the matter?'

'They're burning Wells and Freud, I doubt anyone will feel the loss of my work.'

'Sure they will. Look at me.' I continued to look into my cup. Her knees nudged mine so I almost spilt the contents. 'It's just a display, you know. The books, they'll survive the bonfires.'

I looked up at her then, really looked at her. 'Emilie has the means to leave Berlin,' I said.

'Oh.' She slumped back. 'When do you leave?'

'I don't. I can't leave.'

'You have to.'

'No, I won't leave you.'

'This is your life. Emilie's life. You don't have a choice.' Then, after a pause, 'Did you tell her?'

'I told her the truth so that she could leave if she wanted. She won't. She called me a misguided fool.'

'She's not wrong.' Frieda smiled. 'In other circumstances, she and I would be great friends. For what it is worth, I agree with her. There's nothing here for you anymore.'

'Frieda,' I said, and she looked up. 'Now who's the fool?'

She tipped her head to the side ever so slightly and all I thought about was running a finger along her jawline to her chin to pull her closer to me.

'You know I have to say it: you have no other choice, Henryk. You have to go.'

'Does it make you feel better?'

'Better! What? Telling you to leave, perhaps forever, with your wife? Go and live happily ever after, leave me behind?'

'Then why?'

Our faces so close, separated by the ribbon of steam. 'Because perhaps you need to hear it. From me.'

'Permission?'

She nodded.

'If I needed permission to leave I would never have stayed. It's not as clear as that and you know it.' I placed my cup on the floor.

'The country is in ruins,' she said. But as her mouth moved with the words I was looking, really looking, into her eyes and the unspoken connection from before kindled to life. It was a connection that held nothing concrete, just a deep, albeit slightly uncomfortable, recognition. I didn't understand it, but I knew that this was the force of us.

'It's not the country or some misplaced patriotism. I'm staying because I cannot walk away from you.'

'Yes, you can,' she almost whispered. 'If I can walk away from you, then you can walk away from me.'

I smiled.

'I can walk away. I can,' she said, more to herself this time.

I'd leant so far in I was squatting in front of her and her breath was hot on my face.

'Who are you trying to convince?'

'All these words mean nothing,' she said.

'I know, we talk, but—' I cut myself off. I was at war; I wanted to kiss her lips and work out what I meant through them. But if I did I would lose the contact with her eyes and there was a magic in luxuriating in her gaze. 'I do love Germany,' I said for want of other words. 'The old Germany, I mean.'

She smiled and moved back to take a sip of her drink, then placed it beside mine on the floor. 'You are just like Yeats.'

She did this so often, catching me off-guard with a remark that must make sense to her, but made none to me. I made a mumbled, incomprehensible sound. I admired the shape of her shoulders and the tilt of her head, her jaw.

She laughed. 'You confuse the love of your country for the love of a woman.'

I sat back. 'Your evidence?'

'Take "Leda and the Swan". It's about the rape of a country, not of a woman. His love is all about Ireland. A dreary spot of land he calls home. You place me in your way. Instead your love of Germany is what keeps you here, not me.'

I took both her hands in mine and rubbed my thumb over her knuckles. Slowly. 'Don't insult me.'

'They say Yeats loved women, but what he really did was love his country, a broken country, over anything else.'

'Is that wrong?'

'No, I'm just putting forward the argument that if you searched your soul you would see that I represent everything that makes you think of Germany, the good and the bad.' She looked away. 'And therefore you cannot leave one without the other.'

'That is true, but I am not leaving you. The country can go to hell.'

'It already has.'

'Well then, have you finished?' We were nose to nose and if I moved at all I knew I'd lose eye contact and we would continue our conversation physically.

She pulled back. 'No,' she said. 'I haven't finished.'

'Carry on then, please. Don't let me stop you.' I placed my hand over hers again and pulled her closer, my legs weaved in between hers, touching.

'The best lack all conviction,' she started.

'While the worst are full of passionate intensity,' I finished for her and traced my thumb over her wrist.

'Exactly. That represents men,' she said.

'You are saying I have no passion?'

'No, you have no conviction.'

'Really?' As I spoke I could feel her lips touch mine, a featherweight of expectation. But I was losing her eyes and they were brighter and greener than ever. 'Yeats represents humanity, the human condition, *man* not men.'

'Well, as you well know . . .' She touched my chin and lifted my gaze, which had dropped to a strand of hair fallen to her shoulder. 'I have both intense passion . . . and conviction.' She smiled.

'You,' I said. 'You are a break in the mould.'

She kissed me, pressing her entire body into me. She proved her point as my hands were given permission to explore the rest of her body.

And as our bodies spoke, in rest and exertion, we didn't part.

MIRIAM

She takes out the dress and sits with it on her lap beside her gently snoring father. The poems, the collection, *when all is ruin once again.* The stark reality of the Berlin Wall falling, the impossible happening she had left, and . . . the hollow faces of the Holocaust, *to be carved on a stone* . . . to not be forgotten. She unfolds the letter.

Maybe the dress was not Mum's at all? The glimmer of hope in the dark has Miriam reading the letter again, she doesn't even know where Lublin is.

She touches the dress, her fingers running over the coarse cotton. She plays each finger in turn along the stripes as though she were playing a piano. Thumb, fore, middle, ring – now ringless, she thinks – baby, and then back again. The whiteness of exposed, shrunken skin on her ring finger shimmers under her father's light.

She walks her fingers across the stripes of the uniform until she gets to the pocket. A thread stands out from where Miriam found the letter. She tries to poke it back in and searches with her finger. There must be something more to this.

As her fingers poke into the frayed pocket they touch only fabric and are tainted by the smell of misery.

10

HENRYK

Frieda left my side first. I think she had to because, after all, I always left her. We sipped water.

'You have to go. It's just before curfew,' she murmured.

'I could stay,' I suggested half-heartedly.

'We both know you can't.'

She dressed lazily, her blouse not buttoned but tucked into a skirt with nothing underneath.

I wrapped my arms around her from behind and pressed my nose into her hair. 'In another world,' I said.

'In another lifetime,' she sighed. 'You know the line in that Yeats poem that sticks with me most?'

I shook my head to bury further into her hair.

'*The ceremony of innocence is lost.*'

'Drowned,' I corrected and kissed the skin on the back of her neck I'd uncovered.

'*The ceremony of innocence is drowned,*' she said.

I nodded as I blew on the damp skin my kiss left behind.

'*The ceremony of innocence is drowned*,' she said again. 'That is so true.'

'I have to go.'

'You have to go.' She turned her head so I could kiss her mouth again.

MIRIAM

The smell of the dress hangs in the air as night falls around them and, although defeated, she checks each corner of the pocket for anything, anything at all that would make sense of why her mother had a uniform dress with a single letter that means nothing to Miriam and, as far as she knows, is nothing that her parents ever mentioned. And as despondency takes hold, her fingers uncover a flap of fabric inside the pocket itself, and she can feel another piece of paper.

Sitting up in the chair, she tries to grasp the paper hidden in the pocket with her fore and middle finger, but it doesn't budge.

'There is something else here,' she says to her father. She returns to her mother's sewing box and takes the scissors again. This time she grasps the handle and takes them back to her father.

With shaking hands she leans over the dress, cuts each stitch and follows the seam to open the pocket up to a flap. She uncovers three more tiny, folded, matchbox-shaped papers.

'There is more,' she says and holds down the flap of the pocket with the scissors. She carefully unfolds the paper.

It is paperback-book sized with a corner missing, tiny script written in pencil over both sides of the thin paper.

It appears to be written completely in French.

Unfolding another, the writing is on the thinnest paper she has ever seen.

'Did you write these?' she asks, but he shows no sign that he can hear her. Miriam cannot skim-read it, the writing is too small, but the flicker of hope turns into a flame; they are in French.

Mum. Who neither read nor spoke anything other than German. These are not *to* her and, she thinks with relief, they cannot be *from* her.

But who?

She turns on the main light and moves closer to the lamp beside his bed, switching on its glare. The third one is as tiny as a wallet, both sides are written on. She studies it closely, it is written in German.

Henryk,

I am alive. At least I think I am alive. This is the worst kind of hell if I am dead. I saw you – I know it was you – as I was pushed on to the wagon at the platform. There were over twenty of us in that little space, six dead bodies before we even pulled away. But I saw the prominence of your jaw as your head turned, the tension betraying your fear.

I remember resting my head on your shoulder, my nose touching the sensitive skin just under your earlobe. The smell of you here – this small spot – hidden away from the rest of the world, was mine and mine alone. Its memory fragranced by your cigarette and the music of the words as you read to me. You looked left and right – I'd like to think looking for me, but maybe you were too scared to look for me.

Icicles have formed over my heart and cannot be melted until I see you again. I feel you are alive, for I know you are strong and can withstand so much.

I can taste salt on the air, I imagine the waves, the sand. There is no space here. There are people literally under my feet, or by my side or on top of me if I cannot keep my footing. I breathe recycled air.

I can barely describe what I see. My only thought is that you are somewhere better, that you are not suffering. To think of you in these conditions is worse.

I will try to find out what has happened. No one seems to understand or hear me. Everyone is milling around with no purpose in their own worlds of pain and loss, trying to adjust to the unfamiliar rules.

Once I know where I am I will try to send word for you.

I am sorry.

Miriam places the letter down. She had just been to the platform, Dad had been there too.

'The letter is to you,' she says.

He says nothing.

'Maybe this one is from Mum?'

But the handwriting looks the same as the first letter. She puts the two together and picks up the next letter, but she cannot make out any of it. French, again. The same handwriting.

'Or Frieda?' she says, trying the name cautiously. He makes no response.

She knows she shouldn't hope, but maybe, just maybe, he'll come back, if she can find something for him to live for.

Her head is full of questions but her hands go to the scissors. She lifts the dress and the bag with the sheet inside and takes it to the dining room table. Removing the placemats, candlesticks and table runner, Miriam places the sheet down first and the dress on top. Turning on all the lights she touches the collar and the cuffs.

Excitement flows through her, like a small child.

She traces her fingers along the seams and tries not to notice her battered and scabbed hands. She opens the buttons and moves a hand inside the dress to flatten it between palms, but the seams of the dress stand apart, raised as though something were in them.

'There's more.'

She looks at the dress exposed, laid out; a cadaver waiting to be cut open. She slices through the stitches along the seam of the collar and finds another piece of paper, she sets it to the side, and another and another. The entire collar is stuffed with paper.

Cutting into every seam, she places each sheet she finds to one side and continues snipping at the threads to reveal letter after letter. As the next hour passes she finds many hidden in the main bodice, the waistband, the sleeves and every hem.

She works to uncover the past.

Unpicks old words. Old wounds.

The stale smell of the dress permeates, and makes her head feel as thick as the cotton.

She looks at the stash of loose paper discovered. There are so many. Some are large, others just a scrap the size of her thumb. Some have printing on them, either letters or typed print, others written in the margins of a page ripped from a book. One written on the back of sheet music. Most are folded small. Some are rolled up to the size of a finger.

When she is sure that she has found everything hidden in the dress, she starts to flatten and count them. She picks up each one in turn. Many are written in French, so many that she makes two piles of French letters. Finding one in German that she can read, she lifts it up into the light.

Henryk,
I write to you, but I write also for myself. For I know that
if I do not I will be lost amongst the crowd.

My heart is breaking – I do not know if you are being treated better, but I fear for the worst. You do not deserve this. I do not know if you are alive, if you are suffering. The thought of you suffering makes my skin crawl worse than the lice that torment me.

Maybe you didn't get on the train, maybe it wasn't you I saw, maybe you escaped and are with Emilie and happy together. Maybe you got over the border, maybe you are . . .

The sentence is left unfinished.

Emilie. The letter mentions Mum. Miriam's heart sprints and soars. She couldn't have been there. *Escaped. Happy together . . .* The world feels like it is spinning on an axis, about to career off on its own. But Dad has a tattoo. He couldn't have escaped. She reads on. The words now written in pen, faded grey.

This thought of you together fills me with hope, yet it tears me apart that you do not think of me, or want me. That I am here and you are happy. I am torturing myself with thoughts while the camp is torturing my body, my spirit.

I knew going home was a bad idea. I ran to you that day. I knew to help you and Emilie escape you'd need something to barter with. I feared for the future. As soon as you had the ring and the diamonds I had taken from my mother, you and Emilie would be free to leave.

Once you left I would not see you, you would not need me. You would be gone, safe, but not with me. I would be left behind and as every footstep moved me to you, fearing the stomp of marching boots at my back, I knew whatever happened we would be apart.

I do not know if I stalled, I like to think I didn't, but maybe I did. Stayed at my mother's, imprisoned by glass whereas now I am imprisoned by a brick wall, electric fences and barbed wire.

I wonder if we would have been, had there not been a war.

Did the war create us or ruin us?

When you didn't open on my knock, I feared I was too late, I had led the wolves to your door. But Emilie answered. She opened the door and told me to leave. I was so jealous, fuelled by sadness and loss, at her beauty, her simplicity and more than anything, how she had you first. I barged my shoulder into the door and knocked her into the room.

We all stood there breathing fast and shallow. It's amazing how quiet fury can be.

I placed the diamonds in Emilie's hand. I tried to convey so much to her, but she looked at me as if I was going to rob her.

'Leave.' That was all I could say, so out of breath, so emblazoned with emotion it was all I had. I fear she took this the wrong way. But she saw me looking at you and took the diamonds and vanished. She knew what this meant. I am sure she was as relieved as I was devastated.

Then the knock came at the door.

This isn't Mum's, and the relief is buoyant in Miriam. Maybe Mum did escape? But the fact these letters and the dress itself exist means that someone else loved Dad when he was with Mum, and somehow Mum had the dress. The headiness makes her legs shake.

What has she found? And did Mum *know*?

Her eye is drawn to the mantelpiece and the large, silver-framed photograph of her parents on their wedding day standing outside the Church of the Redeemer, arm in arm, looking happy. The church must be derelict now, having stood in the death strip between East and West. When she had planned her wedding, she had wanted it there, the same church as her parents. But with a river on one side and the death strip the other, it was inaccessible. She chose a smaller church nearer the outskirts of town instead.

With pillars and arched doors, the Church of the Redeemer was beautiful and sat on the riverbank like a stranded ship.

Was anything she knew true?

She takes the framed photograph and piles of letters back to his room. His breathing is ragged and his hands and arms tremor slightly.

'Don't leave me, Dad. I've found letters. They are to you, but . . .' With no other information than that to tell him she hastily picks up another letter, written on a triangle slip of yellowing paper ripped from a larger pad.

Henryk, I am in Ravensbrück –

'Ravensbrück,' she says aloud. She says it a few times, seeing if he has any reaction at all. She then looks back at the paper and continues.

The salt in the air is from the lake, not the sea as I had supposed. I am sure I lived close by in Fürstenburg during the holidays when I was a child. Louisa's grave is up on the hill overlooking it. I feel better in some way that I have found my bearings – I do know where I am, but there is no escape from here. I cannot shake the feeling that I am so far away from everything. The women are cold and hard. They close off, shut down to survive. I know this, yet I cannot do the same; if I lose heart then I lose everything.

I have a red triangle on my dress, it depicts 'Political Prisoner'. I even have a red cross striped in paint on the back of the old coat they have allocated me. None of the clothes fit. I have no idea why I could not have kept my clothes.

I feel like a walking target. They are free to kill without cause or warning.

A young woman, older than me yet not old, was attacked by the Blockova's dog so badly, the Blockova shot her. In the head, just like that. The woman did nothing I did not do.

I cannot understand it.

I do not even know her name, nobody will.

'The brutality,' she says to her father's sleeping form and reads the last two lines again. 'Who are these from?'

She places the letters together with the four she has been able to read. She paces the room, comes back to them time and time again, as though the movement of her body will help her mind focus. 'This is by a woman . . . is this Frieda?' Now instead of relief, she cannot understand who and why and how and the thoughts rattle around, more confused and with more questions than before.

'*A walking target,*' she says aloud. '*A political prisoner.*' And she recalls the television showing the pictures of the East Berliners shot at for trying to scale the Wall. East Germany killing their own.

The cost of freedom.

She thinks of her freedom. What will it cost her?

After looking through the piles of letters until her fingers ache and her head thunders, she rests back in the chair, the letters in her lap.

The letters in French sit unread all night and she watches them, as if she can somehow transform them into German, or that she may be able to read them by the morning. Are the ones written in French from the same person?

The thoughts of the letters and their content swirl in her head, so that past and present have fused into one mass of something indecipherable.

11

MIRIAM

She dreams of Mum, growing older and fragile. Until, like tissue, her skin flakes and starts to shed. Pages first fly around her like a storm, peeling off, until Mum dissolves. Pages turning into words and finally single letters fly. She tries to grab them and put Mum back together again but can't.

Awake and unwilling to close her eyes lest the images have free rein, she watches the December morning slice through the window. When she can hear traffic and a bin lorry crash and wheeze along the streets, she gets up to begin her day.

Answers.

Miriam needs answers, before it's too late. *He* knows where to find her. It's a matter of time, and there's no way back. She collects a pile of the French letters into a handkerchief and places them carefully in her bag.

'I love you, Dad,' she says, a ball of emotion holds firm in her throat. 'I will be back soon. I promise.'

Miriam takes a taxi rather than the bus and arrives before the library has opened. She is one of the first admitted through the double doors and her initial thought is that she needs a French dictionary.

As she sits with an enormous French–German dictionary in front of her she unwraps the handkerchief and takes out one of the many letters, wrapping the rest back up. She starts at the beginning. She writes a word, checks and scratches it out, before trying again. One sentence seems to take an age to decipher. And time is not on her side.

The library is almost empty, there are a few people talking, but no students, no pages turning or pencils scribbling.

She puts the dictionary back on the shelf and walks, letter in hand, to the desk. A young librarian with glasses perched on his nose and another pair around his neck busily shifts paper.

'Hello, I was wondering, can you help me?'

'Probably,' he says, not looking up. 'What are you looking for?'

'I am looking for someone who can translate some French letters for me?'

He looks up. 'The French dictionaries are over there.' He points where she has just been.

'I've been there, but what I am after is someone who knows the language and can help me.'

'This is a library. I deal in books, *not* people.' And with that he turns away and rustles paper on the other side of the desk, his back to her.

A hand rests gently on her shoulder. She flies around and the letter falls to the floor.

'I'm sorry,' says a man, bending to pick up the paper as she backs into the desk. 'Here.' He hands the letter back.

'Thank you.'

'I saw you with the dictionary over there?' He points. 'Are you having problems that *Schmutz* here cannot help you with?'

The librarian huffs, but continues with his filing.

'No – yes, I mean . . .' she says.

The man has large eyes and thick lips. He is being kind, Miriam thinks. She's not sure what to say. Sometimes there are no words, but she tries a few to see what happens. When she does, the words come out in a rush.

'I have a letter that is to my father. He is dying and my mother has . . . already and this . . .' She motions to the letter. 'I just don't understand and I don't read French. My father did, but . . . I don't have time to work out each word . . .'

He smiles gently. 'I am sorry to hear of your father?' he asks, and she sees two large hearing aids pushing his ears forward slightly. 'Bit deaf, you see.' He points to an offending ear. 'So I didn't catch all you said.'

Miriam brings her hand to her mouth in apology, then realises he would probably need to see her mouth to hear.

'From what I heard, you are looking for a French person, or someone who can help you with your letter?'

She nods.

'My nonna speaks French.'

'That's very kind, but . . .' she starts, but her protestations aren't heard.

'Nonna and Opa were born in Strasbourg, you know, on the Rhine? Stunning there. We went there a long time ago, when I was a boy, but Nonna . . . It's very sad.' The man takes her by the elbow. 'She stayed with him in the East, he was unwell when the Wall was built so she stayed.' He leads her around the circling stairs and up two levels, talking the entire time. 'Likes the area called the "reading room", does Nonna, but you need to be quiet here.' Miriam smiles as he says it loudly. 'Be good for her to do something, after the Wall, you know, well . . . it's been hard on her, I think. Mum and I help out, but she's been on her own too long. She's started harassing the librarians about trying to return the stolen books back to their owners, believes the library has been built on the back of fascism and the books do not belong to them.

It's a lost cause, to be honest . . . the owners of the books are probably long dead. I think Opa's death hit her hard . . .'

Miriam is about to offer condolences, but she sees the woman from the bus, Eva, sitting at the same table in the chair Miriam had sat in when she was here last week. Wearing a red T-shirt covered by a navy cardigan, and beige trousers, she has thick, black boots that come up to her shins, and her hair partially covers her face, which is lowered, inspecting something through a magnifying glass.

'Nonna,' he says triumphantly as they reach a large, round table.

Miriam can see that Eva is poring over pictures and two newspapers that are strewn across the table. She doesn't look up.

'Nonna,' the man says again. 'This lady would like some help with a letter, in French, she thinks.'

'Jeff,' Eva says irritably. 'I'm busy.'

'I know, but it won't take a minute, Nonna. You can help her,' Jeff says with enthusiasm, despite Eva's expression.

'Hi,' Miriam says tentatively.

'I'll leave you to it,' says Jeff, patting Miriam on the back and making a thumbs-up gesture. 'Good luck.'

With a sigh, Eva looks up. 'I know you,' she says, the words practically bristle from her lips.

'Yes, I met you the other day, here . . .'

'Miriam, right?'

Miriam nods.

'Funny to run into you twice.' The word 'funny' sounds hostile as Eva leans back in her chair.

Miriam, unsure what to say, waits.

'I don't believe in coincidences. Who sent you?'

'Oh, no one. Your grandson . . .'

'Grandson?'

Miriam turns around to the empty space the man vacated. 'Jeff?' she says.

Eva nods. 'Jeff is . . .' She leans forward resting her hands on the table. 'You were talking about your father when we were on the bus.'

'Yes, and thank you so much for your help.'

Eva sighs.

'Also, I found some letters and I cannot read them, they are written in French. Jeff offered your assistance to translate them, maybe? I would pay of course.'

'How much?' Eva looks at her until Miriam feels beads of moisture form on her top lip.

'Um, well – you see, there are quite a few.'

'How many?'

'Around twenty or so . . .'

'Fifty,' Eva says, unmoving. 'Fifty *West*marks.'

Miriam offers her the letter in her hand, but Eva doesn't take it, so she places it on the table and rummages in her bag. She pulls out half of the French letters, wrapped in her mother's handkerchief.

'I have about the same amount again at home. How quickly can you do this?'

'I suppose Jeffrey told you that I have nothing to do?'

Miriam smiles.

'I can do these in a few days for you; you'll want them sooner?'

'My father is . . .' She pauses. 'Old now, and I think these letters hold something for him that he is searching for.'

'I'll do it. I can work on them for you. Write your address here.' She passes a clean sheet of paper and pencil over.

Miriam bends and with shaking hands writes her father's address.

'Miriam what?'

'Voight,' she says, and writes her name down under the address.

She goes back into her purse and pulls out two twenty-Westmark notes. 'I'll give you the rest . . .' But Eva waves a hand at her.

'Come to the library Wednesday. I'll have some of these done for you, and bring the rest.'

'Thank you.'

But Eva turns back to her magnifying glass and photos, and doesn't answer. The letters sit on the edge of the table and Miriam finds it hard to walk away from them. Nothing happened as she had expected. Should she return for the letters? But they are useless if they can't be read.

The German letters sit on her table at home, she can read them, she'll go home and try and work it all out that way.

She walks away and as she nears the top step, turns to find Eva unwrapping the handkerchief. Miriam exhales heavily and walks down to the lobby. Jeff is talking to a young boy at a table as she passes.

He stands and comes to meet her. 'Could she help you?'

She nods. 'Thank you. You know, I've never met a socialist before, she's quite . . .' But Miriam cannot find an appropriate word.

'Socialist? Nonna? Oh no. She still has *East habits*, you know. She came over with one bag and her old Trabant, but the car's in the garage. I can't make the ruddy thing go. You know what it's like?'

Miriam doesn't, but smiles sympathetically nonetheless.

'She thinks the walls can hear, does our Nonna. No one can be trusted, you know the thing. She'll be fine once she's settled. Maybe helping you will be just the thing. You need a hobby in later life, that's what Mum thinks anyway.'

Miriam nods to the boy watching them. 'Thank you, Jeff. I'll let you get back to your day.'

'See you again,' he calls.

On her return home, a food parcel is in the hallway from the Smyth sisters at number 2. A large pot of something and a few rolls on top. She opens the door and the white feather floats down in front of her to the floor.

Collecting the food, she locks the door and replaces the catches, then steps over the fallen feather before she lifts the heavy, still-warm pot into the kitchen. The smell of stew wafts through the air. She takes one of the rolls and nibbles it as she walks back to the door.

To replace her fallen feather.

She finds an appointment card on the floor. It's Hilda's card with the medical centre logo. A note is scrawled on it: '*Dr Kenny: Tomorrow 9 a.m.*' It's signed '*Hilda*' and there is a cross under her large scrawl. On the other side she has written, '*Taking care of you too.*'

Miriam places it on the kitchen side and returns to her father. She moves him, offers him water and then goes straight to the table. She picks up a letter at random and notices something: a tiny number written in the top corner. She looks at another, then another. Every one of them has a number.

She spends the afternoon putting them in order and marking which letters are absent or in French with a white slip of paper. She wraps the remaining French ones back up in another of her mother's handkerchiefs and leaves it to one side. A package she will deliver to Eva on Wednesday. It feels like a lifetime to wait.

She finds the next letter in the sequence that she can read.

Dearest Henryk,

I had the last scraps of bread in my jacket – the one you gave me as we were parted. I am ashamed that I did not think of you being without a jacket. Now all I think about is how the wind must have whipped your skin, how your second-best cardigan was not enough to protect you wherever you were going. I am sorry, I am shamefaced and so selfish. Even if I had argued with you, it would still have been over my shoulders on the journey, fast losing the heat of you.

I do not know how long we travelled, but there was no food, no water, nothing. Just bodies: women, young and old. We waited for news, we clung on to hope when

107

someone would claim we were going here or there, some-where better than where we currently were. We talked at the start, tried to find similarities – who we were, where we were from. We didn't talk about our losses, the absence of children in a space of so many women was enough, and we were thinking positively about how partners, children, parents would all be waiting at our destination. I did not speak the truth, I hoped we would be reunited.

I said you were my husband.

The lie tasted so sweet on my tongue, the adrenaline of it. I talked much in those early days, all lies, but they nourished me.

After the first night, we were sure they would tell us where we were going but by daybreak, we were still at the station. Waiting. We heard talking, jeering, boots, shout-ing, crying. We heard the voices of the ones we had loved and lost, a communal suffering. Still we did not move.

The second night, we started fighting. Where would we sleep and how. We were so packed in that we were standing only. Propping each other up.

The guards rolled back the doors once, we thought to give us water, or food, but they fired their weapons into the sky, making us cry out in alarm, and ordered the bod-ies of those who had died to be rolled out on to the tracks. By the time the train finally screamed, metal on metal, there was room for us all to sit.

We had stopped talking. Everyone was lost in a void. Women held photographs to their chest like drops of water.

There was a gypsy on the train, on her own – the only gypsies I have ever seen were in a crowd. She plaited the fringes of her scarf over and over. She was beautiful. Dark hair and long, like waves of black silk or thick black paint, dark eyelashes and thick eyebrows, she looked the same age as me.

After a few days she cried out, 'We die!' She was loud after the wagon had been so quiet except the murmurs of the dying and the prayers of the living. 'We die, all of us die.' The gypsy's voice rang out loud and strong and foreign. 'Death to everyone! We are going to hell!'

She spoke Dutch, and although crass and strange from her mouth, just to hear another language again . . . It may have only been days, but the sweet joy of hearing Dutch filled me with warmth after the German threats and insults. Even though the gypsy was talking about the fiery pits of hell, the language was welcome.

Still I only watched her, several of the women kicked her, told her to shut up or called her 'vermin', 'scum'.

A large woman slapped her hard across the face.

Her cries stopped.

The last crumbs were in my pocket, the wagon rocking, holding up against the wind.

Everyone was trying to sleep. The comforting bliss of being elsewhere. Not here. Eyes closed, dreamless, or just hoping that when we opened them we'd find that the reality was just a dream.

But the gypsy, her dark eyes were open. She stared at me as I touched the dry crusts of bread in my pocket, not too much that they turned to ash, but enough so that I knew they were there.

When I could not wait any longer, I looked directly at her as I picked one crust up and placed it in my mouth, like it was a decadent chocolate.

I did the same with the second piece. She didn't waver, watching me. Once I'd chewed and chewed and swallowed, she smiled a small smile, relaxed her entire body as if dissolving into the panels of the wagon and closed her eyes.

I started praying in the wagon, not to a God that I did not believe in, but to a truth, a right in the world that will help me survive the wrongs.

This is my punishment.

For Louisa.

The taste of the bread has gone but the feeling of cruelty survives. Who am I?

'I don't quite understand this. She said she was your wife? Languages and cardigans? And to not share the bread . . . *Who am I?* indeed,' Miriam says and looks at Dad who is dressed in a clean nightshirt, creases and folds still visible on his immobile body.

'You were never warm, were you?' she asks, tucking the knitted blanket closer around him.

'Can you remember how Mum would click her tongue, not in a tut, but more in disbelief every time you wore a cardigan to the beach on holiday?' She smiles.

'Can you not wear a short-sleeved shirt, at least?' Miriam says in a higher tone like her mother's, but then stops her imitation.

Dead.

She sees her mother saying those same words, standing in the hallway of their holiday rental in a flowery dress and enormous hat.

'No.' And, 'I'm a lizard, me, can't absorb heat from the sun, even when I sit in it. Hey, Miriam? Your papa's an old reptile!' He would look to her to laugh, which she duly did to break the thread of strain pulled taut between them.

When the cardigans lost their shape and holes emerged through the elbows, her mother would darn them and buy another, so he could transition to the next one and the next. Never without. An evolving wheel of green and brown cardigans, all in some form of disarray, and the watch, she realises now, hidden underneath.

On their summer holidays, Miriam would walk up the beach from the sea and drip salt water on to hot sands. Dad would be sitting under an umbrella, a kerchief knotted on his head, socks on his feet and more often than not, the cardigan. All the other dads were wearing shorts, their bellies large and brown.

'I loved you, Dad,' Miriam says, walking to his old wooden chest. She rummages around for a cardigan in the worst shape she can find. Green. Holes in the elbows and a threadbare sleeve.

'I'm moving you,' she says, turning his body on to first the right side, sliding the fabric of the cardigan under him, then rolling him back over before manoeuvring his other arm into the sleeve. It isn't an easy task. His arms are stiff and unyielding.

Yet, although wonky, he is in his cardigan. The small change brings out the man he was, rather than the body he is confined in.

12

MIRIAM

The next letter. A page of text, maybe from a French book, but the handwriting, in German, runs in the margins and across the blank back too. She moves the lamp slightly to try to illuminate the page as the room darkens.

Henryk,

I have become numb; numb to humanity, indifferent to loss.

They held me down, hard at first then less when they realised I was in too much shock to move. And a woman, like me, shaved the hair from my head.

She had no hair. Recently shaved too. She wore a white kerchief, prisoner stripes and a black triangle.

I knew at that moment all was lost. Do the guards even force them? Will I be doing this soon? Volunteering even?

It took a surprisingly long time to cut my hair off. The scissors pulled and sliced through my thick locks,

fistfuls at a time. All we heard was the metallic scraping,
metal to metal, cutting through hair.

And Miriam recalls the sensation of scissors cutting through her hair . . .

It was the end of her first work Christmas party, when she was employed by a large school as their administrator. She had worn a wrap-around red dress. Black tights and black heels.

Unbelievable, now, to think she had dressed up in such a way, her hair curled and in a scrunchy. Incredible to think back on herself as impossibly carefree; a life of before, when she could have a great time, laughing and dancing with her colleagues.

Being employed and being Axel's girlfriend and very quickly his wife had happened all at the same time. It was a whirlwind romance: love at first sight, just like her parents. He had taken most of her attention, right from the beginning. He was attentive, charming, funny and sensitive. Having lost his father when he was small and been raised by a callous and cold mother, Axel needed her and she loved the feeling of being needed by him.

She stumbled into the house later than she had intended, after bouncing her way around at a dance where a rather sullen DJ played the new Bowie record repeatedly until asked to stop. Her feet ached and her face hurt from smiling as her co-workers got more and more drunk.

She entered the quiet house, trying not to make noise. Slipped her feet out of her shoes without putting on the light and was about to take her coat off.

'Had a nice evening?' Axel said, coming out of the living room and making her start. He switched on the light.

'Oh, Axel, it was so much fun,' she laughed, shaking her coat off and sprinkling him with rain.

'So much fun, you say?'

His eyes were dark and he stood under the light so she couldn't see his face.

'Do you know what time it is?'

'It's late, I am sorry.'

'I have been sick with worry,' he said, monotone.

'You have? You knew I was out with the girls.'

'The girls?'

She nodded, feeling guilty without cause, and hoping the schnapps she had drunk wasn't too noticeable on her breath.

'The girls,' he said, and left the room.

She stood still, waiting, for what she wasn't sure.

'You know,' he said, returning with something in his hand that she could not see. 'Dane's wife used to say that she had been out with the girls. But it turned out she was fucking another man behind his back.'

'What?' Miriam stepped back, alarmed, and saw his eyes were red, from crying, she imagined. 'Axel, it was a Christmas party, you were invited. I haven't . . . I wouldn't . . .' she said stunned.

He brought a hand to her face, she flinched back.

'Are you scared of me, Miriam?' he asked, touching her cheek.

A silver thread wound its way into her bones. She shivered and shook her head.

'I would never hurt you.' He pulled her hair loose and wrapped it around his fingers. It was long and weaved across his pale skin. 'I would never hurt you.' He leant in and kissed her tenderly at the same time she heard the unmistakable slice of scissors. 'You won't ever leave me, will you? You can't leave me when I need you so much.'

She stepped back, alarmed. The hair that had been woven through his fingertips was still there. Scissors glinted in his other hand.

'I couldn't understand why,' she says to her father, getting up to turn him. 'I still don't.' That was the first time he had ever . . . she can't think of the right word as she mulls it over, straightening the sheets and smoothing Dad's hair.

Axel didn't hurt her, he didn't hit her, but . . . he had frightened her, taking scissors to her hair was nothing in the scheme of things, but it had only got worse. Unable to face the interrogation about her day, every day, Miriam left her job, leaving her friends and her freedom behind.

She picks up the letter and continues, unsure she wants to know what was done.

The journey from prisoner to inmate took place in the time it took to cut my hair. It wasn't the hair itself, it was the person cutting it.

Another prisoner, newly arrived, had protested, she lay comatose and bleeding on the ground while a further prisoner shaved her head too. My blonde hair falling into a sea of dark.

The woman cutting my hair was dead behind the eyes. I wanted to ask her how long she had been here, yet I could not bear to know the answer.

The gypsy, the one from the wagon that I refused to share my bread with. She and I have stuck together.

Her name is Hani.

Hani thought that her hair was being cut before she was hanged or killed, maybe. She didn't understand and some terror or story had invaded her senses that they were preparing her for death. She would not sit, she thrashed and screamed and cried and bit and scratched. A big guard hit her across the face so hard Hani flew across the room, hitting her head on a chair. Everyone was silent. I got up to help her as she wobbled to her feet.

The guard slapped me across the back of my newly shaved head. The noise reverberated across the room, across my skin, and shook me a little.

You do not help.

You feel it. Each woman looks down, avoiding eye contact, but Hani was up and ready to fight.

The guard walked over, so calmly, raised her baton and struck Hani clean across the jaw, blood and teeth spewed from her mouth like vomit as she hit the ground hard. The guard looked at me. She was challenging me. Will you go to her? she seemed to be asking me.

I did not.

I watched as the prisoners, doing the guard's work, stripped Hani of her clothes, each item removed efficiently, as another cut her long hair off, roughly.

It took the time for my body hair to be shaved and a 'uniform' allocated to me, before Hani came around. We were not allowed to put our uniforms on, just carry them. The room chattered with shivering, naked women.

'Photos,' she said, but it was hard to understand with her missing teeth. 'Where are my photos?' Bringing her hand to her mouth she found her face had changed shape.

'Mama, family, God, my photos?'

She looked around her, pulling on the guard's clothing, begging, searching. The guard called a dog to heel. The German shepherd, whom the guards fondly called 'Daisy', was a large, drooling dog with teeth bared, and had been called to bite and growl and menace us since we walked in. The guard looked ready to let the dog at Hani.

At that moment, another 'political' prisoner had got hold of a pair of scissors and threatened a guard, her arm around the guard's neck, scissors pointing into his skin. It was a last attempt and she knew it, you could see it in her eyes. The guard towering over Hani turned to watch the scene unfolding.

Without thinking I said, 'Up. Quick now.'

Hani looked so shocked to hear words in a language she could understand, she stood straight up.

She's a head shorter than me, she looked up with oversized eyes as a puppy would at its master. A broken puppy.

As the guard, so confident in her own authority, had turned her back, she didn't see Hani try to attack her, and she did not see me step in the way.

'They are cutting our hair to stuff pillows and mattresses,' I said. I spoke fast, in beautiful Dutch, enjoying the nourishment of a language across my tongue again. The words melted like butter. 'They are not killing us. They are using us to help the war. You hurt her she will kill you.'

Hani was seething, but the language had captured her. She was listening.

'The photos are gone,' I said with a lump in my throat. 'You love your mama?' She bobbed her head, captivated by my mouth creating the words that she could understand.

'Then she lives here.' I touched her chest, suddenly aware how naked we were, avoiding her tiny breasts. I had never seen another woman naked, it is strange how insignificant this was.

'Not in a photo,' I said as I pulled us away from the crowd that had formed around the guard and the woman's attempt to take control. The dog was set free and attacked. I did not look as the dog snarled, tore and bit. The screams echoed for days after.

Avoid the dogs.

I grabbed Hani's hand and pulled her body in front of mine. Blue welts grew red across her back from where she had hit the chair, they shone from the swelling, a fountain of blood poured from her face.

We passed through the showers with no issue. Hani was allocated two shoes, both for the left foot. I managed to keep my boots.

Once this ordeal was over we covered our heads and bodies again. The clothes are full of lice, the fabric scratchy, ill-fitting; it looks like we are all wearing our mothers' clothes.

I found Hani's hand in my own. It stayed like that as we were shoved and pushed into rows of five, marched and counted and marched some more and then thrown into a 'holding' tent. The number of women in this small space must be in the high hundreds. There was no space for us yet we were pushed in by the volume of others behind.

I do not know if she held me or I held her, what I do know is that neither one of us let go.

We have been starved, attacked, shaved, beaten, humiliated and only when we are treated worse than livestock do we realise that we have survived thus far. We realise we have names, and it seems that we have each other too.

The crumbs of bread from the cattle wagon were long gone, but they weighed heavy on my mind as I rested head to head with Hani, both leaning back against the side of the tent, a small space where we could sit. We were so tired we rested together and as I did so, letting my head lie heavy, I prayed for a miracle.

Shocked and untethered. The letter, raw, unfiltered and devastating. Miriam waits to comprehend the horrors she has just read, on paper that has survived all this time.

And time, for Miriam, rushes ahead so that her vision is blurry, and slows so that the flicker of an outside light feels like one long, slow blink.

Praying for a miracle.

A tick of time.

Axel kneeling on a towel next to her while she was in the bath, smoothing bubbles over her skin.

A beat of absence.

Axel wringing the sponge in his hands. The bubbles frozen. The water cooled.

A drum of loneliness.

A cold so deep her bones ache.

As she dried, like a dog, naked on a blanket. On the floor.

13

HENRYK

It was almost two years to the day, from our first kiss, when everything changed. I was leaving to meet Frieda when Emilie returned from work early.

'I can't do this anymore,' she said, resting her back against the closed door. 'They found me today, they asked about you, where you were, when I would be expecting you to return.' She breathed heavily and her legs gave way. She tucked her feet in, her arms wrapped around her knees, and rested her head back into the door. 'I can't do this anymore. I can't pretend that you and Frieda . . . that it's . . . that I—' She stopped suddenly and I sat next to her and pulled her into my arms.

'Who found you?' I asked.

'That's what you heard? From what I just said?' She took an exhausted breath then continued, 'It was them. The SS. They came to *my* work. They came to find *you*,' she said.

'What did you tell them?'

'Nothing. I said I hadn't seen you since you left the university. They asked where I thought you would be, who you were staying with, friends you may have.' She paused.

'Did you mention Frieda?' I panicked.

She bristled and pushed me so I was thrown off balance and top-pled over on to my elbow.

'No. No. I did not mention the fact that *my* husband has a lover.' She pulled knotted hands through her cropped hair. 'That he chooses to gallivant off with her rather than stay here. With me. That you are more concerned about *her* safety than you are for your own wife! Henryk, it is *you* who is putting everyone in danger. Leave the girl alone.' Then she asked, more gently, as though it was an enormous effort, 'What are you doing?'

I said nothing, resting my head on the door as she had a moment before.

'Please, you have to end this *thing* with Frieda. She's young, she'll forgive you. But we must leave. Now. I don't think we will get another chance. My friend Margot, she can help us. Please, Henryk, see sense. If they can find me at work, they can find us here. Then what?'

'They aren't after you,' I said slowly, watching her pacing her thoughts out, step by step. 'They are after me.'

'And in being after you, they will also want me. Can't you see, I am your wife! I am harbouring a wanted man.' She took a shaky breath. 'Take back your political ideals, say you have converted – *join* the Nazi party. For heaven's sake, what does it matter?'

'What? Never. You know I would never. Ever.'

'Then leave with me, now,' she said, bending down. 'We can be a family again. We can forget all this happened. We can have a baby. Come away with me now. Let's start over.'

I saw the desperation. Her tears flowed down the beautiful chan-nels of her face, but behind her tears, she knew. No matter how much I should leave, how my head was saying that if I stayed, death was the only option, Emilie knew I wouldn't leave Frieda.

'I can't,' I said.

And Emilie, my beautiful wife, let out a frightful yell, a howl. A screech that would befit a cat. 'Then leave me,' she bawled. 'Leave me alone. Make your choice, Henryk . . . because this' – and she motioned around with her hands – 'is all I have. I'm not her and I never will be. So go—' She launched her arms at the stack of books next to the chair, and they toppled to the ground. Grabbing one, she was about to throw it at me, but hurled it to the floor instead. Then stormed into the kitchen.

'To hell with you, Henryk, and Frieda. Both of you be damned,' she sobbed.

I stacked the books back up and was about to go to her in the kitchen. She had put her apron on and was scrubbing at the work surface. Dashing tears away with the back of her hand as she worked. Her apron untied.

I watched her until tears stung my eyes. I closed the door silently behind me, walking fast and keeping my hat pulled low, my eyes down. Aware that at any moment a hand could rest on my shoulder and I would disappear into a night fog.

MIRIAM

Reading the letter somehow brings Axel alive, unbidden and in the room. *Numb* was how the letter described it. Numbness settles like film over her skin. She spends a long night unable to keep the chill from her limbs and by the time the grey morning seeps in, her body aches and she cannot peel off the sensation of being both wet and cold.

She doesn't move from the chair, other than to care for her father. She doesn't speak.

The oppression of *him*, as though they were sharing the same air. Right. There. Keeps her from answering the door when somebody knocks.

'Hello,' a voice calls through the letter box.

She doesn't answer.

'Miriam? It's Hilda. Are you in?'

She rises from the chair, the dress unfolded and draped on her lap like a blanket. When she opens the door, Hilda is on the other side.

The eclectic pattern on Hilda's skirt catches her eye as it sways.

'You missed it,' Hilda says. 'Your appointment, nine a.m., remember?' She consults her wristwatch. 'It's one thirty.'

'It is?' Miriam opens the door fully. 'What day is it?' she asks and yawns widely, which is followed by a shiver. But looking at Hilda's face she rubs her arms vigorously and puts a mask of normality on her face.

'It's Tuesday,' Hilda says. 'Dr Baum told me some of your history. Why didn't you tell me?'

'Dr Baum?'

A variety of expressions pass over Hilda's face as she walks past Miriam into the living room. It seems she goes from concern to trepidation to confusion with such rapidity that Miriam smiles.

'I like you, Hilda,' Miriam says. 'Your face is honest.'

'Miriam, please,' Hilda says and sits. Miriam follows suit. 'I cannot tell you how serious this is,' she continues. 'Dr Baum is thinking of sending your father back to hospital; he thinks you are unstable. I can't say otherwise, neither can you . . . You didn't attend. God, Miriam, you are not helping yourself.' She pulls fingers through her hair. 'The meeting is on Friday,' she says with finality.

The fog clears and the room comes into sharp focus.

'Please, Hilda, I forgot . . . nothing sinister, I promise. Can I see another doctor to explain? Dad cannot go back into hospital . . . not now.'

Hilda sighs so heavily, Miriam can smell garlic on her breath.

'Okay – right now. See if we can fit you into the open clinic. Last chance, Miriam.'

'Let me just check on Dad. I'll be there.'

'I'll wait.'

She follows a step behind Hilda, unable to keep up with her pace. Hilda says nothing on the walk. Miriam follows the green and purple flowers of Hilda's skirt as she is frog-marched across the busy streets, the trees hold the low clouds like leaves.

They wait at a pedestrian crossing beside a mum with a pushchair. The child is howling, red-faced, tear-stained. When the lights turn green she pushes on ahead, the toddler using its entire body to break free from the restraints of the pushchair. The mum walks with speed and deliberation. Miriam wonders if the mum can hear the plea in the child's voice or if she has become numb to it, and at what point the child will give up.

In the medical centre, recently refurbished, the smell of paint mingles heavily with the old and the sick, plus the heating makes Miriam want to leave almost as soon as the doors open. The waiting room is a thoroughfare, people bustling around, coughing. Window cleaners are polishing the glass of a full window that frames the car park.

Hilda marches to the reception desk, looking as comfortable here as Miriam imagines she does in her own home, and motions for Miriam to sit while she confers with the receptionist.

Eventually she comes over and says, 'The doctor will call you when he is available.'

'Thank you.' Miriam is sitting between a man puffing on a pipe with his leg in a cast and a mother clutching a child with red-raw cheeks and teary eyes. She watches Hilda's receding figure.

The noise of the centre bustles along, interrupted by coughing fits and a loud retch.

She picks up a discarded magazine and puts it down. She crosses and uncrosses her legs. She plays with the pleats in her skirt, flattens, then separates each fold.

The child whimpers, moulded into his mother's body. She soothes him with her voice and Miriam is reminded of the box, the mother and child, and Eugenia hiding . . . waiting.

She looks up, aware of someone. She scans every face and looks out of the glass doors.

He is standing there.

Arms folded, hands tucked into his armpits.

Watching her.

Like the sun, his presence is borne with such force that to gaze directly at him would blister.

She stands, then turns.

'Frau Voight – room 6 please,' a male voice calls into the open-plan waiting area. Miriam knocks into people as she runs through the pharmacy attached to the medical centre. Away. As fast as she can. In the opposite direction.

'Frau Voight,' the voice rebounds around her.

She runs until her legs numb and she's running on feet alone. Not looking back. At the top of the hill she doubles back on herself, there is no one there.

She allows herself to walk slower, count the steps, focus on moving forward. Keep going.

'Keep going,' she says to herself. 'Almost there.' She continues to try and soothe herself with her voice. 'Couldn't have been him. Couldn't have been him.' Her feet move faster and her words run into each other. 'Was it him?'

'Scissors and sorry, in sickness and cold, Hani and gypsy and bread and cold. Missing and shivering and no more, and don't leave don't leave don't leave.' Talking to the rhythm of her feet.

'Miriam,' Lionel calls to her as she keeps following the drum of her feet 'home' to the stairs.

'Fr*äu*lein,' he calls again. She stops on the beat of home. 'Letter for you.' He passes her a manila envelope.

She holds it away from her body. 'I don't want it,' she says to Lionel.

'It's from an *Easterner*, she said she was a lady friend of yours. She was insistent that I gave it to you. In person.'

Miriam looks at her name on the front. Not in *his* handwriting. She holds the envelope closer.

'You be careful, pet. Can never be too cautious of those Easterners hanging around now. My cousin over in,' he points over his shoulder, 'had terrible trouble with the . . .' But she turns away.

The feather in the door, safe.

The water in the tap, hot.

Her hands bleed, peace.

She places plasters over some of the wounds. The wooden block of knives in the kitchen and the sewing scissors she shuts away in a drawer. Yet her fingers pull and tug at the skin. She digs the nail of her thumb into her wrist where a graze has scabbed over and pushes it as deeply as she can, drawing it across her skin horizontally, watching her skin go from pink to white under the pressure. Pink to white then red, pulling at the broken skin until it bleeds.

The silence of the house thrums in her ears and she finds a loose eyelash irritating her eye and starts pulling them out, more and more. Until she is blinking them away with tears.

'Dad,' she speaks into the silence.

'I saw, I mean, I know, but I cannot be sure. I . . .'

'Miriam,' he says and lifts his arm to the side and there is a tiny space in the bed. She doesn't think twice.

'Dad,' she sobs. She moves on to the bed; the air mattress shifts and groans as she moves awkwardly into his straight body. The cardigan buttons remind her of twisting and playing with them as a child. She draws circles into the buttons with her finger. Around and around.

His arm closes her in. He is frail and she can feel the bones of him as she moves into his arm.

'He's back,' she says.

14

MIRIAM

The days and nights become unfocused. They seep into each other like a watercolour. The only determination of time is her father, he is drinking, he is eating tiny amounts. And he talks, mumbles and sometimes calls out.

'Frieda. Frieda. Frieda.'

His mouth opens and closes and most of the time no words leave it, but his whole body is fighting.

She hopes she can help him, but as she rubs the chill out of his hands, and massages his arms and legs, she knows caring for him is the only thing she can do.

When she brings herself to open the envelope given to her by Lionel, she finds a small note and three pages of elaborate writing, large and legible, and the letters from the dress attached to each one.

A small note on the front.

> *I need to speak with you about the letters, please contact me.*
> *Eva*

Miriam puts it to one side and allows herself to be drawn into the world of the letters. A world in which *he* doesn't exist.

Henryk

I have no pockets in my uniform. The fabric falls off my shoulders. I have nothing, yet I have everything. By luck or intent, I still have my ID card under the sole of my boots and the ring. I can feel the shape of it. A circle burned into the pad of my toe. I have the means of escape. I can leave this place. Now I am in, I can find my way out, find who I need to speak to to try and leave.

I need to see the Kommandant while my features still resemble those on my card. Before I morph into the others. Before I become faceless. I need to find my way free, so I can find you.

I keep my head low, following the cobbles, randomly aligned. If you don't watch where you place your feet, it is easy to slip. I could feel the cobbles beneath the soles of my boots, I felt grounded. Where once many must have bled and died laying this path I am standing atop. Still breathing, still alive.

The salt in the air reminds me of chasing Louisa across the beach, avoiding the waves, running as fast as I could, my shorter legs no match for her long ones. Hair streaming behind her. The fresh sea air, the lavender garlands we made together. The smell of her last summer.

Here the salt air is tainted with the smell of people. This place was not designed to hold us all. The guards must be outnumbered one hundred to one, yet we do nothing.

The ten-metre wall, the barbed wire, the inmates behaving like guards, the guards like dogs. Salt in the air, the taste on the skin. Fir trees and manicured lawns we saw on the way in.

This is Ravensbrück.

Miriam looks up from the paper and shivers, not from cold. The voice from the letters is haunting and she cannot help but wonder if this voice is coming from someone long dead.

She takes the coffee table from the living room into her father's room, bashing her knuckles on the door frame. She sets the letters down in order as the words repeat themselves unbidden and Miriam can hear the internal workings of this poor woman. She's in Miriam's head and there is nothing she can do about it.

'She didn't fight, there was no one for her to trust,' she says to her father. 'Should *I* have fought back?'

The question feels heavy, a black stone in her stomach. 'No one would believe me even if I did.' The truth stings her eyes.

She sees the image of the irate toddler in the pushchair and of herself pushing and pushing against something just as unyielding. Only not a pushchair, but a man, restraining her with arms and legs and worse. He held her with the force of what he could and would do to her if she broke free. And who would believe her if she spoke out? Who could she trust?

We cannot trust anyone.

'He's back,' she says.

She picks up the next letter in sequence, it is in German, but so difficult to read, written around text in writing as light as dust, Miriam stops and starts, rereads sentences and tries to puzzle her way through it. And the thoughts that slice through the text drag her back to a reality she cannot bear to face.

> *Henryk,*
> *The holding block was just a tent, its sides battered by wind and rain, blown open, its roof capsized and dripping water. We had no bowls, just two spoons. We placed our spoons under the drips and drank rainwater. Tiny spoons of rainwater. It took two long days to steal a bowl so we could eat.*

Everyone stealing and hurting and vicious, all looking for space. Our currency. Once you have space you don't give it up.

The soup is water, rarely vegetables or anything I can recognise. We get bread, which is like a pebble, and 'coffee' too. The soup and coffee are pretty much the same, although we are more accepting of there being bits in the soup than we are in the coffee. I mush the bread in my mouth then give it to Hani, her mouth is so sore and without teeth, she is still struggling to eat.

I've been here a month. Today is my birthday: twenty-one. And yet I fear there may not be a twenty-two.

The routine so familiar now I do not have to think, I pass through each day, my body moving to the beat of the camp. My mind and heart elsewhere. With you.

I am almost there, transitioning into one of them. A walking zombie. I do not eat without a guard telling me to, I do not move, I do not rest or sleep or talk without a guard telling me to. I have no mind of my own.

I miss you

Love, Frieda.

'*Frieda!*' Miriam reads it again and moves closer to her father, picking up his hand and wiping her other gently across his face. She looks at her father's thick, white hair, liver spots that freckle his face, his broad nose, thin lips. She studies him, drinking in the last of him.

'Dad, can you hear me?' She takes a deep breath. 'These letters are from Frieda.'

When he says nothing for a few minutes, she kisses the back of his hand 'I'll find out what happened to her for you, I promise,' she says, and knowing this means reading the terrifying words makes her hands tremble, yet she continues. For him.

HENRYK

I left the apartment, I left Emilie there sobbing and raging at me and I went to Frieda. But every footstep judged me. I stopped on every corner. Should I go back? I turned, walked a few steps, then stopped again. For a wanted man, pacing the same street in a frenzy of indecision didn't exactly make me inconspicuous.

Emilie was right. I was married to her. She was in danger because of me already. Yet she stayed. She knew about Frieda and yet she stayed. The guilt was bile, raw acid, and it burned in my throat. Who was I? What kind of man does that to a wife he adores?

And yet . . .

I loved Frieda. In ways that I had never experienced before, and it was *because* I loved her as much as I did that I knew I couldn't do this to her too.

No more.

Emilie was right. Frieda would be okay without me, better in fact. Much, much better. That thought made me panic. And the panic made me run, drawing yet more attention to myself. My heartbeat pushed me further, the wind soared in my ears, breath ragged and pulsing in my chest.

I had to let Frieda go; she needed to be free from me. And then I would leave with Emilie. Try and do better for her, at least.

Waiting for Frieda to open the door, I was cold and slick with nerves. This was the right thing. It was the right thing and the only way . . .

Frieda opened the door, and the resolve to end things froze solid in my chest. And in that pause, Frieda greeted me with her lips on mine and then her hands, her fingers on my skin.

She pulled me into the apartment and shut the door. And although my heart held an unwanted tick, and the knot in the pit of my stomach made me feel sick, the decision I had made only moments before seemed a distant echo.

I left it all behind and melted into Frieda, willing to lose myself in her touch.

'I missed you,' she muttered, the rich cadence of her voice deepened. With her lips on mine, she pulled me on to the bed.

MIRIAM

In text that seems to be pressed harder into the page, Miriam reads:

My boots were stolen today; with no boots, I have no ID,
with no ID I am lost.

She hurriedly finds the next letter and reads with as much speed as she can. She collects the magnifying glass from her mother's sewing kit to try to ease the process. Axel fades, a paintbrush swirled out in water, and she focuses.

She has found Frieda. Now all she needs to do is find what happened to her.

Dear Henryk,
The holding tent knows no peace. Hani and I lean head
to head, her shoulder on mine, both leaning back into the
fabric that grows warm from our touch.
    Hani asked me why I lied in the wagon when I said
I was Emilie and it made me think . . .
    Isn't love simultaneously as violent, turbulent and
wild as a storm and yet as fresh and calm as the sky in

its wake? The kind of love we have makes us feel we can climb mountains or wrestle snakes, even though we cannot. Our love made us think we could take on the Nazis. I think our love has made fools of us. I am here . . .

I looked around at the women, the noise and smell, the flap of the tent hitting an old woman just inside of it.

Flap, whack, flap.

. . . And you are not.

Hani asked about you and I flattered in my portrait. I made you taller, broader, younger, because I could. I told of our love-at-first-sight romance, although it is not ours, it is your story, your history, how you met Emilie.

Miriam swallows hard. The idea that this woman used Mum's story, her parents' love, and made it her own fills her with a deep revulsion.

There is nothing else she can do but read on.

Hani is one of nine children; she speaks Roma and her Dutch is basic.

She said that no one was particularly pleased when she was born and since then she has, as she says, 'Turned up, stayed put, stood up, shouted out and told the world that I am here.'

The Nazis were not particularly pleased about this either.

Her parents tried to marry her to a cousin when she was fourteen and he no older, but she left the family, went to school (hence the Dutch) and got a job. She had money and a room of her own, but never having slept in a bed alone, she found the cotton sheets cool and crisp on her skin. Coming from a family where there was always someone to share a mattress, Hani found living alone hard.

She went home one day and her whole family had gone. Aunts, uncles, grandparents – everyone. She floated around with nowhere to go, got arrested and now she is here.

She says, 'I rather share my bed and know I am living than be alone and thinking I am always alone. I may as well be dead.'

And I miss you. I miss you and the times we promised each other we would have. I have never woken up to you, nor have we spent the night together. Always snatched moments. I want the tiny things, the things that matter, the things that everyone takes for granted. I want those things, I want to not be alone.

And now it is too late.

I mushed the last of the day's bread in my mouth and gave Hani the full amount, rather than swallowing a little myself.

HENRYK

A heaviness folded over me as I lay on Frieda's bed in tangled sheets, she was draped over me like a blanket. Her soft breath tickled my neck, as I made waves with my fingertips over the back of her arm, illuminated in the half-light. She was becoming lean from sharing her rations with me.

'If there could only be one, I choose you,' I said.

She opened her eyes, but when I turned to face her, her expression was dark.

'You can't choose me. I am not a choice,' she whispered.

'You are for me,' I said, and kissed her on the forehead, clumsily, as she pulled her head away, her body still resting on mine.

'No. You have Emilie.'

'And I have you.'

'Yes, but . . .'

'There is no "but", Frieda. I love you.'

'You can't choose me, Henryk.' Her voice went quiet. 'I am not enough.'

I was about to counter that, but she placed a finger to my lips and then closed them with her own. The kiss was a practical solution to stop me responding, yet her lips shivered as they pressed into mine.

I was covered, yet exposed, as the heaviness of her limbs rested upon me. I looked to the ceiling, pondering my fate, and as tears fell, great sobs joined them, wracking my entire chest open like a cleaver.

Frieda sat up and drew me into her arms, she held me cradled into her naked body.

'Henryk, what's going on?'

I couldn't speak, I couldn't find any words to explain that what was happening was breaking me. I had placed a sentence on us all. The bombs were getting closer and the weight of my guilt was like a mortar poised to fall over my head.

Yet I couldn't keep apart from Frieda, and by being there I was putting her at risk too. I didn't know who I was anymore and the fracture inside me tore open as Frieda kissed my tears and brought her head to mine. I sobbed openly as she held me.

She kissed my lips until our breath was shared and when she straddled her legs around me and drew me into her, I deepened our kiss, not wanting to be a singular being anymore.

Moving on top of me, she didn't let me go. She lifted my chin so I could see her. Her eyes so deep, I tried to turn away, not able to look into her beautiful face. To know I was causing such hurt, that soon it would all be over and it would be my fault.

They were coming for me, and that meant her and Emilie too.

I kissed her neck. 'I'm handing myself in,' I said, and it was a great weight that lifted. 'I'll hand myself in tomorrow. You and Emilie will be free.' I drew her as close to me as I could. I couldn't look up into her face, so I buried my head in her chest.

Her heart beat angrily at me.

'What did Emilie say?'

'I haven't told her. I didn't know myself until I was kissing your neck.'

'Then you go to Emilie, you pack a bag and you leave, just as she planned.' She pushed a hand on my chest.

'I can't.' Tears threatened again. 'This way you are both safe.'

'Safe? And what about you? You just said if there was only one—' She shook the thought away. 'But there isn't, there are two. And there is you. It's time you understood that we both love you. We need you to survive. You're saying you'll offer yourself up; that's suicide!'

'I can't keep hurting you. Both of you.'

'Look at me, my love. You are not hurting me. This is my choice as much as it is yours,' she said gently. I turned my head back to her. 'This isn't something you have to take as yours alone. Hurting Emilie hurts you, therefore it is hurting me.' She kissed me on the forehead. 'What did you say on that bench at the Spree?'

She drew my face up to her lips and kissed the tears as they fell. I nodded, the inaudible shrieking within me contained by Frieda's heaviness surrounding me with her arms, her legs; her heart beat hard and I felt it in mine.

And like a switch, an utter exhaustion dulled the ache in my body and I placed my hands on her thighs.

'I said you were light,' I mumbled as she moved her body over mine, pressing herself into me so that I was breathing through her too. Fully compressed by light itself. She pressed her mouth on mine to stifle the new sobs, the deep anguish that was crushing my chest.

'Without darkness there is no light,' she said in my ear.

'But, Frieda, I am the darkness, look at—' But she cut me off.

'Give me a few days, Henryk.' She said my name so that I felt it resound deep in my belly, lower.

'A few days,' I agreed.

MIRIAM

'Miriam.' Her father's voice punctuates the dark. She rouses herself, having dozed off curled up in the chair.

'Miriam, I . . . you. Frieda,' he says again and lifts his hand. She holds it and tries to wiggle her absent toes.

'I . . .' he starts. 'I. Killed.'

Her feet scream back into life, then tingle.

'Frieda,' he says.

'Frieda? She is here in the letters,' Miriam says.

'I. Killed. Frieda,' he says and deflates into a grief so raw it cannot be heard.

15

MIRIAM

I killed Frieda.

Miriam rocks on the spot.

'No.' A reflex response. It's not true. It can't be true.

'Look, Dad.' She places the letter on his chest. 'It's a letter, a letter from Frieda. It was hidden in the dress. She loved you. Dad, can you hear me? You didn't kill anyone.' But she looks at the page.

How did the dress end up in Mum's wardrobe? She reels back into the chair. She cannot make his statement untrue.

Her father could never have killed anyone, not him. He was incapable.

He collected spiders in cupped hands if one had crawled into the house. He protected it from Mum poised with book or shoe, and rehomed it.

He spoke to wasps or bees and thanked them for taking time to visit. *Her* father could not even hurt someone, let alone kill them.

She collects the letter from his chest.

'It isn't true,' she says. The next letters, transcribed by Eva, will prove her right.

Henryk,

We have moved. We hoped to get a place in a block. There are so many women in the holding tent and the blocks are made from brick and stone, sheltered with a corrugated iron roof.

My boots were taken in the holding tent. I was barefoot for two days, then we found some shoes on the body of one of the dead. Hani now has a pair of clogs that fit her feet and I have shoes again.

Hani and I are in Block 15, but we did not have a bunk to start with. The wooden shelves attached to the wall were full of women. Six to a shelf. The sound of cat cries, calls, nightmares, shouts and taunts pulls and pushes. The shelves are stacked. There are three shelves up and eight across on each side of the block, A and B.

When we arrived, there was no space for us so I talked to the Blockova, an old hardened prostitute. She hit me so hard my head reverberated against the side of a shelf and I was tossed into a small space in the centre of the bunk just behind the entrance. I came around to find myself in a toilet, a small sink, Hani behind me, and a mirror in front of me.

In this toilet cubicle, above the toilet, are makeshift shelves. The shelves women have created; they look sturdier than the others. There seems to be space here too. We found out that they have 'lost' two women in the last few days and we sit and take in this wonderful sight, three shelves and now six people.

For we have been welcomed. Without question.

A large lady, in voice and spirit, helped mop the gash on my head and I saw my reflection for the first time.

I wouldn't believe it was me. I touched the mirror several times thinking it was an illusion. Feeling your own shaved head and seeing it are two very different things. My eyes were hollow, the red of blood on my cheek bringing out the green so I looked almost demonic.

The older lady is called Wanda, her hands work as fast as her mouth and she had a bandage for my face. She cleaned and hugged Hani – who couldn't understand a word. She too was mesmerised with her reflection and studied the place where her teeth had been.

Wanda introduced us to Stella, a little girl, no more than seven or eight. She still has most of her baby teeth, two gaps at the front. Stella sleeps in a bunk with a young woman, 'Bunny', who I do not think is her mother. Bunny hums all night to keep her dreams soft.

'Bunny is silent. She hasn't spoken since they brought her here,' said Wanda.

Then there is Eugenia, who comes across as cold, but may be just hardened by life here; she has been here a long time. Two years! She must be in her mid-twenties, as I assume Bunny is, yet Bunny looks like she could be no more than a teenager, or she could be into her late thirties. I kept looking at her for clues, but the kerchief on her head, the bleak, dark space behind her eyes and the fear make it hard to place her in age. She looks like someone who has seen too much.

Hani and I have no blanket and only one bowl between us, we have nothing to offer, but to Wanda this doesn't seem to matter. She is so kind. We are grateful. I'm not sure if we would have been made so welcome if Wanda had not taken us both under her wing. Wanda

*seemed enchanted with Hani's beauty and her inno-
cent look of being unable to understand all that goes on
around her.*

*Hani and I are invited to sleep in the top bunk. I
have a thousand questions passing through my mind, but
I feel overwhelmed by the kindness. My face throbs from
the blow and Hani and I are lying down wrapped in each
other's arms. The first time I have lain down in many
weeks. It feels so nice, I cry. The first time since I left you.
My eyes heavy from tears, dry and hot. I rest.*

These women, this place. For Miriam, there is no point of reference
for all she is reading. She cannot imagine it, yet she is reading it. And
millions experienced it.

'You've done nothing wrong,' Miriam says to her father. 'You cannot blame yourself. You didn't do this.' She raises the letter. 'This is . . .
Maybe there aren't words for this.'

HENRYK

It was the 10th of April 1944. A Monday. The last time I saw Frieda.

We had been arrested two days after all laws ceased and one man oversaw an entire city.

Our journey started on the Schildhornstraße in Berlin. I was sure we were going to be shot, right outside the flat Emilie and I had been hiding in. But we were told to walk instead. The sun felt like ice as it emerged through a deep fog, blurring the edges of my vision.

We walked for hours, all familiarity behind us. Stopping only for more houses to be emptied of their occupants. As Hagelstraße turned into Fontanestraße, we stayed on the road, lined with tree stumps and burnt-out army vehicles.

A procession of footsteps chattered, a train moving on its tracks. The houses that lined the streets had been boarded up. All doors and windows were blocked, yet there was scattered glass on the ground. People attacked from above and within. Behind the facade of empty, derelict houses, people hid and prayed, thankful that today it was not them. I, too, had believed I was safe within the confines of four walls. But those walls had come down and I was out in the open with nothing but Frieda by my side. Surrounded by officers marching along the pavements, we became part of a throng of people under siege.

Ahead of us someone had fallen.

'*Schwein!*' a male voice barked. To my left an officer swept diagonally towards an elderly man who had collapsed over a suitcase. The officer, in perfect green uniform, gleaming boots, spat on him.

'*Du faules Schwein.*' He struck the man on the back of the head. One blow that propelled the man forward, his hat fell off and a shower of white hair emerged from under it as his face impacted on the case. I moved with the crowds and looked down at him. Frieda pulled me on, averting her eyes. I turned and she grabbed my arm harder, but I moved towards the man against others passing me.

Frieda held back.

'*Zurück in der Reihe,*' the officers shouted to me, but there was no line to return to, there was only the hobbling mass that bumbled along.

Away from the fallen man.

'Henryk.' Frieda had caught my arm again, she was looking at the officers as they were watching me. No one stopped, they kept pace, all eyes forward. The officer brushed his fingers across the rim of his hat, before stomping on the man's back.

'*Aufstehen,*' he screamed, red-faced, then looking at his comrades he laughed and they laughed along with him. I paused.

'Henryk,' Frieda whispered on tiptoes, touching her lips to my ear. 'Please.'

The officer stepped away and the fastening popped as he took out a pistol from its holster.

'*Aufstehen!*' He motioned with the pistol for the man to get up.

'*Bitte warten,*' I shouted and pushed Frieda away. I placed myself between the old man and the officer. 'Wait.' I bent down. 'Wait,' I said again, more to myself this time. Hovering my body over the man, he smelt both damp and old. His coat was too short and his forearms poked out of the sleeves, his feet clad in house shoes, barely soled. The suitcase was made of beaten leather, the stitches frayed at the edges. I was focused on the suitcase, waiting for the shot. Waiting. But it was Frieda who reached me first.

'Come sir, please,' she said, placing a hand on his back. 'They will shoot us all.' She picked up his hat and wedged it on his head.

'He is fine,' she said, looking at the officer with the pistol still pointing at us. 'Please lower your aim, this man just needs help.' At her words, I lifted the man to his feet. Placing both arms over my shoulders and all his weight on my back. Frieda picked up his suitcase.

'*Nein*,' he said so close to my ear that it startled me. He pulled free of my arms and slouched back to the ground.

'*Nein!*' he shouted, grabbing his case back from Frieda and holding it to his chest like a shield. The officer repositioned his pistol and aimed it at the man.

'*Die Juden*,' the officer said, shrugging his shoulders as if it couldn't be helped. I pulled Frieda to me and we turned away as a shot rang out. We shrank from the noise and hurried ahead, getting lost in the crowd. The buzzing in my ears did nothing to dull the mocking bell of laughter from the officers.

We raced along, keeping pace. I held her into my body, our combined heat amplified as we ran from what we had seen. Eventually we slowed with the crowd, she placed her arm around my own and walking became less cumbersome.

Once our hands had cooled together Frieda spoke, reverting to French to allow our words a whisper of privacy.

'What do we do now?'

'What *can* we do?' I said, shaking my head in defeat. She looked at me quizzically then dropped her hand from mine.

She watched the people mill around us and for the rest of our long walk I was just as disconnected from her as they were.

MIRIAM

She moves on to the next letter. They hold answers, but as Miriam reads she becomes lost in a sea of words, in a world so removed from her own that she easily forgets the questions.

> *Henryk,*
> *The first day waking in Block 15 was blissful. The sun shone and we were greeted with 'hellos' and 'sweet dreams?' Rather than shoves and shouts. The roll call was long but the sky was blue and optimism filled Hani and me. Now that we have been allocated a block we can work and this lifts our spirits more. Women work, they get on, it is what we do and Hani and I have become part of the 'sand team'.*
>
> *The others in the block are not part of a work detail. They are known fondly as 'the Rabbit Girls'. From what I can gather they are human guinea pigs, women experimented upon. There is an aura of protection around them from the women. Hani and I look quizzically at each other, not really understanding.*

Bunny does not leave her bunk at all. Bunny, Wanda and Eugenia sew and knit for the war effort while Stella plays outside with the other orphans.

But, I am keen to move and feel blood pumping through my body. Sedentary and stiff over the past weeks, moving will be a blessing. It will be good to feel part of something.

HENRYK

We woke together under the bridge of Gleis 17, numb, into a cacophony of fear. Roused with one command. Men to the right, women to the left. There were no children here. We were a flowing tide about to hit a jagged cliff edge that would send us in two different directions.

No individual wanted to move, yet we were all *forced* forward. It wasn't until the doors of the wagons slid open and I saw there were already people in there, I knew it was over. They must have been locked in the wagon overnight, shut away like cattle, but they didn't run or try to leave their wooden cells. When daylight seeped in, their faces peered out at us, afraid, curious, bleak.

I should have held her tighter. I should not have let her go. I should have found a way to prevent what happened next. But to hold her would be to break her. The ribbon of terror unravelled in me. I knew it would slink into her, and she had to remain strong, for we were both going on.

Alone.

Shakespeare said that for those who love, time is eternal, and he is right. There is an endless sense that wherever she goes I go too. As long as I live she lives within me. I wish I'd said that to her.

But I didn't.

What I said was, 'Your hands are cold.'

Those were my parting words.

She smiled. Her hands slipped from mine as fingertips reached, finding only air. I stumbled and was forced to look away as I knocked into someone. I turned and when I turned back she was gone.

MIRIAM

'Rabbits? Experiments?' She looks at the next letters, on tiny scraps of paper as thin as tissue, they have rolled over themselves and she struggles to keep them flat. 'What did they do to them?'

> *Henryk,*
> *We work, we eat the tiniest food, enough to keep us alive, but only just, not enough to satisfy any hunger. Wanda has found us another bowl so Hani and I no longer share. This means we get to eat more now. I still mush Hani's bread, it is getting harder to stop before I swallow the full amount.*
> *The sand eats at my skin. It is senseless work to break the spirit. We move sand and it moves straight back. My hands hurt too much to write and I have run out of paper.*

Dad grunts, shivers and then shakes. Tremors grow like a wave through the entire left side of his body, becoming more violent as Miriam stands. But just as she is about to get the midazolam, the tremors slow and he shivers again, teeth chattering.

'Hold on, Dad,' she says, adding blankets and smoothing his cool hands.

'So cold,' he mutters, and she lies on the bed with him.

'I'm right here,' she says as his body relaxes. Night seeps in through the window, an unwelcome presence in the room. 'I'm right here,' she says again, but fear crawls up her legs, and the oppressive dark makes her think of *him*. If he's back, then he's back for her.

They are running out of time. Just like Frieda ran out of paper. Yet there are more letters, and she feels a sense of dread forming word by word, letter by letter; this cannot end well.

'I'll find out what happened, but please, please stay. Just a little longer. Please.'

As his snores fill the room, she slips out of the bed, gets another letter from the pile and reads in the small light of the lamp.

I traded my bread for a long, thin pencil and I write to you in the safety of the bunk. The 'rabbit girls' are ignored by our Blockova, an intimidating woman of size and voice, yet she doesn't attack in spite. She doesn't need to. You only need to show the whip to a beaten dog.

The 'rabbit girls' are mainly ignored by the women too. Some offer Bunny and Wanda any additional bread they have saved or stolen. Others make playthings for Stella, from a small sheet of cotton a doll is created, which brings a smile to a young face.

Bunny and Wanda offer sewing and mending, creating pockets on the inside of uniforms is Bunny's speciality. Her fingers are so nimble. I am entranced by them as they work.

I am safe with these women.

I feel exhausted by my day, the routine, the expectation that I may be shot or injured, beaten or moved into holding cells or punishment blocks. Women dragged away, screaming to no avail. We all stand and watch and are thankful that today it isn't us. Friends do nothing. Yet, when the woman returns, so emaciated it's impossible to know how she still breathes, her ribs pushing out from skin, her friends wait with soup, bread and warmth.

I write at night, my eyes tear and sting from trying to write by only moonlight. Wanda snores, Bunny and Stella curl into each other, Bunny humming. Hani is wrapped over me as I write, lying on my side, squeezing as many words as I can on to one sheet of paper for you.

I hope we can burn them together to forget the past and pave a way for the future.

Occasionally Eugenia's head pops out from the middle bunk and we talk. She tells of the Allies, talks of liberation and the other ladies in the camp and how they are making small moves to try to save themselves and others. Regular transports take prisoners away. Some believe to a sanatorium, Eugenia thinks it is to death. She talks of names added to this list and how hard some women work to get their names, or those they love, off the list. It seems the Blockova has control of the blocks and sends names to the guards who form the lists. One way or another, the women leave the camp.

Eugenia promises news that the Allies are on their way. Russians or Americans will liberate the camp, and soon. Neither of us believe this to be true. There is no liberation and to believe in an end to this is folly. We continue as we do: we work to survive. It is so nice to talk, to communicate like women. We talk and talk until one of us falls asleep. I feel richer in my heart talking to Eugenia.

I place my letters in the folds of the straw mattress and pray they will still be there on my return.

I have Hani's warm body around me and this moment is squandered in sleep. It is my time to dream, to think, to give thanks for all that I have. There is no God, there is only soup. I am, with my pencil, making a mark on the world, however insignificant. I exist. They cannot eradicate me.

16

MIRIAM

As Miriam reads, a sense of hopelessness invades her. These women *believed* that something would be done, that other people would save them. She tries to sleep, but sees a silent woman tucked up in blankets sewing pockets and seams, everyone broken or battered. In comparison, her own troubles seem pitiful.

She dozes off just before dawn and dreams of snakes. Long, worming snakes in her stomach, weaving in and out of her skin. She grabs and pulls at them, but she cannot catch them. Smooth and sleek, they just slip back into the skin and writhe inside.

Miriam wakes as her nails dig into her stomach. She jumps up, fetches the scissors from her mother's drawer and takes them to the soft warm skin of her tummy. As soon as she sees red lines the internal snakes shrink and dissolve to the dreams they were.

She is disturbed by a knock at the door, and opens it just a crack, then enough to see Eva on the other side. Eva, with her hand up, poised to knock, paused in motion. Dressed in a deep-blue cardigan, grey-black trousers and heavy boots. Her coat and bag are cradled over her arm, with Lionel by her side.

'Your intercom isn't working,' he says, sweat slick on his forehead. 'Don't suppose you know why?'

'Umm . . .'

'This' – he looks to Eva, who remains silent – 'this lady, here, couldn't get in when she buzzed. Had to walk all the way up here with her, you know. To be safe in these times.'

'Thanks, Lionel.'

'While I'm here, let's have a look at this, shall we?' He manoeuvres his bulk past Miriam and lifts the intercom phone. 'Well, petal,' he says, levelling her with his gaze. 'It's unplugged.' He places the plug back into its socket and gives her a glance that says 'don't do that again', before tipping his hat at Eva and walking away.

'Would you like to come in?'

'Actually, I was wondering if I can talk to you,' Eva says, looking straight at Miriam, her gaze strong. Miriam covers her stomach with freshly washed hands. 'I may have been a bit . . . forceful at the library the other day.'

'Forceful?'

'I just wasn't, well, it's very difficult to trust people.'

'I understand.' She opens the door wider to invite Eva in. 'I suppose I have been privileged, I don't know what it was like on the other side of the Wall.'

'Have you been reading the letters?'

'Yes, the rabbit girls . . . It's horrific, that this happened and—'

'You didn't make it to the library yesterday,' Eva interrupts her.

'No, I'm sorry.'

'Did you get my note?'

'Yes, and thank you for the letters too. It's quite a story, but I don't really know—'

'Can I buy you a coffee? The shop at the end of the street?' Eva interrupts again.

She thinks of her father resting and nods. 'Coffee would be lovely, let me just tell Dad.'

The coffee shop is open, the inhabitants laughing, talking. Living. Miriam walks in and the smell of Christmas invades her senses. She softens in the warm glow of cinnamon and coffee beans.

Eva finds a seat at the back of the shop in front of a large, open window; even though it is early, the view from the window is grim and dark. The breeze is a welcome chill to the hot fuzz of people and coffee. Miriam orders a coffee in a large glass with cream and cinnamon sprinkles; a small biscuit and long spoon are placed in front of her.

She orders Eva the same and scans the room before perching on the edge of her chair. She wishes Axel could just be there. Just there. Because if he's there, he cannot be everywhere. Miriam fidgets, looks up and jumps at the slightest noise or movement from the people around her. Within minutes her body is tense and aches, confined within the chair.

Eva takes a bite of her biscuit and crumbs fall into her lap. Miriam watches as she flicks them away with the back of her hand.

'Thank you for helping me with the letters,' Miriam says.

'You are paying me, and . . .'

'Yes, I owe you money, don't I?'

Eva waves the question away.

'It was a good thing I met Jeff, or you may have found me slaving over a dictionary trying to put the words together.' She knows she is talking fast and almost nonsensically, but cannot find a way to calm down. 'Do you have a family?' she asks. 'Other than Jeff?'

'My husband died a few years ago, he was a doctor. A very good man. His daughters are grown now. Jeffrey is Renka's son, she was the oldest,' Eva says, stirring the cream into her coffee with the long spoon. 'They stole through the tunnels when he was a boy. I hadn't seen them for almost twenty years.'

A long silence casts a shadow over the table as Miriam listens to Eva's breathing slow down. Her hands are darkened with age, yet long and thin.

'Do you have a partner, Miriam?' Eva asks, her mouth full of biscuit.

Miriam shakes her head and sips at her scalding-hot coffee.

'No,' she says. 'Well, not exactly.'

Miriam thinks of the night she left *him*.

'It's . . .' she starts. 'You see . . .' she tries and then settles with, 'It's a bit complicated.'

That night, the phone call from the hospital still ringing around her head, Miriam had washed her hands thoroughly and tiptoed into their bedroom, thinking only of her father, alone, dying, a few hours away.

The soothing sound of Axel's snores offered her peace. He was in his usual position, asleep in the bed as he would be dead in his grave.

The soft, cream blanket, usually found at the foot of their bed, was placed on the floor, folded over and over on itself until it made a small rectangle. The size of a dog basket. Her bed for the night.

Dogs and bitches get the floor.

She turned and left the room.

Her toes had crawled for purchase on the side of the bath as she teetered, trying to access the top shelves of the cabinet where her medication was stored. Away from her.

Axel was the only one who could be trusted to ensure she received the correct dose. After the last time . . . when each bitter pill seemed sugar-coated, a sweetness to abyss.

She opened the old box at the back, and amongst an assortment of medications, anti-depressants, anti-hallucinogenics and sleeping tablets . . .

She saw it.

After years of not knowing where it was, Miriam, looking for an escape, any way to free herself, had found one.

Her ID card.

If she could prove she was a West German citizen, she could get back into Berlin, she could go home. No matter that they lived in

Wolfsburg, still West Germany, the guards at the checkpoints would need proof she wasn't an East German stowaway.

She gathered it in her nightdress, close to her heart, and silently walked down the stairs, avoiding the second-from-top stair and its hollow creak. She placed her feet into her shoes, took her coat and bag from the rack, and pulled the front door shut tight. There was no thinking. Her feet left the house.

'Sorry, Eva, what did you say?' She feels the room pulse towards her and imagines her exit through the mass of bodies and tables should *he* enter the café here. Or be sitting there. Or behind her.

'Just saying how complicated most relationships are,' Eva says. 'Nothing is ever as straightforward as people say it is: books and movies, people are just skimming over the edges. I suppose that is because most commercial art is made by men.' Eva smiles, a twinkle in her eye.

'My mother once said to me, when I was contemplating what to do in life, *Men make art and women make babies.* I failed at both,' she says. Then adds, 'At the time I thought it was stupid, but maybe she was trying to caution me.'

'Caution you?'

'To know my place.' Miriam tries the coffee again and scalds her lip in the same place. She takes a bite of the biscuit instead.

'Can I ask you about the letters?' Eva asks. 'How did you come by them?'

'They come from a dress, a uniform I think. I found it when I was tidying Mum's things.'

'Is it your mother's?' Eva asks.

'I don't think so. One of the letters mentions Ravensbrück, maybe Mum went there, but the letters? Mum never spoke French, let alone read or wrote in it . . .'

'Is she not around to ask?'

Miriam shakes her head at the same time as taking a sip of coffee. The cream splashes up on to her face. She wipes at her mouth with a napkin.

'I'm sorry to hear that. How long?'

'Three years. From cancer,' she says. Her hands shake and the coffee spills over her fingers.

The music is quiet and the voices swarm around the café like bees as Miriam waits for the shattering feeling she has grown used to when thinking about Mum. But the feeling doesn't come. She waits for it as she sips her coffee, the cream sweet, she licks her top lip as the warmth of the café seeps into her.

Eva rustles in her bag. 'Would you like one?' She offers a clementine. They sit eating and watch the cars and people wash by.

'And your father?' Eva says eventually.

A man in leather shoes walks past her, Miriam springs up.

'I have to get back,' she says.

'And I thought I was jumpy. Are you okay?'

'I have to get back to Dad, before it's too late.' She consults her watch. Time has passed.

The noise of the café becomes deafening. Happy faces, laughter, perfume, couples sitting face to face. Guilt crawls and takes hold in her throat. The crushing, banging and bashing of the coffee machine. The grinding sharpens her senses.

The door opens, a bell tinkles and the weather intrudes with the sweep of a wet umbrella, held by a man in a long black coat.

The man is as tall as Axel, but it isn't him.

The coffee turns bitter. A spiderweb of fear she cannot swallow past.

'Sorry,' Eva says. 'I apologise if I said something out of turn.'

'Oh no,' Miriam says, putting on her coat. 'But I must get back to my father now.'

They leave the café together. 'Can you come back? I left the letters on the table for you.'

'I came with a few more for you too.' Eva gently takes Miriam's arm and slows her pace to match her own. The weight of Eva on her arm is comforting and eventually the panic Miriam felt on leaving subsides.

They walk together in silence, watching their footing on the leaf-strewn street.

The house is still and as she stands by her father, she whispers, 'Eva is here, Dad, she's helping me. To find Frieda for you.' She squeezes his hand tight.

'This is the dress,' Miriam says in the dining room where she has put the bag with the dress in it. She opens the clasp and pulls the sheet out, offering it to Eva, who steps back.

'You do it,' she says.

Miriam flattens the dress out on the table.

'A miracle,' Eva says. 'Where did you find the letters?' she asks.

'Here.' She points to the pockets and the frayed seams, the collars and cuffs.

'They used to adjust the dresses,' Eva says, her fingers trace the bottom of the dress. 'The uniforms, so they could carry their own spoons and sometimes a photo of a loved one, a letter.'

'I read that in the letters. Bunny sewed secret pockets or something?' As Miriam says her name aloud she realises that these letters are real. Bunny is real. These are letters depicting lives that have been lived and lost. Miriam feels an overwhelming sense of inadequacy at reading something so personal, and wonders how Eva feels about translating them. Sharing this with Eva brings a comfort, a shared experience, maybe even a friend.

Eva walks along the table, smoothing her hands along the fabric as she goes.

'Can I get you a glass of water?'

Eva doesn't answer.

Miriam goes into the kitchen and returns with two glasses of water.

Eva seems to have aged, her face is still wrinkled in the same places, but the lines have deepened. Her lips narrowed. Her fingers smooth the pocket. Miriam hands her a glass and she takes a sip, swallowing hard.

'It's incredible such a thing exists. So many members of my family died in camps,' Eva says quietly.

'I'm so sorry. The dress got to me too,' Miriam says. 'Especially the smell.'

Sitting abruptly in a chair, Eva seems to shrink in front of her. She places her hands together and shakes her head, looking at the dress.

'It's horrendous. I don't know how you are managing translating them, but I certainly . . .' A loud bang at the door makes both jump. Miriam sloshes water over her top and Eva looks wide-eyed towards the hallway. Neither of them move.

Another knock propels Miriam into motion. She opens the door to Lionel panting with an enormous bunch of flowers in his arms: red roses with foliage. Expensive.

'These are heavy,' he complains. 'What is wrong with your intercom again?'

'Nothing,' she says, and takes them from him. He is right, they topple in Miriam's arms.

'Who are they from?'

'Those stairs . . .' he pants, holding his hand up to stop her speaking. 'You're welcome,' he says, brushing green leaves from his shirt, and walks away, muttering something under his breath.

'They look pretty.' Eva appears by her side, composed. 'An admirer?'

Miriam shakes her head.

'Can I help you? Get a vase maybe?'

'No, thank you.' Miriam places the flowers down on the kitchen side as if they were an unexploded bomb. She finds the card:

Until tomorrow, my wife.

'Who are they from?' Eva looks over her shoulder.

Miriam picks them up and squeezes them in the bin, stems snapping as she forces them further and further in. She closes the lid and steps away, brushing her hands together, the plasters on her fingers join themselves together. She collects the bin liner and takes it out to the main bin downstairs.

Eva waits for her return in the kitchen.

'Can I help?'

While she washes her hands, Eva puts the kettle on.

Miriam winces as she places her hands under the steaming hot water, then washes them with soap. The kettle screams and she looks at it. At the boiling water, thinking of the blistering it could cause to her skin, and the peace she would find after.

Eva takes the kettle off the heat while Miriam rinses, before using a nail brush along the palms and fingertips, ripping off the plasters, rinsing again with water that streams hot. She allows the water to run red before Eva places a hand on her shoulder.

'That's enough,' she says.

'It wasn't an admirer,' Miriam murmurs.

'I can see, but it's enough now.' And she reaches past Miriam and turns off the tap before placing a towel in her hands. 'May I see?'

Miriam unravels the towel, showing her bleeding fingers, the skin peeled back on her fingernails and the scratches and grazes along her wrists.

'May I help?' Taking her by both hands, Eva guides Miriam to the living room and into the high-backed, gold-studded, olive chairs. She dries each hand with a towel, stems the flow of blood and replaces the plasters to Miriam's muted instructions.

'What's tomorrow?' Eva asks.

'They want to take Dad away to the hospital, I think. There is a meeting.'

'What will happen?'

The question is left in the air.

'The flowers,' Eva starts, 'are from your husband?'

Miriam nods.

'You aren't together?'

'No,' she says. Then a second 'No', with more conviction.

'All terrible things do pass with time, I promise you. Your fingers will heal, and the damage inside will too. You just need time,' Eva says and collects her bag. 'I have some more of the French letters here.' She draws out a bundle. 'I should be going now,' she says, looking at the dress and then at Miriam's hands.

'Of course.' Miriam gives her the other half of the letters and a ten-Westmark note. 'Thank you, and I am sorry you had to see that.' She nods to the kitchen.

'Never apologise. Can I perhaps . . . If it wouldn't inconvenience you, well, perhaps I can call again?'

'Please, any time.'

When Eva has left, Miriam takes the new letters to her father's side.

There are so many letters of all shapes and sizes and many more to read. Grateful for something to do with her hands, she picks up the next letter, happy to absorb herself in Frieda's plight rather than think about her own.

17

HENRYK

I am resting in pieces, but I can hear Miriam.

Her tiny voice speaks, but not to me. I try to listen, to find my centre once more, but I am turning and turning and I lose her words in the dark.

I am adrift. I can feel my toes, I try to move them, but they are too far away. My legs feel confined and strange but they are there. I am lying on a bed. I cannot place where I am, all I know is that I *am*.

And although I know that Frieda is gone, I also know that she has not faded for me. I must know all that happened, I must know the weight of my crime, the judgement and the sentence.

All that happened to her was because of me.

I hear Miriam again. 'Frieda,' I call. But my mouth won't form the words. Not today. '*Please*,' I scream, but the scream just reverberates inside my head and spittle runs out of my mouth. I feel it slide down my chin and cool there.

MIRIAM

To not think about *tomorrow*, Axel or anything other than the letters, Miriam reads long into the night.

> *Henryk,*
> *The Blockova said I could see the Kommandant. After all this time, it felt useless. I had nothing to say now. The reason I wanted to talk to her had gone now we were in Block 15. But you cannot decline to see the Kommandant if she calls for you.*
>
> *I felt naked walking to her office. I had not bathed in days; there was no water for bathing, because we needed it to drink. It was so hot. I smelled like bodies – hot, dirty bodies. I washed my hands to rid myself of the sand and grime and the little water left I drank. I pinched my cheeks and licked my lips to try and plump them up. I had sand in my teeth.*
>
> *The Blockova caught me, vanity is punishable. She whipped the back of my hands. My eyes watered from the bite of it.*

The office was quiet, and I was faced with a woman: blonde hair, clear skin. Pressed, dark uniform.

I could be her.

I think we are but a circumstance apart. Lipstick, hair lacquer, her hat pinned on to her hair. I pulled off my kerchief revealing patchy hair growing thick and light. I realised I was staring. I did not know where to start. I cried tears I didn't know I had.

I spoke words that crippled my heart. My shaved head, my broken hands, my empty stomach reveal who I am. I will do anything to be free. Even disown the name I had taken so easily.

The truth is ugly.

Only eight weeks ago I answered to the name Emilie Winter – I chose to be with you, as Emilie hid away. I was proud to stand next to you. To be arrested with you. To walk with you, even if it was to here.

I am ashamed, but I stood and emulated all that I hated.

'My family are pure Aryan,' I mumbled.

Her impenetrable face, marbled, watching me.

'Heil Hitler!' I said. The salute, one I had not done for so long, felt like treachery, treason of the heart and mind.

I was selling my soul. My only worry: was it enough?

She had papers in front of her.

'How long have you been here?'

'Eight weeks, ma'am.'

'What do you want?'

And in that moment, although I knew I wanted a bowl and a better job than shifting sand; I wanted the Blockovas to treat us better; I wanted the women in charge not to be criminals; I wanted to DO something.

I said very quietly: 'Please, I want to go home.'

'Women do not get released from Ravensbrück.'

That was it.

But just as I turned to leave, she called me back.

'It would be nice to have eyes and ears in the camp, you understand? Bring me information, illegal behaviour, rule-breakers, slackers, there are several underground goings-on. Women "hiding" within blocks, spouting lies.' She looked up. 'I can make things better here for you if you help me. Do you understand?'

I nodded.

'Return next Wednesday with something to tell me.'

I left.

I was marched back to the block. I thought of Bunny, Wanda, Stella, Eugenia. What was the price of my freedom?

HENRYK

I was forced into the wagon, forced with so many men. I looked for Frieda. I stood by the barred window and looked out for her. We all clambered to see out of the window to catch another glimpse of those we had been parted from.

We saw nothing.

I rested my head back on to the wood of the wagon. The door was shut tight. *What had I done?*

I was sent to Auschwitz. I did not know the meaning of 'Auschwitz' as it is talked of. I only knew I was in hell. Every night, I would close my eyes and there we were under that bridge, Gleis 17, waiting for a future, never knowing that future would be apart.

And for me, this time that all have forgotten, or chosen to forget, is entwined with Frieda, and to pull on a thread is to lose myself in the tapestry where I bit a man's hand for the bread held tight within it. Where I threw bodies into the crematorium, not questioning if those bodies were dead or alive.

MIRIAM

She places the letter face up and looks at the four names that jump from the bottom of the yellowed and curling page. *Bunny. Wanda. Stella. Eugenia.* She wonders if any of them got out alive and who was this person, Frieda, who could even think about giving up such vulnerable and broken women?

Is Eva right not to trust anyone? When Miriam herself believed her parents always told her the truth, now the lie bleeds into every memory she has. Who were the people before she called them Mum and Dad, and who was Frieda to them?

> *The 'rabbit girls' are all in pieces. Their legs operated on.*
>
> *Wanda has a scar through both her legs from inner ankle up to knee.*
>
> *Eugenia has a deep scar, a loss of a lot of flesh taken from her left leg.*
>
> *Both their legs have healed.*
>
> *Bunny, however . . . the sweet smell of rotting flesh is strong, it is the heart of our bunk. She covers her legs with a blanket. Her legs have not healed from whatever*

*they did to them. She will never walk again; she doesn't
have enough bone left in her legs to stand.*

*None of them talk about what happened, aside from
Eugenia, who whispers in hurried urgency. Her stories
make my blood run cold, even now, putting her words to
paper, a spike of fear runs along my skin.*

*Operations without consent, waking in agony, shards
of glass in their legs, broken bones, the smell and then the
infection.*

*On Eugenia's round, only she and another woman,
Katya, survived – all six other women succumbed to the
infection forced into their skin, bone and blood supply.
Many died on the operating table.*

*They couldn't move – restrained in the bed, with legs
not their own. No water, no painkillers. They lay there
and prayed for death.*

*Katya survived. A drunken doctor stitched up her
legs and she was released back into the main camp. Four
months later she was 'chosen' and killed. Her legs were
proof that they had used her as a human guinea pig.
Many of the other 'rabbits' who survived have suffered
the same fate.*

*On Eugenia's release, she found the broken space in
Block 15 and made a small bunk from the wood found
in the upper loft space where other 'rabbit girls' were hiding. The women pretended not to see the rabbit girls, they
are like the forgotten war-wounded; left alone to tenderly
lick their wounds.*

Yet the guards are always looking to smoke them out.

*The broken bunks, our space, is their sanctuary, and
the camp women have kept the rabbit girls a secret. It's*

one of the only times, Eugenia says with pride, that the women have stood united against the guards.

Fear, Eugenia thinks. It is fear that keeps their secret. Because the women know that so random was the selection for the experiments, it could so easily be them.

Eugenia kept her leg clean by using water from the sink, which has now dried up. She escaped knowledge and detection. Soon other rabbits joined her, although many died. Eugenia went back in to rescue Wanda and Bunny, and Stella joined their group the following day.

The guards want 'the rabbit girls'. They want to destroy the evidence.

Tomorrow I will hand them in. Three lives for the price of my release.

Wanda.

Eugenia.

Bunny.

And what will happen to Stella without Bunny?

I am awake, not fearing tomorrow, but I am doing what I have fought against all my life. One life is worth more than another. My life matters more. Because of this I can barter my life for theirs. A position of advantage. I am no better than the guards who kill with batons and guns. I am no longer Frieda. I am superior.

I will stand on those who have shown me kindness. I will stomp on them to leave. I think of my empty stomach, my own pain and I know the Nazis have won a war, whether in victory or not, they have won the war over humanity. Turning everyone against each other.

Eight weeks is all it takes.

Can you forgive me?

Can I forgive myself?

A disgust so deep pulls Miriam away from the letter, she feels tainted by it. By its roughness and an honesty that scares her. She looks at the remaining letters and considers burning every single page, every word removed in flame and smoke. Imagines the match scratching a flame into the air, taking each letter in the corner, flames igniting the paper into life. To eradicate the past, the present so almost at its end. Then the thought of her teetering on the side of the bath comes into focus, the cool bath under bare toes, and what she had considered doing to escape Axel. If anyone had given her an opportunity, or the means to leave . . . would she not have taken it, also?

Instead of setting them alight, she thinks of her father's words, '*I killed Frieda.*' And she knows no matter how difficult, she will see this through. She must, so he can rest in peace.

18

HENRYK

To look back is to relive.

To relive is to die a thousand deaths again. I barely survived it once. I would get lost in the labyrinth of black eyes and a loss of humanity that so startled me. We were nothing but animals, and within the barbed-wire walls, surrounded by the weakest mankind has made, we were slaves. Not to them, but to ourselves. Slaves for survival. Slaves to the next mouthful of food. We would kill for bread, all of us. He who fights hardest and longest wins.

I was covered in lice, watching them crawl along my skin. Did Frieda fight back, pick them off, shake them away, scratch? Or did she resign herself to their torture like I did?

I did what I had to do to survive, I tell myself that, but I know that I would rather have died than become who I became.

That is why I didn't go back. That is why I am paralysed. I cannot think that Frieda would have done the same, I cannot know if she was so compromised.

Even though I smiled, I laughed and I enjoyed my life, I was also hollow. She holds something that cannot be returned, only shared.

For a time, I willed the memoirs, maps and reports to tell me she was shot in the back of the head, perhaps. Even though the crevice that opened for me at the thought was black and red and cindered as if on fire, it was peaceful.

And it meant that Emilie never lied to me.

It meant it was over. But I fear the opposite was true.

Emilie did not know the horrors that existed within me; she did not want to hear, she chose not to look and I cherished her the more for that.

Auschwitz was like a cancer: it ate and changed everything into one thick, black mass. An abyss.

Emilie found me in the hospital and I returned to her side. We had been married nine years, she took me back after the camp was liberated when she did not have to.

As a husband, I did not recognise myself. As a man, I was lost. Nine months was all it took.

After six months in hospital, I returned to the small room Emilie called home. As one of the very few married couples who had both survived the Nazi regime we were considered fortunate and many women in the large building we inhabited visited us. I remember nothing but an endless sea of women at the door and my wife at my side. For months I was, apparently, inert. I did not move unless told, eat or speak unless I had to.

Emilie told me many times that she thought about leaving me in that room. So deeply absorbed in my own trauma I had no ability to do anything when everything needed to be done. Emilie stayed because she had made a promise to, she always said. 'I promised to stand by you, Henryk, even though I would leave you ten times over if I could.' My wife never minced her words, but even in their harsh reality I was lost.

So, am I a weak man?

Yes. Of course I am. I am weak because I am strong, because I took from those weaker, when in every other circumstance, I would never have done so. I am weak because in giving Frieda myself I gave her a promise that never needed words: I promised that I would love her, and although I have, I have done so only in private, in words of my own heart.

Maybe I should have tried to find her sooner. Maybe I couldn't really have loved her, because if I had I'd have gone back for her. Tried, even. Looked and turned over every stone to find the woman I loved. Maybe. But life is not a love story, it is not a fairy tale.

There are no happy endings.

MIRIAM

Leaving the apartment later than she intends, she hurries past shops belching out people, bags in hand and full of laughter. Miriam looks at their faces, scans each one. Checking none of them are him.

The tomorrow of his note has arrived and she doesn't know when or how she will see him, but she knows she will.

After shaking herself dry in the medical centre, she finds conference room seven from Hilda's directions. The sign is black, it has peeled away at the corners. She represses the desire to pick at the tip of the '7' as she stands facing the white door, hearing voices within.

'Excuse me.' A woman, glasses around her neck and a pad of paper in her hand, moves past her and opens the door, which propels Miriam forward. The chatter and the humidity roll over her as the door closes her in.

She is greeted with the eyes of everyone in the room. Everyone except the man pouring the coffee, the man with his back to her.

The man in his best shirt. He turns.

'Morning, Mim. Coffee?' He holds the pot up.

She backs away and knocks into the wall.

He puts the coffee down.

He's here and she cannot run.

She is stuck. Frozen.

But she is also back: all the way back to a month ago; before she had left; before her father was dying; before the dress; before Eva.

'Oh, sweetheart. I have been so worried.' Everyone around the table is looking at him.

Miriam looks at him too. He is clean-shaven and wearing a shirt and suit trousers.

He is also in jeans and a sweater, casually leaning against the fridge, telling her that she couldn't go. That he wouldn't let her go to her father. That she was his and his alone. That she couldn't abandon him as his mother had done. Leaving meant she couldn't love him.

She says nothing and no one in the room moves to her aid.

She can hear the mechanical whirr of the fridge, his words sharp and pointed. No. She feels the cotton of her dress against her legs, her toes on the cool linoleum. Her back against the wall.

Axel pours a cup of coffee, turning his back to her, and she scans the room for other familiar, perhaps friendlier, faces.

'What's he doing here?' she hisses to Hilda, sitting next to her; the floral bouquet of Hilda's perfume blocks out the stale smell of confined bodies, and Miriam holds on to that smell to try and stay present.

'Who?'

She points to Axel.

'He's here to support you.' She smiles as Axel delivers Hilda a coffee.

'Can you make him leave?'

'Now that everyone is here,' Dr Baum says, 'I think perhaps it might be time to begin.'

There is a scrape of chairs and a flurry of activity.

Axel returns to his seat, opposite Miriam.

Hilda touches her on the arm. 'There is nothing to worry about.'

She wrings her hands in her coat sleeves, aware she is overdressed but a frost has settled over her stomach and works its way out.

Please, she had begged. Actually begged to be let out of her own home. To go to her dying father's side.

'Miriam. Miriam,' Axel said. 'Going back now, what good will it do?'

'He's dying,' Miriam murmured.

'So let him die in peace, my love.' He moved towards her slowly and touched her gently on the cheek.

'But . . .' she said meekly.

'Welcome . . .' Dr Baum looks around like a pastor at the podium. 'I would like to start by thanking you all for . . . well . . . in the weather . . . the current parking issues . . . time from your, well, whatever you would normally be doing.' As he speaks, he feels each word in his mouth before committing to it.

Before his first sentence is over, Miriam wants to scream.

The clock on the wall has no second hand, time passes in hours rather than minutes here.

Axel is directly opposite her, across the table. He looks the same, but slightly different. Familiar, yet with the novelty of not seeing someone for a while whom you normally look upon daily. His dark hair slicked back revealing his widow's peak and a healthy dusting of grey just above his ears. She cannot tell what mood he is in. His lips are relaxed, his jaw doesn't twitch. She studies his face, trying to predict what will happen next.

'Let us start the meeting, and do this in a methodical, maybe more of a linear way, so that we are all aware of the current situation, as it happens to be, and all the possible alternatives that we can, perhaps . . . the options that are available to Herr Winter, should the opportunity arise and the members of this meeting agree.'

Miriam watches Dr Baum and feels lost to the conversation already. She concentrates on his words, yet finds none of them make sense.

Understanding Dr Baum feels like studying a map with no reference point.

Everyone introduces themselves, while Miriam snatches glimpses at Axel calmly sipping his coffee.

She also sees him on top of her, sweating, pulsing, pushing, searing, scrambling, chasing, catching, teasing, hurting, laughing, finishing, apologising, crying, holding; promising.

Her head is spinning and she cannot stop her heart from racing. It's going to beat out of her chest, or she is going to collapse in the plastic chair.

The heat of his skin, clammy, wet, pressed against her mouth, his lips on hers. She tries to push against him, but he doesn't move. His mouth working on hers, prising her lips open, pushing his tongue into her mouth.

Dr Baum draws her back into the room, and she looks at Axel, sitting still, smiling pleasantly. And, like vertigo, she plummets back to a time before, as well as being aware of what is happening now; as though both are happening at once.

She sees the charming, middle-aged man in front of her, but she also feels her husband move his hands up her skirt. Grabbing her bottom and digging his nails deep into her so that she rises to meet his body. She can feel it happening, as though Axel's hands from the past are still groping and squeezing at her skin.

'One second,' Dr Baum says, holding up a hand. 'I see we've fallen out of sync.'

Then everyone looks at her.

'Miriam,' Dr Baum continues, 'do you understand, comprehend or indeed apprehend your role in this meeting, as such, although perhaps meeting is not its name . . .'

Miriam drifts off into a haze.

Dr Baum looks at Miriam, who is unsure if she needs to speak or if there was a question posed to her.

'Miriam. I am clearly asking you, if you would be so kind, to explain your role in the room today.'

Miriam looks to Hilda for help, but none is offered.

'I'm here to speak on behalf of Dad's wishes,' she tentatively says.

'Yes, the wishes of your father as you see them.'

'That's right, his wishes.'

'Well, technically, no. Not his wishes as his state is one in which his wishes are not easily identified or articulated. You are basing your assumption of his wishes on your own ideology and inference, I suppose?'

'Based on knowing Dad.' She feels defensive.

'Ah, yes, but . . .'

'She hadn't spoken to her father for a decade,' Axel says. Miriam glares at him and his face lights up in a smile.

Axel had written to her father, once, before her mother had died. Telling him that Miriam hated him, blamed him for her current difficulties, which he catalogued in detail. Axel wrote that Dad's *episodes* (which she had disclosed to Axel privately) were a trauma that Miriam needed medication to overcome. Axel had written it out in a long letter, stipulating that Miriam was a bad wife because her Mum had been a 'raven mother', abandoning Miriam for her career. The letter was barbaric, it was hideous, it was lies. But it was lies that would hurt her parents the most. Miriam had watched Axel seal the letter and lock her in the house as he went out to post it. And there had been nothing she could do.

But every night while she watched Axel sleep, she waited for a noise, for the front door. For her parents to come for her, because she knew they wouldn't believe the letter. That they would know she was in trouble. That she was stuck. They would come for her, and they would help her.

After a week she became frantic, checking the post like a maniac, walking down the street, lifting the receiver of the phone – waiting . . . wondering. After two weeks, she accidently cut herself while chopping carrots, the pain had shocked her. But it had shocked her out of the loop of why her parents hadn't come for her.

Was Axel right? Did they not love her at all?

After a month and not one letter from her parents, not one phone call and no one to come to her door to rescue her, Axel had taken her to the doctor.

He had taken her to this doctor.

Dr Baum is talking and Miriam is trying to hear him through the clatter of pain that comes from the feeling of being abandoned, exactly when she thought she would be saved.

'Thank you, Herr Voight. So, Miriam, I wonder how in fact you think that you know of your father's wishes, or are able to adequately represent them in this room.' Dr Baum raises his eyebrows.

'His what?'

'Why are you here? is what Dr Baum is asking, love,' Axel's cotton-soft voice.

'Do you want me to leave?' Miriam asks Dr Baum.

'I think the question here is, do *you* want to leave?' he counters.

Miriam is completely torn by this, more than ever she would love to run from the room, away from Axel watching her. But she thinks of her father, and she draws strength from the letters, what the rabbit girls went through, the operations and the doctors. If they can survive *that*, she can keep her head in a meeting. She shakes her head. 'No.'

But, why did her father not come for her? When they must have received the letter – the letter that would have so hurt them.

Miriam knows it would have killed her mother, that her mother died thinking that Miriam hated her.

It wasn't true.

The meeting continues and Miriam tries to breathe slowly. The woman who came into the room a little before Miriam is writing something, her pen scratching the paper furiously. A nurse with a plain, round face, named Sue, is eating biscuits noisily. Hilda is listening, Axel is listening and Dr Baum is talking . . . about hospice and hospital and her father leaving his home.

Confused as to where the conversation is heading Miriam interrupts. 'But there is nothing wrong with the current arrangement.'

'Frau Voight. I am aware you are not taking your medication,' Dr Baum addresses her in what she knows is his *sympathetic* tone. 'I can understand you may well be feeling . . . well, you might naturally find yourself in an unnatural state.' He sighs and looks to Axel who nods conspiratorially, then continues, 'A state of mind that cannot manage the nature of the discussion that is taking place.'

'Why can things not be as they are?'

'The meeting here, today, is testament to the fact Herr Winter's current situation, or environmental care, if you prefer, is not appropriate.'

'Isn't it?' she challenges. 'He is safe, yes he's dying, but he's doing so in his own room, in his own home, with his daughter by his side. This isn't forever, it may not even be for tomorrow. Let me care for him, please. Besides, I have Hilda.' Confidence she does not feel comes out strong in her voice, but once she has finished, her breathing is ragged and her blouse is stuck to her skin.

Dr Baum takes a deep breath and looks to Hilda. 'Okay, nurse, what is your position?'

Hilda leans forward as Miriam rests back in her chair.

'I think Miriam is doing an amazing job, but I'm sorry, I have to agree. I think as Herr Winter is stabilising he may need more long-term care and the pressure put on Miriam is high. I would suggest the hospice is a suitable alternative.'

'Hilda?'

Hilda turns in her chair. 'I'm sorry, Mim, you did an excellent job when your father had the seizure, but,' she lowers her voice and Miriam becomes aware that everyone is watching her, Axel just across the table, 'it looked like you had drunk an entire bottle of wine, and you've missed two appointments with the doctor, one I escorted you to.'

Betrayal, harsh and brittle, snaps Miriam into speech.

'I am caring for my father, that is what I should be doing. Not taking medication that makes me numb or dribble or sleep.'

'I have to say, that alcohol is in itself a substance which some may define as numbing,' Dr Baum interrupts. 'And I cannot think that any medication that would lessen the paranoia or psychotic episodes is any worse than being inebriated.'

Miriam recalls the snakes in her stomach; only a dream, but the scissors . . . the scissors were not.

'You say you care for your father,' he continues. 'But being drunk does not show any of us that you can put his needs before your own.'

And like a runaway train, the meeting continues. Miriam has nothing to say. Eventually Dr Baum draws this unique form of torture to a close.

'The matter is decided, Miriam. I am sorry you do not like the decision, but Herr Winter will transfer to Ruhwald Hospice at the earliest opportunity.'

185

Axel shakes Dr Baum's hand before holding the door for the note-taker and disappearing behind it.

'Can I go now?' she asks Hilda.

'Yes, Mim, you can leave. I'm sorry, the transfer to the hospice will probably be tomorrow.'

'Tomorrow?'

Axel meets her in the corridor and places his arm around her shoulders.

'Not what you wanted, eh?'

She doesn't speak and they walk out of the medical centre together. Her hands seem to swell and sting as the cold air hits them. Rain patters lightly on the cars.

She walks on. Axel follows.

'Go away.'

'Not until you are safely at home.' He pushes open the door an older man is waiting to enter, Miriam skips past the old man and out into the car park. The man drops a bag as he walks past which stops Axel from leaving.

'Let me help you with that,' Axel says, bending to pick up the bag.

While Axel is helping the old man, Miriam backs away. She moves behind one car and then another. The gated car park has a pedestrian exit. She sees it. She takes one look at Axel, shaking hands with the man who thanks him for being such a 'gentleman'.

She turns for the gate and runs.

Her breath runs hot in big gasps through her body. She sees the bus, its green outline means a way out. It's about to pull away from the stop, she just makes it and bangs on the door. Miriam tries to calm her impatience as the door wheezes open. Not looking back, just focusing on the bus, she steps on as soon as the gap of the door is big enough for her to slip through.

Her fingers trip and fall to find the change. The driver rattles out a ticket for her and she sits on the lower seats back to the window and sinks low.

19

MIRIAM

Pushing the heavy main door open, the familiar smell of polish, carpet and air freshener greet her. She is home. She checks behind her again; he is not here.

She heads to the carpeted stairs. Feeling the weight of tears promising to fall, needing to escape. Miriam rushes up the steps, desperate to lock herself safely away.

Up the stairs, key in hand, she sees Eva sitting on the floor opposite her door. Miriam exhales a breath that judders.

'Hi, I hope it's okay, I thought you might want company today.' Eva has two shopping bags of food in front of her. 'As Jeff told you, I have nothing to do,' she says with a smile, 'so, I bought some food.' Miriam folds herself to the floor. Her legs too heavy to move another step.

'How did the meeting go?' Eva asks.

'Not good.' Her voice fatigued. 'I'm done. I can't do this anymore.' Miriam stares at the front door, her father waiting inside, but cannot move herself to him.

'Do what?'

'Life. This.' She gestures to the door.

'You don't have a choice. You have your father.' She holds Miriam's hand. 'He needs you.'

'He does,' she says remotely. 'Will you help me find out what happened to Frieda? It's all he's living for now, I'm sure of it.'

'And you?' Eva asks, standing and helping Miriam to her feet too. 'What are you living for?'

She doesn't answer.

'I'm living for him,' she says finally, looking up. 'My father. That's it. I have no one else.'

Eva places a hand gently on her shoulder. 'You are not alone,' she says, swallowing hard, and hugs Miriam.

'I don't know what I would have done without you. These letters, knowing you are reading them too . . . they are just so awful, but I couldn't have worked it all out without your help.'

'I have a few more,' she says, tapping her bag. 'Let's go in.'

After checking on her father, Miriam leaves his door open. She finds Eva in the living room, placing a selection of pastries out and pouring golden breakfast tea from a pot.

'Have you eaten?' Eva asks.

'You didn't need to do this,' she says and Eva looks wary. 'I mean . . .'

'I can go if you would prefer?'

'Oh no, it's just . . .'

'I don't want to intrude, but if I'm honest, it's nice for me. Jeff said he spoke to you the other day, at the library.'

'He said you came over from the East, but you told me that yourself, he said you needed time to settle.'

'In the East, the Holocaust never happened. It was never talked about. The communists believed that East Germans were in no way to blame, even in part, for the Holocaust. Every citizen was completely exonerated from blame, thought or examination. And the victims left without any support. Communism was peace-loving. We had to believe these fictions as fact.'

Miriam listens, it's the most Eva has said. Only the other side of the Wall and the world was such a different place.

'Reading these letters, they feel fresh and yet incredibly long ago. A time forgotten.'

'The letters are awful, just terrible what people do to each other.' She picks absently at her fingernails until Eva starts watching her. She tries to keep her hands still, but focuses on weaving the tie of her blouse over and around her fingers instead.

'She was just twenty-one, in the letters,' Miriam says, swallowing. 'But still she was going to expose the rabbit girls. How do you live with yourself after doing something like that?'

After a long pause Eva asks, 'Can you remember what it was like being twenty-one?'

'No, it was a lifetime ago.'

'Only just a woman and responsible for yourself and the opportunity to leave *there*? We like to think we wouldn't, but all of us would. It's about survival, and that is why so many people don't share their stories, because they don't want to be judged by those who cannot possibly *know*.'

'Do you know? From personal experience?' Miriam asks cautiously.

Eva picks up her cup with a tremor in her hand and spills tea on her trousers.

'I'm sorry, I shouldn't have pried. It's not my business,' Miriam says, rushing to take the cup.

'I wanted to ask you, if I can,' Eva says, drying her trousers with her handkerchief. 'I've been thinking about the dress and you cut away all the seams. Can I sew them back together?'

Miriam looks at the woman, her legs crossed at the ankle. Her back straight, her face serious, worn by the sun but still full; her smile brightens.

'It just feels wrong to leave it empty and cut open like that. After all, it has been preserved so well,' Eva says, a little bashful.

'Yes of course. I'll read and you can sew?' Miriam fetches the dress from her father's room.

Eva says nothing more and takes up the dress.

Miriam watches her as she folds the dress in her lap, then threads a needle that she finds in her bag and bites the end of the thread with her back teeth.

'I married Axel at twenty-one,' Miriam says slowly. 'I was naïve and very young.'

'It is easy to judge with older eyes.'

Miriam would scream at her younger self, '*Don't do it. Don't marry that man!*' But she knows she wouldn't listen. At all.

'They were so young,' Miriam says and finds the next letters from the table where they are scattered like snowflakes. 'It plays on my mind about Dad. I have no idea what he saw, but I'm sure now that Mum wasn't there, she just couldn't have been. It makes me think about what they must have gone through as a couple, with these letters to Dad. Frieda really loved him, I think.'

'The best relationships endure the hardships to test strength. Your mother and father prove this? All the challenges will make the relationship, or break it if it isn't strong enough.'

'I understand,' she says. 'If you don't have hardships until later, it is more difficult to break the ties.'

'Exactly. The honeymoon ends, sometimes it never starts.'

'This is so sad.'

'It's life.'

The silence vibrates around them.

'I need to know what happened to Frieda,' Miriam says, picking up the next letter. 'He deserves to know.'

She reads as Eva sews. The next, written over the top and back of another letter which consists of two scrawled lines in different handwriting, in German, is dated the 31st of May 1944. The paper is yellowed and very creased.

I stood in front of the Kommandant, and my hands, black with dirt, wrapped themselves around the kerchief.

'I wrote to your family. The Haseks from Charlottenburg. They were prompt in their reply.'

She picked up a piece of paper and handed it to me. It was my father's handwriting. It was short:

Dear —

Thank you for your letter regarding the heritage of a prisoner of yours. I am sorry to say that I have no daughter. My wife and I were not blessed with a child.

Yours truly,

Otto Hasek

I went to hand the letter back to her but she dismissed me with her hand. I looked at the brevity, and I saw the fear in his scrawl. He doesn't recognise his daughter; he won't help me, he worries about a reprisal. I wondered if he did this to Aunt Maya too, turned his back when his words could save his family, and my hands shook as I swayed. Then I read the last line. 'My wife and I were not blessed with a child.' He didn't recognise Louisa too? How hard is it to speak of the daughter he lost? My sister. I crumpled the letter in my fist.

'Coward,' I said.

The Kommandant looked up.

It was over. I had wasted her time and worse.

She charged me with twenty-five lashes and the bunker. She said it in one breath, her shoulders softened and although pointing to the door, she dropped her head looking back at her desk. Next order of business.

I held the letter tight in my hand, as if clutching it might save me. A guard stood from where she had been sitting, unseen by me, and walked to me, swinging her baton.

My mind had to process so much so quickly the world slowed. I wanted to run.

I kept reading the words that sealed my fate.

No one has returned from the bunker and stayed the same. Most die soon after their release from the tiny cramped cell. Twenty-five lashes.

The guard smiled. Lipstick perfect, hair curled just so. I wanted to retreat but my feet froze. I was going to the bunker. Would I see daylight again? Or would I die there? Her shoes squeaked as they moved across the wooden floorboards. The leather rolling over wood.

The door opened behind me and I was prepared for a pair of hands to grab me.

The Kommandant looked up and I fell to my knees.

'Please . . .' I said.

'What is this?' She was looking behind me and standing up.

Two children around eight or nine years old, filthy dirty, ran into the room. They moved straight past me to the desk where the Kommandant stood and started talking about missing their grandmother.

'Where is she? We need food, we are starving much and there is no food for us. Grandmother . . .'

'What are they saying?' the Kommandant asked the guard whose journey towards me had stopped.

I looked behind me, the door was open, the attention was on the orphans, maybe I could leave? I backed away.

The children noticed the quizzical look on the Kommandant's face and moved further towards her. There was a glass of water on the table, half full. Beads of condensation rolled down it on to the desk. I hadn't noticed it, but when I did, I couldn't stop looking. One of the children darted for it. Splashing most in her haste, she gulped, then offered it to her sibling, who drank greedily, giving the glass back for the smallest drops at the bottom. The Kommandant had small dark circles on her uniform where she had been splashed by the water and the papers on the desk also succumbed to a light sprinkle.

'What is this? How did you get in here?'

The children just looked at her.

'Out. Now. Throw them in the bunker too.'

The children must have understood 'bunker' as they grabbed on to her.

'I don't understand them. Get these children off me.' The guard plucked the children off the Kommandant.

'Wait,' the Kommandant said, wiping down her skirt. 'You,' she said, pointing to me.

There was silence as everyone turned and noticed that I was still present. I thought perhaps I should have left when I had the chance.

'You can choose who goes to the bunker and you can choose who gets the lashes. Considering you are such a supporter of the regime, you can decide how the punishments are divided.'

A panic so strong it swished around my stomach. 'Kommandant,' I said, thinking, trying to find my voice. Their small faces, grubby and pink, eyes wide, watching the guard with the baton and me. 'They are just asking after their grandmother. They lost her and are hungry,' I said.

The guard picked up her baton and looked to me. The children cowered on the floor.

193

'You understand them?'

'Yes, they are speaking Dutch. They are looking for their grandmother.' And to the children I said, 'Hush, little ones.'

'You speak other languages too?'

'Yes, ma'am. Many.'

'Why, a little linguist!' She laughed with the guard and made a tiny motion with her head. The guard swung her baton at the back of the bigger child. He fell to the ground with a howl. The younger jumped on top to protect the fallen one. The Kommandant looked on as the guard tried to drag the younger away from the boy lying prone.

'Stop,' the Kommandant said. 'Tell the children to go back to their block.'

I did and said that they would find their grandmother there. I lied because it appeased them and they were both looking at me. The boy sitting, the girl squatting beside him. I lied because it made them listen. I lied because doing so may not take me to the bunker. I lied to delay my punishment.

'Shall I take them back to their block?' I asked.

'Yes. Yes.'

'Come here,' I said to the children, taking their small hands inside my own. We turned to leave.

'Wait . . .'

I turned back, thinking the guard was coming for me.

'There are women arriving from all over Europe. It would help to have someone tell them how we work here.'

'Of course, anything to help,' I said quickly.

'Report back here tomorrow. We shall find some use for you. Six a.m.'

'Thank you, ma'am.'

And what possessed me to do it I do not know. But I lost the grip on the little hand in mine, brought my hand out and up, palm down, I stamped my foot and shouted:

'Heil Hitler.'

The children looked at me like I was a monster and I lost the other hand in mine. The guard smiled, a knowing, pitying smile. I turned and left. The children followed me, but as soon as the sun, white and hot, bore down on us, they ran.

I watched as their small frames wearing only rags ran off. My heart sank.

After the children were out of sight, I walked back towards our block. The sun was hot on my head and neck, but had never felt so good. A few minutes earlier I was looking at the bunker and what was sure to be my death.

'This is . . .' Miriam stands to place the letter back down on the table, having no words to convey her feelings at the letter she has just read.

'It says somewhere in there *the truth is ugly*?' Eva asks.

'But this? The children?' Miriam asks. 'My father couldn't have known about these letters. He wouldn't still be thinking of someone who could even consider condemning such vulnerable women, mutilated, bed-bound women. No. And children?' Miriam shakes her head. 'This cannot be the person *my* dad is talking about, he cannot love . . . this.' She emphasises her point by shaking the letter.

'You are probably right,' Eva says. 'But, as you well know, love is sometimes not what we once expected it to be.'

20

MIRIAM

'These letters are so important, but,' Miriam says, 'they are so hard to read and I had no idea. Did this actually happen? People treated each other this way?'

'That's why so many of the stories are lost. People who experienced it cannot find the words, and those around them do not want to hear. Words hold a lot more power than we realise,' Eva says. Then, speaking more to herself, she continues, 'Even the darkest words will find the light.'

Miriam picks up the next letter. 'I suppose what is lost can always be found.'

> *Henryk,*
> *After the Kommandant, Stella launched herself into me*
> *and held my hand.*
>
> *'Hello, pretty lady, you take me home now?' She*
> *swung her arm in mine.*
>
> *The little Dutch children found me by Block 20. The*
> *older one spat on the ground.*
>
> *'You lied,' he said.*

'I am sorry – have you tried looking for her in the revier?' I shrank at the thought of the camp hospital: revier, a place of agony and death, not always from illness.

'Yes, but she is not sick. You told us you find her, you told us you help. You lie.' He spat again. 'Everyone is always lying.'

Stella watched the children, her hand safely tucked in mine. I wanted them to go away. I feared how much Stella understood of this interaction.

'Maybe we can look for her together. I will help you.'

'No. We not need your help. You are one of them.' The younger child pointed to the guard. 'You are one of them!' She said it louder and I wanted to make her shut up. The insult vibrated in my chest.

The children held hands and turned from me.

Stella looked up, seeking an explanation, which I did not give.

I called out to their receding backs.

'Tell me your grandmother's name, I will help you if I can.'

The boy called back, 'Grandmamma.'

Miriam takes a long shaky breath, before composing herself enough to pick up the next letter.

Henryk,
I returned to the block where Bunny was quietly sewing and Stella jumped up on the bed next to her, playing happily with a new doll made from a dirty cotton rag tied in little knots to make a head, hands and feet.

I sat in Eugenia's bunk and told her I had a job.

Eugenia sat straighter and gave me her full attention as I explained.

Henryk, I am worried, this place . . . it would be better than shifting sand, but it feels like a change and I am worried what they will ask me to do. But as Eugenia said, it's not like I was given a choice.

At roll call Hani joined me under a clear sky at the Appellplatz, where we stood for hours before soup. The guards counting us, recounting us, making us stand. If anyone fell they would start again.

'It always takes longer in winter,' Eugenia whispered in my ear.

'Longer than this?' I asked, and she nodded.

I was about to relay this to Hani, but she had a deep frown on her face and avoided my eye.

I held her hand, but she pulled away.

'What's wrong?'

'You lie,' she whispered. Then, 'You lie,' shouted loud enough for the guards to look at us. Eugenia told us both to be quiet and the silence returned.

Hani shifted from foot to foot, her hands clenched then unclenched as she crossed and uncrossed them. Whatever the matter with Hani was, it would boil over, and soon, I thought.

Finally, the roll call over, we walked back into the block. 'What is the matter?' I said.

'You. You are the matter,' she said, and grabbed my arm. 'You NAZI!'

'Hani, shut up. What are you talking about?' I whispered as I collected soup from the vat into my bowl and pulled out the spoon attached to my dress.

'*Paulo and Brigitte, you know them?*' she asked, still loud, collecting a ladle of soup, but pulling away too fast so that it spilled down the side.

'*No.*'

'*The children, little baby children, you chose Paulo to be attacked.*'

I tried to explain to her. To tell her that I hadn't made the decision. That I had been asked, but the guard had chosen to attack Paulo. Hani was upset.

'*He has marks over his back. You say you help them find their grandmother. They go for help and they find you. You tell Kommandant you help her. You choose Paulo to take your punishment. You SALUTE!*'

'*Hani. Shut. Up.*' I said. Her voice carried and it felt like everyone was watching us.

'*You liar, you lie to me, again.*'

'*No, I didn't mean to. Please keep your voice down and I will explain.*'

'*Give you time to lie again?*' she replied. '*Who are you? You look like a picture postcard. You could be Nazi.*'

I touched the top of her arm. '*Please, listen.*'

'*Don't touch me.*'

'*Fine, but listen and I'll explain.*'

She quietened, but I didn't know what to say. We were surrounded by people, although talking in Dutch, still you never knew who was listening.

'*The children,*' I said. '*How do you know they are telling the truth?*'

She slapped me clean across the face. It didn't hurt my skin, it was a slap to the stomach, ice cold, followed by a stare. It's the worst attack I've ever experienced. It stung my heart more than my face.

'I love you, I trust you,' she sobbed. 'You leaving, is that it? Leaving me here?'

'No, but I did try to leave,' I said. I was trying to eat soup. An hour before I'd felt famished, but now I could not stomach even a spoonful. I slid it over to Stella, who took it happily.

'Can I share with Bunny?' she asked, and she took the bowl away back to the bunk. After we both watched her leave, in hushed whispers I told Hani everything.

She was silent.

'Please talk to me,' I begged.

Hani finished her soup and walked away without a word.

She hasn't said another word to me. I have been frozen out. She is asleep with her head where our feet normally go. I have lost something I didn't know I had, nor earned. I don't think I've ever felt this alone. I don't know if she'll forgive me or if I deserve it. I suppose tomorrow will tell.

'The letters.' Miriam takes a deep breath. 'It's just so incredibly sad.'

Eva walks to the table, placing the folded dress on it.

Miriam smooths her fingers across the coarse fabric. 'It's awful to imagine such conditions,' she says. 'And the letters keep reminding me of things.'

Miriam tries to find some words to describe what she means. Eva waits.

'Like the standing in Appellplatz,' Miriam begins. 'My husband used to set a timer, you know, like a cooking timer, he'd read about it somewhere, to help us work out some issues we were having. He'd have his say then I could have mine, I think that was how it was supposed to work.'

'He timed you?'

'Yes. I cannot remember what issues they were now. But I had to stand, while we talked, so that I could give him my full attention. If I teetered or swayed he'd reset the timer.' She can hear the mechanical crunch as the egg timer, in the shape of a chicken, was wound back up to thirty – always thirty – minutes.

Eva's face changes and she sits opposite Miriam, folding her hands on to her lap.

'It got worse and worse,' Miriam says. 'There was no way I could do it. It sounded so simple. Just stand and we can talk. He did it, stood and talked to me. But I had to look up at him and well, I just kept coming over all wobbly.' Miriam glances at Eva. 'It's not anything like this,' Miriam says, lifting the letter in her hand. 'I'm . . .' She runs her fingers along the stripes of the dress.

'Miriam,' Eva says.

She doesn't look up. 'I'm sorry, I don't mean even for a second to compare this to . . . what the rabbit girls went through, or the letters, my father even. It just reminds me of things, that's all.'

'It sounds like you have had a terrible time,' Eva says, leaning forward.

'He wouldn't let me sleep until I had achieved it. Thirty minutes,' Miriam says, her voice trembles. 'That was all. But he wouldn't let me sleep. I was begging him, just to allow me some rest and I could do it,' she whispers. 'I was sure I could do it.'

Miriam felt the ache in her neck from looking up at Axel, she felt the skip in her heart as the black spots came over her vision, she screamed at herself, just a few more minutes.

The egg timer was down to five, she could see it.

Five more minutes and it would be over. It ticked, like a clock, but faster, like the heart of the chicken.

Tic-tick-tic-tick-tic.

Five more minutes and she could rest, she could sleep.

'So, what do you think?' Axel asked.

'Yes,' she said. 'I think yes.' She had no idea what she was agreeing to, the complexities of his argument were beyond her scope. There was no room for anything else. Just stay upright. Just keep standing.

'Woah,' Axel said, holding her by the shoulders as she fell into him, eyes closed, trying to come back. The black circles surrounded her.

He sat her gently on the sofa, their sofa. Their new-beginning sofa. And brought her a cup of water from the kitchen.

'How are you feeling?' Concern etched into his face.

'I'm very tired, Axel, can we do this some other time?'

'Do what?' he asked.

'The discussion. I agree to what you said, but can we resume it, if you have anything further to ask me, perhaps tomorrow?'

'What discussion, my love?' He looked so confused she placed a hand on his cheek.

'The – the egg timer, the focus on . . . I am just really tired,' she said.

'Miriam, where have you been?' His voice was quiet.

'Right here,' she stuttered. 'I felt a bit faint talking to you.'

'We talked and I went to bed hours ago. You said you were coming up, but I came back to find you here, talking to yourself, mumbling about something you had lost. Have you lost something?'

Miriam shook her head until the black spots came back into her vision. 'No. We were talking, you made me stand . . .'

'I made you stand?'

She nodded.

'My dear, why would I do that?'

She had no answer. But she could feel his words worm their way into her and muddle what she thought she knew.

'With the timer, I felt faint.'

'I was asleep, you woke me, again, with your muttering. I think,' he continued, 'this might be another of those moments we were talking about at the doctor's the other day.' He stood up and walked away.

'No,' she cried and stumbled after him, falling to the floor. 'No, Axel, please.'

The mechanical whirr and then the click of the camera propelled her into the foetal position. 'No,' she cried.

The camera wheezed out a picture and Axel flapped it in the air. 'As the doctors say, we need to collect evidence if we can have a hope to help you.'

Miriam didn't move. The carpet spun around her. 'I'm sorry,' she said. 'I'm so sorry, Axel.'

'It's all right, my love. In sickness and in health. It's bedtime, my wife,' he said in a lullaby voice. 'Shall I carry you up?'

When she said nothing, he walked out of the room. She heard his footsteps pound on the staircase.

'Don't be long,' he called.

She opened her eyes and looked up to the mantel. The camera was there and next to it, right beside it.

The timer.

'And?' Eva prompts after she falls silent.

'I was medicated,' she says. 'No one believed me. I didn't believe myself. I am sorry, it has nothing to do with the letters, the camps. I am being ridiculous.'

Eva opens her mouth to say something but Miriam interjects.

'I need to check on my father,' she says, shrugging away the heaviness in her neck and shoulders. 'I've been sitting too long,' she says to herself.

'Are you all right, Miriam?'

'I am tired, so tired.'

'Would you like me to go?'

'If you would like to,' she says, and supports herself on the wall feeling light-headed. 'I need to check on Dad.'

'You've had a very long day,' Eva says, following Miriam into the hall.

She walks towards her father's room and Eva moves towards the door.

'Thank you for making it better,' Miriam mumbles and watches Eva's shadow retreat into the hall.

Later, Miriam washes the dishes, her hands performing a mundane task as her mind wanders, skips and jumps to the details in the letters.

She picks up a bottle of red wine, thinks again and replaces it, instead opting for the open packet of codeine. She imagines swallowing the bitter-tasting pills.

Lingering at the window she looks down at the street, a shadow crosses the path. *Axel.* Closing the curtains so that the rings clatter on the pole, she checks the door is locked. Checks her feather is there. Miriam lifts one of the chairs from the living room, it is heavy and she waddles it so that it rests behind the door. 'He's back,' she says, turning the lock, again.

Miriam spends the night in the chair by her father, the decisions made earlier in the day circling her. She can hear a tic-tic-tick in the hum of the air mattress that she hadn't heard before. *Tomorrow.*

She holds her father's hand and leans back into the chair. Her eyes close and she longs for the blanket of sleep to envelop her.

'The ceremony,' he whispers, and her eyes open to his voice. 'The ceremony of innocence is drowned,' he says.

'Yes, Dad. Yes, it is.'

'Miriam. Miriam. You. Are . . .'

'I'm here. I love you, Dad,' she says and waits, watching his every movement, but he snores and rests, and soon enough she does too.

21

HENRYK

In my first clear memory after Auschwitz, the sunlight reflected on the grass hurt my eyes. It was green. So green that it shone like gold. So sharp my eyes wept. I was bringing a damp handkerchief to my cheeks and praying that someone would move me indoors.

Then a pink hand touched my knee, a tiny, but heavy, little pink hand. It was followed by another and then a little pink person appeared, a face at knee height. Her dark hair and dark eyes set within a moon face gave her a doll-like appearance. She smiled at me, a toothless grin. My face cracked and something came back.

I smiled.

I realised I was sitting in a chair on the grass, gravel surrounding it. The sun was not hot, but a comfortable warmth that reached the bones without stinging the skin. It must have been late autumn. There were voices around me but they were like the birds chirping: slightly irritating, easily ignored.

I leant forward and looked past my knees and down. My shoes were on the wrong feet. I wasn't wearing socks. Sitting on the grass, one leg underneath her and two hands at my shoelaces, fingers absorbed in the knot, was a little girl.

My little girl.

This was Miriam.

MIRIAM

She watches the flame burn ever closer to her fingers, the bright flame kisses her raw skin. She waits. They would be here any second. The heat licks at her fingers, intoxicating on her open skin, her fingers shake as she strikes another match, then they calm, become steady.

The smell is delicious.

Fire and its ever-powerful ability to destroy and blacken everything. Turn everything to dust. It would be a beautiful way to go. Watching the apartment go up in flames, caressing the old chair, journeying up the walls. Sucking the oxygen from the room. Once ignited, fire will steal everything in its path. She considers how it would be to fall into unconsciousness while watching the work of the flames as they dance in her parents' home.

The strike of a match stops the tremors of her hands. A task that prevents her from harming herself.

She watches the flame eat through the stick, moving closer and closer to her fingers. A knock makes her jump, she drops the match to the floor and instinctively stomps it out.

They are here.

For him.

They arrive with a stretcher. It's a reversal of how he came home from the hospital, a fortnight previously when she had agreed to bring him home. The hospital was no place for him. People should be able to die in their beds, surrounded by their things. The medical professionals had said. And now they are taking him away.

Instead of relief when the paramedics leave she feels only loss.

They take him away, safely pack him into the ambulance. She kisses his clammy head, holds his hand desperately, not wanting to let him go.

Miriam fully checks the apartment. It is empty, the kind of empty that fills your ears like water.

Submersion empty.

The white walls, the large furniture, the space. With nothing to do. Alone and pointless. She waits, for what she is unsure, she looks out into the never-changing sea of wet and dark.

By late afternoon, having heard nothing about her father's transfer, Miriam continues reading the letters, translated large and bold by Eva. There is nothing else for her to do. She picks up the next one. And as she unfolds it, she knows that nothing will end well.

> *My first day in the new job, translating letters in 'Canada', a large storage unit with all prisoner belongings. Some belongings stay, others go back to those 'in need' but most are labelled and put away. My job is to read letters in other languages and translate in a few lines the information I can.*
>
> *After I had finished and the sun pinched at my eyes, I was greeted by Stella.*

'Stella? What's wrong?' I asked, looking at her creased face.

'Your Hani, gone.' She was breathing fast, 'Pretty lady, please you help her?'

I bent and kissed Stella on the top of her head. Inhaled the innocence lost, and gathered myself.

'Let's go,' I said with an assurance I did not feel.

But a week has passed and still no Hani.

I am sleeping alone.

The Kommandant sets me to work interpreting letters; I'm looking for addresses and locations of those being sought by the SS.

Canada is full of clothes, jewellery, money. There are medical supplies here as well. Pills with no labels, everything has its place. Yet possessions do not matter in Ravensbrück.

My other job, aside from reading the letters they find, is to write to families telling of the death of their loved ones. The forms are pre-printed, I write the names and addresses on them. I get to sit and read and write. I thank Aunt Maya every single day for teaching me because French, Dutch and Polish have saved my life.

I get to wash twice a day and I have access to so much paper. My letters to you can be longer now. When I write, I do so not to you, because I cannot know you will receive them, I write to the memory of you and that keeps you alive, and the language that I fell in love with; with you.

I ask everyone I know and all the people I meet about Hani. I think of the children and their 'grandmamma' and I cannot get the look of disgust from my mind. Finding Hani seems to have taken a deeper meaning, I trade my food for information. I look for Hani like I am possessed. I am sick to the stomach, I do not eat and struggle to rest; I am exhausted. The work I have is much better now as I fear I would have fallen asleep in the sun and the sand. I would have died there. Here I am safe. I sit next to an old school teacher. She is quiet but will nudge me gently if I fall asleep when the guard comes back around. I do not know her name. I do not want to ask it. We work in silence.

I sleep alone, and although there is more space, I cannot rest. Her presence in this place has been all I have known. I am without a shadow, alone in the sun.

Miriam cries next to the empty bed. How much effort Frieda went to to write letters to her father, and now she is all alone. She feels such sympathy for the woman, her father's lover, that she cannot stop the tears from falling. For Miriam knows what it feels like to be all alone.

The next letter is the one about Eugenia, which in its rightful place comes next, and she realises with a sinking heart that the following letter will complete Eugenia's story and she doesn't want to hear it at all. The silence grows around her like a storm. She thinks about the flames, the matches, and this steadies her, remembering the mother and baby with the little socks, waiting for something. She reads.

Eugenia sucked in a deep breath, nodded her head to herself then on her exhale she talked, fast, her words joining together, stumbling over each other.

Eugenia jumped out of her skin and bashed her head on the top of the box. She felt the soldiers before she heard them, moving like shadows, then the putrid smell of smoke.

The baby cried out at the din, but the mother quietened it as Eugenia's skin crawled with fear. She could taste burning and could touch the smoky tendrils as they snaked around her. Imagining wisps penetrating the box like long skeletal fingers. She feared being burnt alive.

'Search. Search,' they shouted.

The main door opened and the crash of objects followed. In the room, she heard heavy boots and it felt like the soldiers were standing on her lungs.

A jack in the box before it pops up, every sinew of her body pulled so taut. She couldn't trust herself not to spring out.

The footsteps moved away.

Then the lid of the box opened.

The woman and baby. Opened to the day. Eugenia shrank away from the light and curled as small as she could into the dark recesses of the box. And at this angle she could see higher, she saw them.

Their deep voices shouting a mockery of empty words.

They pulled the mama up by the hair. Her breast was still out, the baby sucking hard to stay attached. The force brought the baby to his feet. He stood. Alone. Shock still.

But the mama, she screamed and screamed and kicked and flew at the men, stretching out to her baby.

They held the mama easily, despite the effort she put in to get to the baby. One of them carefully picked him up. Held him in his own thick hands. The mama screamed again. The baby cried too, hands reaching for each other – hers long and thin, his small and fat.

They shot her. In the neck. She folded on top of herself like a blanket.

The baby outdid his mother in the screaming, a caterwaul of noise escaped his bright red lips. Eugenia sobbed. But the baby scratched, he bit and kicked at them. Hands outstretched to the mama on the ground. They had a harder time holding the baby than they did the mama. He flapped around in the man's arms, trying to get to the floor. To his mama.

Another man must have pulled out his gun, but Eugenia heard, 'Don't shoot, you'll waste the bullet or miss and hit me!'

They laughed. Laughed like it was a game.

The baby screamed, constant.

'Then-his-skull-went-crack, against the side of the box,' Eugenia said it so fast, it took a while for me to register what she'd said.

The silence was held within our bunk. We heard Stella's gentle snores and Bunny pulled her closer.

When the soldiers left, Eugenia got out of the box. As fast as she could.

The mama was on the floor, face down, shot in the back of the neck; Eugenia turned her. Her eyes were open, body straight, arms outstretched to her baby who was also on the floor, crumpled, one shoe off his little foot.

His round face was broken, wonky, his baby eyes closed.

Eugenia pulled on the mother's arms and dragged her, leaving a long smear of shiny blood on the floor. It took some effort to pull and push and the mama fell heavily into the box. She was tiny, so skinny and young. Her eyes . . . vacant. Eugenia got back out and picked up the baby. His head fell back. Floppy and wrong. His little mouth was open and she saw two tiny little teeth. He smelled of milk and blood.

Eugenia placed the baby into the mother's arms. Snuggled them in as tight as she could, even tried to wrap the mama's arms around him. Eugenia placed one of her hands on the baby. And used her jacket as a blanket over them both. Eugenia tried to close the mama's eyes, but she was unsure if she should. Maybe she needed to watch over her baby in heaven.

Eugenia tucked them in and closed the lid.

Eugenia looked up at me, as I scribbled away.

'I do not know their names,' she said. 'They don't exist. No one who loved them will know how they died.'

And Eugenia took another deep breath, picked up the patch of cloth that was resting in her lap and sewed a running stitch along its seam, as methodical and precise as ever.

Henryk, her story seems to whisper in the crevices of my mind. After all, fear is contagious. I tell myself that although we die in body, the memories of us will live on. In the hearts of those who know and love us, for as long as they live, we survive. Eugenia lost everyone that day, so I entrust her memory to you, so that she does not have to die twice.

Yours, always.

Miriam feels sick, the snakes that fed through her skin slime and shiver inside her again, from what she reads, not from a dream now.

The baby.

A thought. A flicker, a flash and then gone. *The baby.*

Tears swim in her vision. She gets to the bathroom and washes and washes and washes her hands.

Eugenia believed she no longer existed. What about her? What was she doing to prove her worth in life, to live when all these incredible women died?

Darling Miriam, my wife, my love.

She can hear his voice, feel the texture of his hands along her cheek, then moving to the back of her head, caressing her neck.

I will never, ever hurt you.

She can feel the kiss as his lips pressed themselves into her neck.

My most precious wife, I will always be with you.

She hears words spoken in love, but words which have left more than a scar.

She looks into the mirror until her features blur into his words and she can feel his breath on her neck, and hear his voice.

'What are you going to do, Miriam?' she says to her reflection.

22

HENRYK

The world came back into focus quickly after I met Miriam for the first time. I became a father and a man. I sorted out the wire that hung corner to corner in our little room, so that when Emilie was hanging up the towelling for Miriam's nappies she didn't have to balance on a footstool with half its leg missing. I held and hugged and fed and looked at the small person I had, unknowingly, created. And I looked at Emilie, with Miriam's arms wrapped around her neck like a monkey, radiating in motherhood, and felt proud that I had given her something.

Something good.

Miriam's appearance in our lives changed everything. We were parents, and I followed Emilie's guidance and found my feet. I was watching Emilie settle Miriam on our mattress; the abandoned cot in the upper hallway of the block felt too empty to fill.

Emilie was singing whilst rubbing circles on Miriam's back, and the nagging feeling that I had had for a few weeks came clattering over me and took the air out of my lungs.

'Emilie,' I said in hushed tones as she shuffled around, busy with her hands. She rarely stood still and never made eye contact. I wondered what she had been through, pregnant and alone. I wondered if she could ever forgive me. 'Emilie, I need to try and find Frieda,' I said.

'Why?' she asked. 'What good can possibly come from that?'

'I have to try. I have to try and find out what happened to her.'

Emilie was pottering around not looking at me. 'Emilie, please. Let's talk about this,' I said.

'Why? Henryk, why are you doing this again? We have a baby, a future!' She shook her head, took a deep breath and came and sat in the chair opposite. 'You really want to know?' she asked.

'Yes.'

Emilie took my hand in hers. 'Henryk, Frieda died, in the hospital after the place . . . the place you were held. After it was liberated,' she said. 'I'm so sorry, I didn't want to tell you this way.' She tried to hug me, but my body was completely stiff, unyielding to her touch.

'No,' I said. In our one-room apartment, in the aftermath of the war. Everything seemed black and yet brilliant white.

'I'm sorry,' she said.

'No,' I stood. Pacing the room, ready to run. I wasn't sure where I was going. 'No,' I said again. 'How can you know?'

'I know,' she said sadly.

'You *can't*.' I ran my hand through my hair and then over my eyes. 'How? How did she die?'

'Henryk, please calm down.'

I was walking from wall to wall, a caged animal.

'I found you, at the hospital, you remember? She was there too.' Emilie looked at her feet. 'She died in the hospital.'

'No!' I shouted. Then I collapsed in the chair. 'Emilie why are you saying this to me?'

'I didn't tell you straightaway because, Henryk, you couldn't even feed or dress yourself.' She took a breath. 'She was dying. Henryk, she wanted to come to you, but she couldn't. Here . . .' She stood quietly and walked over to the old chest.

It had been the only furniture left in the apartment when we acquired it, mainly because it was too heavy to steal. She dug to the bottom and removed a sheet.

I stood as she placed it on the table, and carefully unfolded it. I remember looking and thinking that Emilie must have known what I had done, otherwise why confront me with *this*.

A uniform, I presumed my own, was folded on the table.

'It was hers.'

'You wanted me to know that she was there, that I had done this to her. I killed her, Emilie.' It wasn't loud, the confession. It was silent, a whisper. Emilie tried to pull me into her soft body, but I couldn't yield. I was transfixed by the empty dress. An uninhabited uniform, the evidence of what I had done.

Emilie was still talking. 'I cared for you, I wanted you to get better, for me and for Miriam. I didn't want to set you back. I know I should have told you sooner, but I didn't know how to. So please, you need to let it go. It's over.'

In such a jumble her voice seemed to journey around me. *Look for her*, I heard. Look for her. Yes, I thought. I shall. But how? The dress was empty.

'Where is Frieda?' I asked.

'She died.' A worried look entered Emilie's eyes and she dragged me to sit with her and get me to focus on her face, but the dress, laid out, the stripes, the stitched pocket. I kept looking at it.

'She didn't die,' I said.

'How many people did you see who lived in *that place*?'

I turned to her, her dark eyes were on me and I held both her wrists in my hands tight. 'She wasn't there. She didn't die.' Emilie pulled away, but I didn't let go of her wrists.

'Look.' She pointed to the dress.

'Please, tell me this isn't true. Please, Emilie. Tell me you don't know where she is, tell me anything. I'll do anything, anything, but please. Tell me it's not true. Please.'

She held my gaze steady. 'I am so sorry, Henryk.' She matched my intensity with her own, and I was empty.

Hung-empty. A void. Blank. An utter bleakness clouded my vision, turning everything two-dimensional, space sucked out colour like a vacuum. Everything and everyone now a series of featureless shells. All flat, like the empty dress.

Nothing moved as I held on to Emilie, holding her eyes with my own, but just before I was about to crumble away into dust, her eyes flashed towards Miriam.

She stood quickly and went to Miriam, fast asleep, her bottom in the air, thumb in mouth. I watched Emilie fuss over the sleeping infant.

Emilie was lying about something, but why?

Was she sparing me a worse pain, knowing *how* Frieda died? Was there something she hadn't told me?

Or was she ending something I never could?

Dazed and confused, I left the apartment and walked around the graves at Heerstraße Cemetery. I looked at the grieving, shell-shocked faces that mirrored my own. *It wasn't true.* And as I walked, without sleep, I knew that she was alive.

Because lights that bright do not just go out.

MIRIAM

The sky is dark when she returns to the letters, tears soaking her face and a vortex opening deep within her.

Things cannot be unheard or unseen, the images seep into her, and although she tries to detach, she wasn't there, she cannot manage the images of the baby as they appear from the letter.

As the clock inches forward, and she hasn't heard from Hilda, Miriam notices that time itself has changed: 4 p.m. used to be time to tend to her father, now 4 p.m. is nothing; 6 p.m. turning him, but now, nothing. Not having heard from anyone, and with nothing to do, her day is empty.

She finds the cord to the phone disconnected.

Shunting it back into its socket as fast as she can, knowing she may have missed the call after waiting for it all day. She calls Hilda. There is no answer.

She calls the hospice.

'Hi, can I please speak with the nurse for Herr Winter, Henryk Winter. He arrived by ambulance today.'

'No Herr Winter, I'm afraid,' a deeply nasal woman says.

'He . . .' Miriam is cut off. She dials again.

'I'm Henryk Winter's daughter, he was due to arrive with you today.'

'As I said, we've had no new arrivals today.'

'Wait,' Miriam says. 'Can you check again, please?'

A huge sigh comes across the phone line. 'As I said, no new arrivals today.' There is a pause down the line and a shuffle. 'We had a Herr Winter pencilled into room four, but he didn't arrive.'

'What do you mean, didn't arrive? Where is he?'

'I don't know. Look, the manager has gone home for the day. Call back tomorrow, I'm sure she'll have more details for you.'

Miriam calls Hilda, again. No answer, again. She leaves a message trying to sound calm, but her voice comes out pinched and when she hangs up she feels like crying. She tries the medical centre, but they are closed. She doesn't leave a message. She scratches her thumb and pulls the tiny bit of skin she uncovers with her teeth. She looks at the phone, and picks it up.

Shredding her thumb with her teeth, she dials another number. A number that once was her own.

'Where's Dad?'

'Hello? Mim? Is that you?'

'Where is my dad? What have you done?'

He yawns down the receiver and she can hear him stretching. 'Was he transferred today?'

'Yes,' she says, suddenly unsure why she made the call.

'Then he's at the hospice surely?'

'You know he didn't get there. Where is my dad? What did you do?'

'Miriam . . . Darling, have you taken your medication today?' She places her weary hand on her forehead and takes it off quickly as the skin on her thumb burns to the touch.

'Please, Axel, just tell me where he is, he needs me, and I'll take the medications, I'll do anything.' The silence on the other end of the line goes on and on. 'Please, Axel,' she begs.

'The professionals and I all agreed you are not of sound mind. And this, Miriam, this is you returning home, being my wife, taking the medications and getting well.'

'What did you do to him?' Miriam's mind runs around a thousand scenarios. 'Please.'

'Do you agree?'

'To come back to you?'

'Yes, to come *home*.'

She bites down on her thumb, hard.

'Axel. I'm not coming home,' she says it. For the first time, out loud. There is only static at the other end. She can hear the change in him as the pause grows.

'You may not have a choice soon anyway.' His tone is playful. She imagines his smile. Frostbite. Her fingers hold on to the handset so hard the phone sounds like it's cracking against her ear. Axel laughs.

'I have to go, Mim. I'd call the doctors if I were you. You are accusing me of what? Stealing your father from an ambulance? I'm tired of all this erratic behaviour. You are paranoid.' And she gets dial tone in her ear.

Hands still shaking she calls Hilda, but with no answer, she hangs up. She paces up and down, walking past her father's empty room each time. Nothing.

She puts on her coat and shoes, but having no idea where she would go, she returns to the phone. She redials the hospice.

'Do you know where else the ambulance may have taken my father?' she asks, desperation bringing her voice out high.

'The ambulance is attached to the hospital. Try there and ask for the paramedics. Ambulances do deliver patients into hospital, maybe your father is there?'

After about ten rings to the hospital emergency department, someone answers. After talking to three different people asking the same questions and being placed on hold again and again. After peeling back the skin on her fingernail with her teeth, and digging her nails deep down into the broken flesh of her wrist until her stomach feels like it's spinning, she finally gets an answer.

'Yes, Herr Winter was redirected to the emergency department after he deteriorated en route. He has since been transferred to ward 71, where he has stabilised.'

'Can I see him?'

'Visiting hours finish at eight thirty.'

'Thank you.'

Miriam picks up her bag and leaves.

At the hospital, day or night, lights, hubbub and noise. She buzzes on ward 71 and is shown to her father's side. He is as white as the sheet he lies on, an oxygen mask over his face, his mouth ajar, asleep. She sits, holds his hand and stays by his side, folding and refolding the pleats in her navy skirt.

Being back in the hospital again. She remembers the night she left Axel and feels a little better that she didn't concede on the phone and say she'd return.

Over a month ago, she got off the bus and entered the hospital. She found herself sitting on a plastic-covered chair that crackled as she moved, with such a high back she was unable to look up without getting a stiff neck, dressed in only her nightie and coat. Awake and listening to what she thought were her father's last breaths. The beeps on the monitors soothed her. Each wave of nurses offered hot drinks, food and blankets as they cared for her as much as for the man in the bed.

And now she is back: same green, plastic chair, same watchful eye on the monitors, but this time she knows that Axel is at her back. Before, she thought her father would die and then she would too. But now, she thinks maybe her father might be okay, but in that way, there is no escape for her. She will have to deal with Axel too. And she has no idea how to do that. It was stupid to call him. Her father's heartbeat traces lines across the screen and she wonders what Axel has lined up next.

'I need to be less crazy,' she says out loud, and laughs at the irony.

She is shooed out of the ward at nine thirty, having overstayed her welcome with the nurse in charge. All her questions were answered with 'tomorrow'.

'Will he be okay?'

'We'll find out tomorrow.'

'Will he go to the hospice?'

'We can ask the consultant tomorrow.'

'What time can I come back?'

'We'll call you tomorrow.'

But in the back of her mind, she isn't sure he'll make it to tomorrow and the relief and fear that come from that thought bring tears to her eyes and a pounding in her heart. She leaves the ward feeling like she's just run a marathon.

In the hospital corridor, she sits on a bench placed within an alcove, a grey filing cabinet on both sides, she feels oddly safe, unwatched. And thinks about staying here until that elusive tomorrow has arrived.

But she hears footsteps and she smells him before she sees him.

'So, you found him then?' Miriam stands and tries to step around Axel, who seems to grow into the vacant spaces, no way around him.

Not looking up, focusing her eyes only on the floor. He places an arm out to stop her moving, but all she has done is shift her weight from foot to foot.

'What antics, Miriam. I mean what *will* Dr Baum say?' She makes to move in the other direction, but he catches her wrist and pulls her into him.

'What am I going to do with you?' He smooths her hair. 'Because you really are not well, are you? Such a shame. Hilda called me, love, to say your father was here. Not one person believes in you.' Her mind rushes as his words penetrate.

'Hilda called you?' she tries to say, but is abruptly stopped as he kisses her. She tries to fight, at least she thinks she tries to fight. But suddenly her limbs feel like jelly. *What is the point*, she thinks.

Axel guides her behind the bench and she realises what is happening. She is stuck, no one can see her.

There *is* a point, she thinks, and Eva believes her. Eva knows. Miriam pushes against his chest; her whole being pushing against him. Nothing. Like pushing a wall. He is still holding her wrist so tight that she cannot move under his hands.

He turns her around so that she is facing the wall, a picture hangs there, it's of the sea at sunset and two people paddling along the shore. He presses himself into her and her cheek touches the cold wall, the picture hangs in a pine frame and the back of it is bowed so that it touches the wall too.

He breathes heavily into her ear, she feels his breath and shivers, a full-body revulsion, trying to tug her arm free, he places it in the small of her back.

'Now then, this is a familiar sight,' he says, kissing her cheek and moving her slightly to the right, away from the picture and closer to the corner. He touches her neck with his hand and runs a fingernail along the crevice of her throat. 'Very familiar.' He swiftly kisses her on the cheek. 'I have missed you, Mim.'

She looks away, trying to turn her head, but he forces his body into her and she feels crushed between him and the wall; suffocated.

Then he pulls her skirt up and a 'chink' of metal chimes on the floor. She doesn't notice it until he pauses, he pulls on her so that she almost topples backwards and collects the item that fell.

'What's this?' He holds a glinting bit of gold in his hand, but it's too close for Miriam to see clearly. He glides her down the wall to the floor. She is completely covered, by his body and the bench. He is right on top of her. She sees a ring, her wedding ring, at eyeline now.

'What is this?' he says and tugs at her wrist hard. Her ring, she must have forgotten to remove it from her skirt when she took it off days ago.

Miriam can feel the cool dampness of the floor on her cheek. He grabs at her underwear as she tries to turn to move him off her. He holds her chin and guides it to face him, pulling on the muscles in her neck until they tremor in pain.

'You know how much I need you,' he says and allows her chin to rest back on the ground. 'My wife. I cannot live without you, my love.'

She looks at the floor, it is cut into squares all neatly in a row, flecks and tiny outlines that look like scattered daisies. At walking height, Miriam thinks, the floor is plain green. But it isn't. She looks for patterns, she counts the flowers, tiny white blobs she can see. She struggles to move herself, to move away from him. He holds her hand against her pelvis, pinning her down, positioning himself over her.

'Hush, hush,' he says, breathing hard.

Then the pain.

It moves within her like a red-hot wave, again and again.

Not ceasing.

Each crash tumbling over the last.

Red. Black, then, finally, white hot.

A tiny scream escapes from her lips with spittle and she watches as the flowers all bleed into one another. The floor, after all, is just green. He leans over her, pressing his entire body on hers and she, once again, feels unable to breathe. He is hot from the shower, fresh and clean.

'I have missed you so much.' He says and uses her to move himself up. He stands and she hears him rearrange his clothes before bending to her again. He picks up her hand and kisses her knuckles.

'I will never hurt you, Mim. I love you.'

Then cold steel, a band, is forced on to her finger. Her wedding band, in its rightful place, back on her finger.

She lies alone for a moment, expecting his return. But he has gone, she hears his footsteps receding. She quickly pulls herself up on the bench, then leans on the cabinet.

The picture. The couple on the beach, the clearer-than-clear sea, has shifted on its hinge and now looks as if viewed from the cabin of a boat. She straightens it and, staying close to the wall, staggers away.

23

MIRIAM

A man dressed in blue scrubs sees her. She keeps walking, but he must ask her something, though she can't quite hear him. She just knows she needs to put one foot ahead of the other. But the man is at her arm and with gentle pressure guides her through the empty hallway.

'I'm Karl, a porter here, are you a patient?'

She shakes her head.

'You look like you've had a bit of a fright.'

She realises her tights are ripped, her skirt is too high, she tries to pull it down, but her jacket hangs at a strange angle over her shoulder and she can't make the angle with her arm, which feels heavy and numb, to pull her skirt lower. She leans into the man's shoulder.

'I need to go home,' she says.

Many people speak to her. Touch her. Then they start speaking of her as if she were no longer there. When she can locate the voice to the person and the person to the location in the small cubicle space she says quietly to no one in particular:

'I'd like to go home.'

'We'd like to examine you, if we may, to see if you have any injuries. You're obviously in shock,' says a nurse, taking Miriam's arm out of its jacket and attaching a cuff and a cold stethoscope to the flex of her arm.

Miriam watches the nurse look at the scars on her arms.

'I'll do some vitals and then get the doctor to come in and have a look at you,' she says as the cuff deflates and Velcro snaps back into life.

'Does anywhere hurt? Any pain?' she asks and places a thermometer in Miriam's mouth.

She shakes her head. And the thermometer knocks against her teeth.

'Good. Doctor will be with you shortly.' The nurse, a wide woman and short, takes the thermometer and walks away, closing the curtains around the bed once more.

Miriam looks around her and shivers. Her jacket is half off and she pulls it around her fully and buttons it up. She is sitting on the bed fully clothed, her tights hang like wrinkles against her skin. Her skirt is bunched. She gets off the bed, and although feeling light-headed stands steady and finds her underwear tucked into her skirt. Torn. She bends to remove her shoes and take off her tights and alongside her underwear she places them both into a brown paper bag, used for vomit, she presumes. She folds the top of the bag over, twice.

Miriam perches on the end of the bed and the plasters on her fingers are wonky and have collected blue dander. She takes each plaster off and stretches her fingers slowly. Pulling her wedding ring off, again, she places it in a yellow bin with a red lid on the table beside her. The ring gives a satisfying thump as it lands at the bottom of the bin.

She bends to tie her laces back up when the curtain springs open. A doctor of epic height and stance looks at a chart in front of him.

'Miss, I am Dr Evellor.' He turns and pulls the curtain closed behind him.

'Do you have any injuries? Have you fallen? Hurt your head?'

'No, no. I think I'm okay.'

'How is it that you have found yourself in the emergency department then?' His smile is wide and genuine, and he sits at the bottom of the bed, placing the chart down. He looks at her.

'I would like to go home.'

'Have you been visiting relatives? Some bad news, perhaps? It has been noted that articles of your clothing were torn?'

'Yes, I took them off. I would like to go home now, I am feeling fine. I am sorry to waste your time.' She stands.

'Please sit. Let's be thorough, shall we? What happened to you before you arrived in my department?'

Finding there are no words she smiles and meets the doctor's eyes. They are bright blue, but red-rimmed. Tired.

'My husband hurt me a little, that is all. I will be fine. I now need to go home to my dad.' Then she realises, her father is on the ward, she doesn't have anyone to return home for.

'Hurt you? Where?' He writes on the board in front of him.

'It's nothing.'

'Did he hurt you sexually?' he asks in the same tone.

'Yes,' she says, thankful that someone could name it. 'Yes, he did.'

'Do you think he intended to do this?'

Miriam nods.

'Thank you. Now, if you don't mind, I am not going anywhere, but I would like you to feel a bit more comfortable and I am very aware that I am a man, and discussing injuries you may have sustained during intercourse may not feel appropriate for you. My colleague, Sarah, will be with you very shortly. Until that point, can I ask you to tell me if you need anything?'

'I'd like to go home, please.'

'To your husband?'

'No, my parents' house. I left my husband.'

'I'll leave these forms for you, can you complete them and Sarah will be with you shortly. If we can check you over, give you a clean bill of health, then you can get on your way.'

She completes the forms, leaving the majority blank. Her marital status – unknown. Her medical history – complicated. She feels in a moment of rare clarity that her medical history may just have been the consequence of her marital status.

Sarah arrives in a red-headed blur, she stammers and blushes. Miriam feels more uncomfortable than ever, so declines an examination, declines blood and swab tests and declines contraceptive advice.

'I don't need that,' she says as kindly as she can.

'Because you have been hurt and attended to today I'd like to ask if you would like to speak to a police officer, there is a female officer who can take a statement from you. Or at least discuss your options?'

'I really don't need anything, honestly. This is not unusual, Sarah. He just caught me off-guard, that is all.'

'Don't you think it wrong, though, that he can do this to you?'

Miriam looks at her askance.

'I mean, if you spoke to the police there would be a record that he harmed you. If you let me look at you for injuries, they could press charges. He could be punished for hurting you in this way. Because it is not okay.' Miriam says nothing. 'I'll get you a glass of water and a biscuit. Have a think and I'll be back in a few minutes. Is there anyone you would like me to call for you?'

Miriam shakes her head, 'No, thank you.'

Sarah pulls the curtains closed, cutting out the vision but not the sound of people all around her. She thinks about the consequences and she thinks about 'on the record'. Maybe people would believe her.

When Sarah returns, she agrees to the examination and the talk with the police officer following that.

The wide and older nurse, perspiration on her top lip, with a name tag with 'Dawn' on it and a sticker of a yellow sun, stays throughout the process. Miriam thinks Dawn looks like she needs to see some sun herself. Almost grey from head to toe, uniform, pallor and hair. Only her black shoes shine.

Cold instruments prod with as much care as stainless steel can command. Miriam is numb all over, so although it smarts, she finds the humiliation worse. She thinks of the rabbit girls, the stainless-steel scalpel making cuts to their legs.

She thinks of Hani, lost. She thinks of fighting back, of being on the record. Just like Frieda did when she wrote the letters. All the letters. Miriam takes deep breaths and imagines the faces of the women lost. Each woman she can see so clearly. And Stella, little Stella.

Dawn stays with her while her genital injuries are catalogued meticulously by the doctor on a diagram of the female anatomy. Miriam has never seen it so bold and vivid on the page before, almost like a flower.

Once Sarah has completed her findings, she turns the clipboard. Miriam looks at what she has found and wants to tear the page out. Remove every line, every red mark, all the hatched lines depicting what, she didn't know. When Sarah asks if she can talk through the injuries, new and old, so Miriam understands what all the red markings are, Miriam averts her gaze.

'So, the hatched lines are scar tissue,' Sarah starts. 'And the thicker lines are the tears that are recent. Miriam, how often has your husband done this to you?'

'A while,' is all she says as Sarah recommends a course of antibiotics to prevent infection which Miriam agrees to. Her head feels full, her mind imprinted with the diagram of genitalia in black, covered with the doctor's drawings, marking out all her imperfections in red.

When the female officer arrives, she has no idea what to say.

She speaks the truth. All of it. Dawn at her side speaks quietly, gently telling Miriam to slow down or rewind a step. She is calm yet firm and Miriam listens and explains the best she can, feeling more and more that everything should make sense, yet nothing does. Every question judging her further.

Finally, the police officer gives her a card – Officer Müller.

She says, 'You have been very brave.' Like a dentist would say after a long procedure in the chair.

When Sarah gives her the tablets and calls for a taxi, Dawn helps Miriam to the door.

'I hope you get home safely,' she says as they wait for the cars to move along and the taxi to come around to the entrance. A plume of blue smoke settles low as patients litter close to the entrance, in their wheelchairs, holding drip stands, dressed in hospital gowns with cigarettes in hand.

'Can I say something to you, some advice that my mum once gave me?' Dawn asks.

Miriam watches the rain mist around them, seeming not to fall but to rise, as if the tiny drops were suspended in the air.

'She used to say that if you give a man what he wants, he'll never take what he needs.'

Miriam says nothing as a black car turns into the entrance space. She opens the door and gets in without looking back.

The shame washes over her in huge heavy waves, she goes straight into the bathroom, deposits all her clothes into a small pile and turns the shower to a scalding heat. It burns her scalp like tiny needles.

Looking down at her body, she feels his handprints, like tar, marking her body. Where he touched her, where he hurt her, his paint on her canvas. His hands on her body. The shower cascades like oil over water, she cannot erase his unwanted touch.

Her hands scream and withdraw from the water as it burns through the broken skin. It takes days for the smell and taste of him to leave her, no matter how much she washes.

She once tried bleach, but it looked like her skin had been removed with sand paper and then set upon by bees. It singed her nasal passages too, it was all she could smell for five days, long enough for him to evaporate, at least from her body. But the scars and the scratching lasted an entire month.

Sitting on the side of the bath, a towel loosely draped around her, she watches as beads of pink water cascade down her legs, swallowed up by the dip in her ankle. She allows tears to fall.

Then, wrapping herself back up, she returns to Dad's room and stands at the window for half a second, taking a glimpse at the same picture, its scene unmoving, yet everything has changed. She shuts the curtains tight and moves around the empty house, touches things, but doesn't move anything. Her father's absence fills each space and makes everything foreign.

She scrubs and scratches and her skin stings. She tries to remove *him*, she settles for distraction and sits carefully, looking at the letters, each as individual, as beautiful and as tragic as the last. Except these won't just melt away like the women described within them. The untold women with untold stories.

Laid out on the table, her parents' table. Having been held captive in a dress for decades. She wants to free them, to find out how they survived.

If they survived.

24

MIRIAM

Dearest Henryk,

Wanda Bielika and Bunny are from the same village, Lidice. The Nazis did what they did to Lublin a year later: they tore it to the ground.

Wanda told me, when we had a rare moment alone outside in the shadow of a block, that she had known Bunny before they met here.

She was a young mum called Neta-Lee. Wanda discovered it was her when they were lying side by side in the special treatment section of the revier.

A woman called Jacosta, also on the Lidice transports, was lying on the other side of Wanda and knew of Neta-Lee too. She was not dumb or mute. She married young, childhood sweethearts, they had four children.

When the Nazis came to town, they stood the husband and all the children against the wall of the house, the babies calling for their mummy, small hands reaching out.

She begged the guards to shoot her, to take her instead. To spare the children. The guard laughed. Five shots. The family lost.

When the rabbit girls in Wanda's group had been bathed, but before their legs were shaved, Wanda tried to talk to Neta-Lee, using her name. But she said nothing.

As Wanda was older she never thought she would make the selection process as all the other girls were young, with thin, long legs. But she was selected and enjoyed the bath full of warm water. They were so amazed, Wanda recalls, they splashed and laughed and for the first time in so very long, felt like women.

Afterwards, in clean beds, clean shirts, a nurse came by with a razor to shave their legs.

The next morning, they were given a tablet and the world became blurry. Wanda remembers the walls moving as if they were liquid. She was taken to a sterile room, strapped to the bed. Unable to move at all.

When she woke, her legs were in a cast up to the groin. She could hear others screaming out, but she felt fine, tired but fine. But when she awoke that evening, her legs felt like they were on fire and she couldn't move. A woman in the opposite bed had hiccups, continual hiccups, when the hiccups stopped they took her body away.

They all had different number and letter combinations on their casts – no one knew what this meant. It is the thirst she remembers the most. By night her lips were bleeding. One of the women from another bed who had been there for a few weeks came around with a bucket of water. She was hobbling on a cast too, she brought water to all the parched mouths and left a trail of blood and brown pus from the cast in her wake.

This, it turned out, was Eugenia. The next few days were laden with pain and screams; three women died within the week.

The doctors came around by day, checked their numbers on their clipboards, didn't speak at all. Eugenia came around at night, bringing water.

Bunny also lay in the bed, silent, but had her eyes open, listening. She refused the water offered.

Wanda looked at me. 'That's why we protect Bunny. We must. She has been through so much. It's our duty to help her.'

'That's why she needs Stella?' I asked.

'Stella keeps Bunny alive, I think. All the love for her own children spills over into Stella.'

When Wanda came back from the bandage change, Bunny lay stagnant, Wanda thought she was dead. Wanda reached out and held her hand, to help her find the ground again and Bunny didn't let go.

A week later Eugenia was discharged. She continued to bring food from the bunks to Wanda and the other rabbits and delivered items through the window. They all watched as Jacosta died. Her jaw locked shut. The nurse plunged a syringe into her heart so she did not 'suffer'.

Eugenia said she had heard the guards were planning to destroy evidence of the experiments, she cautioned Wanda to be vigilant. That night the nurse came around again, she had a needle. When Wanda awoke, the nurse was over her. Wanda screamed:

'I am not a guinea pig. I am not a guinea pig.' It woke Bunny and by morning they were the only two who had survived.

Eugenia planned their escape. Bunny could not walk.

Wanda was more fortunate and could stand. To be in a place like this and not be able to move. It was a death warrant for sure.

Eugenia came in carrying a chair she had found and they tied Bunny to the chair with a sheet. Eugenia and Wanda, as the guards watched, carried Bunny back to the bunk. The guards saw them and laughed. Two women in casts, barely able to walk, carrying a mute on a chair.

Mutiny was the only power they had left and they were determined to save Bunny. Wanda would not leave her behind.

Soon more and more women came and arms helped to hold Bunny, to get the rabbits to safety.

They made some shelves in the old toilet area and Eugenia sewed the skin back up on Bunny's leg with her perfect running stitch. Wanda's legs, it appeared, had been shot: black circles front and back and bruising up to her knee.

Wanda showed me her scars, her legs deformed, the skin still bright red, raw and new.

'We have to stay alive, for we are the only witnesses.'

Miriam recalls the hatches, the drawings the doctor made in red pen. She too has scars, but these are even less visible, and even less believable.

Does anyone know or remember Wanda? Miriam doubts it and the thought makes her sad.

She gets some pens and paper from her father's office, replaces many ledgers back into the desk, and piles the books and paper to one side. She has time now, waiting for her father to die, or for Axel to get her again. She tries not to think about which will come first.

She uses her father's good pen and stares back at the letter. Her hands shake so much the ink drops and splashes, and as she presses the pen on to the paper, the nib bends slightly at her hand. Her fingers stop quaking. They are quiet. She becomes entranced by them as they work. Moving the pen across the page, tracing Wanda's words.

A deep sense of peace cloaks Miriam, stilling her busy mind.

On second reading and really looking at the finished letter on plain paper, the letters are beautiful. Written as she supposed they were meant to be. As Eva has restored the ones written in French, Miriam will do the same for the rest.

How Frieda must have imagined them. Rather than squat writing pressed into space that could never contain the volume of thoughts. The pages overflow with love and grief.

'*If you give a man what he wants, he'll never take what he needs.*' The words of the nurse seem to echo in her head. She feels foolish and petulant to have been talking to the doctors, the police, about Axel. Look what happened to the 'rabbits', and they didn't complain.

Axel had sex with her, she thinks, that is all, yet she went crying to the police. Maybe Dawn was right, that her actions caused his needs to take over. That she deserved it, again. Of all the things the police must hear, her whines and worries must seem so petty.

She continues writing, feeling shame at her own actions. It is a new sensation, it pricks her skin like a rash. Not shame from what someone else has done to her, but shame at what she has done to herself. She writes until Wanda's words exist again, then calls the hospital.

Her father is stable and off the oxygen. Miriam is relieved and then cautious. Like being pulled toward and instantly repelled against something. The hospital. What if Axel were there again? What if he didn't just hurt her, what if he were able to do worse? Her head spirals into the 'worse' she's experienced before. She continues to write out the letters with diligence and intensity.

When her hands ache and she has rewritten many of the letters, wrapped them in cloth and placed them in her handbag, Miriam gets up with no real purpose, and walks into her father's study. Taking off her jacket and rubbing life into her arms, she starts to collect his papers and put them away. She sorts them and places them back into the desk and the folders just behind it. She works without stopping until she can see the floor space and there are only a few small piles left on the desk to go through. She pulls out her father's chair and sees a book has fallen; she retrieves it.

Yeats in English.

She flicks through the pages, the spine is broken and deeply lined. She opens it to a poem and a scrap of paper falls out.

> *When darkness drops, I am your light.*
> *Frieda.*

The poem, 'The Second Coming', is full of pencil markings and lined with notes in her father's writing, all around its margins.

She sits in the chair with the poem on her lap, and reads and rereads it and the note.

From Frieda.

Her father had been searching for her; after all these years. Miriam swallows hard. He must never have found her.

25

MIRIAM

'Merry Christmas,' Eva says, slipping off her boots and placing a bag of food on the ground. 'I have a present for you.'

'Christmas?'

'It's Christmas Eve.' Eva is wearing a red dress and a deep green jumper with her usual heavy boots.

'It is?'

She follows her through to the kitchen.

Eva takes out all the vegetables from her bag, some coffee and a newspaper.

Miriam picks it up and leafs through it. A picture of the church catches her attention. *The Church of the Redeemer is opening its doors tonight*, the headline reads. *After almost thirty years shut away, there will be a service this evening at 8 p.m. All welcome.*

'The church,' she says, holding the newspaper for Eva to see. 'They have a service on tonight.'

'Are you religious?' Eva asks.

'No, but my parents were married here. Now that Dad's not here, I'd like to go, I think.' Axel would never find her there.

'Perhaps I could accompany you?'

Miriam looks at her. 'Okay.'

'Here, I got you something,' Eva says, and places an envelope on the side, before rustling back into her bag. 'I still have a few more to go, but I'm almost there. And I also have this.' She hands Miriam a small parcel wrapped up in pink tissue paper.

'Merry Christmas,' she says as Miriam takes off the sellotape at each end first before unwrapping.

She finds a scarf the colour of autumn folded over on itself. It is the softest fabric Miriam has ever felt between her deeply battered hands.

'Do you like it?' Eva asks.

'It's . . .'

'I know it's bright, but I can't stand pastel colours and, well . . . I always said that pale colours are poor relations, if you know what I mean.' She laughs as Miriam smooths her fingers across the fabric. 'I thought maybe you could do with a bit of colour?'

'It's beautiful.'

'Go get yourself dressed and I'll make dinner . . . if that's okay?'

Miriam looks down and realises she is still in her pyjamas. She smiles and stretches.

After changing she returns to the kitchen, where there is a substantial mess of tomatoes, saucepans, knives and an eruption of what must be broccoli all over the work surface. She shakes her head and takes a piece of carrot from the chopping board and chews on it.

'Mum would have a fit to see her kitchen like this.'

'I promise I'll clear up.'

'No, I didn't mean it as an insult, just . . . it's not a problem.'

'I love to cook, so this is a treat for me. It's hard to make an effort when you are on your own, so cooking for someone else is nice,' Eva says, searching the drawers for a spoon. Miriam points out the cutlery drawer. 'And it's Christmas!'

'Can I ask, how long have you been alone?'

'My husband died five years ago,' Eva says.

'Do you have children?'

'My husband had two daughters before we were married: Renka – who has Jeffrey, whom you met, and Clotilde . . .' Eva swallows hard. 'I am a grandmother three times over.'

'Are you close with your daughters?'

'Well, Renka fled with Jeffrey so long ago it's been hard to keep in touch, and . . . Clotilde . . .' Eva changes the subject. 'How did the transfer go?'

'Dad's in the hospital, he didn't make it to the hospice. He's sick.'

'Oh no, Miriam, I am sorry. What is wrong?'

'Pneumonia. I saw him last night, he was stable. But I'd like to give him that closure, to find out what happened to Frieda.'

They eat in the dining room, the letters at one end of the table and them at the other. The rain taps gently at the window as they eat in silence. Miriam's thoughts twist and jump around, but she finds the more she eats, the calmer her mind, and she focuses on the meal.

'Wine?' Eva offers, and pours herself half a glass.

'No thanks, I . . . I'm not sure that's a good idea.'

'Because of them?' And she nods to the door.

'Yes, I had a drink, well, more than one, and Dad got sick, so now it proves I'm unstable. And Axel, well, he enjoys that. It's bait for him really.'

'Fuck 'em.'

Miriam laughs, unsure if it's her laugh itself or Eva's expletive that surprises her, she laughs more.

'What?'

Miriam laughs all the harder.

After the plates are empty, Miriam stands.

'The food was lovely, Eva, thank you. It's nice to eat with someone. I always eat alone.' She collects the dinner plates and they both walk into the kitchen.

'Always?'

'Yes. When I was with Axel I was always too nervous to eat. It's hard to eat nervous, so I would eat before he came home or after he went out in the evenings.'

'Your husband sounds like a tyrant,' Eva says. 'The things you said the other day.'

'Please ignore me, I was being dramatic.'

'No. Actually I've been thinking,' Eva says.

'Please, Eva. Not today. I can't talk about it.' She feels her dinner contract in her stomach.

'Okay,' Eva says. 'I don't know very much about you other than Axel. Tell me, what was your father like?'

She smiles and speaks uncensored. 'He was wise. Smart. In the best of ways, not just intelligent, but he knew his own heart and he was so honest. I loved him.'

Eva gulps.

'I just said *loved*. Past tense.'

'Yes.'

Miriam takes a deep breath. 'I love my father, but all I have are memories of when I was a different person and now I know he was there, all the memories seem to change.' She sighs. 'I haven't spoken to him in so long.'

'From what I can see, you have been busy fighting your own demons. Your father will know that.'

'I've missed so much.'

'Will you divorce Axel?' Eva asks, running water into the sink.

'I'm not sure that's a good idea.'

'Why?'

'He would go mad. He's silent scary, if you know what I mean.'

'He's dangerous?'

'Yes. He makes me think I am completely mad and the trouble is everyone else believes him. I even missed Mum's funeral because of his lies, I only got there for the wake.'

'How do you know he was lying?'

'I just knew. That was three years ago. When I got the call that Dad was in hospital . . . I couldn't allow that to happen again. Mum had Dad, but Dad has no one.'

'You love your father very much,' Eva says solemnly. 'And by being here, that takes courage.'

'No, I was with Axel for over twenty years, I am very, very stupid. I believed him. It's only now that I can see he is lying, but it's easy to get drawn back into that. And the more resistance I put up the worse he'll be.'

'That's why no divorce?'

'Yes, if I fight it'll be hell.'

'What about now?' Eva turns from the washing up, soap suds up to her elbows.

'What do you mean?' Miriam picks up a towel and starts to dry the crockery that drips bubbles.

'Do people believe you or him?'

'Him. Always him. If you met him you'd believe him too.'

'Never. This *man*, I'd see him.'

'Keeping as far away from him as possible is my plan.'

'But maybe you can fight back?'

Miriam says nothing as they work quietly, clearing the kitchen in a calm silence of solitude and company combined.

'Shall we call a taxi? To go to the church?' Eva says.

'Oh yes, I almost forgot.' And Miriam scrambles around getting ready.

'I'd have driven, but my car . . .'

'Jeff said it wasn't working?'

'No, it's still not fixed. Garage don't want to touch it until the New Year now.'

'I'm sorry.'

'Me too, have to rely on public transport.' She makes a face.

Miriam smiles and picks up the phone to book a taxi.

The taxi driver drops them off by the Wall. There are people walking arm in arm, but Miriam doesn't see a way to the church. Paying the driver, they follow a couple and find a whole panel of wall removed.

Miriam's steps are cautious and slow.

'Are you okay?' Eva has flushed cheeks from the cold and her fingers are red-rimmed and glow. She rubs at them as if rubbing in an ointment.

'Had a run-in with Axel yesterday, and I'm a bit sore, that's all, I'll be fine. Let's keep moving, it's cold.'

Miriam and then Eva duck under the loose metal bars that keep the rest of the Wall standing and find themselves on the death strip.

'This is eerie,' Miriam says to Eva by her side.

'You know, I dreamed about walking through the death strip every night after this wall was built. I hate walls, doors, anything that will keep me in,' Eva says.

Miriam looks at Eva as they step through the sand, once immaculate, now full of footsteps.

She works out the tangle of thoughts in her head to try and create some words.

'In another life, I'd live by the sea: all that space,' Eva says. 'Over the Wall, there is no space, every day you are looking over your shoulder; waiting . . .' She leaves the sentence in a knot as Miriam checks her watch in the bright light overhead.

'I used to come here with Dad,' she says, pointing to the tower. 'We are early, let's go up.'

Inside, the spiral stone staircase leads up to the bell tower. Their shoes on the cobbled steps vibrate through the air, water drips from somewhere and the windows that had looked out on the river are all boarded up.

'It is very dark. Watch your step.'

The nape of Miriam's neck tingles, hearing her own voice refracted around her.

'Stairs are a bitch to old hips.'

Miriam smiles briefly. 'It's worth it . . . come on,' she says, and even to her own ears she sounds flat.

They reach the railings which overlook the river, there are empty beer bottles on the floor and cigarette ends everywhere. The frost in the air stills the water and both sky and water merge into darkness.

She stands in the silence and looks at Eva, who is crying.

'Are you okay?'

'What you said earlier, it's hurting me so deeply.' She clenches a fist to her stomach.

'What is?' Unsure what to say, she turns back to the view.

'You've left Axel, yes?'

Miriam nods.

'So why not divorce him? So he cannot say or do again what he is doing. He is breaking you, even though you have left.'

And although her thoughts jolt at Eva's words, her focus is on the drop.

Will it feel like flying if I fall?

'I can't,' she says dreamily.

Will the wind whip or kiss my skin?

Eva says something, but the words sound tinny and lost. A pinprick of words from a distance.

The absence of anything other than that moment.

Flying, falling.

The end.

Miriam leans forward, pushes her weight through her hands.

'Miriam!' Eva's voice brings her back to her feet, her hands loosen and she looks at Eva, who trembles and grips the handrail until her knuckles show white.

Miriam suddenly sees the incredible drop below her feet. Looking down makes her take a step back, away from Eva.

Away from the edge.

Miriam shakes her head and turns to the inner sanctuary where the bell used to be but is no more. Her eyes sting and she feels disorientated. She looks past Eva to the white slip of moon.

'Are you a man or mouse?' Eva asks.

'I'm neither,' Miriam says cautiously.

'Exactly, you are a woman,' Eva says. 'And God only knows there is nothing stronger than a woman. You are acting like a coward, like a man, and you run and hide away like a little' – her fore and middle fingers walk through the air, the moon allowing her hands to shadow their image – 'mouse,' she says.

'You have *freedom*,' Eva continues, pronouncing the *free* so that it elongates like smoke into the air. 'Axel will never give up and you'll lose your fight and go back.' Eva turns around to go down the stairs.

'No. I did stand up to him, at the hospital, he hurt me and I even spoke to the police.'

'The police . . .' Eva tuts loudly in the confined space, it sounds like a penny rebounding off the walls.

'What else can I do?'

'You can divorce him, or he will keep playing with you till you stop running.'

'I'm doing my best here,' Miriam says. 'It's not easy and to be frank I'd rather just die after Dad than deal with any of this.'

'You want someone to fix your problems, but not to deal with them yourself. You left him – that is a woman – but you will go back.'

'No. No I won't.'

'You will until you take control.'

'How? How are you the expert?' Miriam asks.

A pause grows and the drips in the tower become amplified.

Eva continues on the same thread. 'You think like him, you are used, abused, but he has left something in here . . .' She points at Miriam's head '. . . and you forget what thinking from here is.' She jabs Miriam in the sternum. 'I cannot . . . I cannot watch you do this to yourself. No more. I'm sorry, Miriam, I will return the letters I haven't translated. I can't watch this happen again.'

'Again?' Miriam asks, but the emptiness at Eva's words pulses in Miriam's chest, echoing like the tower itself as Eva's footsteps recede until they are gone.

Miriam looks down over the railings, really looks down. She stays there a long time gripping the bars.

Hard.

26

MIRIAM

She watches her step on the wet stairs as she descends from the tower. Despite numb toes she moves with speed. Turning each way, looking for Eva, her breath coming fast from lips white-tipped with frost. She moves towards the church, its domed roof lost in the night sky, she hears noises within and a slip of light filters through cracks in the door.

Miriam follows the trickle of people as they go into the church, it smells empty and damp and cold. She sits close to the door and looks at the broken and cracked floor tiles, once terracotta and green cut into diamonds but now smashed. She cannot recall any of the service. She sits until the people next to her stand. She stands, then sits when they do. She leaves just after them. Alone.

After the church, she gets a taxi with a decisiveness that she finds stimulating and terrifying equally. She travels through the Berlin streets: street lights bright and atmosphere buoyant as bars and clubs swell and throb to the dance of Christmas.

Miriam goes to the hospital in the dark for the last of the visiting hours. When on the ward, she takes out the bundle of transcribed letters and sits; the air is heavy from the whirring machines and clunky radiators. She kisses her father's head and squeezes his hand, he has a tube up his nose and it curls around his face. He has been shaved. His skin is soft and he smells baby-lotion fresh.

If these are all the letters she has from Eva, then she will share them with her father; he deserves to know. And if Eva cannot help anymore, Miriam will find someone who can. Eva's words clang in Miriam's heart and she feels guilt that she cannot live up to Eva's expectations.

'I would always regret not doing this, but even now we are on pretty shaky ground, Dad. I hope you hear me, I hope you understand. I have these, from Frieda.' She unfolds the thick paper and reads from the beginning.

'*I am alive, at least, I think I am alive . . .*'

After she has read many of the letters, a tear falls down his cheek. She dries it with a handkerchief.

HENRYK

Miriam reads to me. I try to focus, to hear what she says. Time stops ticking and starts to flow and soon it races away. I know there is something I must hold on to.

We moved back into our old home in 1946 as Emilie had wanted, we lived within walking distance of what was left of our friends. If Emilie had asked for anything I would have done it, whatever she wanted.

She worked at the hospital to support our family. She was happy, and I did everything to keep it that way.

But I will always remember that time, in the tiny apartment, her face looking at me as I returned to her from Frieda. Sitting in the chair, her small frame shrouded in blankets, plucking at the fabric with both hands. I walked into the room and she looked up, disappointment and loss creased her eyes, and if there was a moment where I wished the ground would shake, in which I was removed from her life, and Frieda's, I asked a God I didn't believe in to grant it to me then.

Back in our old home, her face still contained her grief and everything we touched contained the memory of Frieda, and I wanted to claw back what I had lost.

She would look away and not look at me again for hours at a time. I would never ask for forgiveness, but I could do everything to give Emilie the life she had always wanted. We had Miriam, and that changed everything.

For fifteen years, I stayed home with Miriam. I marvelled at her incredible growth, her intuition and resourcefulness, and the years flew by so fast, although I remember the days to be long.

When she was at school, I'd walk her there, stand by the blue gates as she chatted with her friends, whom I liked very much. Girls and boys like colourful flowers growing together, an eternal spring; it was a privilege to watch them bloom. They'd ask me questions about life, sometimes love, and I would happily help with French or English homework.

As I was leaving one day, a teacher stopped me, he knew me by sight as Miriam's dad. He asked me if I could join him in his office.

'Miriam tells me you were, or perhaps you still are, a teacher?'

'Yes, I used to teach.' Immediately I was on my guard, felt imprisoned in the confines of his office, a boiling cup of insipid tea in my hands, sitting so deep in a seat I could see the imprints of my bony knees through the fabric of my trousers.

'Miriam is an exceptional student.'

'Thank you, I am proud of her.'

'Obviously, she'd achieve more if she talked less.' He laughed. The desk was full of papers, magazines, books. Herr Blundell, his name on the door. He was Miriam's head of year, I think, or maybe I didn't know that then, only after.

Time fills in the blanks as we know them to be, rather than as they were.

'She's a lot like her mother,' I had agreed, because Miriam was such a sprightly thing, at the end of the day I couldn't wait to sit in an empty room and let it fill up with the silence that had been driven out by the chatter of both mother and daughter.

'I have three teenage girls,' said Herr Blundell. 'It's a rocky road to travel as the only man in the house, I can tell you!'

'I can imagine.'

'We blame hormones, a lot.'

'Women have it rough.'

'So, you don't have a job now?'

'No, I'm at home with Miriam.' I felt I needed to qualify that somehow and added, 'I used to teach at the university.' His expression changed and I regretted my words.

'Impressive. Were you published?' Herr Blundell moved all the magazines and books to the floor and revealed a chair that didn't seem to be there before, on which he sat.

'Yes, for a while, anyway.'

'Would you be interested in a job?' he asked sincerely.

'No, not really. If I'm honest, I don't think I'd be up for it.'

'Health problems?'

'Something like that,' I mumbled, placing my undrunk drink on a stack of magazines. 'I have to go now.'

'If it helps, I was there.'

'Where?' I struggled to remove myself from the chair and the question invited time to try to get up without sinking back into it again.

'Buchenwald, first,' he said, and it was like a fist into the gut. I deflated back into the chair, winded. 'Then Auschwitz-Birkenau.' He unbuttoned his collar. Three buttons down, he pulled his tie to one side and his shirt the other way, revealing one letter followed by five numbers. Just like the one I had on my wrist.

'The bastards decided to brand me here.' He pointed to his chest.

'Why?'

'I fought back,' he said. Then he buttoned his shirt back up and replaced his tie, so that it was once again straight. 'This school is a family, and if you wanted a teaching job, you would be very welcome.'

'Does Miriam, I mean, do the students know you were . . . there,' I said, pointing to his chest.

'No. I teach history, but not my own history. The way I see it, I am a lynchpin to help the next generation understand and prevent this happening again.'

'Most people don't talk about this,' I said, finally pulling myself out of the chair and standing up to my full height.

'I know, but I see no shame in sharing this with anyone. You know why?'

I shook my head.

'Because it wasn't my fault, nor, if I am correct, was it yours.'

'I think you have been mistaken,' I said, and left the room with my heart running so fast my feet were numb after only a few steps. The smell of the teacher's office lingered on me, as did his words: '*I fought back.*'

MIRIAM

Back at home she goes straight to the pile of German letters. Picking up a tiny scrap, she switches on the lights and reads. She doesn't know what the difference is between the German and French letters. If Eva stops translating, what will Miriam miss?

I asked Wanda if she wanted a piece of paper to write to her family, but she had no one to write to. Her family were all separated by the time the war started. She had four children and six grandchildren. She speaks of an idyllic life. She is fifty-six.

We are her only family now.

She is a mother to us all. I imagine her wearing an apron in front of a stove, smelling of warm dough. Her children and grandchildren must have that image of her, milling around, waiting for whatever she had baked to cool enough to eat. She has lost them all. She sits in her bunk and she cares for us.

Wanda wraps her wings around us all, and still has the girth to offer a hug that feels like home. A home I had with you. She is the glue and right now she holds me, and paints a future that is not so bleak.

Miriam rereads the last letter. If Wanda died, would anyone know she had gone? Would anyone tell her stories, could anyone name her children? Eradicating the whole family is like removing the roots of a tree, if you remove the roots everything is destroyed.

At least I have lived. Miriam places the paper back on the table. Lived. She cannot think of a way in which her life can be defined that way. How has she lived? She doesn't know. She knows that when she dies, no one will remember her either. She has done nothing at all, except be a 'wife' to Axel and a daughter to soon-to-be-dead parents. Orphaned. And now, without a friend. She understands why Eva left her at the church, she would walk away from herself too. She is pathetic, just as Axel has always said she is.

Christmas is as lifeless as a plastic flower, drooping in the condensed hospital heat, and the ward is full of limp spirit. The decade-old tinsel wilts on the walls.

She arrives early on Christmas morning. Her father has a yellow paper hat from a cracker perched on his head, which she swiftly removes. There is subdued cheer as Miriam sits next to her father, and all the visiting hours are consumed with her reading to him. She reads to him from the letters and starts to see a pattern. The French letters in Eva's handwriting are personal: love letters; the German ones are more about the camp and the women within it.

Miriam feels a rush of affection for Frieda, who must have known her father so well, and then thinks that if Eva has been translating the love letters it must have been difficult after recently losing her husband.

Miriam hadn't thought of Eva in any other way than as the translator of the letters. She was present in Miriam's life and Miriam hadn't even thought to check Eva was okay with what she was doing. Or to understand anything about her. The letters are so sad. Miriam loathes that she didn't check on the woman who has been her only friend.

Her father squeezes her hand, turns his head to her voice, he says, 'Thank you.' His Christmas present to her. The sound of his voice, he is there . . . somewhere. She reads poetry again, just like she used to when he had episodes. She reads just to hear his voice. He only says two words, 'Thank you,' but they are enough to give Miriam some cheer.

When the nurses give her father medication and his snores are rhythmic, Miriam picks up the next of Frieda's letters written on sheet music.

Hani has returned, sterilised.

Skin slick with sweat, frozen to the touch. She has been gone for two weeks. She bleeds heavily.

Hani doesn't say what happened. She climbs into the bunk and moves into my body, as always. We stay that way all night. My body heat warming her back, then when she moves, warming her front. She is never warm all over.

We try to feed her up, we try to keep her warm. Stella sings to her and smooths her growing hair. There is something magical about Stella and for a while, she joined us in our bunk, telling Bunny she was on holiday with Hani at the seaside, telling of waves and seagulls.

'Everyone look. It's a rainbow. Do you see?'

We all had to say we saw the rainbow before she continued.

'We have rainbows on my holiday, Bunny. Hani, tell me the colours of the rainbow.'

'Rood,' said Hani.

'Red,' I interpreted.

'I know, pretty lady – I speak Hani now.'

I laughed, Eugenia laughed, Wanda dried her eyes, for we could all see the rainbow now.

'Red makes us cry when it leaks out,' said Stella and she rattles along without breath. 'The whip, the dogs, they make everything red. Orange is the sun, it no longer shines bright. The sun is sad, because the people are sad. Yellow is the sand, in my eyes, between my fingers, between my toes. Sand bites all over. Green is very rare, like smiles and photographs. Pretty lady, your eyes are green, they sparkle. Bunny's eyes are brown. Hani's eyes leak a lot of love.'

And they do.

'They say my eyes are blue. I cannot see my eyes.'

'Your eyes are blue, Stella,' said Eugenia. 'Blue like the deepest sapphires, the most brilliant blue of the sky.'

'Blue air tastes like salt if the wind blows. We are by the sea, a deep, blue, wet sea. Hani, what colour is next?'

'Purper.'

Stella laughed, repeating her again and again. Hani laughed too and the air suddenly lightened.

'Purple. The colour of bruises when the red doesn't come out of the skin, but weeps underneath. Bunny is like a bruise, she cries on the inside.'

Bunny nodded her head, yes.

'Where is grey in the rainbow, Aunty Wanda?'

'There is no grey, Stella.'

'Yes, there is. The rainbow holds all the colours of the world.' Then to Eugenia, 'Genia – where is the grey?'

'The grey is at the bottom, the smallest colour before it blends into white.'

'Here there is more grey,' said Stella. 'The sky, the concrete, the wire, the uniform. The dead.'

'But we are not here Stella, we are on holiday, on the beach,' Hani said.

'Miriam Winter?' a kindly nurse in a navy uniform asks her as she is about to leave. 'Can I have a quick word?' She escorts her into a side room and sits on one side of a sofa and offers Miriam the other.

'I have some good news,' she starts. 'We can transfer your father to the hospice Wednesday or Thursday probably. He's responding to the antibiotics and I'm sure you saw the tube in his nose, he is on enteral feeding, and the physiotherapy can be done in the hospice too, to help clear his lungs. He's doing okay.' She smiles. 'If you ask me, I think he has something to live for.'

'He does,' she says. 'Yes, he does.'

Two days later Miriam leaves the hospital at the shift change. She walks out of the ward mingled with the nurses and up the silent streets for home. No one around. Not one person. She notices a purple sign illuminated by the street lights. *Purper.*

'Abbott, Abbott and Co.' The white lettering by the door to the left in the window lists:

Residential property
Wills and Probate
Family, Marital, Divorce.

Miriam walks in to a chime and three male faces rise to her entrance. She leaves hours later with a stack of brilliant-white paperwork, which she puts down carefully, like a bomb, on the end of the table.

Maybe she has something to live for after all.

27

HENRYK

The job offered at the school motivated me to look for something. Miriam's school was the best Berlin had to offer, but Emilie encouraged me to find something at the university. I was, after all, a professor.

A French book in my hand, my new briefcase at my feet, it was my first day. A group of exceedingly smart-looking young men and women sat looking at me and I crumbled. I broke down without saying a word. I didn't return.

A few months later I caught Herr Blundell in the courtyard after walking Miriam to school.

'Herr Blundell, is it?' I called.

'Herr Winter,' he said formally.

'I apologise about how I left your office, you must think me terribly rude. I'm afraid you startled me and I didn't know what to say.'

'That's fine. I'm used to talking about it now, I suppose.'

'You were mistaken though, I do not know what you went through, not at all.'

'That's okay, people deal with trauma differently. I should have been more sensitive.'

'No, there's nothing to be sensitive about,' I pressed. 'The reason I stopped you today was . . . well, is that job still on offer?'

'Yes, of course, please call me Peter.' He extended his hand out to me. And it was 'Peter' until his retirement. I was a pall-bearer at his funeral, two months before carrying Emilie's casket up the same aisle. I worked at the school until my retirement and to all intents and purposes had a full and happy life.

That is, until I thought of Frieda.

MIRIAM

Christmas passes and she thinks of Eva, of freedom and of living a life; her life.

On the day her father is due to transfer to the hospice, Miriam takes four codeine tablets and heads straight for Mum's room.

The smell of memories overwhelms her, but with some sense of purpose she starts by packing away the dresses. Taking each out she lays them on the bed, and sorts them to go to the charity shop – they are too good to be hidden in a wardrobe forever.

Once Mum's wardrobe is completely empty and the shoeboxes arranged around her, she opens the drawer and finds a pair of silk gloves. The silk threads soothe her inflamed and volatile skin, so much so that, in her narcotic-induced state, she feels sure she will never take them off.

She also finds Mum's apron, folded and pressed into a drawer. She unfolds it and places it over the kitchen door. Where it should be.

She takes two more tablets, emptying the pack, and goes to bed, only waking up to a knock at the door. The codeine has yet to wear off and the effect has given her the feeling of a heavy rug across her shoulders.

Like a hug, but better. A hug that doesn't want to let go. She holds on to this feeling for as long as she can.

'Hello, Hilda.'

'I can come back another time. I just have a few things to collect.'

'It's okay. Come in,' she says, although she is aware she is slurring her words a little.

Hilda moves and talks at quick-fire speed. 'Seems to be responding; stable; physio in the hospital.' Miriam watches as she deftly collects the deflated air mattress and other medical bits that have littered the room.

'Dad shouldn't be in hospital, especially after you know he was in a concentration camp.'

'I know. Oh, Miriam I am so sorry, if there was anything I could do,' she says and stops moving.

'You could have backed me in that meeting. Said that Dad could stay here,' she says and rubs at a fallen tear as it slides down her face.

'You don't look well,' she says.

'No. So that's it, as far as your visits go?' she asks, and as Hilda is about to walk into the hallway Miriam stops her, not wanting to be alone. 'You called Axel.'

'He called me. He said you two had patched things up after the meeting and I needed to get a message to you.'

'He met me at the hospital.' Choosing her words carefully, she says, 'He *assaulted* me. I spoke to the police and . . .'

Hilda is looking at her cautiously.

'They call it *sexual assault*,' Miriam says, trying the words out and flushing scarlet.

'I—' Hilda begins, but Miriam doesn't let her finish. Her voice slow and methodical, she continues.

'I trust people, but everyone believes Axel. Not me. He hurt me. He continues to hurt me and no one cares. I am not crazy. I told the police everything. Dr Baum is wrong,' Miriam says.

Hilda interrupts, 'Problem is,' she says, 'you have a noted medical history of psychotic episodes, paranoia, self-harm.' She looks pointedly at Miriam's hands, which are covered in white silk gloves. 'And your husband has been a registered carer for you,' Hilda continues. 'And you were filed as a missing person after you left him in Wolfsburg. It was all on your file. I should have looked.'

'None of it is true, Hilda. You did the right thing. You helped me to care for my father. You helped me make up for some of the things I have done. I am not mad. I will prove it to whoever listens. I am sorry.'

'Can I ask you, why do you think Axel is doing this? Because I would really like to believe you, but it doesn't make sense. Why go to these lengths? What's the purpose?'

'I wish I knew.'

'What are you going to do?'

'Eva says I should divorce him, but I don't really know, keep away, I suppose.'

'Who is Eva?' Hilda asks and Miriam realises that she has no idea.

'A friend,' she says.

'Any further forward with the letter, in the dress?' Hilda asks.

'No. No. I don't think so. I think . . .' Miriam rubs the silk glove across her face and is greeted by the faintest smell of aloe vera from Mum's Atrixo hand cream. 'I think maybe I am lost. I don't know anything anymore.'

'Do you not think you may need some help? I'm not talking medi-cations,' she says. 'Just someone you can trust, talk to even?'

'I can't go back to Axel. He is a very bad person to me, Hilda.'

The honesty of her statement holds true in the air and Miriam, coming out of her fog a little, feels better. 'He is a very bad person,' she repeats.

'There are other people you can trust, Miriam, not just Axel. What about Eva?'

'She doesn't trust anyone, either,' Miriam says petulantly. But in the back of her mind she thinks, *Eva trusted me*. Miriam continues, saying sharply to Hilda, 'I trusted you and *you* called Axel!'

'He called me,' Hilda corrects. 'I am so sorry, Miriam, really I am. I should leave now.' Hilda turns to go.

Alone and clearer in thought, Miriam walks to the table and all the letters. She picks one up and places it back down. She paces the house, trying to find some cohesive thoughts. Remembering her harsh words with dismay. This will all end, and soon. No more Eva and soon no more letters, no more Dad. But there will always be Axel . . .

And with Eva's words in her head and Frieda's voice in her heart, she completes the paperwork from the solicitor.

She puts the radio on and checks the door multiple times before she trusts herself to sit and pick up a flaking, thin letter, almost brown at the edges, and the counterpart Eva has transcribed, attached.

> *Henryk*
> *Twenty-five days later, I am told, I have returned to the light. I am held now as I held Hani. Hani is better and she tries to warm me, nothing can warm me now. I am very near death. I can feel it. I cannot write again, I have Hani and Eugenia at my side.*
> *I love you.*

Miriam reads back and over again. The previous letter was about rainbows. She looks through the pile, this one is numbered in sequence. She looks to the next for explanation.

A knock at the door makes her jump. She expects it to be Eva. She raises the letter in her hand as a greeting, but she sees two male police officers, in pristine blue uniform.

'Frau Voight? Can we come in?'

She opens the door wider and drops the letter on the mantel. They smell of men, a smell that conjures the image of a mechanic's workshop:

of denim and wood. They are both holding their flat hats in their hands as they walk in, their heavy boots making imprints on the pale carpet.

'This is Officer Snelling and I'm Officer Nikolls,' says the older one. 'Can we sit?'

Miriam motions to the dining room chairs as she perches on the edge of another one.

'Our colleague, Officer Müller, advised us of the' – he reaches into his jacket pocket and pulls out a notebook, flicking through the pages, he removes a pen – 'attack. The attack you sustained on the twenty-third of December.'

Miriam looks to her feet, clad in tights, her toes covered in silk.

'We spoke to Herr Voight this morning. What with Christmas and you not answering your phone, we thought we would do this the old-fashioned way.' He smiles showing large teeth. 'Herr Voight has an entirely different version of events.'

'Of course he does,' she says.

'Would you be able to go over what happened in your own words?'

'Do I have to?'

'We could get a female officer to attend, if you would feel more comfortable. That won't be until tomorrow, though, I'm afraid.'

She shakes her head.

'He frightened me.' She swallows hard as the younger officer, who hasn't uttered a word, takes out his notebook and makes notes with a scratch of his pencil. Officer Nikolls looks directly at her. She talks to her toes. 'He twisted my arm and pushed me into the corner, behind a cabinet. He tore my clothes and forced me to the ground. You have the rest?' Her face feels hot and she looks at Officer Snelling making notes. He nods without looking up.

'Thank you, Miriam,' Officer Nikolls says. 'But I need to tell you that your husband states that at around seven p.m. he received a call from you inviting him to meet you at the hospital. Did you call him?'

She swallows a lump the size of a mountain and runs her gloved fingertips across her lips.

'He has phone records to prove that a phone call from this address was answered by him and the conversation lasted the duration of three minutes.'

'Yes, I did. I wanted to find out where my dad was.'

'What do you mean?'

'He was meant to go to the hospice, but he didn't get there and I called Axel because I thought he might know.'

'Why would you think Axel would know? It says here you have been separated a month, was he in contact with your father?'

'No. My father is dying. I assumed when my father was missing that Axel had been involved. He's . . .'

'Your father was missing?'

'In the ambulance, they took him to hospital, not to the hospice, as he was unwell.'

'And the professionals didn't tell you. Did you try to contact them?'

'Yes, and when I found out he was at the hospital I went straight there.'

'Did you inform Axel you were going there?'

'No.'

'How did he know where to meet you?'

'Hilda, Dad's nurse, told him.'

'He says you asked him to meet you?'

'Did I?' Miriam thinks, what did she say on the phone? She remembers holding it tight and the bite of his smile heard through the phone line. She shakes her head. 'I wouldn't have told him to meet me. I am sure.'

'When we spoke to Herr Voight he said you and he like to partake in "risqué" sexual interactions.'

She sits back, stunned.

'Sometimes in public areas. Sometimes, quite . . .' He looks through his notebook again. 'Rough. He maintains that you did have sexual intercourse, but that it was entirely consensual and initiated by you.'

'That is not true, he hurt me. He always hurts me.'

'And we have the hospital report that shows this. However, it is your word against his, so this becomes a domestic dispute. As such, our involvement tends to escalate these situations. And the problem here is that you are husband and wife. It would be hard for a solicitor to make a case when there are previous relations between the two of you. I presume these relations were consensual in the past?'

Miriam nods. 'But not for a long time,' she whispers, then louder to the officers: 'If he were not my husband, you'd call it rape, right?'

The younger of the officers clears his throat, and scratches at day-old stubble on his cheek. 'Did you clearly say no?'

Like the final nail in the coffin, her shoulders slump back in the chair, raising her feet off the ground. 'No.'

'Try to push him away? Physically hurt him?'

'I was scared,' she says quietly and thinks of Dawn's response. Maybe she did ask for this.

'Scream?' suggests Officer Nikolls, trying to be helpful. 'These would be clear signs, you agree? For your non-consent to this specific interaction between the two of you.'

'What *did* you do?' Officer Snelling looks directly at her and Miriam takes a deep breath.

'I accepted it, just like I always do. I just lay there and tried to be elsewhere. I wait for it to be over. If I fight it's worse.' She stands. 'But it doesn't matter. We are married, maybe I did ask for it. I apologise for wasting your time.'

They both remain seated. 'Our job,' says Officer Snelling, 'is to support the community – vulnerable people, like yourself. I think the main issue is keeping distance between you and your husband should you not wish for his assumption to happen again. He mentioned that you have some further challenges, and we have a record of you as a missing person for a time.'

'Yes, well, I do not wish to waste any more of your time. Thank you for coming all the way out here today.'

Finally, they stand. 'Cases like this are complex, but unfortunately, in the circumstances, there is no further action we can offer you. Perhaps your doctor could offer you some support, friends maybe?'

She waits for them to move and follows them out without a word.

'If you have any further questions,' he says, and offers her a card with his details on it.

'Thank you.' As she looks up they are walking down the hall.

She closes and locks the door. She finds the feather on the shelf and places it carefully between the frame before pacing each room.

28

MIRIAM

Miriam runs the water in the bathroom sink and contemplates its still surface, reflecting her image back to her. Dashing the water away, unused, she puts Mum's silk gloves back on. And back at the table she picks up the next letter to read on.

> *Twenty-five lashes.*
>
> *My punishment for morphine, three jars of anti-septic, one roll of bandages, sanitary towels and a tiny wooden carving of a rabbit. All but the morphine made it back to the block. It was the last package. I had discovered the morphine and had hoped this would ease Hani's pain. It was the riskiest thing I had stolen over the course of the week from the abundance in 'Canada'. Bunny had sewn a pocket into the inside of my dress, each item had been hidden there – this was the final one. I had told myself no more, I couldn't risk it. But Hani, cold, in pain, screaming into the night. I had to try and get it for her.*

I got caught.

Twenty-five lashes to try to save my friend.

Twenty-five lashes.

The wooden stool had leather straps. They stripped me and put me in rubber pants. I was forced over it, face down, almost kneeling, but not. It was indented and I held on to it as my calves and shoulder blades were strapped, buckled. Secured. I lost all control, I thought I was going to die.

Twenty-five lashes . . . I cannot remember past ten. The body can endure more than the brain can. My brain gave up. I felt my skin slice open, a searing knife. They were standing around watching; they talked as the skin on my back to my thighs was split.

Scars fade, but what remains is this:

I saw a guard's feet, his trousers had a perfect crease down the centre. I do not know what happened, maybe my blood splattered him. The whipping stopped. He knelt beside me, smelling of cologne and cigarettes. Rust blood. Someone held my wrist and felt for my pulse. I was eight lashes in, eight times the whip had broken the skin. I cannot tell you more than this. I do not want to remember. But the guard had stopped at eight. His hands cupped my chin and turned it towards him, tears and snot and dirt on my face. I looked to him as my saviour. The lashings had stopped.

'Open your mouth,' he said to me.

I did, and he spat in my mouth.

'Continue,' he said.

I remained silent until I passed out, the blackness was a blessing. For is this what it is to be called human?

When I awoke, I was in a tiny room alone. The first time I had been alone in months. I was bleeding, my skin had opened like an envelope on my left thigh, I hurt in every way.

I was cold. My soul frozen, my limbs blue and in shock.

I found my uniform and pulled it over my broken body. I could stand, I checked myself at every step, I was still okay. I could move. The room was four steps by six steps. I could lie down.

A woman in the cell next to me saved me some food, we talked. I cannot remember what we talked of. I slept and I walked and I dreamt.

Miriam exhales, having not consciously done so for the length of the letter. She sits stunned for a long time before spending the rest of the day writing the letters on plain paper in her own hand, merging them with the last of the French letters.

Later in the day the phone rings, reconnected for the call she is waiting for.

'It's Sue here from Ruhwald Hospice, Miriam. Your father has joined us this morning, the transfer went well. He is asleep now and resting, but if you wanted to stop by this evening, I think he'd like that. Would you like me to tell him you will visit?'

'Yes, please.'

The hospice smells of lavender, fresh-cut flowers and gravy. The Christmas decorations hang brightly and the Christmas tree is real and twinkles in the entrance. Everything is either sunflower yellow or deep blue, which contrasts so radically with the red decorations and green tree, the entrance feels like a colour wheel.

She is shown to his room, which has a view overlooking Ruhwald Park. No one asks her to leave. She is given a mug of tea, and biscuits, she even gets an evening meal: a deeply rich leek-and-potato soup and fresh, crusty bread.

The chair is a fabric living-room chair. Miriam raises her knees and reads the letters aloud. She doesn't know if he can hear her, he makes no movement and looks pale today.

Miriam takes time to turn him and offer him water, although he is hooked to many different pumps and monitors. By the end of the day she has read the bundle of letters she brought with her and he seems at peace.

'I won't stay tonight,' she says to Sue, 'but I'll be back in the morning, is that okay? I'll be back tomorrow, Dad,' Miriam says and squeezes his hand, which is warm. And to her surprise he squeezes back. Firmly. And doesn't let go. She perches on the side of the bed so as not to break the contact between them.

She feels more positive on the way home. Recalling the letters, she feels an urgency to get home and get some more of them written up to take to her father, and to read what happens next. She was right not to destroy them, her father needs to know. She walks past the closed solicitor firm and pushes the thick envelope through the lower letter box, it lands on the mat on the other side of the door.

No turning back now.

One way.

Miriam breathes freely and walks home, enjoying the night air, hoping Eva will be there, so she can tell her that she is going to fight back.

No messages and no Eva. She continues reading the last of the letters Eva brought with her at Christmas.

Dearest Henryk,
Losing you without losing you is so terrible I cannot bring
myself to believe you are gone. That we are apart. I didn't
get to say goodbye, although I am not sure I ever could.
For us there is no end, no goodbye.

Miriam looks up, this letter is scrawled over a triangle of paper. There is no end, there is no goodbye. She cannot imagine having to say goodbye to her father. Yet she supposes that this is exactly what she has been doing for the past few weeks. She has been gradually showing her goodbye, her love, her care.

Miriam cannot stop thinking about Eva: why did she choose to stop helping, and what did she mean by 'again'? She feels selfish and stupid for behaving so recklessly. She knows nothing about Eva and yet Eva has been reading these letters too.

Feeling sick at her own selfishness Miriam reads on.

I need you, Henryk. I need to look into your eyes just
to prove to myself that we are true. That you do exist,
because right now I am floating, drifting through a dead
sea with only one outcome awaiting me.

I am doing this all alone. I have lost you, not that I
ever had you. You chose Emilie every single day, and for
the way you love her, I admire you. It reminds me of all
that is right in the world. The feeling of pure joy of your
love. Imparted to others as well as myself. I reflected light
that made me shine, the moon to your sun.

I am forever in shadow.

Just like Louisa. She was bigger and better and
brighter than me. I was always in her shadow. I idolised
her, my parents adored her. I came second.

There was one thing that I wasn't second in though, one thing I could always do. Every winter we would go to the frozen lake and I could skate. I loved the scratch of ice under my feet and the wind blowing my hair. I was free, and most importantly at that time, I was first. Louisa didn't like the lake much, and I was cruel, pushing her, taunting her. I am not proud of myself.

Louisa was worried one day about the ice being too thin. The day was as bright and as cold as snow. I wrapped my blue scarf around my neck, it was long and it floated behind me like a ribbon as I took off. I left her behind, sitting on the bank, pulling on her skates.

'Frey, wait.' She must have called me many times. I was floating, beautiful. I was free from being in the shadow of Louisa. But when I turned back she was gone.

She fell through the ice. She died. And from then on I never left her shadow.

Henryk, you made me feel like I was first, even though I wasn't. You saw me, but you always chose Emilie. I have never been enough for anyone, but Henryk, I always chose you.

If we survive this, can WE survive this?

Because I want you, all of you. War or not, do we exist in anything concrete at all? Or do we just exist on a metaphysical level where souls collide but fingertips remain separate?

Henryk, I wish so much to talk to you. Because we have made something, I am sure. It flutters within me, and after the lashes, to have survived is beyond a miracle. But we have made a baby.

A baby. There was a baby?

Miriam reads and rereads the last letter and spends the entire night sitting up in bed.

Thinking.

Of her own baby.

Of how she grew and expanded, how everything changed. The small flutters to the almighty kicks. The tiny hiccups in the middle of the night. She thinks of all those things, and then she thinks of them in a place like Ravensbrück.

Wrapped in blankets, she cannot feel warm.

29

MIRIAM

The next day she takes the letters to her father, and as she reads further, her mind is on Frieda, pregnant, in Ravensbrück. She recalls all the worries, all the tensions, and how her own body changed. She places those worries in Ravensbrück and, though she cannot fathom why, she cries as she reads, every letter seems to have changed.

Now she reads as a woman who must have known pregnancy and death in the same breath. Every word transforms her into a human, alive. She cries, but reads.

Her father interrupts her. 'Miriam,' he says, and she jumps out of the chair shifting the letters from her skirts. He squeezes her hand tighter.

'My second coming,' he says slowly, 'is at hand.'

'Don't be afraid, Dad. I'm right here.'

He wheezes as she sits by his side, and as she listens to him breathe she thinks of second comings, of second chances, and she picks up a clean piece of paper and writes the address of the editor at *B.Z.*, found on the day's newspaper that flitters around the ward. Miriam writes a letter asking for information about Frieda. She lists Frieda's age at incarceration in Ravensbrück, Frieda's father's name and all the personal details she can recall from the letters. She asks for anyone who knows her, or knew her, to come forward. She encloses her address and telephone number and twenty Westmarks to place the advert. Miriam posts it just outside the hospital.

Finally, she drags herself home, full of words and worries and the past. Heavy on her feet, she walks into the building. She feels darkness seeping in. Two questions, like ivy twisting and curling:

What did happen to Frieda? And where is she now?

The end of the letters, she presumes, is also her father's end too. This is what he is holding on for. She wonders if the advert might yield more answers before she gets to the end, but with some of them still in French and many still with Eva, maybe she will never know.

She shuts the main door behind her and checks it holds fast when she pushes against it. Locked. Lionel must have gone home for the evening. Moving up the stairs at a steady pace, she feels prickles of fear rising with every step. She shakes them away. Although not as mentally unstable as they all would have her believe, she thinks, maybe her father is better off being cared for by someone else.

She cannot shake the sensations of fear and tries to calm her breathing. She thinks she can smell him. That smell of him. Soap and something else. But she knows it's her mind, it plays tricks. She has made the step towards divorce, this will be over soon. She thinks back to the solicitor.

Six months, they said, unless there are financial difficulties, which there won't be. He has his money and she has hers now, well, Dad's.

Six months until freedom. She almost loses her footing on the stairs and grabs the handrail.

'Six months,' she says aloud. Maybe, just maybe, she can manage this. Maybe there is something to hope for.

She grips the handrail harder, seeing her knuckles protruding out of her skin, white. 'Six months.' She pulls herself up the stairs. Opening the door, the feather floats past her vision and she collects its soft, downy plume in her hand. Rubbing it gently in her palm, she relaxes, shuts and locks the door and replaces the feather.

Removing her shoes, she allows her toes time to luxuriate into the thick, soft carpet.

The hospice, like the hospital, has a way of getting into everywhere, and her feet feel swollen and tired. She removes her coat and hangs up her jumper, gathering her handbag close to her she walks into the lounge, switches on the lights to place the letters on the table. She is over halfway into the room before she looks up.

She cannot place what she sees. Her brain scrambles, trying to make sense of the person sitting at her parents' dining-room table. A person who shouldn't be there.

Her bag falls from her shoulder and she grabs it with both hands.

'Like what I did with the feather?' he asks.

She backs away, nudges into her father's chair and sits abruptly.

'Leaving so soon? Aren't you going to ask me why I'm here?'

'Axel?' Her mind is racing to work out how he got in and how she can get out. 'Do what you like, Axel, I don't care.' He looks at her, unmoving. 'It is time to leave.' She steps aside so that he can walk past her to the door.

'Oh, come on. Don't be like that. I bought you flowers and chocolates.' He points to the table where an over-large bunch of lilies lie in their wrapping with a small box of chocolates beside them. 'For the *misunderstanding*,' he says, and runs his thumb down her cheek, tilting her chin up to him. 'You still feel me, don't you? My imprint inside of you? When you walk, when you sit down?' He laughs and she tries to look away but he is holding her chin.

Miriam stands so still she thinks she may have forgotten to breathe. He kisses her lips softly. And for a millisecond she thinks about launching herself at him. Ripping that smile off his face with her broken fingernails and pressing her fingers into his eyeballs.

He must sense the wave and steps back, pulling an envelope from his back pocket. A white envelope, folded in two. The way he holds it means she knows exactly what is inside.

'You promised,' she says. 'You promised you'd get rid of *them* for me.'

'And you promised to love and obey me.' He smiles and dangles the envelope just out of reach.

'It was important, to know they were gone. You kept them? All this time?'

'Can't throw everything away that you used, now, can I?'

'Those were . . .' she stutters. 'Different.'

'Oh darling, have I disappointed you? I just thought, now you are *healthy* again you may want them back. A memento, if you like?'

'I don't want them, Axel. Leave.'

'I wasn't staying long. Evidently you're not in the mood to play nice. Enjoy your evening, Mim.'

Her attention is on the envelope as it hovers above her head. Miriam feels disorientated, the envelope has the same effect on her as a hypnotist's watch.

He looks at her and then back at the table. He places the envelope against the huge bouquet. It rests slanted on its crease against the black paper of the flowers. He taps two fingers on the table before turning.

'Hmm?' he says, as a question, an expectation. Long and slow he strides back to her. She waits. The smell of him conjures images she is unable to stop. The pain, the endurance, the fear. Just that smell and she's back at the beginning. He bends and kisses the top of her head. And takes a deep breath.

'You smell good,' he says.

And then he is gone and she rocks on the spot, left in the bruise of the room. She hears the door open and shut, but doesn't trust herself to turn around in case he is still there and his leaving was just an illusion, a trick. She doesn't want to feel that relief, turn and then see him again, to think it's over, but then it's not.

She waits. Holding her breath, every sinew stretched taut to break-ing point. Every sense crying out for some sign of him. He is still in the air. Stale. The lilies bold and strong.

When her legs begin to tremble, when her toes ache and her teeth groan from the pressure of being clamped shut, she turns, as ready as she'll ever be to come face to face with him.

But the room is empty. She checks through the house, every single room, checks the windows are shut, the curtains drawn back. She feels the same rush as a child might checking for monsters under the bed.

Only this time the monster is real.

The envelope compels her back to the table. She circles it a number of times, straightening the curtains, removing the flowers and then circling back to gather the chocolates, putting both items in the bin, until all that is left at the end of the table is the envelope. She picks it up in both her hands. The weight of the small item feels heavy, and its heaviness is comforting. It is time, she thinks.

She walks to the bin and opens its lid. The faces of the lilies look up at her, she looks at them until they morph into open-mouthed snakes. She closes the lid with a bang.

In her bedroom, sitting on the end of the bed, she opens Axel's gift. A rush of excitement floods her as they tinkle on to the bed sheets. She puts the envelope down. She licks her lips.

The scissors have landed open on the bed, their gold handle and the screw in the middle, faded gold, almost white. Their blade sharpened to a point. Scissors that were hers; never to cut paper or thread, but to cut away at her own pain. She only ever used these, something about their beauty and size and precision. These scissors were hers and hers alone.

She draws up her blouse and sees the scars along her inner arm, an eclectic design.

She takes the scissors and opens them into one long blade. The room becomes fuzzy around the edges, she feels held in time. The point, gold, presses into her pale skin.

Scratch. She flattens and then slides the blade, and everything oozes out.

Red.

She breathes fresh air, as if she is no longer drowning. She places the scissors back into the envelope and takes them to the dining-room table and puts them next to the letters from Frieda. It doesn't take long for the pale skin of her arm to throb, for her to feel again, and as soon as that ache returns she wants to grab for the scissors and take them further, deeper, to allow the thoughts to disappear, maybe for longer this time.

She turns on the radio in her father's room and the living room and his study. She switches on the TV and the nine o'clock news is in full swing with images of Brandenburg Gate and how East and West will celebrate the new year as a united country.

The apartment is full of noise as she sits, pulling out the scarf Eva gave her, weaving the fabric over and across her fingers, in and out. Over and over again. Her entire body exhausted, spent and sated. She feels heaviness in her limbs, as if part of the furniture itself. Her bones turning into the wood of the olive chairs. She guides the scarf over her forearm.

She thinks of Eva.

Eva caring for and bandaging her fingers. The fingers healing, scabs rising and not being picked apart. The fabric is kind on her skin, she misses her.

When sleep evades her, she gathers the feather from the hallway and places it in the envelope with her scissors. She tries to quell the discord within her. Apathy, yet the desire to place the beautiful gold metal against her skin again. Knowing the scissors exist, their exquisite point tucked away alongside her flightless feather . . . she gathers the next letter, content to be swallowed up in Frieda's story, to forget the power of her own hand.

Henryk, I'm scared.

You exist within me, literally, now. I cannot tell you in person that I am carrying a child. Your child. I felt it stirring in the dark, it was my only light. Each flutter of movement bringing me closer to the world, bringing me back from the depths of my own hell.

Yet our love made something. How long I can keep it growing I do not know. Whether we survive this is doubtful.

My future is bleak. I have no idea what to do. I cannot tell anyone either, I would endanger all around me. And Hani, whose womb was blackened and removed with steel, having mine ripe and growing life?

I cannot do that to her. I need her, I need her so much right now, because she KNOWS that I am selfish and cruel and she sticks beside me anyway.

I hold on to her body, alive and holding mine, and I hope you have someone to hold you.

Miriam feels the familiar sensation growing from behind her eyes. She can smell hospital, she can smell Axel and she can feel the baby inside her. The weight, the tiny hiccups, and the kicks that made her feel whole, somehow.

She stands and walks the room. *I hope you have someone to hold you*, and he did. He always did. Her father had Mum. They were together.

They visited her, just after it happened. Both together, hand in hand. Her father held her tight. Mum dealt with the baby.

They left hand in hand, shoulder to shoulder. Both crying the tears Miriam could not. She sat with Axel's arm around her. A coldness held her, and she felt emptiness so entirely she was almost transparent. The absence seemed to slither then boom, its weight heavier than any noise. And Miriam stuck under it.

30

MIRIAM

She turns up the heating and puts her father's cardigan over her shoulders. His smell brings her back to the present, the letters and Frieda.

Henryk,
We have created something. More than either of us combined.

The child grows strong within me. I forget it exists in moments of the day. I have joined Hani at work at the Siemenslager. The factory is warm and we sit in chairs with backs and arm rests, and wind thin wire over spools. It is good work and the manager oversees us, not the guards, so there are fewer beatings, and above the noise of the factory we can talk in whispers and not be heard.

The baby is quiet in the day, but as soon as I lie down or when I eat – it kicks out and wriggles. I am fascinated by it. I can even see the movements through my skin now. My muscles and fat reduced to bone, however my belly protrudes. It grows. In a place of death there is life. It is strong. I imagine its dark hair and brilliant eyes. Holding my hand, looking up at me, looking like you.

My memories are broken. For surviving now is my only aim, for both of us. I listen to Eugenia and the talk of Allies, the talk of rescue or release, and I believe. I believe that it is possible for us, because I have to survive to bring this child into the world. I have to survive to bring it back to you. For we deserve an ending better than this one.

I hold on to our memories, but they are sand slipping through my fingertips. I hope we can create new ones together.

'But she never did,' Miriam says, placing the letter down.

In the early hours of the morning she gets some sleep and wakes from a heavy slumber. She showers, allowing the water to rinse her skin. The blood still pours from the wound, working its way down her arm like a vein. She sits uncomfortably on the top of the toilet and places four Steri-Strips along the wound which hold it closed, then covers her guilt with a large, white, gauze plaster.

She opens the windows to a bright, freezing-cold morning. Allowing the pungent smell of Axel and the rose-pink lilies to leave through the windows, she places the feather and the gold scissors, wrapped in their envelope, in the bin liner. The plaster pulls at her blouse. A reminder.

She makes two phone calls. The first to check on her father. She is told he slept well and is doing better. The second, a gruff voice answers and tells her he'll be over to the apartment at some point today, he cannot give her a time.

Hanging up, she takes the bag outside, cumbersome and heavy, she places it in the bin and instantly wants to clamber in and retrieve the scissors.

'Morning, pet.'

'Morning, Lionel, how are you?' His big bulk is moving towards her, she has the bin lid open, on tiptoes, undecided. He stands beside her and lowers the lid for her, despite being able to do so herself, but she is grateful.

Gone.

'I'm good, thank you. How is your father?'

'He's holding up,' she says, turning her back to the bin. Turning her back on the past.

'Give him me best when you see him.' He squeezes her shoulder and turns to walk away.

'Oh Lionel, before I forget.' She gathers herself, present. 'I'm having a locksmith stop by today to change the locks. Hopefully I'll be back in time, but can you show them up if not?'

'Sure thing. Your husband mentioned he'd lost his key. Better to be safe than sorry these days, right?' He turns back and she walks beside him into the main foyer. 'When I was a lad, we always had our doors open, anyone could have just walked in. Mind, we didn't have much to steal in them days.'

'You let my husband in?'

'Yes, just before I was getting off home. Was lucky really, five minutes later I'd have been halfway home myself. He had such beautiful flowers, I thought you'd be pleased to see him. He said it was a surprise.'

'Surprise indeed,' Miriam murmurs. 'Lionel, my husband and I are separated. Please do not let anyone into my' – then thinking about what she is saying – 'my father's apartment without checking with me first. Not ever.'

He opens and then closes his mouth and Miriam shakes her head as she walks back up the stairs.

Back to the letters. The next two are written on the inside of an envelope, the waxy strips burnt amber, and covered in writing on both sides.

Henryk,

There is a pressure in my chest. I imagine this is how a lion feels before it releases a roar which shakes the ground. I do not roar, nor do I cry. I cannot relieve this pressure. It builds and builds, then falls away only to grow again but from deeper, stronger, bigger.

Wanda has found a new vocation. There is a block opened for babies, a nursery, where the mums can be with their newborns and still work.

Block 22 holds infant babies, mothers can work and return to feed their babies in their break. They are cared for by the prisoners. Wanda is one of them. This fills me with dread. Parting with our child? I cannot imagine. While it grows within me it is safe. As safe as I am.

I cannot survive what is to come. The death of our child. For here there is only death. No child is born and lives, even most in the nursery die. I listen to talk of liberation and think about walking back to you. Then I see the shadow of Emilie and I know that my happily ever after does not exist.

All outcomes are impossible.

I try to survive the day, every day. For it is my hope that I see you again. A small foot nudges me from within and I am reminded that you exist, that we exist.

Until tomorrow.

She picks up the next letter without pause.

Wanda looks at me as if she knows. She talks of bowels, bowls and bread. She bores us with detailed descriptions of them all. The value of a bowel movement entrances her as if we were babies again.

But every now and again she looks at me, maybe it's just my perception of her look, how I am interpreting it, but it's different, as if she knows.

She has changed in the past weeks while I have been recovering from the bunker. Since starting the job she has told stories, stories that had they come from anyone else I wouldn't have believed.

A three-kilogram baby born. A mother given a glass of milk at birth. A mother washed and cared for during her delivery.

Eugenia covers her eyes and pretends to sleep. She cannot believe that things are changing, that there is some humanity in this place. She cannot believe it to be true. She cannot let herself have hope. Block 22 disproves her belief that all Nazis are monsters.

Eugenia and Wanda are at war over Block 22. Some days no peaceful words are passed between them, yet under the words and tensions there is utter devotion.

Wanda talks of nurses and caring for babies. She talks of the cloth they are swaddled in, paper as nappies. Mothers queuing up to see their babies in their breaks. She talks of holding them, soothing them, she talks of chubby hands, rosy lips, healthy newborns. Every word like nectar to my soul, soothing my worries away. I pray she is right.

Three kilos?

Miriam's baby had been measured in grams. Held, soothed, but not chubby, not rosy and not alive.

Unable to keep reading the letters, unable to walk down the path that leads to that day, the day she lost him, Miriam goes out to meet her new solicitor, David Abbott. She doesn't check the streets; she doesn't care anymore. David Abbott accepts the hefty cheque she has written and says that Axel should have received notification.

He is stuffy and old and in every respect a typical solicitor; she feels grubby just being around so much handled paper. The floor, the table, the chairs, everything covered in yellowing paper. His fingers, his eyes, his not-so-white hair, all tainted yellow.

She walks home contemplating her name, she had changed it to marry and she will change it to divorce too. There feels some symmetry to it. Like going full circle, back to the beginning again.

In the hospice, she reads more letters to her father, in her own hand the letters are easier to read and she gets to the end of them quickly. She makes conversation with the nurses, she helps to care for her father and he talks, very quietly. Words she cannot understand, but he is talking. She takes that as a good sign; she sees her advert in the paper and holds on to some hope that someone might know something of Frieda.

Finally, back at home she finds a new key on the desk with Lionel and a bright, shiny new lock on her door. Inside, on her dining room table, the invoice is folded over. Beside it is a note in Hilda's large handwriting:

Sorry to have missed you. Please call me, Hilda x

The next day follows peacefully. Miriam walks to the hospice, she tends to her father's needs, then takes a bus to the library to find Eva, to apologise, to understand, but mainly to feel like she doesn't exist in a vacuum.

The library is closed.

To distract her hands from pulling the tiny line of new skin apart on the underside of her arm, she walks into shops with garments and bags showcased in the window. Long, oblong bags with tassels and bright dresses in the latest fashions. Miriam smiles as she purchases some gloves, silk gloves, unaware of fashion choices; what she does know is that she is missing colour. She buys a pink scarf, the identical colour to the deepest shade of the lilies. A reminder that she made a choice and she did it alone. And returns to the till with a purple scarf too, thinking of Stella's rainbow.

Her taste for freedom slightly satisfied, she returns home, pours a glass of wine and reads more letters, each one taking her further and further into something that feels inescapable.

> *Stella.*
> *Her blonde hair was dark with dirt, twisted and knotted. In her skinny arms, she held something. I couldn't see what it was. She was singing it a lullaby, the tune to 'Silent Night', but the childish lyrics unrecognisable.*
> *Slowly she lifted her head as I watched her. She saw me and smiled. She held out her bundle, covered in a blanket, towards me. She looked elated, her eyes shone. Bright as buttons.*
> *'Dolly,' she said.*
> *It wasn't a dolly.*
> *It was a baby's dead body.*

Miriam folds the paper back into its creases and places it down on the table.

She remembers the eyelashes, so long and dark. The fingernails, a deep purple, but long, the tiny mop of dark hair. The weight of him heavy, but not enough. Not enough to breathe his first breath, or for her to see his mouth open. Or to see his eyes.

It takes a long time for the words to make sense in the next letter. Her mind flits and flutters back to that night, then draws her back just as fast.

Henryk,

I want to write about Wanda, but I don't know how. After I found Stella with the dead baby, Wanda became lost. Hani helped Stella, she led her by the hand and they dug a small hole to lay the baby to rest.

Wanda started muttering, she mumbled, she lost her bowl. She did not talk to us anymore. She went to Block 22 each day and she cared for the babies.

Wanda smuggled out babies, almost dead babies. Shallow breathing, glassy eyes, floppy, skull fusions visible through paper-thin skin. She tried to mash bread in her mouth and mix it with water to give to them. This did not work. Every morning we had another dead baby to bury.

Eugenia and Wanda had an enormous row. We tried to stop it, the women in the block tried to stop it, the Blockova failed to stop them. The guard hit them both with the butt of a rifle. They were both dazed, but even that didn't stop them.

Wanda kept bringing the babies home. She placed them on her naked chest and covered them with her clothes. She explained to us that the warmth from her heart would help them. It was no good. By morning they were gone.

Eugenia gave Wanda an ultimatum, stop or she would tell the Kommandant. 'The mothers of the babies have a right to see them for the last time, to say goodbye,' Eugenia said. 'By stealing them you are denying them this right.'

Wanda stopped bringing the babies home.

Wanda stopped returning to the block at all.

Wanda was lost.

I tried to speak with her, to help her see sense.

The guards designed Block 22 as a death block for the newborns. The conditions enforced by them would kill the babies. Wanda now knew this, as Eugenia had all along. No access to their mothers, only feeding from famished women twice a day, cold and alone at night.

Wanda spoke of rats and vermin on the babies when they opened the block in the morning. The newborns freezing without blankets or clothes. Dead in their beds. Ten in a row like sardines. Wanda and another prisoner would go through each one of them in the morning, looking for life.

Half of them died, but by noon more babies had arrived, pink and chubby, fresh from their mothers' wombs.

The mothers leaving their newborns in a postpartum fog. A miracle to survive the birth and deliver a healthy child, yet immediate separation caused despair as nothing I have ever heard.

This separation was as good as death for the infants. Yet Wanda continued to go, to hold the babies. Hani is the only one she lets near her. They walk together.

The next letter rolls up and Miriam struggles to keep it flat.

I had a dream that all was lost. I was strapped to a bed, the baby pulled from me. Dead or alive I do not know, just gone. Whisked away. Never to see its face. Never to see your face.

Wanda died yesterday.

She threw herself into the electric fence. We found her there in the morning. The guards were taking pot shots at her back. Her lifeless body hanging by the threads of her uniform.

We couldn't retrieve her for fear of electrocution ourselves. At evening roll call she was still there. We shielded Stella's eyes and walked on. But this morning she was gone. Eugenia is silent, Bunny is silent. Hani and I sit in silence. Stella cries into Bunny and will not eat.

What will become of us?

We sang for Wanda. That is all we can do.

All her family lost before her, all the memories she has of them, dead. And now she has gone and taken her memories with her. With Wanda's death comes the end of any legacy her family had. Wiped clean away.

A chosen death here is an all too painful reminder of where we are all heading.

31

MIRIAM

She writes out the German letters long into the next day and collects them beside the French ones. Knowing she can read them to her father, so he can know. Really know what happened to Frieda.

When she arrives, the hospice is quiet and calm, her father pale.

'He had a visitor today,' Sue comes up behind her.

'Who?'

'Your husband.'

'What?' Miriam is shocked and she leans back against the wall as Sue speaks.

'Yes, your father was not very happy, he had a partial seizure. His left side, arm and leg, shook for a few minutes. We got in quite quickly with the midazolam and it's wearing off now. He's okay, but I suggested to your husband . . . Axel, was it?'

Miriam nods.

'I suggested he not come back unless you are here too.'

'Sue, can you not let him in if he does. Axel, he has a bit of a vendetta.'

'Against your father?'

'Against me. He's belligerent, he won't give up.'

HENRYK

'He's belligerent, he won't give up.' I can hear Miriam's voice. He was here, I want to say. That *man*. He told me what he was going to do to my little girl. But the confines of my inert body cannot let me move.

I want to battle, to shout, to scream, to move in any way to stop him. I could feel the pressure moving through my chest and into my head, a scuttle of beetles. I wanted to explode just so I could stop hearing his voice. His words. So I could get to Miriam.

I am imprisoned in this body. The nurses gave me something. The taste so strong, like peppermint, cherries and bitter too. Everything grew wobbly and flat. I was back on the bed, Axel had left and I knew I needed to tell Miriam.

But I had no way of doing so.

Miriam grew up so fast, I'm not sure I realised this until I was sitting in a too-loose tux, in a freezing cold church. Miriam at the altar in a white taffeta dress, violets in her long, dark hair. My little girl had grown up and I hadn't noticed.

She left the house in silence, and Emilie and I both pined for our most precious daughter in different ways. Emilie was always at Miriam's house, but I couldn't go. I saw the look in Axel's eye and I wanted to take her and run away. Emilie thought differently, and Miriam's relationship grew with her and stagnated with me. So that when I did see her I could see the change. Her downcast eyes, checking with Axel before opening her mouth. I saw it all too clearly, but when I spoke to her about it, she wouldn't listen to me.

Emilie didn't see it, Miriam didn't see it, but I did.

After years of living down the road and after Miriam lost the baby, they moved to Wolfsburg.

Axel and Miriam were moving away, together. I hoped that I could go and see them. I offered to help, but all my approaches were denied. It was the move that stopped Emilie talking to Miriam. She went there once, unannounced, and was turned away. She required an invitation, but none came. The phone calls became less and less.

Miriam had been in Wolfsburg a year when Emilie got sick.

Miriam didn't come home, she stayed away. I hadn't heard from her, not once. In the whole time Emilie was ill, then when she was dying. I sent letters, I called, but I was just as powerless at keeping Emilie alive as I was at finding Frieda. And Miriam wasn't there.

She missed the church service for Emilie.

At the wake, I saw her across the busy room. I went to go to her, but Axel stood in my way.

'Don't think that's a good idea, do you?' he said, and I don't remember what I had thought, just that my daughter was in pain. I was in pain and with only one wing each, crippled by the loss of Emilie, I thought we might hold each other up.

Axel placed a hand on my shoulder and steered me to a bar and ordered me a drink. A glass with a small amount of brown liquid was presented to me.

'I don't drink,' I had protested, but he insisted and he was hard to refuse. I cannot remember why or what he said, but it was like a trance. I did what he said and regretted it later.

The threat of unknown consequences enough to drive you to actions that are not your own. I knew Miriam was in a lot of trouble, but I couldn't find my way around Axel to her.

'She's struggling, obviously,' he said, close to my ear, and I turned to see her sitting looking lost, pulling at the sleeves of her clothes. 'You have to admit you weren't close.' He was probably right, I thought.

'She's a bit upset with you, to be honest?' he said, placing a hand on my shoulder.

'Why?'

'I think she has it in her head that you . . . well, the stress of Emilie always working so hard, and looking after you when you were . . . indisposed.' He raised an eyebrow as if I should know what he meant.

Then something shifted into place and everything came ratcheting down on me.

Axel continued, 'I think Miriam is upset because Emilie, well, maybe she could have had an easier life?'

'Miriam blames me?'

'Blame is a strong word. Give her time and if she wants to, she'll come to you. A bit of time,' he repeated.

The alcohol was rushing through my head and of course I was to blame, I had caused Emilie so much hurt and pain. I could never take any of that back and Miriam knew that too. I watched Miriam over Axel's shoulder as he talked. I couldn't turn away from the wilting flower my child had become. Axel talked nonsensically then about grandchildren for me in my dotage, but I couldn't imagine a future where my daughter would want to be in the same room as me. And then they were gone. I hadn't even spoken to her.

My daughter.

After that when I tried to call it rung out, and the post was returned, unopened, to sender.

MIRIAM

She goes home to pack a bag.

She feels the release as her teeth break the skin and the blood oozes across the white nail bed.

She places her white gloves over her ripped fingers, then goes to the letters, only five remain.

Miriam plans on packing them, but instead she is drawn in to reading just one more letter.

> *Henryk,*
> *The transports happen more and more frequently, lists calling people up in the morning who are gone by the afternoon. No one knows where. Everyone fears the lists. We are all treated the same, so many women, a collective. Yet when they select we are individuals, one number means nothing, another death.*
>
> *Hani and Bunny have sewn all my letters into Wanda's spare uniform. They did this as a gift to me and I am never more relieved that I write to you in French and German so they do not know what I have written. But they are hidden in a dress now, where once they were*

stuffed under the mattress. Hani and I share the spare
dress, for it keeps away the cold.
The weather has turned.

A knock disturbs Miriam and she opens the door, hoping to see Eva. The intercom buzzes. Momentarily distracted by the noise she glances to the phone. A foot blocks the opening and a push from the other side pulls the chain to its maximum with a 'ching'. Miriam pushes against the door, but it won't close. She takes a few steps back and watches the chain, so bright and new, as it grips to the door. A foot leaves the gap and she moves forward to try and shut it.

The chain slackens and the door bursts open with force as Axel propels himself into the flat. She's off-balance and falls back against the wall. His smell washes over her in waves and she breathes through her mouth, trying not to taste his warmth. He closes and then bolts the door. The carpet thick under her feet she steps back, her toes sinking into the thick pile trying to find some leverage, something that will keep her rooted to the spot.

'Divorce?' he laughs. '*You* want a divorce?'

She knows fighting makes things worse. She knows he loves it when she says no, when she fights, but she cannot just roll over. Those days are gone, she hopes. Her body starts quivering like a drop of water poised to fall.

'Yes,' she says. 'I am divorcing you.'

'Oh, no Mim, you are going into the hospital.' He moves closer to her, but she stands upright, as tall as it is possible for her to be.

'As soon as I can get you there. I chose you, of all the women that were available to me, I chose *you*. You belong to me. See this?' He lifts his hand and the movement makes her flinch back as if hit. His wedding ring, gold and worn, catches her eye. 'This means you are mine.'

'No, Axel. I'm not.' And she takes a step towards him to try to make him move out of her way, but he remains static and she has just walked closer to him. She doesn't move and neither does he. He has a smile on his lips. A smile that doesn't touch his eyes, a smile that is as dangerous as a threat.

'Please leave,' she says. He lowers his head, then bends his face into her neck, he breathes into her ear, long and slow, like a whisper, a promise. She tries not to flinch.

'Leave,' she says again, but the quiver in her body shakes her voice too.

'No,' is all he says. 'You can leave, of course, I won't stop you.' Then he bites her earlobe hard, she jumps as if electricity runs through her veins and he laughs. 'But where would you go? You have no one now.'

And the truth of the statement hurts Miriam more than she thought it could. 'The fun I'm going to have with you before you get shipped off.'

'I'm not going anywhere, the doctors . . .'

'Will be lining up to sign the forms themselves.'

'I'm not mad.'

'Not yet, but see these?' He holds a bag with a few jars of something in his hand, it wobbles around so she cannot get a good look at it. 'You'll be in such a comatose state, not one doctor in the country will disagree with me.'

'What is that?'

'Your father's medications, from the hospice,' he says with pride.

'You want to drug me?'

'As if this is a new thing to you?'

She waits, hoping she'll comprehend what he is saying soon.

'I wasn't ill in the first place, was I? Why? What did I do?' she says.

'I did what any loving husband would do,' he says with such loathing she recoils. 'Come on, Mim.' He nudges her shoulder. 'Fight me.' She stands still and looks at the skirting board in the kitchen, focusing on the dust that has accumulated on it. 'Come on, you whore, you want it, that's what it is, right? Let's play, just like we did before you left.' She shudders, 'Ah, you liked that, right?' He gently guides her into the lounge.

'Leave,' she repeats.

'Look.' He reaches into his pocket and pulls out some polaroid photos.

She looks away.

'This is my favourite one, do you want to see?' He moves her head, holding her by the chin. 'Look at you beg for me.'

She can see the image of herself and she tastes bile in her mouth. She turns her gaze away as he examines her in the flesh against the picture. 'Hmm, things seem to have changed a bit.'

He takes a step away and puts the picture back in his pocket. Placing his jars of drugs on the table he pulls out a dining-room chair and sits on it backwards. Resting his arms over the back.

'Wife,' he says quietly, then gets up and moves the chair around. 'You look so very sad, come to me and tell me what's wrong.'

She doesn't move.

'*Now.*' He shoots spittle and words together and without wanting to step forward, she does.

'Sorry, Mim, you have to know how hard this has been for me, with you so *unwell* and me alone, day and night. Well, you know what I get like. It has really been the lowest ebb for me without you. Do you forget so easily?' His face softens and he rests his head on his arms.

She considers his face, like looking at oneself in the mirror: at a glance the reflection holds familiarity, but the closer she gets, the more she can see the changes, until he becomes a blur.

Abstract shapes of light and dark.

When she refocuses on him, his eyes are almost kind, open and damp at the edges. But it is an illusion, this kindness, caught like a freeze-frame in a flash of lightning, and in its wake, the thunder.

'Forget who was there with Michael.'

At *his* name, she stops. Stops thinking entirely, blank.

'You forget who cared for you, who brushed your hair for you, who dressed you, who stopped the "counsellors" from sinking their teeth into you. You forget so much. You forget him too, do you?'

She shakes her head, no. No, she doesn't forget him at all. Axel takes her hand in his, it's clammy and warm and he pulls her into him. He tries to get her to sit on his lap, but she pulls back so he leaves her to stand.

'You remember his face? What we called him? You remember?'

He gives her a few minutes, and she loses herself in the memories of her son. The day she buried him. His tiny body.

He lets go of her hand and claps his together. 'I have a proposition.'

Miriam is reeling at the change of tempo and cannot comprehend where his bright spirit came from, how he changes so fast.

'I will sign your divorce papers now.' He lifts the envelope she hadn't seen in his hand and takes out the papers. 'But you must sign yourself into the hospital, voluntarily. What do you say? That way you get treatment and I know you are safe. Compromise? That's how all the best marriages work, right?' He finds the right page, his pen poised. She watches him, about to give her freedom, and she cannot want him to sign it more. *Please*, she thinks, *just sign.*

'So.' He is quieter now. 'What do you say?'

She goes to say something, although she's unsure what it will be, and when she opens her mouth to speak, 'Why?' is all that comes out.

'Well, let me tell you a little secret.' He pulls on her arm again, but she withstands it. 'Fine,' he says as she won't move closer. 'I am getting tired of the *caring* husband ditty, think I'd do better as the husband to the *mad* woman in the asylum. It's worked out all right for a lot of people before now.'

'You are mad,' she says so quietly it is almost to herself.

'I could always be the *grieving* widower.' He tilts his head to the side. 'That might suit me pretty well too.'

301

And then, suddenly, as Miriam is trying to understand what he is saying, her heart and mind are drawn way too far into the past, to the smell of rain on fresh earth.

He continues at a completely different tempo again, enough to give her whiplash.

'You know when I first met you I was mesmerised. Mesmerised.'

She sways and he grabs her hand, and this time the pull brings her into his lap.

'What do you see when you look in the mirror now?' he asks.

'I don't look in the mirror,' she says honestly.

'Why?'

'Because I hear your voice, I hear your words.'

'And what do I say?'

'You say . . .' She doesn't need to hear the words, she knows them, she feels them. She cannot get away from the sound of rain on the umbrella and she feels completely disorientated. 'Michael,' she whispers.

He speaks clearly and firmly. Monotonous. 'No, I do not say Michael, my love. You have faded away again.' Then softly, 'Yet I love you anyway. Can you remember how you had such bright, black hair, so long and dark? How I used to wrap my hands in it?'

She remembers the pull on her hair and on her neck.

'It's falling out now, Mim. You have less hair than your dad.'

And it's true, she puts her hand to her head.

'Do you hear anything else when you look in the mirror, any other voices?'

She shakes her head, stands and turns her back to him.

'Turn around, my love, let me look at you.'

She does.

'When I met you, you were perfectly slight and immaculate. Beautiful. Take off your top,' he demands and his shift in tone has her trying hard to focus on what he is saying.

She is still under an umbrella, the rain hammering on its fabric, the white casket being placed into cold, wet, soggy earth. She cannot free herself from the image. She tries to remain with Axel.

'You still there? Seeing him, how blue he was. They say new babies are pink, but I just can't see it; he was almost purple, wasn't he?' He comes over to her and unbuttons her blouse.

'He had eyelashes,' she says quietly, 'and fingernails.' He had slipped from her body; she had never heard his heart beat.

'It's a shame you couldn't have kept him longer. You know, to "term". I think that's what they mean when they talk about guilt.' And he pulls her blouse over her shoulders and down her arms, the fabric feels like ice cubes and her skin goose-pimples at its touch.

'You liked my little present, then?' he asks, lifting her arm in his and examining the large plaster.

He kisses her on the cheek. 'I am pleased,' he says, dangerously quiet. He has a slight stubble, but it doesn't scratch, or she cannot feel it if it does. Then he steps away and says louder and buoyant, 'At least we knew *I* worked.' She's heard that before and covers her breasts with her arm. 'But you. You couldn't keep him, could you?'

She shakes her head. 'I'm sorry, Axel.'

'I know you are.'

Her tears don't fall, the sorrow is too deep. With dry eyes her tears fall from her heart.

32

MIRIAM

Axel walks away from her, leaving her adrift like a buoy without an anchor.

She looks down at her half-nakedness. And places her hands on her stomach, the way she did when she was growing a child. The way she did when it was empty again, and her hands were full of grief that her arms were not heavy.

She remains standing as she hears him bashing around. Waiting for his return with acceptance, he'll tell her what to do, she'll do it and then he'll leave.

When he returns, he sits in front of her and eats nuts, he offers the bowl out to her, she declines. And bends to collect her blouse.

'Just remember, Miriam . . .' He picks up the pen and takes it over to the papers hovering over what Miriam can see is a dotted line.

She can endure this, she thinks, for freedom. She thinks of Eugenia and Wanda, both in agony, carrying Bunny on a chair, the guards watching and laughing. They did it one step at a time, she can do this. Just let him do what he wants, then it'll be over, then he will leave. He folds the paper up and places it with the pen in his breast pocket.

'You used to be so beautiful. But now look.' He points to his lap. 'I can't seem to get it up for you, keep it up, I'm not sure what you've done. I'd never hurt you, old girl, you know that, right?' She nods. 'But at the hospital, well, it's the only way, you see.'

She doesn't see.

'I'm sorry, love. *Miriam!* he shouts and she flicks back to him. 'Sorry it has to come to this.' He takes an envelope out of his trouser pocket.

'Turn around,' he says.

'Axel . . .'

'On your knees. Lie down.'

She does.

She hears a zip undoing, his belt unbuckling, she waits for him. Just as she always has. Just as she always will.

The night she left him, he had made her pay for asking to go to her father. After getting the call that he was in hospital.

Axel had made her beg and he took another polaroid, another damn picture to prove to her she was weak and disgusting and a whore. Begging him just so it would be over.

She knew it was the end, that moment of knowing, it would end. He would kill her, and if he didn't she would do it herself.

In an instant, the past seemed to have cleared and she realises she is on the floor. She changed the locks, she has filed for a divorce, and yet here she is again, exactly where she left.

'No,' she says, thinking of Eva. *Fight back.* Miriam stands abruptly, so he is on the back foot.

'I thought this might make you reconsider.' He opens the envelope and tips paper over her. She shrinks away from it, unsure what it is. But when the paper flies past her vision she knows, familiar yet broken.

'What is this?'

'This is what happens when you leave. I had no choice, Miriam, just know there was no choice. Your psychosis comes from this. This destruction.' But his words fade as she realises what is in front of her.

Her only picture, the footprints on pale blue paper. The photograph from the hospital too, scattered around her.

'You needed to cleanse the house of all the pain. The memory that broke us. You took too much medication, and . . . well, it's lucky I found you, right?'

Suddenly he is too close to her, surrounding her like a swarm of bees, she cannot hear what he is saying or understand any of it.

'Come back to me, my love,' he whispers. 'It's not too late to try again. A new baby, what do you say? You're not too old yet, right?' She looks at all the paper on the floor and up at the man in front of her. He's played his hand, he looks euphoric.

'After Michael,' she says, hushed and calm. 'I couldn't do that twice. There will never be another baby for us,' she says.

He looks confused. 'But we tried for years.'

'I got pregnant six months after Michael. I had an abortion. I had my tubes tied. I was never going through that again.' She cries. 'I couldn't do it again.'

He looks at her. 'Oh, my Mim, what did you do?' He wipes away Miriam's tears with his thumb. He bends and kisses her softly; it's a kiss from the past. She kisses him back, full of passion and pain and loss of their child. Longing for a life she had hoped for.

He kisses her long and slow and deep and moves into her open body, he removes her trousers and she steps out of them. She moves closer in to him trying to sink into a touch she hasn't felt in years; into the love of the man she married; into her own dreams.

He breaks away and slaps her across the face. She steps back, stunned, but he hits her again so hard she falls to the floor.

'You disgust me,' he says. 'You liar. Did you murder him too?'

'Who?' She touches her cheek, the skin tingling like shards of glass.

'Michael. Did you murder him like the other one? Abortion.'

'No! I loved Michael, and you know it.'

'Couldn't have kept him till his time though, you gave birth too soon.'

'It wasn't my fault, I tried. But you remember, before we lost him, that night, what you did to me? You hurt me.'

'And I've not forgiven myself, but the doctors said it was no one's fault. That we couldn't have done anything to prevent it.'

'You shouldn't have raped me,' she says quietly.

'Raped you? *Raped you?* Miriam, I am your husband. Look at you, you are practically naked and throwing yourself at me and look at *me.*' He gestures dramatically. 'I don't want you at all.'

'You just want to hurt me.'

'Hurt you? When *you've* broken *my* heart?'

'I can't hear this anymore,' she says and pulls on her trousers. 'I don't care that I have nowhere to go. I cannot be around you, Axel. Divorce, hospital or jail. I do not care. Anything is better than this.'

She moves to the hallway on wobbling legs then grabs a coat from the rail.

She doesn't hear him behind her. She doesn't see his hand raised. She doesn't see the look in his eye. But she feels his sweaty hand as he grabs the back of her neck, and she feels the door slam her in the face.

'Miriam, Miriam, Miriam,' he says, as she reels from the shock of impact and is turned so she faces him.

Fingers clutch at her neck, she cannot move. Her limbs have given up the fight, and the more she tries to push back against him, the tighter his grip, until a red haze falls across her vision.

'This will not do,' he says and bends so they are eye to eye. Her back is now at the door.

In a millisecond she moves, lunging forward and up, knocking into his nose with her forehead. He stumbles back and blood seeps through his fingers as he covers his nose with both hands. Miriam cowers away from him, up the hallway, away from the front door to her father's room.

Trapped in her own home.

He is dripping blood from his nose, his eyes are black.

'I . . . I . . .' she stammers but no words come out.

'If I can't have you Miriam . . .'

He moves towards her, and instinctively she backs away, but trips over the step to the bathroom. He grabs her ankles and pulls her underneath him. Sitting on her chest he places both hands around her neck and blood drips on to her face. His full body weight is crushing into her. She cannot breathe and although she is kicking her feet and scratching at his hands, trying to move . . .

Nothing happens.

The black of his eyes seeps into her until she is surrounded by his darkness. She cannot see anything.

Her eyes open, yet only black crumples around her.

Her body stops fighting.

Her hands loosen on Axel's wrist.

She drifts away, into the velvet sea.

HENRYK

I could not find a way to really know if Frieda died, in all those years.

I thought of her often, but I saw uniforms. I heard laughter. I tasted flames and human ash. My feet cramped and froze over and my body refused to move. I sat for hours, rigid, my mind willing my body to move, but it would not. My nose burned and my eyes watered, then dried so that every blink felt like sandpaper, drawing blood-tears. Not for anything could I make myself move, even if Frieda was just across the street.

In the end, after years of torturing myself over my desk with maps and memoirs, to see if anyone mentioned her, the radio came to my aid:

> 'We interrupt this broadcast to bring you breaking news that protestors are destroying the Berlin Wall. Although police are present, this is seemingly a peaceful protest. People young and old are using hammers, rocks or bare hands to remove the Wall. No one is said to be hurt, but the Berlin Wall is coming down . . .'

And as if the newscaster's voice melted the chains tying me to my desk, I stood, gathered a few things in a bag, took out the money in the safe and placed it in my wallet and left the house, leaving the key with Lionel at the desk.

But I didn't get far.

33

MIRIAM

A voice shouts at her. A voice from the land, way off in the distance. An enormous crash reverberates around her and the noise stuns her back.

The pressure around her neck falls away. She feels the carpet under her back and Axel, no longer holding on to her neck, sags on top of her. Miriam pushes against the dead weight, but cannot move him. She sees a shadow towering over her. She cannot think straight, but knows that someone is there.

Eva!

Eva lifts the intercom phone over her head and brings it down over Axel again. It chimes, and the splintering sound makes Miriam turn her head away and vomit. Axel's body slumps to the side.

Pushing Axel completely off, she wiggles free.

Eva grabs her under both arms and hauls Miriam to her feet. She sways and wobbles, leans against the wall and slides slowly to the floor.

She watches Eva take off her own coat and wrap it around her. Then wipe Miriam's face with the sleeve of her dress. She can still see spots across her vision, but she is held by Eva's arms and sits stunned, looking at Axel prostrate on the floor.

'Is he dead?' she whispers.

'No, he's breathing, look.'

She sees his chest rise and then fall, with it a grunt. She stands and staggers back, straight on to Eva's feet.

He remains on the ground.

'Shall we call the police?'

'Maybe an ambulance.'

Miriam looks at Eva, whose face is full of worry. 'It looks like you need one, Miriam.'

'I'm fine,' is her reflex response, but Miriam is unsure if she is even whole.

Eva covers her in the coat and buttons it up, then taking her by the hand and elbow she guides Miriam out of the apartment and down the stairs.

She finds herself facing the doors of the entrance hall, looking at the lights from outside reflected a thousand times like stars trapped in the glass. Eva passes her a telephone and mimes for Miriam to talk.

'Operator, what's your emergency?' a female voice says.

'Ambulance,' Miriam croaks.

She watches as Axel is loaded into the back of an ambulance. He has a white blanket over his legs, an oxygen mask on his mouth and blood all over his face, flaky and darker against his pale skin.

She has a blanket over her shoulders and Eva by her side.

'How did you get in?' Miriam asks; her voice is crushed and deep, and very sore.

'I came by the other day, the locksmith thought I was you, and I didn't correct him.'

'You have a key?'

She holds the gold key into the light. 'I'm sorry, I was worried about you.'

'Excuse me,' a paramedic interrupts, 'can we check you over?'

She allows herself to be poked and prodded, she answers questions and the response from the paramedics is that she needs to attend the emergency department, for observation. They feel the tender swollen skin on her neck, her bright red cheek and the lump on her forehead, and say there is a risk that swelling may cause further damage to the voice box, possible head injury.

'Axel went to hospital,' Miriam declares. 'I am going nowhere near him.'

'Well, if you have any symptoms of dizziness, vision changes or your neck feels any worse, then make sure you get checked out.'

'I'll make sure she does,' Eva says to the paramedic.

Miriam takes Eva by the hand and squeezes it between hers.

'Thank you for coming back.'

The paramedics pack up their belongings and say, 'Happy New Year' before leaving.

The main hallway is suddenly cold. Miriam shivers uncontrollably and continues to do so until she is back in the apartment. The smell of vomit and rust is overpowering and Eva goes around opening the windows.

Eva helps Miriam wash the blood off her face and hands. Miriam, feeling exposed without clothes on, covers her arm with the large plaster, but Eva doesn't draw any attention to it as she warms a thick towel. Miriam dries and dresses quickly with Eva's hands helping her button the clothes where her body still shivers. Dressed in layers of T-shirts and jumpers, Miriam places her mother's silk gloves on her hands.

'These are beautiful,' Eva says.

'They were Mum's.'

'Your father never tidied her things away after she died?'

Miriam's hands shake so Eva covers them with both of hers. 'Beautiful,' she says.

'I want to keep them that way, and it seems to be working.'

'Your hands?'

'Yes, they are a bit better, and I stood up to Axel. Eva . . .' Miriam sobs. 'I'm sorry.'

Eva holds Miriam's hands for a long time before speaking. 'I saw his face, you did stand up to him, didn't you?'

'Yes. Yes, I did.' The shakes and sobs do not cease until Miriam is sitting with a scalding coffee in her hands, trying not to spill the contents over the gloves.

Eva collects the tiny shards of paper from the floor without questioning what they are, she places them carefully on the dining-room table next to her letters.

'Where would you like these?' She holds up the bag of medicines.

'I suppose the police will want to talk to me, maybe this is evidence? Leave them, I think.'

'Why would the police come to you?'

'Because Axel, well, he didn't look in a good state. And . . .' She wants to say that they might believe her now, but the tremor of uncertainty pulls inside her. 'You don't think he is dead, do you?'

'No, he'll have a great headache and a broken nose from us both. He should consider himself very lucky he didn't get worse.'

'We'll get into trouble.'

'With whom? He was going to kill you.'

'Will you tell the police that?'

'The police have better things to do with their time,' Eva says, about to walk into the kitchen.

'Please stop, just sit.'

'I can't. I have to do things, get things done, if I stop . . .' She pauses. 'I was very scared I was too late. I saw Axel come in, I buzzed but you didn't answer. Your security guard who thinks he is the fucking Stasi wouldn't let me in.'

'He let my husband in though,' Miriam says, shaking her head.

After a silence that seems to reverberate across the entire room, Miriam squeezes out a small voice and gets Eva's attention.

'What a mess.' Miriam shakes her head.

'Actually, I think you are quite courageous. When I was in jail, after falling foul of the Stasi "intelligence", I was regularly taken in for "routine" questioning. Solitary confinement, sleep deprivation, no light.' Eva takes a long deep breath before continuing. 'Once a month I was taken in for forty-eight hours. It was less after my husband died. I think they were just trying to cement his loyalty to the party,' she says, brushing the word 'party' away with disdain.

'One of these "routine questioning" occasions,' Eva says, 'I really thought I had reached the end, but then I knew something, something bigger than all this.' She gestures dramatically. 'It was as small as a tiny golden speck. Light. It gave me a cause, and I saw that in you when we were at the church tower. You can kill anything if you surround it with a wall.' Eva presses both her thumbs and fingers together to make a circle. 'But if there is a tiny light, if there is hope . . .' She separates her fingers. 'You can survive anything. The letters and finding Frieda gave you a cause, and I wanted you to keep fighting, no matter what.'

'So you told me I was a mouse.' Miriam laughs, but her voice squeaks on the rush of air and they both smile.

'I wanted you to keep fighting,' Eva says. 'I was very scared you wouldn't. Clotilde didn't.'

'Clotilde, your daughter?' Miriam says stunned. 'What happened?'

'I don't know. I don't think I ever will. She stopped fighting. She stopped seeing me, and I never saw my grandchildren again. Filipe was ill for a while, but I think watching his daughter submit to her Stasi husband . . . It was too much. I couldn't save her.'

Miriam turns away to allow Eva the privacy to dry her eyes and gather her composure.

Miriam speaks carefully, 'You saved me though, even though I have done nothing to deserve it.'

Neither woman speaks for a very long time.

'I had a thought,' Miriam says eventually. 'The letters should be in a museum or published, or something, they are such a timeless thing. The women, the stories, shouldn't be lost.'

'They are not lost, they are with you now.'

'Yes, but others should read them too.'

'Maybe. See how you feel after you read them all, they are yours so you can decide. I saw your advert in the paper, about Frieda,' Eva says. 'That's why I came over – you need to read all the letters. I think you will have your answers.'

'Why?' Miriam asks. 'She died, didn't she?'

'I think,' Eva says carefully, 'I think you should read them all and then you can do what you feel is right.'

Eva stands and brings Miriam the final letters. She places them down on the table next to the dress in its bag on the chair.

'But first, let's eat something. I'll make another pot of tea.' She looks at the bag again. 'It's amazing how it survived for so long.'

Miriam hears Eva pottering around the kitchen, filling the kettle, and sinks further into the sofa. Closing her eyes, just for a moment . . .

HENRYK

I was sitting on the bus with all the commuters going from Charlottenburg to Checkpoint Charlie. The black suits and briefcases, the newspapers full of yesterday's news, and idle chat became the noise of my future. I was finally moving and I couldn't help but smile, I even tapped my toe as we were jostled around. I would find out what happened to Frieda, and for no reason at all, I knew that journey would start at the Wall.

I was ready after all this time. To face what I had done, to finally *know*, when a volcano of pain started behind my eyes. What if she was alive? She would look at me and see. See all that I had done.

That I threw people into the crematoria, that I never checked if they were alive.

The volcano erupted into my face, pulsing my skin like magma.

That I did not fight, I did not stand up for what was right.

Cleaving my head.

The heat swallowing me whole, a heartbeat and I would fall deep into the flames. Sucked away with only ash to rise.

To steal some bread, to last the night.
The heat to my heart shivers.
Though so many died. How many did I kill too?
It burns its way down my arm.
So it is over. It must be over.

34

MIRIAM

She sinks to the sea floor, under darkness. Frieda's letters move around her like tiny shoals of fish. A rust-black anchor held tight around her neck embeds her to the seabed. The letter-fish scatter, the anchor rises and her eyes open to a crash.

She sits, suddenly, prepared for what, she doesn't know. The blanket that has swaddled her falls across her lap.

'Miriam Voight,' a voice calls.

'Yes.' Her voice comes out so pinched, she places her hands on her neck, then withdraws them as if hot.

She answers the door and the police officers, the same pair from after the 'incident', are on the other side. Concern etched into their faces.

'Thank heavens,' says the younger, Officer Snelling. 'We were about to break your door down.'

'I . . .' Miriam squeaks, then whispers instead, 'I was asleep.' Her words come out muffled and swollen. 'What time is it?'

'It's early, we are sorry to call on you,' says the elder, 'but I needed to check you were okay and to collate some evidence to investigate the incident that went on here last night.'

Miriam opens the door fully and they follow the same tread, sit in the same seats as before and collect their black notebooks together. Synchronised policing.

'Do you need to see a doctor?' says Officer Snelling. 'I hear you sustained some injury yourself.'

'The paramedics said I would be okay at home,' she stammers. 'I am sorry, my throat is so sore.' She looks around for Eva, but doesn't see her.

'My friend, have you seen her? Was she downstairs maybe?' Miriam tries to look around the officers. The house is tidy, the kitchen light off.

They both look at each other. 'No, haven't seen anyone.'

'We will be quick, if we can. We are here because your husband made a complaint at the hospital. He says you hit him on the head, he doesn't know what with, he lost consciousness, is that correct?'

'Yes, but . . .'

'You called the ambulance, and he was taken to hospital.'

'Yes, is he okay?'

'He has some stitches, a broken nose, but aside from a concussion he'll be fine.'

'That's good,' Miriam says, although not sure what she means when she says it.

'What did you use to hit your husband?'

'I didn't hit him.'

'Who did?'

'My friend, she arrived and she hit him and she saved me. Axel was trying to kill me.'

They write judiciously in their books. 'Can you show me where you were?'

Miriam stands and sways, then shakes.

'Are you okay, Miriam? Have you taken anything? Drink, drugs maybe?'

Miriam shakes her head. 'No, I'm cold. I'm not sure I'll ever be warm again.' She walks them to the hallway, points to where she was and explains that Axel was on top of her. 'He was bleeding all over me.' She looks at the carpet. The beige carpet.

'Why was he bleeding?'

Miriam turns and gestures to the door. 'He tried to strangle me by the door, he bent down, so he could see me. I think he wanted me to die, he wanted to watch me die.' She shivers, not from the cold this time. 'I made his nose bleed, and I ran away.'

The officer, Nikolls, points to where Snelling has crouched at the end of the hall.

'Yes. Then what?'

'I thought about locking myself in the bathroom, but I tripped on the step and he grabbed me, he sat on my chest and . . . and . . . I was about to pass out. His blood was all over me.'

'Then what happened?'

'My friend arrived and hit him on the head, he slumped off me and we ran downstairs and called the ambulance.'

'What did she hit him with?'

'The intercom phone.' She turns to look down the hall again, she sees the place where the phone was, but the space is empty. The four screws that held it poke out of the wall, but the phone itself has gone. Miriam looks around her, goes into the kitchen, switches on the long fluorescent lights that flicker and blink. She turns to walk out and away from the kitchen and bumps into the younger officer.

'Where is the phone now?' he asks.

She doesn't answer, she walks into the lounge searching for one thing. Then his room, Mum's and her own. She opens the study door and it crashes into the bookshelves.

'Where is the phone?' The older asks her. Miriam opens the front door and checks down the hall. Nothing.

'Wait a second, Miriam, please come back inside.'

'It's gone,' she croaks.

'It's okay. Come back inside and we can talk further.'

She turns and sways down the hall in a daze, she looks at the floor where Axel had been on top of her.

'Where's the blood?' she asks. 'He was dripping blood, it was all over the carpet, here.' She points.

The younger officer bends down again and touches the carpet, 'It's damp,' he says and lifts his fingers. He looks to the senior officer and then back to Miriam.

'When did you clean up?'

'I didn't.' She pulls her glove off and scratches at her hand, palm to wrist, deep scratches that pull the skin and tear at the air.

The officer places his hand over her own. 'Come back inside and let's start from the beginning.'

'I didn't, I changed and washed him off me. I didn't clean the house. It must have been Eva.'

'This is your friend?'

'Yes, Eva.'

'Eva what?'

Miriam can't remember.

After some time and a lot of questions later, Officer Nikolls, who had kept quiet thus far, says, 'You don't know a contact number, her next of kin is a Jeffrey at the library. You don't know her name. You don't know anything about her apart from the fact she is at the library, and lives around the corner somewhere, has just come over the Wall from the East? She has translated letters to your father?'

Miriam nods.

'Where are the letters?'

'On the table.' Miriam points.

The table shines like a chestnut. A brilliant brown. Completely empty aside from the shards of paper that Miriam recognises with a start are the pictures of Michael, and the bag of her father's medications.

Miriam stands and touches the table, runs her fingers across its smooth surface.

'I don't understand,' she says.

'Let's go back to what happened tonight, shall we? Your husband arrived . . .'

They ask her questions for what feels like hours. Miriam doesn't know what to say anymore.

'Your friend hit Axel on the back of the head?'

'With the phone,' Miriam adds.

'Once?'

Miriam nods quickly. Then remembers that no, she hit him twice. She doesn't correct herself. She thinks of Eva, who saved her. Where is she? Miriam feels jittery and jumpy and cannot sit still.

She shows the officers the markings on her neck and finds it soothing that her voice is so deep and broken and every time she hears herself she knows it happened, she is speaking the truth.

'We will need you to come to the station later,' Officer Snelling says. 'To take photos of your neck, and perhaps with a bit of rest things may make more sense to you, as I am aware it is early and you have had a shock.'

'I am the evidence, right? I am not making this up. I am not ill. I have been hurt, physically hurt and I have a broken voice and a bruised neck,' she says more to herself, a list of comforts: it did happen and it wasn't all in her head. 'They cannot put me away now, can they?'

'Put you where?'

'The hospital. Axel came over and offered to sign the divorce papers if I would sign myself into a mental facility. I said no, I'm not crazy.' She stands and picks up the bag of medicines from the table. 'He said he would drug me, make it look like, I don't know what, then I would be admitted. I'm not crazy,' she says, aware she has said this too much and the officers are looking at each other, again.

'These are the drugs he said he would force on you?' The officer collects the bag from Miriam's hand and looks at the bottles.

'Henryk Winter.' Officer Snelling looks up.

'That's my father.'

'How did Axel get these?'

'He said from the hospice.'

'Your father had medications here too? When you were caring for him?' Officer Nikolls asks.

'Can I take these?' Officer Snelling interjects.

Miriam nods. 'You believe me, right?'

'What we need to do is discuss this with our sergeant, and talk further with Axel tomorrow. We'll need you to come to the station to go over the events of this evening, but I think we should leave you alone now. Will you be okay?'

'Yes,' she says to their retreating backs.

On closing the door, she sees the dust on the skirting board, the light-pink stains on the beige carpet. Eva may have tidied up, but Miriam will clean until the carpet is beige again.

She opens every window and cleans every surface. She sets about making the house look right. The windows open, she hears calls of merriment from New Year parties that have yet to stop. The air is cold and black.

It isn't until she looks at the dining-room table she remembers the letters are gone. But in a tiny mound, the only picture she has remains.

The shiny surface looks foreign now from the sea of white letters it had become.

'That's it then,' she says aloud to the space around her.

She tries to place the little mound of paper back together. But she cannot. She pours the shards into an envelope in her father's office and writes Michael's name on the front. She places it on his desk with his paperweight on top. Returning to the living room she sits, finally allowing the tears to fall.

35

MIRIAM

She sips on herbal tea, checks her voice is audible and picks up the phone. The apartment is pristine, the windows ajar and the frosty breeze clean and cold.

'Hi Sue, it's Miriam Voight.'

'Happy New Year to you,' she says.

'And to you.'

'Is everything okay, you don't sound good?'

'Yes, fine,' she croaks. 'How's Dad?'

'He's okay, no real change, although he has asked for Frieda again today. Is that your mum's name?'

'No, Frieda is an old friend.'

'He's settled and has sat up a few times. He's still very disorientated, but we've changed his feeding tube today, the tube looks horrible on his face, so you'll see that when you next come in. But it'll give us some more scope for better sustenance, think that will do the trick. Poor man has been starved to death. What they do in those hospitals, I'll never know.' And with that Miriam hears a crunching on the other end. 'Sorry, Miriam.' Sue's voice is muffled. 'Just about to have a break and thought I'd have a quick bite, but it's a bit crumbly.' She laughs.

Miriam can't help but smile. 'Thanks, Sue.'

'See you tomorrow?'

'Yes.' But as she places the phone down she cannot think of a single reason keeping her in the apartment: Eva has not come by, she has no letters, she doesn't know what happened. She has nothing keeping her here.

In the outer hallway, she stumbles across a police officer, tall and thin, not one she has met before.

'Miriam Voight?'

'Yes.'

'Would you mind coming down to the station to answer a few questions about the events that took place last night?'

Miriam shakes her head. 'I don't want to,' she starts.

Lionel appears at her side. 'Is everything all right, Miriam?'

'Yes, thanks, Lionel.' She takes a deep breath, the eyes of the officer are hard. 'Will I be back tonight?'

'I should think so.'

'Do you want me to tell anyone where you are?' Lionel asks.

'Only if she comes by.' Miriam doesn't want to mention Eva, it doesn't feel right that she should get into trouble when she was the one to save her life. She hopes Lionel understands.

Miriam is directed to a police car outside with an officer behind the wheel. She has her handbag on her knees and her coat neatly folded over the top. The car is clean and the seats deep. The journey is short, but Miriam feels unsettled and more nervous than she thought possible.

In the station, she sits on a plastic chair. Pictures are taken of her neck, and of her hands, the bruises and cuts, scabs and broken fingernails shine up against the white, so that once the pictures are taken Miriam wants nothing more than to cover them up and hide them away.

She is shown into an interview room and invited to sit on another cold and hard plastic chair, this one grey. The desk in front of her is pockmarked: black cigarette burns, scratches, blotches. The officer's skin resembles the table, and seems to have been around as long as it has. He sits opposite her with a sigh.

Nothing is said for a long time, then the door opens and another officer joins them, a pressed white blouse and blue pleated skirt with sharp, small heels. Miriam recognises her at once. Officer Müller; the officer who saw her at the hospital. She smiles at her in relief when she sits down and places a file on the table.

The officer with the pockmarked skin speaks into a recording device and places it on the table.

'Frau Voight, please can you tell me where you were on the night of December thirty-first between six and nine p.m.?'

'At home.'

'Alone?'

'No, Axel, my husband, he arrived. I don't know what time, around eight, I think. He barged through the door.'

'Barged?'

'Yes, I opened the door thinking it was someone else, but he pushed his way through it, he broke the chain. He locked me in with him.'

'In your father's home?'

'Yes, that's right.'

'What happened then?'

She can't find the words to pave the way forward. Her mind circles.

'Did you talk, argue, eat?' Officer Müller offers her a lifeline and her voice is soft and gentle as Miriam tries to find words to accurately recall the evening's events.

The Rabbit Girls

Miriam speaks directly to her, and although she remains aloof, Miriam hopes she understands.

'He brought the divorce papers – I filed for divorce after what happened in the hospital.'

Offer Müller nods and Miriam takes this as consent to continue and an acknowledgement that she remembers her.

'He said he'd sign the papers if I consented to attending a psychiatric evaluation. He wants me to be sectioned. I asked him to leave.'

'You asked him to leave?'

'Yes, after all that happened in the hospital I realised that to be taken seriously I needed to tell Axel, no.'

'So, you told him you didn't want him in the house, because an officer recommended you did that if he should be difficult?'

'Yes, well, the officer didn't say I had to, but he suggested that I wasn't being hurt because I didn't call out. I've never said "no" to Axel because right from the start it didn't really matter what I thought or wanted anyway.'

Miriam waits for what she is sure will be the past rising, shrouding her, suffocating her. She takes a deep breath, waiting to be plunged back.

Nothing happens.

She continues to speak to Officer Müller, who sits almost completely still. She is young with blonde hair tucked up into a bun and clear skin, her hands are folded in her lap.

Miriam, aware that she is talking a lot and not coherently, continues. The rasping of her voice not only hurts, but each sentence lowers it further. And still she is present. Sitting on a plastic chair, the smell of cleaning agents, stale coffee and smoke. Nothing else.

She feels a little intoxicated by the fact that she said 'no'. She did say 'no' to Axel, and not only that, she also told the police she said 'no' and they recorded that she said 'no' on their device. So that people will hear that Miriam did say 'no' and she meant it. This tiny thing, a speck of sunlight, makes Miriam sit up taller.

'Did he leave?'

'He refused. He said I could leave, but where would I go? So again, I told him to go. I tried to stand my ground. This is my father's and my house after all.'

The older officer in low tones says, 'So you chose to stay?'

'It wasn't a choice. Where would I have gone? Who would I have gone to? My mother died. My father is dying. I have no one. I have *no one*,' she repeats.

Officer Müller passes her a small box of tissues. She tries to compose herself, but she howls instead, her entire chest feels like it is collapsing and her throat feels swollen and worn away to nothing.

An arm appears on her shoulders and Officer Müller bends so she is in Miriam's eyeline; she smells fresh, like linen.

'I'm sorry you have had to go through all of this, Miriam. We only have a few more questions for you. Let me get you a drink. Tea? Coffee? Water?'

Miriam lets out a small hiccup. 'Tea, please, with a dash of milk,' she says, and like a drop in the ocean she realises. She didn't pause to wait for Axel to order for her, or to check with him first. She answered with exactly what she wanted. 'Tea,' she repeats, and smiles.

She isn't alone. She can't be because, finally, she is beginning to know herself. When the officer returns with a tray of hot drinks, Miriam sips hers and warms her hands on the cracked cup.

'I'm sorry,' she says, finding her voice again, her throat soothed from the tea.

'It's not a problem, you have been through a lot.'

Miriam smiles, knowing she has been through nothing in comparison to others.

The older officer starts talking again. 'Back to Axel offering you a chance to leave. Can we go back to that? I'm wondering why you didn't call the police?'

She sees Officer Müller look over at him and roll her eyes, which gives Miriam some confidence to speak frankly.

'Why? He was in my house, doing nothing but talking to me, and you don't know Axel, he's a very patient person. If I call the police when Axel is doing nothing I look crazier than ever.'

'So you stayed.'

'Yes,' she says, and she notices her shoulders roll and her hands wind themselves in the inner silk of her coat. 'Otherwise I'm giving him what he wants. He hurt me in the hospital, assaulted me. He used that, he said it showed my neurosis, how sick I am, he used the truth and turned it into a lie.'

The male officer opens his mouth to speak but Miriam continues, 'Do you know I have been married for over twenty years? All this time with a man who has been set on destroying me. I have lost my job, I have been given medication that made me sleep, some made me swim through the day. Some of the pills made me dribble and drool like a dog, others made my mouth so dry my tongue felt it had been made from sandpaper. This was all him. He made me take those pills and he manipulated the doctors to keep prescribing them. He called himself my carer, took me away from my family, and I was too drugged to notice what I'd lost. So I want a divorce and now I'm sitting here. Will you arrest me?' Her voice breaks and she sips the last of her tea.

'Miriam, this is just an interview to find out your version of events,' Officer Müller says.

'My *version* of events *is* what happened. You know I'd rather be in prison for the rest of my life than with that man. I'd freely go to the mental institute, but for the medications. I can't stand not being able to think.'

'Miriam, are you listening to me?' She stretches her hand across the table palm down. 'You are not in any trouble here. We have seen the bruises on your neck, and the injuries, the damage to his nose, the scratches on his wrists, are all linked to him choking you. What we need to know, and this is serious, is the intention behind the attack on him. He says you hit him with the telephone, is that true?'

'No, I was blacking out, I couldn't breathe, I thought I was going to die. Then Eva must have hit him, because the pressure eased off my neck and Axel slumped off me. It was ages before I could see again and when I did Eva was beside me. She saved my life.'

'How did this Eva get into your apartment?'

'She has a key. I got the locks changed after Axel got into my apartment the other day. Eva has a new key.'

'How long have you known her?'

'Not long, she is an old friend of my parents'.' Although not entirely the truth, Miriam doesn't think twice.

'Where is Eva now?'

'I don't know,' Miriam says.

'Do you have another address for her, a telephone number? She'll need to corroborate these events.'

'Will she be in trouble?'

'I don't think so, but with this type of situation . . .'

'Is Axel going to make trouble out of this?'

'He has made a complaint, yes, but I can't see us being able to pursue this further, seeing as he attacked you.'

'In your own home,' adds the older officer. 'He says he signed the divorce papers and left them with you, is this true?'

'I don't have them.' She shakes her head, overwhelmingly tired; crying is exhausting. She tries to focus, but her tea has made her warm and as the officers speak, she can feel her eyelids close.

'We can see you are very tired, Miriam. We will be in touch.' Officer Müller touches the file in front of her. 'We have all your details. And can you ask your friend to come down to the station, so we can have a chat with her too. Your security guy' – she consults the paper in front of him – 'a Herr Lionel Ambrose, he's stated the presence of a third party, a woman, so it should all line up. But we do need to talk to your friend.'

'Sure.' Miriam stands as the officers do. 'Thank you.' She shakes both their hands and moves on wobbly feet. 'I'm sorry for all the tears,' Miriam squeaks, her voice gone.

'You'll need to check your neck with a doctor.'

As the door opens and Miriam is rustling with her coat she hears a familiar voice.

'I am Eva Bertrandt. I tried to kill Axel Voight.'

Miriam looks to the front desk and there is Eva. Her voice deep and loud in the empty room. In her arms is the intercom phone and she passes it to the officer on the other side of the desk as if it is a baby.

'No, Eva,' Miriam says, but her voice is inaudible. 'Eva,' she tries again, and clears her throat.

She takes a step towards her, but the older officer has crossed the room in a few strides and he ushers Eva to the opposite side of the desk and away from Miriam. Officer Müller puts an arm out to stop Miriam moving towards her.

'She didn't kill him,' she whispers. 'She saved me. Axel's not dead, is he?'

'No, he's at home, resting.'

'Then tell her, please?'

'It's important we listen to her.'

'But she's trying to protect me.'

'Why? You aren't in any trouble.'

'She doesn't know that!' Miriam wheezes a response that is inaudible even to her.

'Go home, rest up and we'll be in touch.'

'What will happen to her?'

Officer Müller steps closer to hear Miriam, who repeats herself at a whisper.

'She'll be questioned.'

'Can I wait for her?'

'No, go home. It will all work out.'

She holds the main door open and Miriam steps through; as she does the door hushes shut behind her and she is swallowed into the late afternoon, as black as night.

36

MIRIAM

Lionel is asleep in his chair, his mouth open, and heavy snores rattle the newspaper on his chest.

'It's a bit late for you?' she whispers, her voice sounding strange and foreign.

She touches him on the shoulder.

'Why aren't you home?' she mouths. 'It's New Year's Day.'

'Oh, hullo pet, are you okay? Thought them officers had arrested you.'

'No, I'm fine.'

'With all the shenanigans going on, I thought I was better placed here today. Well, until all the residents are back. The Smyth sisters are out at the theatre so I said I'd stay late until they got back. What happened with your husband and that *woman* gave us all a hell of a fright. The whole building's talking 'bout nothing else today.'

'I'll bet.'

'And that woman, an Easterner, no doubt. I did say it before, but that wall may have been a blessing, you know. Now that it's down you never know who'll come through it. Your poor husband.'

'No, Eva did nothing wrong, she saved me.'

But either Lionel isn't listening or cannot hear the croak of voice Miriam is using every effort to push out. 'Came by again today, cheeky blighter, after all she's done.' He stretches in his chair and his buttons pull, revealing his greying vest underneath.

'Told her it was all her fault, you see, that you had been arrested instead of her. Bad lot.' He shakes his head. 'She flew off like a cat that caught the pigeon.' He smiles. 'So you see, there's nothing to be worried 'bout now, petal. You get off up the stairs and I'll keep a look out down here. You find that once the police are round, them Easterners scatter. Bet she was a red and all.' He rests back in his chair.

'Lionel,' Miriam tries again, but points to her throat, to mime that she has no voice.

'Oh.' He sits up and looks at her neck where the scarf has fallen loose. 'Oh pet, that looks terrible. She did that too?'

Miriam says, 'No. It was Axel.' But he can't hear her and just shakes his head.

'Look after yourself, Fräulein, I'll be here 'til the sisters come back. They do love their ballet, them two. Goodnight.'

She walks up the stairs, pulling the scarf from around her neck. Frustrated by her lack of voice, she thinks about how to get Eva out, how to help her. The house is dark, she locks the door.

On the dining-room table is the dress.

Miriam switches on all the lights, the letters are in small piles resting on the dress at the waistband, and an envelope of newly translated letters is at the head.

She cannot understand what Eva was doing. Why take the dress and return it? Why confess to something that she didn't do? Perhaps she knows what she is doing. The woman, from the little she has shared, must have endured so much, but still she kept going, and keeps going.

She looks at the stitching on the dress, it's been patched up as though Miriam had never taken her scissors to it in the first place. The letters, for her, are no longer about finding a woman her father loved, but how a woman can survive these horrors. If she survived. What Eva had said makes her think that whatever Miriam has not read will not be easy. It will not end well.

The letters are all in order, she separates the piles, and finds she only has a few left to read. She wraps a blanket around herself.

Henryk,

Bunny, although silent, is a presence in the camp like nothing else.

Half her right leg is missing, severed from inner knee to ankle, it's covered in a blanket, but you can see the tendons pulsing if she moves. Her bone removed. She has only one where she should have two.

To keep her fingers busy, she sews. Patching army uniforms and sewing pockets. Trying to thread flesh to bone again.

She holds Stella like a newborn, absorbing her innocence, her childhood warmth.

We could not have been more surprised the morning The Noise ground the camp to a halt.

When the wail that hurt our hearts more than our ears came from Bunny.

Rabbits make no noise. Silent animals. Until they scream. A rabbit in pain will scream. A scream unlike anything I had ever heard before.

We were walking back to the block with the soup, Hani and I, and we saw guards in our block. We were about to drop the soup, but we carried on without spilling a drop.

'What's happening?' We looked to each other. The Noise entered my body, penetrated so deep. It hurt me inside, like a fracture. I heaved on an empty stomach.

The guards came away with Stella. Her arms and legs thrashing about. Stella was calling for Bunny. Hani and I dropped the soup and ran. Ran towards the sight of Stella being taken.

But we were stopped. A shot rang around and around, a spiralling noise that deepened and worsened as it sang out. Stella was crying, slumped, a dead weight, they were struggling to hold her.

I rushed to her, she grabbed my neck with both her arms. A vice-grip.

'Bunny!' she called.

Hani went past me into the block. I rocked Stella in my arms and watched the door. The guards were talking amongst themselves.

Hani came out shaking her head and joined us where we sat at the feet of three guards.

'Bunny,' Hani said, and wrapped herself in my arms with Stella.

Goose pimples rise over Miriam's skin and tingle at the nape of her neck. Tears fall silently as she reads. 'Bunny,' she says into the darkened room, shaking her head and blowing her nose.

She checks the time, it is late, but the thought of walking in the night no longer bothers her. Miriam places the unread letters in her bag, and goes to the hospice.

The hospice is locked and she waits a long time, listening to the rustle of leaves from Ruhwald Park. Finally, a nurse waddles to open the door.

'It's late,' she says, and Miriam recognises the voice, deeply nasal, as the one she spoke to when she was trying to find her father after his transfer.

'Sue said I could stay,' she says and ducks past the woman towards her dad's room.

'It's late,' the nurse says again, but she has darted in and gently closes his door behind her. With only a small night light above his head, the room is musty with sleep and dark. Miriam unfolds the bed with a creak and a crash of springs.

'It's only me, Dad,' Miriam says. 'My voice is a bit broken, but it's only me. I'm fine.'

She takes hold of his hand and kisses her father on the forehead. The nasal tube is large and pokes out from his nose, he has been shaved again and looks younger.

'I'm sorry about Axel, I'm sorry about a lot of things. But Dad, I can make things right.'

He smiles, an actual smile, and pats the bed with his hand. Miriam perches on it and holds his hand in both of hers, his nails neatly manicured and his skin soft.

Miriam bends to kiss his head and he reaches his hand and places it on her hair.

'Miriam,' he says, patting her head very gently. 'My Miriam.'

She rests her head on his chest for a long time, unable to pull away, not wanting to either. 'I've put a notice in the paper for you, Dad. If she's alive, she'll come. I know it. Until then, I'll read you all her letters, I promise, but please' – her voice breaks – 'please, if she is what you are holding on for, please don't die. *I* still need you.'

When his arm falls heavy, she wipes her eyes and sits in the comfort of the armchair to read the final letters. Unable to push her voice into sound, she whispers the words, like a promise in the dark warmth of the room.

Henryk,
Stella's number was called to transport. Bunny was mur-
dered in her bunk. Hani and I had a split-second decision
to make. We were sitting in the dust. Eugenia came out
to join us. The guards started to try to take Stella from
my arms.

> *Eugenia, Hani and I looked to each other.*
> *Hani and I stepped up with Stella. We held the sob-*
> *bing girl. She was calling for Bunny. The guard hit her*
> *and her tears fell, but her hands were in ours now. We*
> *walked with her.*
> *Eugenia stepped back. She would not make the jour-*
> *ney with us.*
> *We have been unmanned, disbanded and now, yet*
> *again, we are on a journey of unknown destination.*
> *I did not think of our child, or of my life or of you.*
> *Henryk, I am sorry.*

Eugenia stepped back? What happened to her?

She can understand why Eugenia stayed behind. Why would she step up to an unknown when she knows the status quo? That's why she'd stayed with Axel. If you jump out of the frying pan, you may end up in the fire.

But Frieda made the choice and took the risk. She reads the next letter, a tiny, finger-sized piece of paper.

> *When I stepped on to the train with Stella I thought of*
> *her mother, long dead, I am sure, and how I would want*
> *someone with my child when they die. I finally under-*
> *stood what Wanda was doing with the babies. She was*
> *giving them warmth and love at the very end, something*
> *their mothers were not permitted to do.*

The original letter curls back over itself. She picks it up and unrolls it. The paper so small and flimsy she doesn't want to tear it.

> *We held Stella as she sobbed for Bunny; we sobbed for Bunny too. And for Eugenia left behind, and for Wanda.*
> *We held Stella as she shook in fear. We gave her all that we had, food and stories and songs.*
> *Then she became feverish.*
> *We held her hand when she grew cold. Her wooden carving of a rabbit held tight in her palm. Talking only of her 'Bunny'.*
> *We held her when she died. We wrapped her in our love, but we had to let her go. On the transport to 'Pitchi Poi'.*
> *Now it is just Hani and me. We shake and we sob and we scream in anguish at a forgotten world. But we also look to each other.*
> *What next?*

She doesn't want to read on, she doesn't want to know. But she promised her father and she needs to know *what next*. With a heaviness in her heart that ripples back to the loss of Michael, Miriam picks up the next letter.

> *I am now in Auschwitz-Birkenau.*

'You were in the same place?' she says. 'Dad, Frieda was in Auschwitz too. I wonder if you met each other there?' She places her hand in his and he squeezes tight.

> *This is a special degree of hell. Babies thrown into a roaring fire, alive. Mothers and fathers jumping in after,*

*everyone getting shot. Black flakes fall like snow. Ashes.
The chimneys burn here all day and all night. This is
our fate.*

*By some mistake we were neither stripped, searched
nor showered. We kept our clothes, missed the showers and
stayed side by side. We ended up in a line. A red cross is
painted on my Ravensbrück uniform and Hani's too. We
stood for hours in the line, waiting, not sure what we
were waiting for. A man, a prisoner, with a cap and a
striped uniform like ours, sitting solitary, with a needle
attached to a pen-like instrument. He heated the pen
under a lamp, then dipped it into ink, and marked the
skin on the arm with a series of dots.*

We waited and Hani quaked.

'I cannot let them mark me again.'

*'No, Hani, not now. I need you. Stay by me, we will
be okay.'*

*I moved her in front of me, I held her there with
both hands and I talked to her constantly. When she was
in the chair she pulled away so hard she almost toppled
the table, but I kept her in place. It hurt. The process.
They have marked my skin again. This time with ink
and not with a whip. More scars. We are now 72828
and 72829.*

*But my nine is joined almost like an eight and Hani's
eight doesn't join. Perhaps, if you look from afar, we have
the same number.*

*Then we were put in a block with eight women to
a mattress, women on the floor; it is so packed in here
it reminds me of the holding tent when we first entered*

Ravensbrück. Hani and I stay close, we try to understand how this place works.

All I know: it is a killing camp. We will not leave here.

We look at our numbers, maybe they will save us. But we both know that, just maybe, they can only save one of us.

HENRYK

Miriam is alive. She is alive. My baby is alive.

I hold on to that thought as I hear her broken voice; she is hurting but she is alive and Axel failed.

I try to hold on to this, this hope, as I hear Miriam read all that Frieda went through, for me. I can do nothing. I hear it all now. I squeeze the small hand held within my own. I thank Miriam with a heart full of love for the sacrifice she is making. I know this is my punishment. I must hear how Frieda died from the mouth of my sweet child. But not just how she died, the way she was tortured too. And how she loved me, even though I caused all of this.

I dreamed so often that I would throw a body in, waiting for the belch of the flames, then I would realise it was Frieda. And I would tumble and fall, leaping into the pit to find my love and to seek redemption. Because I am lost. And I fear that Frieda will never be found.

Because it was me. It was my name. My name upon her pure tongue. Her life has gone, for *me*.

And I am nothing, for hell has a name, and it is mine.

37

MIRIAM

She moves to the pull-out bed when he breathes evenly and restfully in sleep. She switches on the lamp and pulls out the final letters. First, a letter to her mother:

> *Dear Emilie*
> *Please forgive us. I know you love Henryk, stand proud beside him, care for him.*
> *I hope the diamond necklace bought your freedom. As I gave it to you, I was looking only at him. For if you had left for safety he would have gone with you. He chose you every day, and in doing so you had my love too.*
> *I hope you are reunited, I hope that you have a future. Please love him with everything you are, there is no shame in needing, wanting, desiring and being fulfilled by another person. You don't have to meet all your needs alone.*
> *Thank you for allowing me into your world, even if it was only for a heartbeat. Take care of Henryk and love him enough for the both of us.*
> *Truly*
> *Frieda.*

How accurately the letter reflects Mum and how honest it is. She tries to calm the fluttering in her chest, for Mum never read this, when maybe she should have. Mum was strong, she cared for Dad, she loved Miriam and she did everything alone. She needed to be needed and Miriam – small, fragile, petite Miriam – always needed her. Dad chose Mum, but are the choices we make for others or for ourselves? What if Dad had chosen Frieda? What if he had never had to make that choice?

Picking up the next letter, its original hard to read in the light, Miriam pores over the tiny script, words squeezed on to both sides of the page.

> *Henryk,*
> *I was woken with force. Hani and me in our bunk with three other women. We slept holding the other so that we could stay safe.*
> *'Please hurry. We need you.'*
> *It was a young girl. 'My mama delivers the babies; we need your help. You speak Dutch, yes?'*
> *'Yes, I do and Hani too.' I was fearful of us being separated so I clung to her.*
> *Hani and I went with her, following her through the maze of blocks which are larger here, thousands of people squeezed in, rather than hundreds. I do not know any of the faces, yet I know all of them. The vacant stare. Accusatory: what was it that allowed you to survive, when my mother, sister, daughter, granddaughter was selected? They died and you live. Why? We all do that. It seems involuntary. Trying to assess what makes someone special just by looking at them. It's luck, it's got to be.*
> *We heard the commotion before we saw what was happening.*

A woman, Matka, was holding up her hands, in peace.

A young girl looked at her, wild, feral, she bared her teeth. She was pregnant and she touched her stomach with one hand and placed the other ahead of her to warn others off.

'Mama,' said the girl. 'This is the Dutch speaker.'

'I need to be able to see what is happening and explain to her to remain calm, baby will not come and the pain will be bad if she continues.'

I explained to the girl that her baby was coming, that Matka was here to help, but she started talking in such broken Dutch I was not sure I could make out many words at all.

I looked to Matka. 'I'm sorry, I'm not sure she is speaking Dutch; I cannot understand her.'

'Is Roma,' said Hani.

Hani talked to her. The words passed through three mouths, from the girl, to Hani who translated in Dutch to me, and then from me to German for Matka while Matka's daughter, Sylvie, watched.

The girl was fourteen years old, Elisabeth, she kissed Hani once, twice, three times and said she didn't know what was happening.

'The Germans put something in me, very painful,' she said. 'Am I going to explode, a bomb?'

Hani explained that it looked like she was having a baby.

Hani and the girl conversed and the girl's face changed as she realised what was happening and allowed Matka to move closer.

Her breathing became more fluid. Matka was very patient with her. I watched her absorbing the situation and relayed everything Matka said to Hani who passed it on to the girl. Hani held the girl, comforted her with her touch and it worked. Elisabeth calmed and in no time Matka instructed the straw mattress be placed on the floor.

In a few loud, long moans, a baby was born, blue and covered in blood. My initial reaction was that the baby was dead, but it quickly pinked up and yelled to tell the whole block it had arrived. Matka put the baby into the waiting girl's arms and instructed her to place it on her chest.

She used strips of cotton to tie off the cord.

The girl smiled, a layer of sweat pinpricked her forehead. She looked at the baby and cried; Hani cried, I cried. It was beautiful.

After a few moments, Matka massaged her empty stomach and more contractions started.

'Is there more?'

'No, just the afterbirth.'

It was delivered without issue. Matka placed it in a cotton sheet and she and Sylvie looked it over.

'What are you doing?'

'Checking it is all intact. It's important.'

The baby and mother were cooing, pure exhaustion and bliss all over the girl's young face, and Hani was at her shoulder.

Then Sister Klara entered.

The baby was ripped from its mother.

The baby was a boy.

Sister Klara took the baby by the legs, it hung upside down. Mouth open – wailing.

'Look away,' Matka whispered, but I could not.

Sister Klara left the block with the baby.

The girl tried to get up to follow, but her legs didn't hold her. Hani and Matka supported her under her arms and she staggered towards the closed door.

There are no babies in Auschwitz.

Hani and I walked back to our block as the sun rose, snowflakes curled and fell among the ashes.

Innocence drowned.

We move about our day unable to remove the image of the baby floating in the bucket outside the block. Matka wrapped the baby with the afterbirth and took both away. Leaving the poor girl, the grieving new child-mum, alone.

Miriam feels a knot, heavy and cold, settle in her chest. She tries to breathe around it, but, like the centre of a web, it seems to hold everything together. To pull on a single thread will cause it to fall apart.

Despite Axel always being there, she had been alone after burying Michael, in a world of grief that no one would talk about and that no one could share. Then she shakes the thought away. And views the letter through Frieda's eyes. Frieda, pregnant and *knowing* that this would happen to her.

The next two letters in Eva's handwriting on beautiful clear white paper. The original in French from a triangle of paper the size of Miriam's palm.

To the baby inside of me,
You were made in love, and I have loved feeling you grow.
I will never be able to look upon your face with peace.

There is no future for us, of that I am certain. However, I know that in another lifetime, in another world – we will find each other again. Mother and child.

Loving your father and knowing you, even if I'll never meet you, have been the best and worst times for me.

They say love is beautiful, love is kind, but it is not. Real love hurts, its ferocity binds two people together even though they are bound to be torn apart. Love is cruel.

You are stronger than I ever thought was possible and just by surviving every day you helped me to see the sky, the purity of a raindrop, the flecks in the sun.

Thank you for keeping me alive.

I am so deeply sorry that there is no more than that.

I will never hear the word 'Mama' or hold your little hand. I am sorry that to be born means you will die. Life has no cause or meaning. But know that despite all the chaos, you are loved. And that will see you through – even if only in spirit.

You have been a guardian angel, saving me from my own destruction.

Thank you.

Your Mama.

Miriam wipes the tears away from her cheeks and feels the ball of emotion in her chest. She looks to her father, his sleeping form peaceful, and wonders at the horrors he has seen, and can understand why he chose to leave it all behind.

She knows he would never have told anyone about it, he would have carried the burden alone. Holding on to the pain as his own cross to bear, for not living up to his own high expectations.

'Have you ever forgiven yourself?' she asks aloud.

'None of this was your fault, Dad. It's so deeply sad, but know that you are forgiven for whatever you have done; it was a lifetime ago. My lifetime, and all you have done for me is enough. I love you.' And she cries further. Picking up another letter, she reads the tiny scrawl.

Dear Henryk

I suppose we are finished. I suppose we are done. We only just got started and now we cannot be.

I will not survive this camp. I am not sure I will survive the birth. I was optimistic in Ravensbrück, but here . . . Here they are so efficient at killing, at murder. I know I stand no chance. I pray, though to whom I know not, that I will survive long enough to see its face. The face of our child. I want to see you again; the baby is the only thing left of you that I have.

I miss the idiosyncrasies, the tiny things I can no longer recall. I see you in my mind, but it is just the shadow of you. You will never grow old or fade for me.

I still feel you, your presence, like a second skin covering my own. I miss you. I suppose that if we were face to face words would be superfluous. We would touch without touching, speak without words. A symphony in silence. I would leave this world with the taste of you on my lips. The feel of you under my fingertips, the contours of your face made granite to my touch. If I had known the last time I held you would be the last – I would have looked harder into your eyes, burned my soul into your own. I would have sparkled in the touch of your gaze, shining bright from the love of it.

I will think of you at the end. I have known you and been known by you.

We are living in an ever-decreasing circle. There is no talk of freedom, no talk of Allies or liberation. All we talk of is home. Our lives, however short, we want to share them with another. To revel in a story of love, or bravery, courage and strength.

At my end, I will think of you and all the hope and possibility that opened to me the moment we met. Thank you for being in my life. To have known you grow old, to hold your hand, to have had a future is gone. But you will have me, in my heart, I have given it to you. For another chance at the same fate, Henryk, I would travel the same road. A hundred times, to have shared our snatched moments.

No more paper.

No more letters.

No more words.

Miriam places the last letter down. The pencil must have made a whisper on the paper as it traced out Frieda's thoughts. What happened to Frieda? And the baby? And as Miriam looks at the collection of letters, despite knowing so much, she realises she may never know. She places the letters back where they were collected and prepares herself for tomorrow.

Early the next morning the sky is heavy and clouds leaden with snow. She gets up to the noise of the hospice and kisses his head.

'Frieda,' he says.

'No, Dad. It's Miriam. I am trying to find out what happened. But first . . . I need to go and help my friend.' Her thoughts leave the letters and the past and look towards the woman who saved her. 'I need to help Eva first.'

'Frieda,' he says again, beckoning her with his voice, then settles, mumbling, 'My Frieda . . .'

She is too early to leave for the police station. With time on her side, she rearranges the letters and places them safely in her handbag. Finding the last one translated by Eva, she notices that the original of this one is different. Although the words are pressed tight on to each page, this letter covers both sides of two pages. The paper, although yellowed and thin, isn't ripped from a book and the words don't have to navigate around other text. This is clean paper; or it was . . . over forty years ago.

38

MIRIAM

Dearest Henryk,
Paper and a pencil are my only solace. I know there is no
future; but now I must tell you all that happened. My
hands shake . . . but I am no longer cold. This is my end:
The last day started at evening roll call. The
Kommandant at Auschwitz stood close then paced away,
his boots reflected the searchlights that had become our
moon.
'Dreckhund!' Obscenities, callous and cold, rang out
like steeple church bells. I thought of my family a lot at
that time. I imagined them sitting around after a dinner
of Bratwurst: I could hear the sausages sizzling and danc-
ing in a thin layer of fat, the skin, browning, waiting for
a knife to break it open and juices to run free. Absorbed
by potato and bread with a smothering of butter across
its perfect white surface.
Famished and frozen, the thought of food was poetry
to a starved soul. Talk of meals eaten, extravagance and
indulgence. The descriptions would make us salivate, and
would satisfy our hearts, if not our stomachs.

The showers had smoked twice that day so the Kommandant was all puffed out, proud as a peacock. Standing too close, I could smell his half-smoked cigarette and the heat stung my frozen nose. He moved in to me. He was so close I heard the leather of his uniform strain as he bent over, lowering himself to my eyeline. Then he turned to Hani.

'Zigeunerin,' was all he said. 'Gypsy.' A fact, but poison from his lips.

I held rigid as the cigarette sighed, extinguished into the pallid coolness of her forehead. The pockmarks of burns grew like acne. He flicked the butt in her face and with a wave of his hand we were dismissed and rushed back into the blocks, dogs at our heels, insults in our ears. I grieved the heat of the cigarette as the stench of life returned. I reached out for Hani's hand as we fumbled our way, sliding around and against each other. She snatched it back and moved forward with the crowd.

I remember stopping at pressure all the way across my stomach. My bump grew like rising dough and hardened beneath my hands. My breath caught.

It was time.

I found my way to the bunk, but got in at the bottom. Lying down with some caution, as a pain grew from my lower abdomen, all the way up to my chest, and ebbed away.

Despite exhausted limbs, empty stomach and a battered soul, I was not able to rest.

The camp slept and peace replaced hate, the world righted itself a bit. Pressing my fingers at the upper right side where I normally could find a foot, I waited, pressure

*of feet against my fingers, I smiled and did it again. There
was no alarm, baby was fine.*

*Pressure grew and my stomach hardened beneath my
hands.*

*The rats started to retire, bored of eating dead bodies
by day, they looked to chew on the living at night. As my
stomach softened I rolled on my side and watched them.
Another tightening. My belly held life and love. Every day
it reminded me what love can do.*

*The scrat of rats were on the hunt, their long claws
clacking, sharp from plying flesh off bone. Hani launched
herself in front of me from the bunk above. Placing her
freezing arm around me she sighed into the warmth of my
body. Taking heat but not giving any in return.*

*I pulled her arm closer and nestled her slight figure
into my chest, careful to move my bump away, as usual.
There were lots of big bellies in Auschwitz, from malnutrition, no one knew I was pregnant.*

*'I am so . . . so . . . humiliated, I hate this.' Hani
said. I knew where this was going, the same monologue in
its varying forms. 'These people are evil . . . Why nobody is
doing anything to stop this? We cannot be vanished from
the face of earth. Never am I going to leave. I'd rather
they got it over now, liquefied me now, than torture me as
they do.' Nothing changed, the test of time was how many
burns Hani could accumulate before her suffering ended.*

*I squeezed her arm, rubbing the chill out of her skin.
The baby gave an almighty kick as a large wave hit and
a small cry escaped my lips. Hani placed her hand to my
stomach and as powerful as an electric shock pushed my
arm away so hard I almost toppled over the side of the cot.*

'*What is this?*' Pure terror distorted her voice. '*You are pregnant?*' Another wave so strong took over my body and even if I had wanted to, I could not reply. I focused on my breathing, like Matka had said to the young girl.

'*What is happening? How?*' I could feel her eyes looking at me. I was pleased the searchlights were moving over another block. The emotion in her voice was enough, I did not need to see it too.

'*A child? Here?*' The fear was in her voice. I struggled with a lump in my throat.

'*What you are going to do?*' She touched my face to bring me back to reality. The wayward thought of the barrel and Sister Klara drowning my little angel brought a whole different kind of shiver through my body.

I placed my lips to the top of Hani's head as she processed all the new information, knowing this would hurt her, but feeling so much lighter that she finally knew.

Hani placed a hand on my stomach and the ripping, stinging, tearing she must have been going through repelled her body from mine. A hand touching an open stove, feeling the flames lick skin, but holding it there anyway. Finally, I felt her relax as she felt my body perform something unique, muscles flexing and relaxing without any conscious effort.

I found myself singing to Hani in a whisper, as I breathed to my baby's rhythm.

Hani cried, I cried. It felt like the end, and it really was.

That night we swayed, Hani by my side, breathing and moving in the small spaces between bunks, her hands in contact with mine. The searchlights, our rising sun, and a crack of a bullet fired at a rat, a woman, a shadow.

The day was tucked up in a blanket of dark. A deep guttural noise escaped my lips, causing panic: noise was exposure.

'Shall I get Matka?' Hani asked, bending down to dry my face with my shirt as I moved on to all fours. A straw mattress on the ground. A huge rise in panic as I realised this journey would soon be over. My child would be born and everything would change. I grabbed her hand and forced her to look at me.

'No, Hani. My baby cannot be taken from me.'

Hani said, so gently, 'But Frieda — if not then is stillborn.' The word was there to shock me.

No one can understand how a baby so helpless can cling to life so hard, submerged in water. Gurgled and burbled until drowned, causing everyone who can hear it to rip apart, the depths of a wound that will never, ever heal.

I grabbed Hani's arm, she looked away. 'I will die before that happens, you look at me and see.' I pulled her even closer. 'It. Will. Never. Happen.' The words between contractions, feral.

'I will stand in front of you both.'

I let go of her arm as a wave channelled all thought to the baby, the baby alive, moving through my pelvis, so close to this world.

To survive meant days or weeks only, then death from malnutrition or disease. Mothers cradling skeletal babies, no energy to suckle from an empty breast. No relief from the hunger, but never from an empty heart. The row upon row of dying babies. Block 22. The atrocities; the innocence; the anguish. Please. No, I thought.

'Beg doctor to take it and raise it. It lives this way, please, sister, allow me to go to the revier to ask for you. Otherwise is death.' Hani's tears fell so large that they touched me in their path and I cried with her. The same question running around and around. 'What are we going to do?'

An almighty contraction, different from the others, came over me. So strong I cried out, not in pain, but shock. It kept coming, stronger and deeper, then a heaviness. My baby was emerging. Another low noise from me was masked as the speakers blasted out, vibrating through the block.

The hunt had started. I vaguely heard numbers, the drum of death.

Each number an end. The speakers woke and the rats deserted. Everyone suddenly changed from the sleep of the almost dead, to the howl of the living.

The rhythm of the numbers, drowned out by shouts, wails and movement.

Hani screamed.

'Frieda!' She grabbed my wrist, yanking it over. My number 72829, black on white. She screamed again and rose to join what was becoming mass panic in the block. The numbers kept coming. Guards shouting, women shrieking, like a seesaw: one then the other.

It all seemed to happen so far away. I knew my baby was coming, it wouldn't be long now.

'They've called you,' Hani said, bending nose to nose with me.

I roared with the power of my body, my body was pushing, pushing my baby into this chaos.

A small group of women from our block gathered. Familiar faces. The speakers stopped reeling numbers, the screams seeming distant.

I put my hand down past my bump; hairs, soft and curled, and my opening. The sacred beautiful place that accepted the love of a good man.

Another wave grew and I could feel the top of the head, hair, wet and hot. My baby.

Hani was the epitome of despair. She spun circles, hands on her head.

'Matka,' Hani said, and she left the bunk. Once she left, the others grew closer. A consciousness of being a woman, when all aspects of femininity were erased, united us. Cool hands, skin to skin, a small snatch of bread shared. Words, beautiful words in the language of love, sheltered me from the horror of the hunt.

Hushed excitement as a small figure arrived. Matka's calm peace descended over me. She gave instructions and knelt by my side. Her hands were warm. My child would be born into these hands.

'Can I look?' she asked.

I nodded as a contraction built, I felt hair and moved my hand so she could see.

'Baby has hair – dark hair,' she said. The words soothed me. Like its father.

A deep fire grew. Another contraction so quick and the baby slid into Matka's waiting hands. Matka moved under me and as I turned she placed a wet, hot, sticky, and surprisingly heavy lump under my shirt on to my bare chest.

'A girl,' she said as she placed another shirt over us both; the top of baby's head poked out. The cloth and

Matka's warm hand around her too. Relief. She was beautiful. So small, but perfect. An overwhelming urge to lick came over me, she smelled of life, of the depths of me, warmth and blood. She squirmed on my chest, head rocking back to open her eyes up at me.

Matka took out some scissors. I stayed the silver with my hand. No. We were one, I would not sever us anytime soon. I felt the thick, hot cord pulsing on my stomach, her heart was beating from my heart too.

For us to be parted was to die. I knew it now. I looked up as Hani returned. I pulled her close so she sat next to me on a soggy mattress now full of birth, the water that nourished and protected my child.

'Look.'

I lifted the top of the shirt and baby opened her eyes, poked a small, pink tongue from red lips and dropped her head back down on to the swell of my breast. We both watched and absorbed her. She nuzzled to my breast and took my nipple in her mouth, placing her hand on my heart.

The feeling of wholeness. It was there, in that moment.

Love.

The speakers continued to scream numbers when a Blockova from another block came in, bat in hand, and pulled a woman hiding under the mattress from the top bunk. The force reverberated through the block and the wails of fear recommenced. The protective circle of women dispersed and I watched the Blockova as she hammered blow after blow. When submission could have been achieved, she continued. One less for the showers, straight to the pile. Human life so worthless. Dragged away by her feet, leaving a trail of thick red, the only evidence she even existed.

And watching that, I knew what to do.

I stood and felt the cord pull, strange against my stomach. Hani inhaled, it sounded like a bullet whizzing past. Matka gave us a blessing, many women started to come closer again, touching, holding and guiding us. My body exhausted and shaky. I stumbled, but did not fall. They held Hani, embracing her in bony hands.

I kissed the top of Hani's head for the last time, inhaling the smell of friendship. I looked into her loving eyes. I felt her pain. My baby and I would not be separated in death, we would die as one. She would spend eternity with me, in my arms, held and adored.

I walked past Hani and Matka, my steps slow, and shuffled my feet into clogs. Legs bare, the shirt covering us to my thighs. Following the blood trail.

'Frieda,' Hani said. All the love for me in one word. I smiled and as I turned away she started to sing. And then they all sang. A chorus of voices joined hers, the words lost in a sea of languages; a lullaby sung, as I walked us to our death.

Tears fall down Miriam's cheeks and drip from her nose and chin. She shakes her head and stifles a sob as she reads the final page.

I didn't get far. Hani came running after me, and then in front of me. The Blockova with a bat and a clipboard in her hand towered over her. She pulled up her sleeve and the Blockova made a mark on her paper and sent her forward.

To the showers.

In my place.

I moved as fast as I could, but stumbled at the last and landed on my bare knees on the ice at the Blockova's feet.

And something strange happened. I felt another contraction, my initial thought was twins. Oh my god, there's another. The baby was out of sight of the Blockova, but I couldn't just have a baby in front of her and not get a response. Matka had followed me and kept a distance. She quickly lifted my dress and clamped and cut the cord as the Blockova's back was turned. When the Blockova turned back to me and saw the blood trickling down my legs and the pool of placenta at my feet, she screamed, 'Revier!'

Matka collected the placenta and wrapped it up in some paper. Other women were holding me, lifting me, the baby didn't make a sound, she lay her head on my breast.

'My friend.' I said to the Blockova, and as I said it I realised that Hani had been my only friend in the world. I couldn't see her now through the mass of grey stripes. I kept looking, I stood in front of the Blockova waiting. Then Hani turned and I saw her for the last time.

I understood why Bunny was silent.

39

MIRIAM

She walks to the police station, her eyes tired and her heart full. She arrives at 9 a.m. and the doors are not open. She waits, stamps her feet and blows into her hands. Thinking of the letters, of Hani and of Frieda.

An officer arrives and opens the doors from within, the air is warm and Miriam feels her fingers, cheeks and toes tingle back to life.

'I'm here to talk to someone about Eva, Eva Bertrandt, I think.'

She is shown to a plastic chair in the main waiting area and the officer leaves his desk.

'Is she still here?'

'Yes, she was kept overnight.'

'Has she been arrested?'

'Not that I know of. I've just got in, so give me a few minutes to get up to speed. Coffee?'

'No, thank you.'

She watches as the hands of the clock move and imagines Eva curled on to a bunk in a small, grey cell, cold and unspeakably alone. Trapped behind yet another wall. She feels the shiver of cold and dread wash over her, then feeling her fingers pink up, she removes her coat and waits.

'So, you're a friend of Frau Bertrandt, is that correct?'

'Yes.'

'Can you come this way, please?' He has notes in his hand and opens them, reading as he walks.

Miriam stands and as she follows the young officer she cannot help but speak.

'I was questioned yesterday and as I was leaving Eva confessed to something that she shouldn't have done. I think she was doing it to save me, but I didn't really need saving. Neither of us did anything wrong.'

'I see,' he says and points to the chair in a similar room to the one she waited in yesterday, only this table is white, shiny plastic.

'From what I can see here,' he reads from his notes, 'she was questioned and kept here overnight. She will have to give a statement if needed in due course and to be available to speak with the police as a witness to a crime. The crime against you, I believe.'

'Not against Axel?'

'Herr Voight seems unable to recall what happened to him.'

'Why?'

'I think the facts that were presented to him, including the injuries to you, prevented his story from having the impact he had hoped for,' the officer says with disdain. 'We also received a supporting letter from a . . .' He consults his file. 'A Nurse Hensher, stating that your husband has shown abusive tendencies and that the concerns about your mental health were not relevant now that you had left him.'

'How did Hilda know anything about this?'

'The letter came with Frau Bertrandt,' the officer says. 'I think it is hoped that this, although serious, will be classed as a domestic incident and no further action is needed. I would caution you, as I will do your husband, to stay away from each other.'

'Thank you.'

Eva comes out into the reception area creased and small. Her face has seemingly shrunk into itself and she looks very old. Her white-blonde hair grey in the fluorescent lights.

'You came for me?'

Miriam doesn't answer but drops her bag and coat on the seat and gives Eva a huge hug.

'You came for me too,' she says and kisses Eva's cold cheek.

Both women stand and cry. The police officer puts a box of tissues on the desk. They wipe their eyes and smile shyly at the other.

'Can I escort you home?'

Miriam uses the police phone to call a taxi and they travel in an overheated car which smells of leather and smoke.

Eva rubs her hands to warm them. 'Would you be very cross with me?' she whispers.

'For what?'

'I saw something in the file at the police station, I may have stolen it,' Eva confesses quietly, moving closer to Miriam as they are rocked by the travelling car. From her sleeve she pulls out a small stash of papers. 'I couldn't let them sit there.' She hands the paper to Miriam.

'These are the divorce papers,' Miriam says so loudly her voice breaks into a squeal, and she coughs.

'Shhh,' Eva says and turns the pages. 'Look.' She points to the place on the paper where Axel's large signature dominates the page.

Miriam looks at the paper and back at Eva. 'Do you think . . . ?' she starts, but turns to the driver instead.

'Excuse me.' She swallows and says a little louder, 'Can we make a second stop, please?' She gives the driver the address and the taxi turns down a narrow street, manoeuvring around the parked cars, before heading back to Neufertstraße.

Miriam looks up at the shopfront and pushes the bell to the flat above. Eva waits in the taxi, running on its meter.

'We are closed,' says David Abbott, wearing a thick, knit jumper and rubbing his eyes. 'Oh, Frau Voight, is anything the matter?'

'Sorry to disturb you, but I have these' – she hands over the papers – 'and I didn't want to post them.'

'He signed?' David Abbott asks, opening the fold.

'He signed.'

Back in the taxi, Miriam smiles. 'Thank you,' she says, although the words are not nearly enough.

'I am famished,' Eva says. 'Shall we have a celebratory breakfast?'

Miriam nods, unable to comprehend that Axel signed the divorce papers.

'Can I stop by my home first, so I can clean up? I have something for you, but I left it at home.'

Eva gives the driver directions to her flat. Miriam waits in the taxi on the meter, with the window down, as Eva disappears behind a red front door in a building like her own. So much has changed in such a short time. A few weeks ago the Wall was still up, she hadn't met Eva and her father was well. However, she wouldn't rewind time. She understands her father better, she has a friend, even Hilda stood by her in the end, and she has a chance at freedom and not through death either.

'Why did you take the letters and the dress?' she asks when Eva is back in the taxi, changed and smelling of toothpaste.

'I was scared.'

'Of the police?'

'Well, yes, but not just that. The last letters, I didn't want you reading them alone. I thought you might wake up and see them and start reading. I wanted to protect you, I think.'

'Why?'

'There is one more letter . . . I have translated all of them and feel I have got to know you too, in the process and . . .' Eva stops talking as the taxi pulls to a stop at traffic lights. She says nothing more until the car has pulled away again. 'I came back the next day to return the letters, but you weren't there. When that man said you had been arrested, I left straightaway to see what I could do to help.'

'Lionel told you I had been arrested?'

'Yes, and I knew it was all my fault. I went to the doctors. I had met Hilda when the locksmith was here, so she knew me a little, and I asked for a letter, to prove you were okay, hoping it would be enough. Then I put everything back in your flat and went to the police station.'

'It is enough. You saved my life, you have helped me. You are my friend. That means something to me.'

'Thank you, and it means something to me too. '

Eva says nothing for a while as the taxi jumps through the traffic. The Palace Gardens and the River Spree are silent, the view from the window, grey. The prospect of a different life, unbelievable.

They pay the taxi and walk slowly up the busy streets. They cross the road along Neufertstraβe and walk a few feet. On the corner of the junction between a bike repair shop and an old Italian restaurant, stands a large, green-fronted building. It has only one small window at the front.

'Here?' Miriam asks, standing back.

'Yes, what's wrong?'

'I used to come here with Mum,' Miriam says.

Eva holds open the door and the smell of rising dough makes Miriam's stomach rumble.

The café is quiet, an older couple sit drinking tea from daintily painted china cups. Pictures of Paris line the wall, with tables and chairs under them in a row along one side of the shop. The heat and the moisture have steamed up the mirror hanging on the facing wall, under which is a counter full of cakes and sandwiches.

'What do you fancy?' she asks, pointing to the lines of cake, and the waitress behind the counter poised with a pad to take their order.

Miriam looks at what is on offer, wiping her hand in a napkin, and chooses an inconspicuous *Lebkuchen*, it smells of Christmas, ginger and warmth.

Eva chooses a much larger cake with icing sugar dusting the top. They take their plates and coffees and sit by the window.

Miriam focuses on her plate, trying not to look around, but aware she is sitting by the window. Able to see the street.

'What's wrong?' Eva asks.

'Nothing.'

Eva takes a sip of her coffee. 'To freedom,' she says.

'I used to come here with Mum,' Miriam says, ignoring Eva's toast and sipping her coffee, the bitter taste dries on her tongue.

Eva takes a bite of her cake.

'In fact, we had lunch here the last time I saw her, not that we ate anything . . .'

And the day was a bright one. Mum had worn a black dress with a grey trim; she looked beautiful, her white hair pulled up on her head in its usual style. Both pushing their food around with their forks. Both thinking the same thing.

'Why didn't Dad come?'

'You know why. We've missed you terribly. You live down the road and we see you so infrequently. He doesn't want you to go any further away.'

'You won't ask me to stay?'

'I can't.' She sighed loudly. 'Axel is your husband, you must go with him, and it's only a few hours on the bus, after all.'

The silence stretched and Miriam, looking at the old spots that had gathered on the back of Mum's hand, tried not to think of missing her, but she couldn't think of anything else.

'I miss you,' she said, tears threatening to fall.

'I'll miss you too. Miriam, what will I do without you?' She raised her napkin to her face and dabbed at the corner of her eyes.

'Please don't cry, Mum. You've been without me for years; besides, you have Dad,' she laughed. 'I don't want to go.'

Her mother took a deep breath. Pushed her food away and took Miriam by the hands.

'Sometimes we must endure things in a marriage to make it work. It will all turn out okay. You will be with Axel, he loves you. You'll have a fresh start in Wolfsburg – it's supposed to be beautiful there, and after losing the baby, fresh air is just what you need to find some happiness again.' She smiled.

Miriam kissed her on the cheek. 'I love you.'

'Let's order a pudding, eh? And celebrate new beginnings.'

Miriam had looked out at the street while her mother had gone to order a cake. *His* red car was parked across the street. Him inside. He had wound down the window so she could see him.

When Mum came back she said, 'They are getting us a chocolate pudding and ice cream, will be a few minutes.'

'I can't stay.'

'Why?' Mum asked, sitting down and placing her napkin over the corner of her skirt.

'Axel is waiting outside.'

'But he said he would pick you up from the house later, so you could see your father too.'

'Look.' Miriam pointed to the window. As her mother turned, Axel got out of the car and rested his arms on the roof, sunglasses shielded his eyes.

'I'm sorry.'

Her mother's face dropped and she looked deflated, sagged at the middle, her napkin askew in her lap.

Miriam bent down to kiss her, but Mum didn't look up, so she placed a kiss on her soft downy hair.

'I love you.'

'Travel safe,' she said, and swallowed hard. 'Will you call me?'

'As soon as we are settled. I promise.'

Miriam picked up her bag and headed for the door.

'I love you too, be safe, sweetheart.'

Miriam had walked across the street, her eyes swimming with tears.

It was the last time she had seen her mother. She had been in Wolfsburg, just two hours away, for five years, and returned only once.

For Mum's funeral.

At the table, Miriam places her *Lebkuchen* down with a clatter. 'Sorry, Eva, what were you saying?' She rubs her eyes with the back of her hand.

'Are you okay?'

'Even though Frieda loved Dad and Dad must have loved her too, it doesn't change anything. I love my Mum so much, and it hurts, it hurts that she is no longer here.'

Eva puts down her coffee and finishes the last slice of cake before picking up her bag. Without saying a word, Eva slides a piece of paper across the table. The letter covers one sheet of A4, and like all the others this one has Eva's translation attached.

Miriam takes a deep breath. 'The last one?'

'Yes.'

She picks up the paper and reads.

> *Henryk*
> *Hani sacrificed herself so that I could live. She was so brave, she died when I should have. Matka helped me. Feed, feed, feed.*
>
> *And then one day the guards left, taking all prisoners who could walk, all the food, and locked everyone else in. I could not move. I could not eat. I stayed.*
>
> *The next day the camp was liberated.*
>
> *We were rescued and the soldiers spoke English and I stayed quiet. I ended up in hospital and the baby grew! It was a miracle.*
>
> *Emilie has come to visit me in the hospital. I am very ill but the baby is well and being cared for in the nursery. I saw Emilie in the doorway of my room. She looked unsure. I suppose I didn't look anything like the 'Frieda' she knew.*
>
> *The nurse who had opened the door confirmed that I had developed typhus. 'She has only days to live,' the nurse warned and left.*
>
> *It feels so strange to hear of my life, after fighting for so long, reduced to days.*
>
> *I am dying, Henryk. I write this to you as Emilie watches on, far back and close to the wall. Our daughter in her arms.*
>
> *I can smell orange blossom, sweet baby milk, and I can see happiness. Pure joy. I am dying, but I am leaving something good behind. You have all my letters, you have our daughter and you have my love.*
>
> *Please don't forget me.*

All I have now are stolen images and Emilie's promise to take care of the baby and to take care of you too.

Emilie returns often without the baby and she holds my hand. She cries. And all I know is that I want you to be with me before I die.

I ask only for you.

Just so I can say goodbye . . .

40

MIRIAM

The air around Miriam seems to vibrate in her ears as if she is surrounded by water. Her feet remain numb, attached to the ground.

'I don't understand,' Miriam says.

'Turn it over,' Eva says.

> *Frieda died 14th February 1945 at 4 a.m. Her baby survives.*

'That's Mum's handwriting!' Miriam looks again. 'Mum knew?' Her head is fuzzy and scrambled suddenly. 'What does this mean?'

'I think,' Eva says, reaching her hand across the table. 'I think this means that you are the baby . . .'

Miriam is silent.

The noise of the café grows around her, but she looks at Eva's clean, strong face, she holds Eva's soft, warm hand and she looks at the letter.

'What?' She stands abruptly, but the blood rushes to her head and the room seems to spin around her. 'I mean – *no!*' She sits. Waiting for something to make sense.

'We can't know that,' Miriam says. 'We don't know if the baby lived, or that Mum even took it.' Miriam looks at Eva. 'Is that everything?'

'Yes, when I took the dress I wanted to check there was nothing else. Anything that may help you,' Eva says.

'And . . . ?'

Eva shakes her head.

'You cannot take her away from me. I mean, this, the letters . . . I've already lost her once, Eva. Please. Stop,' Miriam says and wishes more than anything Mum was alive to put an end to this. She knows it's not Eva's fault, but she translated this.

'You didn't need to give this one to me. I would have been okay without knowing this,' Miriam says eventually. 'Why?'

'You deserve to know the truth. It's not my decision to withhold anything from you. I think your parents protected you a lot. It's not a bad thing, but maybe, maybe you are stronger than you realise,' Eva says gently.

'Why didn't they tell me?'

'I don't know. But think about it, Miriam; if this is true, if you are the child of Frieda . . .'

'*If*,' Miriam says. 'Big if . . . because even if I am, Mum is my mum.'

'She will always be your mum. But think of the strength you had to survive right from the beginning? If this is you, and this is your story too . . .' Eva doesn't finish the sentence. 'I thought you should know.'

The more Miriam thinks, the more she can understand. Her father is calling for Frieda. Maybe . . . But maybe not because he is searching for Frieda, as she thought, but maybe he is trying to tell her, Miriam, that she came from Frieda. Or . . . her thoughts topple over each other. Or maybe Dad thinks she is Frieda? She has been gone so long . . . did Miriam resemble Frieda?

'I'll never know anything for sure, will I?'

'I'm so sorry, Miriam. If it's true then you survived so much and have been so loved.'

Miriam shakes her head. 'Nothing is ever true, is it? The only person who would know what happened is dead. Mum was my best

Anna Ellory

friend. This . . .' She shakes the letter. 'Cannot take that from me. I won't let it.'

'Nothing will take your memories. Your mother, I'm sure, loved you very much.'

'And Frieda?'

Eva stands, moves around the table and pulls Miriam to her feet. Embraced in a hug so deep, Miriam sobs something that sounds like a wail. When Miriam pulls away from the hug she sees Eva's eyes reflecting the sorrow of her own face. The other diners are looking at them.

'I need to leave,' Miriam says.

Eva pays the bill and they walk out into the street.

Miriam stops suddenly and pulls out the last letter again; the hurt in the letter from Frieda seems to break through Miriam's skin and scatter around inside her, as if it were her own. Did Dad go to her?

Did this woman die alone, without him?

Finally, when Miriam feels calmer, she goes to Eva's side, waiting a little behind her, and holds her hand. And together they walk down the street.

Eva says nothing, allowing Miriam the time to compose herself. The Christmas decorations still hang like jewels from the trees and lamp posts.

They walk until the road becomes blocked with bodies. The air is full of chatter as they get to the other side of Ruhwald Park, close to the hospice. Miriam's head feels about to shatter with the volume of thoughts: the letters; the lives lost . . .

The chatter dies down as a voice as clear as a bird flies into the sky. People look up, as if they can hear the voice of an angel.

Eva places her hand in the crook of Miriam's arm. No one speaks. The song seizes time and holds it for all who can hear and Miriam's mind clears. No accompaniment, just a singular voice, singing to the heavens. Transporting Miriam in both time and place.

She recalls one year when her father returned late at the end of term.

'I'm so sorry, did you do it all without me?' he called from the doorway.

'Almost,' Miriam said. He arrived and kissed them both; Mum decorating the top of the tree and Miriam playing with the ribbon on a small gift she had wrapped for Axel. Her father pulled off his tie and dropped his briefcase on the table.

'Is he here?'

'Not yet.' Mum's voice was full of excitement.

'What is he like?'

'Gorgeous,' Miriam proclaimed in a fit of giggles. 'You'll love him, Mum.' The bubbles of excitement rose within her until she couldn't stop smiling.

'What's left for me to do?' her father asked.

'The star, as always,' Mum replied.

The tree was beautiful, silver and gold. The carols on the radio were quiet. Miriam passed her father the star and he placed it at the top of the tree.

'Countdown then,' he said, and Miriam went to the light switch and turned off the main light so they were plunged into darkness.

'Three . . . two . . . one,' they said together as Mum flicked the tree lights and they brightened the room.

The star at the top dazzled glitter. Miriam watched as her father pulled on the strings of her mother's apron and took it off over her head. He placed it over the back of the chair and took her small hand in his. She stepped into his arms on tiptoe and he danced her around the room.

'Mind the decorations,' she said, smiling into his eyes.

Miriam watched as they did a few circuits around the room, so graceful, her mother's skirt billowing around her so that she looked like a fairy ready to sit atop a tree herself. Her cheeks flushed and her hair messily out of place. She hoped one day soon that she would feel how Mum felt, but in Axel's arms.

'Merry Christmas, Emilie,' her father said, and kissed her fully on the mouth. Miriam watched Mum flush in his gaze.

'Merry Christmas,' she said, and stopped to straighten her hair, her father pulling her close.

'Merry Christmas, everyone,' Dad said, kissing Miriam on the cheek, and her heart was full of cheer, elevated because Christmas was near.

The applause from the crowd is slow to start but becomes loud and flamboyant with whistles and cheers, bringing Miriam back to the present.

The orchestra starts up and bodies move slightly as the next song gets underway. She looks and sees a small boy taking a sip of water. He is surrounded by adults, but it is his voice that had carried them away.

Miriam places her hand over Eva's arm as the crowds drift away.

'Are you okay?' Eva asks.

'I have been more than blessed. But right now, I don't know if Dad knew and he deserves to know what happened. Even if it is the end. I promised him.' She walks on a few paces, leaving Eva behind, then returns.

Mum's voice jumps in her head. 'People deserve a peaceful, unburdened passing,' she had said. Miriam takes a breath that shimmers in the cold air. She can do this for Dad.

At the entrance to the hospice, Miriam stops and looks up. The moon is still in the sky, surrounded by what look like bright stars. And it looks, at first, as if the stars are falling, but it is snow. It has started to snow.

Miriam holds her hand out and catches the flakes in the palm of her hand. She looks up and admires the beauty of something so erasable.

'Their ashes rise black, but they always fall white,' Miriam says. 'Dad used to say that when snow fell, the ashes of those we lost fell with each flake, to nurture the ground and land on those they loved. Snowflake kisses, a snowflake touch. When I was little I never really understood, I just giggled as the snowflake kisses turned into Mum and Dad kisses. No matter what, they loved me.'

'I am sure they did. I'll wait for you, if you need me?' Eva asks, but Miriam is watching the snowflakes melt in her hand. She can hear her father's voice, his gloved hand wrapped around hers, his smoky breath mingled with fresh white snow.

'If every flake dissolves, some part of that person moves into you. Giving you a gift, something they had,' Dad had said.

Miriam thinks of the rabbit girls and Hani, Frieda and her mother and all the others lost and forgotten. As the snow gets thicker she wonders if, maybe, the lost have quite a lot of gifts to deliver.

Miriam feels Eva gently open the door and catch her arm. Inside, Eva waits by the Christmas tree as Sue walks down the corridor.

Sue holds both of Miriam's hands in her own and greets her, 'Your father is very alert today,' she says. 'But his chest has got worse again. I think' – Sue directs Miriam into her father's room – 'I think it's time,' she says with gravity.

The room smells faintly of cloves, of Christmas gone. Sue walks in, leans over the bed and takes her father's hand.

'Herr Winter, Henryk. Miriam is here to see you,' she says. And nods for her to move closer.

Sue straightens. 'I'll leave you to it. Christmas biscuits to eat,' she says, stroking Miriam's arm as she passes.

Miriam knows she should start talking. She knows she should explain what the letters said. She knows she should tell her father that

Frieda is dead. She knows she should ask if he knew, that maybe, just maybe, she is his and Frieda's child.

Instead she walks to his bed and leans over to kiss him lightly on the forehead.

She thinks of the poem and Frieda's scrawl from the office, what seems like a lifetime ago, and knows she can bring him peace.

He deserves a happy ending.

HENRYK

It is her. Frieda.

I cannot open my eyes, but it is her.

After all these years.

She kisses my forehead, and I can feel the kisses of the past; her breath hot and static, charged so raw and bright I feel myself spinning, centred only by her lips, her touch. On me. So long ago . . .

A fog, haze and I am floating, leaving behind a body, a life.

'Henryk.' I can feel her swallow, her lips thin then plump back up on my skin. She moves to my ear, her breath makes goose pimples dance over my entire body.

'When darkness drops, I am your light.'

And yes, she is. My light and my dark. She lives.

'I love you,' the voice says, full of tears. 'It's okay.'

Frieda sits on the bench, under the pine trees, her blonde hair playing in the breeze, she rests into my body. She holds my hand, softly yet firm. She smells of fresh snow, of roses, of stars.

And with her hand in mine, I squeeze tight. I swallow and take a deep breath. The voice that escapes my dry lips is not my own, but I say:

'Frieda.'

December 1990

Snow was falling heavily and landed with a humph on the screen, as the old Trabant gargled north. Both women silent, watchful, respectful.

Cutting across white fields, trees and abandoned collective farms, a sign for Sachsenhausen meant they were going the right way; to Ravensbrück.

She couldn't believe how close it was, less than two hours north of Berlin.

She took a long, deep breath and pointed to the spire of Fürstenburg Church as it came into view. They passed Fürstenburg station and she shook her head. She didn't stop shaking until they pulled in on the other side of Fürstenburg. There was a cobbled forest road that led to the camp. Houses with pitched roofs appeared to the left as the lake opened to them, white, vast and frozen, to the right.

Wrapped up in coats and scarves, arm in arm, they walked carefully to the entrance.

High walls and signs in Russian. They couldn't go any further.

Wood pigeons were cooing from atop the mass of linden trees bowed with snow. They stood looking out over the lake, the church spire spiking black through the blanket of snow.

'They lie at the bottom of the lake,' she said. 'All of them.'

The breeze bit into their cheeks and eyes. Neither woman cried. They just stood in silence until feet, legs and arms were numb with cold.

A feather, small, fluffy and white, hovered briefly in front of them, before fluttering across the ice.

ACKNOWLEDGMENTS

This book could not have happened without the support of my parents, who believed in me long before I did and long before I had anything worth believing in.

I owe you everything.

Thanks to Juliet Mushens, who saw something special buried within my manuscript and signed me, worked with me, pushed me and challenged me. This book would not be half as good without your edits, your support and ultimately my sheer determination to not let you down.

To Laura Deacon and everyone at Lake Union, for taking my book out into the world.

To Arzu Tahsin, for edits that made me a better writer.

I could not have done this without my tribe – friends new and old. Thank you for listening to me; feeding me; taking time to care; for not asking 'how's the book going' when I was rewriting (again); for the cups of tea; the boxes of food; the 'shoe-drills' and the incentive to never give up.

Thank you to my Evil Twin; Demo Dan; Shawn and my Krav family. For Faber friends Fran, Mandy and Louise; and new writer friends

Louise, Priscilla, Lina and Liz. All exceptional writers in their own right. 'Mummy' friends, especially Beth Hollington, for truly hearing me and for sticking by me – when others would have told me to quit.

Finally, thanks to Jane Reece for being an exceptional teacher. Fay Weldon for helping me believe in myself and Clint Badlam for seeing the person behind the pen.

ABOUT THE AUTHOR

Anna Ellory lives in Bath and has just completed her MA in Creative Writing at Bath Spa University.